Jerusalem

By the same author

FICTION

Musungu Jim and the Great Chief Tuloko

Twelve Bar Blues

The London Pigeon Wars

City of Tiny Lights

NON-FICTION

Where You're At: Notes from the Frontline
of a Hip-Hop Planet

Culture is Our Weapon (with Damian Platt)

Jerusalem
An elegy in three parts

PATRICK NEATE

FIG TREE
an imprint of
PENGUIN BOOKS

FIG TREE

Published by the Penguin Group
Penguin Books Ltd, 80 Strand, London WC2R ORL, England
Penguin Group (USA) Inc., 375 Hudson Street, New York, New York 10014, USA
Penguin Group (Canada), 90 Eglinton Avenue East, Suite 700, Toronto, Ontario, Canada M4P 2Y3
(a division of Pearson Penguin Canada Inc.)
Penguin Ireland, 25 St Stephen's Green, Dublin 2, Ireland
(a division of Penguin Books Ltd)
Penguin Group (Australia), 250 Camberwell Road, Camberwell, Victoria 3124, Australia
(a division of Pearson Australia Group Pty Ltd)
Penguin Books India Pvt Ltd, 11 Community Centre, Panchsheel Park, New Delhi – 110 017, India
Penguin Group (NZ), 67 Apollo Drive, Rosedale, North Shore 0632, New Zealand
(a division of Pearson New Zealand Ltd)
Penguin Books (South Africa) (Pty) Ltd, 24 Sturdee Avenue, Rosebank, Johannesburg 2196, South Africa

Penguin Books Ltd, Registered Offices: 80 Strand, London WC2R ORL, England

www.penguin.com

First published 2009
1

Copyright © Patrick Neate, 2009

The moral right of the author has been asserted

Set in 12/14.75 pt Monotype Dante
Typeset by Rowland Phototypesetting Ltd, Bury St Edmunds, Suffolk
Printed in Great Britain by Clays Ltd, St Ives plc

A CIP catalogue record for this book is available from the British Library

ISBN: 978-1-905-49041-7

www.greenpenguin.co.uk

Penguin Books is committed to a sustainable future
for our business, our readers and our planet.
The book in your hands is made from paper
certified by the Forest Stewardship Council.

Dedicated to the memory of my beloved sister, Milly
(1973–2007)

Part one: And did those feet . . .

I

Insert document
'The diary of a local gentleman',
21 August 1900 (Empire Museum, Bristol), anon.

It is strange to me that I should feel compelled to begin a
journal only on the eve of my departure from this
God-forsaken place where, truth be told, no civilized man
should ever have made his home (and increasingly, I fear,
none did). How can I explain myself? Let me just say that
this conflict has not lacked for chronicles and, for my part,
I have been paralysed by the most peculiar funk.

Although I make no claims to valour, many have been
made on my behalf. So, should my words be read at some
future time by Mother, Father, Catherine or, God willing,
my child or grandchild, it is important that they – that is to
say, 'you' – should not consider me coward either, for this is
not that sort of confession. You must believe that I have
served Queen and country as I always meant to, with every
muscle in my body, every facet of my wit and wholehearted
passion. Ask any who served under me and they will tell you
the same. Indeed, examine my record and you will see I was
offered invalid's passage home three months since, but
refused it that I might take up this grim post at Standmere.

For my actions at Paardeberg, some called me a hero. But
they were not true military men who know the chaos of
battle and the unpredictability of the desperate human spirit.
Find a dozen sweats to tell you about a hero and you may be
surprised to hear as many different descriptions. One may
tell you about a fine fellow who was one of the first to fall to

3

a Mauser's bullet; another, a reckless type who hadn't the imagination to think himself a fool. But, should you ask a real old fundi, he'll tell you that bravery is short-lived, fear a constant companion and that the greatest challenge facing any hero is to leave heroism behind, to reject coarse lusts in favour of the subtle sympathies prerequisite in a man of God, science and peace.

For my part, of course, I can only tell you what I know, which is this: he is a hero who confronts the truth honestly, off the battlefield as well as on it, who looks terror squarely in the eye and is man enough to recognize the face that stares back at him as none other than his own. It would be remiss, and render this journal unworthy, therefore, if I did not admit that I have been fearful, impotent even, to record the true horror of this place and the dark reflection it throws upon myself, my superiors and the whole of Her Majesty's great Empire. To do so now is my only hope of respite and redemption.

My initial intention for this journal is simply to record some of what I have witnessed. Perhaps that is all I will manage. My wound is festering and Nurse O'Brian – a fine Irish lass but no medic – fears the infection may spread with fatal consequence before I can reach a Cape surgeon. I must confess I am not unduly perturbed by this and I am prepared to abandon myself to Fate (for there's no evidence of our Lord's presence here) – such is my mind. Indeed, I have come to regard the state of my gammy leg as metaphoric of this whole bloody mess. As my wound is to me, so is this war to the Empire. It was initially painful but no more than that. Now, through a lack of care, competence and conscience, it may yet threaten life itself.

If Fate does indeed spare me, however, and carries me home on the breath of its mockery, I believe I must use this journal to begin a thorough investigation of the English nature. It was Kipling who wrote, 'What should they know of England who only England know?' Never before have I felt the import of a general question so personally.

I am a proud subject of a great nation, a nation that has built the widest Empire man has seen and brought civilization, Christianity and prosperity to every territory it touches. Such achievements would surely not have been possible without the distinctive attributes of the English character: singularity of purpose, rigour of planning, compassion for the unfortunate and humility before God. And yet here at Standmere, I see no evidence of purpose, planning, compassion or humility, only chaos and inhumanity.

In my despair, I have spent some time considering the customs of the kaffir. For all his savagery and heathenism, there is much to admire. His society, for example, is organized on a principle he calls 'umbuntu', which means, I am told, 'we are people through each other'. I cannot express how painful it was for me to hear such simplicity! For I fear that in this place we have become less than human, less even than the Negro.

When I return home, therefore, I will –

[Fire damage has rendered the following two pages of the journal illegible]

– but it was the thirst that was most terrible.

I have always been the hardy sort and I managed better than many, though my throat was painfully parched and my tongue cracked and blistered. But some of my men were awfully afflicted with blindness and fever and some even took to drinking their own water, a copper-brown colour and noisome too.

If you thought about it an instant, this battle swiftly highlighted the absurdities of human conflict. There were Cronjé's Boers on one bank of the Modder and here were we on the other, both sides half crazed with thirst as a thousand gallons passed between us every second beneath the crack of the guns.

By the evening of 20 February it was insufferable. We had already lost more than a hundred men and the enemy about the same, but it was water that dominated our every waking thought and the increasing frenzy of our dreams in snatched moments of sleep. I had my men on half rations and they must have been hungry but none had the saliva to swallow even half an ounce of biscuit. Such thirst leads to a certain kind of mania and it was in such a state that I decided I'd prefer to die sated than shrivelled. I summoned Macintosh to my quarters and had him rustle up a dozen canteens. Honestly expecting failure, I did not tell the men what ruse I had planned, but my sergeant was keen as mustard from the off – the wholehearted, instinctive sort who seems perennially primed for a spot of derring-do.

The moonlight might have been daylight to Mac and me, the way our hearts raced, but we made it to the riverbank easily enough and began to fill the canteens one by one. We could hear the enemy on the other side, yapping in that guttural way of theirs. I was quite sure we'd be seen but Mac was calmness personified and we had those tins brimming in no time. Only then did we realize that lugging twelve up a steep ridge between the pair of us was a task to challenge Hercules.

Mac hissed that we should leave four behind but, in my crazed state, I could not agree. What was going through my mind was this: my men would be back in the thick of it at first light, killing and being killed, and I couldn't stand to see another fall in silence, the howl of his soul strangled in his dehydrated throat. If my men wanted to scream, they would scream.

We would have made it had I not tripped at the very top of the ridge and dropped one canteen that bounced noisily down the slope. Mac reached down for me and pulled me up with those thick pig-farmer's arms that had spent a lifetime hauling swine from one pen to another. But the bullets were already flying and one bit into my left shoulder and another into my left calf.

As God is my witness, I would have happily lain down to die with nothing for company but a drink of water, but Mac dragged me up saying, 'Come on, sir. Not far now.' So, I stumbled all the way back to camp, still carrying five canteens, blind with pain but fearful that, if I fell, I must suffer the indignity of returning to my men under the arm of a giant Scotsman, squealing like a piglet.

The men made quite a fuss of us that night as they drank their fill. My sergeant recounted the story a dozen times, embellishing my bravery a little more and ignoring his own with each telling. The next morning I was stretchered out on the convoy for Bloemfontein leaving my chaps in the care of a well-intentioned but green young fellow by the name of Hay. I heard later that he was dead before sunset.

Before Paardeberg was won we lost a further –

[Again, fire damage has rendered the following three and a half pages of the journal illegible]

It is true that Ackerman told me on the day I arrived here at Standmere that I could make any changes I saw fit. He told me this is his house, which is the only permanent building on the site and whose four walls I have rarely seen him leave. His exact words were, 'Policy is to leave the women and their tykes to get on with it and that's exactly what I do. If you fancy a tad of do-gooding, go and do good but, if you ask me, you're wasting your time. We call them refugees but frankly they're worse than kaffirs and they don't speak a word of English.'

He was right, of course, because I have been wasting my time, although not for the reasons he gave me. These women and children – women and children! – have been treated like dogs, but there is nothing I can do. It was not my decision to build this camp on land that is no better than swamp where insects rule throughout the day, spreading numerous hideous diseases. It was not my decision to house these people under perished canvas, rejected by the army, that lets the icy night wind whip through. It was not my decision to appoint one nurse for a thousand-strong population and to equip her with nothing but her own goodwill. It was not my decision to deny these people fresh vegetables and milk, and to provide meat that is already live with maggots. It was not my decision to assign the dregs of the British Army to police this Hades, or that they should have dug the latrines no more than ten yards from the sleeping tents. These were not my decisions but their consequences are unfolding under my jurisdiction and I am sickened.

I have made my protests through the chain of command and I have heard nothing. I have myself witnessed at least twenty infants under eight years old starve to death, twenty more who will do so within a week. And, for my pride and with my shame, I have turned away an American journalist who came to report on these terrible conditions. Was this the action of a hero?

My own fever is now rising and I must stop writing before my nightly delirium overwhelms me. My left leg is numb and I am too fearful to look beneath the dressing. I leave at dawn and it cannot come soon enough. I conclude, therefore, with one thought: this – this *nightmare* – is now all I know of Empire and, for the first time in my life, I am loath to call myself an Englishman. May God forgive me.

2

Prisoner 118

Queenstown, Republic of Zambawi, 2008

The guards frog-marched the new recruit along the dark corridor, their boots echoing a portentous rhythm on the concrete. The shift captain took the lead and four of his men boxed the recruit in a tight formation. The recruit didn't resist, but there was a slight catch in his stride as if he couldn't quite keep time or, perhaps, he was tempted to break rank at any second and run for it. Each man marched with his left arm ticking and his right hand fixed to the ball of the knobkerrie at his waist. None of them spoke. Nothing could be heard but the regular beat of their footsteps, the syncopated jangle of the heavy bunches of keys on their hips and the occasional drip of water from the ceiling.

The four old hands could easily be identified by their scruffy uniforms. But even if you'd caught only the briefest glimpse of their faces, you'd most likely have recognized a commonality: their expressions were like blank pieces of paper, the only distinguishing feature a slight but perceptible sleepiness at the eyes. The new recruit, on the other hand, was pristine. His grey shirt was buttoned to the collar beneath his clean navy tie with the initials 'ZPS' stitched in silver, his shoes were mirror polished and the creases in his trousers marked both his eagerness and uncertainty. His mouth was dry but his lips were wet and shiny and his expression wide-eyed. He looked as if he'd just been unwrapped.

Half an hour ago, the recruit had stood to attention in the governor's office while the others loitered outside, peering through the frosted glass, smoking cigarettes and discussing their new colleague. 'He looks like a Brit, this guy,' one remarked. 'Full of good intentions and bad ideas.'

Another shook his head. 'He'll learn.'

The recruit was twenty-one years old and had only recently left the technical college with a mediocre diploma in education. He had applied for two dozen posts in schools across the country but, due to government cutbacks, there were now far fewer vacancies than teachers qualified to fill them. The only alternative then open to the young man had been to try the NGO schools, but they were almost exclusively staffed by foreigners. These foreigners were either recklessly over-qualified and recklessly overpaid in foreign currency into foreign bank accounts, or they were volunteers with mediocre certificates but, it seemed, no need of a living wage. Typically, the only position open to locals, therefore, was to teach the foreign teachers how to say 'please' and 'thank you' and 'no, I don't want any'.

Such a position was never going to provide adequate income for a young man who was the only breadwinner at his parents' house and had a new wife who was eight months of the way through a problematic pregnancy. So, eventually, this young man had applied to the prison service, which, though similarly afflicted by cutbacks, had not enjoyed the same influx of helpful foreigners. His acceptance had been a relief and he was determined to make the best of it.

The guards stopped outside the iron door at the far end of the corridor. This wing of the prison wasn't like the others the recruit had seen on his brief orientation tour the previous week. Whereas the rest were made up of large, communal units with forty or fifty inmates crammed into each, this one consisted of a dozen two-person cells designated for 'special cases' (typically miscreants held by presidential decree). At present, only two of these cells were occupied. At the other end of the corridor, the first on the right held a short, fat, bald *musungu* who showed few signs of losing weight despite a diet that consisted of little more than righteous indignation. The second was this last cell, which held . . . Well, if the rumours were true, it held a one-time national hero whose name had long been synonymous with the Second Revolution and the President's own.

The recruit's heart was drumming so hard and so fast against his chest that he wasn't sure he could hear anything above it. The air at this end of the corridor was thick with some odour that he was struggling to identify. There was the usual stink of sweat and shit and piss, of course, but mingled with this was something else; something he couldn't name and which was, therefore, terrifying. He turned to the shift captain (whose bright idea this initiation had been) and asked, 'What's that smell, sir?'

The captain, a great bear of a man with dark skin and pinprick eyes, spoke flatly: 'You'll find out soon enough.'

The next thing the recruit knew, his colleagues had grabbed him by the arms and shoulders and thrust him against the cell door. Then the captain reached in front of his face and, with one huge, fleshy hand, grasped the handle of the steel hatch and pulled it back while the other pushed the recruit's face towards the metal grille. 'See for yourself!' the captain whispered.

The recruit looked. His breathing was quick and shallow. The cell was gloomy and his eyes struggled to adjust. The mysterious smell was stronger than ever and filled his nostrils, making his eyes water. The light from the hatch cast a stripe across the cell floor but at first, outside that narrow sector, he couldn't see a single thing.

Then, slowly, he began to make out what had to be a human form: the prisoner, squatting in one corner. The recruit struggled to free himself but the hands and the weight of the bodies against him held him in place. A strange object protruded into the narrow strip of light that bisected the cell. The recruit stared at it. He couldn't make out what it was but it was a rough oblong shape and it was filthy and it appeared to be attached to a thin stick. The recruit tried to lick his lips but his tongue was heavy and dry.

Then the prisoner spoke: 'Have you a good view, Simeon Matete?' The voice had a deep and musical quality.

The recruit blinked. 'How do you know my name?' he asked. By comparison his own voice sounded thin, high-pitched and insubstantial, like the whistle of a half-blocked nose.

His question provoked a rumbling chuckle from the cell. 'I know lots of things,' the prisoner said. 'Many of them for reasons that you would not understand. In this case, however, Captain Makuvitse was kind enough to furnish me with your details. Despite appearances, the captain is a decent man who likes to keep me abreast of the situation. I suspect he is following orders. I suspect our president, although he has no intention to forgive me, does not want his old friend to rot in this hell-hole. Indeed, were it not for Makuvitse's ministrations, my poor wounded foot would have turned gangrenous and dropped off by now.'

Next to him, Simeon the recruit heard one of the other guards murmur, 'He's lucid today.'

Even if he'd had ears like a bat, the prisoner surely couldn't have heard this. Nonetheless, he now addressed the guard who'd spoken as if it were a conversation. 'Edwin Vumba! My friend! Your ongoing concern is endlessly touching. But you needn't worry. I am always lucid. Even in the dark a mirror reflects, you know.'

Suddenly Simeon saw a hand emerge into the shaft of light, holding what appeared to be a paintbrush. The strange smell intensified again. The hand started to dab gingerly at the rough oblong shape at the end of the stick. Suddenly, in a simultaneous rush of understanding, Simeon identified the nature of the smell, the stick and the rough oblong shape: the smell was iodine, the stick was an inhumanly wasted lower leg, the rough oblong shape a toeless foot. Suddenly Simeon could make out the tiny bud-like stumps where the toes had once been. His throat constricted and he gagged, spluttering loudly.

'Simeon Matete!' the prisoner exclaimed, amused and derisory. 'You'll have to toughen up if you're to work in a place like this. With or without toes, my foot is still my foot and still attached to my leg. Although I wish the flies and rats would get the message.' Then, to the shift captain, 'Makuvitse! Is this now the benchmark for your recruits? It's a bad sign, my friend.' Then, to himself, 'Iodine is a colonial miracle. Are we expected to pretend otherwise? I said as much to the –'

The voice cut out as if someone had hit the off switch and the leg and foot retracted into the shadows. The abrupt silence caught Simeon by surprise and he pressed his face harder against the grille to try to make out what was going on. No sooner had he done so than he tried to pull away again but there were still hands forcing him to watch. The prisoner had now leapt to his feet and begun manically to stalk the cell in small circles, his damaged foot thrust out to one side.

Every second or two, the prisoner passed into the shaft of light by the door and Simeon caught sight of his face in momentary glimpses through the dreadlocks that whipped about it. Simeon spotted wild eyes, thick lips, gaunt cheeks and a peculiar flawless, almost childlike complexion. 'What's he doing?' Simeon murmured.

But before any of the other guards could choose to answer, the prisoner began to speak again, only this time the voice that emanated from his mouth was indisputably not his own. This voice came fast, clipped and insistent. Most of all, though, it came speaking an arcane English that Simeon struggled to understand.

'Look here!' the prisoner declared. 'Read for yourself! "The danger is not less real because it is imaginary. Imagination acts

13

upon a man as really as gravitation, and may kill him as certainly as a dose of prussic acid!'' Read it! Read it!'

Simeon watched, terrified but transfixed. He recognized possession, of course, and he'd heard of mediums giving voice to any manner of totem ancestor. But to witness a spirit medium (not only that, but the most famous *zakulu* in the country) speak like this was incomprehensible. What could it mean?

With the final 'Read it!', the prisoner had buckled at the knees and collapsed beneath the door so that he was obscured from Simeon's view. The hands that had been holding him in place finally relaxed and he was able to take a step back. He turned to look at the shift captain. Makuvitse's expression was inscrutable. Simeon said, 'That's Comrade –'

'*That*,' the captain interrupted, 'is Prisoner 118 and that is the only way he is to be addressed: "Prisoner 118" or simply "118". This is a penal institution, Matete, and there's a lot of madness. Some of our guests are here because they are mad and some are mad because they are here, but that is precisely why we have regulations that apply to all men equally. Prisoner 118, however, is a special case. He will tell you all kinds of strange things and it is your duty to report them to me. That's the order from the governor and it is, shall we say?, the exception that proves the rule about our rules. Are we clear?'

'Yes, sir.'

'Then we'll get back to work.'

With that, the captain spun on his heels and made to march back down the corridor.

Simeon turned to the cell door to close the hatch but he found the prisoner's face now pressed up against the grille. 'Simeon Matete!' Prisoner 118 hissed. 'I have something to tell you.' His own bass tone had returned and the sound of his voice had stopped the captain in his tracks. 'Come close!' he insisted.

Simeon hesitated, but at Makuvitse's signal he pressed his

14

ear to the grille. The *zakulu*'s voice was like hot wax slowly filling his head. He closed his eyes and listened.

He stood like that – eyes shut, a little stooped, head inclined – for a full five minutes. Then he opened his eyes, stepped away from the door and slid the hatch shut. He stuck an index finger in the ear that had been pressed to the grille and gave it a quick wiggle. He looked as if he'd just woken up.

Makuvitse was watching him with his eyebrows raised. 'Well?'

'Sir?'

'What did he say?'

'He asked for a book, sir.'

'118 wants another book? No surprises there. What book?'

'*The Golden Bough*, sir. By a man called Frazer. He says it's an old book, sir.'

The captain produced a small notebook from his breast pocket and jotted this down. 'And?'

'And he wants some painkillers, sir. He said the iodine may stop the infection but do you realize that he's in agony? He says he wants some high-strength ibuprofen, which you can buy in the expat pharmacy at the Alliance Française on Machel.'

The captain wrote this down too. 'And?'

'And what?'

'He was talking to you a long time, Matete. What else did he say?'

Simeon took a deep breath. 'He said that my wife has gone into labour, sir.'

'I thought she was still a month away.'

'She is, sir. Or, at least, she is supposed to be. But Comrade . . . sorry . . . Prisoner 118 said that I'm going to have a son. He said that my wife will be scared because he will be born small and short of breath. He said I must reassure her that this is only because the child is eager to get on with things and it's generally a good sign. He said . . .' Simeon hesitated.

15

'Yes?'

'He said I must call the child John Kipling Matete that I might never take him for granted, but never be afraid to let him go. He said that, in the long run, Sibongile and I would be quite OK.'

'Sibongile?'

'My wife, sir.'

'Never be afraid to let him go?'

'That's what he said, sir.' The shift captain wrote all this down. 'And that was about it,' Simeon concluded.

'What do you mean "that was *about it*"? I told you, Matete, I need to know exactly what he said.'

'Exactly?'

'Exactly.'

'Well, sir . . . *Exactly* . . . that is to say, exactly as I recall . . . he said, "The first illness John will suffer as an infant, Simeon Matete, is a nasty dose of glue ear. When that happens, it will be cured immediately if you spit in his ear like this."'

'Like what?'

'Then he spat in my ear, sir.'

Makuvitse looked at Simeon steadily for a moment and said, 'Very good,' closed his notebook and returned it to his breast pocket. Then he smiled broadly. It was the first time Simeon had seen his superior's teeth and they were horribly misshapen and crooked, jutting from his gums at all sorts of angles. But, in Simeon's opinion, the expression made him look almost like a human being for the first time. 'You have a son,' Makuvitse said, as if he'd never heard anything quite so surprising.

'That's what he said, sir.'

The captain nodded briskly. 'Congratulations, Matete. Congratulations.'

3
Authenticity™

London, England, 2008

The Authenticity™ core team was gathered around the table in the timber and canvas yurt that acted as a meeting room in the company's open-plan office in Old Street, London. They were all talking at once, but their boss wasn't listening, which was unusual.

Preston Pinner, a.k.a. '2P™' a.k.a. 'Tuppence™', often said that he'd made his fortune 'just listening and watching'. This was euphemistic and an attempt at self-deprecation. Because Preston didn't just listen: he devoured variations of accent and dialect, chewed on nuances of tone and vocabulary and, frequently, knew what someone meant a whole lot better than they did. He didn't just watch: he dissected expressions, peeled away mannerisms (whether cultural, contextual, culturally contextual or plain vain) and picked apart fashion. Preston had a party trick: he could look at anyone in any context and tell you exactly where they'd bought each item of their clothing, how much they'd paid and, even, their motivations for the purchase. He didn't just watch and listen, he *engaged*.

The use of the word 'engage' to mean 'connect with a person or idea' is thoroughly modern. Ironically, perhaps, this usage often accompanies the absence of the practice. People didn't 'engage' before 1990, they listened and watched. Now, however, they claimed to engage precisely because they did neither. It was the new rule of engagement, and Preston was the exception that proved it.

In fact, when Preston founded Authenticity™, the slogan 'We engage so you don't have to' was printed across the first batch of company stationery. Only later was this replaced by the more nebulous, not to say, meaningless, 'Authenticity™: keeping it really real'. In fact, he had a couple of mottoes. One was, 'The guy with a good idea is only half as important as the guy who recognizes it.' The other, 'Don't worry about what *you* think they need, engage with what *they* think they want.'

It is safe to say, therefore, that Preston recognized the value of listening, watching, *engagement*. But he wasn't engaged right now – or, at least, not in the way he should have been.

Jodie was talking about 'The Game', the nationwide 'urban talent' competition that Authenticity™ had been running in partnership with a mobile-phone network. Regional heats were due to culminate in a televised live final, the winner to be awarded a place on the A-List™, have their track distributed as a downloadable ringtone and be granted the opportunity to perform within the Authenticity™-programmed slot of 'Africa Unite', the government-sponsored music festival that was planned for the climax of the year-long African Authority project.

The Game's early rounds had been a triumph of media exposure, but now it seemed Authenticity™ had hit a snag. According to their partners, Jodie explained, some of the regional winners – MCs, vocalists and producers – were just 'not urban enough' while others were, frankly, 'too urban'.

This provoked a lot of laughter around the table and then a heated discussion as to what exactly the sponsors could mean. The hubbub rose and the meeting was in danger of splintering into half a dozen separate discussions until Errol cut to the chase. 'Fuck it!' he spat. 'We all *know* what they mean. They mean that the white kids what won is too fucking white and the black kids what won is too fucking black, you get me? Urban? It's bullshit, man. Total racist bullshit. Press? Tupps? Tell 'em, bruv.'

The round table was silenced by Errol's impassioned outburst. Unfortunately Preston wasn't engaged. The yurt's canvas was rolled back and his attention was fixed on the muted, big-screen plasma HD on the far side of the office. It was showing twenty-four-hour news and his dad, the junior Foreign Office minister, David Pinner, appeared to be addressing a press conference. There was a standfirst bar across the bottom of the screen that he could barely make out. He had to strain his eyes and read it a couple of times to make sure he'd got it right – 'Prominent UK businessman arrested in Zambawi'.

Zambawi? Preston had barely heard of the place. He racked his brains. Was that the one famous for blood diamonds or weed, for genocide or famine? Frankly, like most non-Western places, it only existed for Preston in the broadest brushstrokes, coloured in by GCSE geography. It might as well have been one of those rogue Middle Eastern states Hollywood invented so the latest muscle-bound action hero could go and rescue it from some or other oppressive regime, or one of those Bosnian towns with names like bad Scrabble hands in which his old man had taken such interest in the mid-nineties. Though Preston had made his fortune engaging, he rarely engaged with the serious news.

He watched his dad now. He couldn't lip-read but he was sure he could follow every word. He watched the minister's mouth form the word 'outrage' and then, surely, the phrases 'strongest possible terms' and 'highest possible level'.

Preston blinked. The language might have been predictable but he was fascinated nonetheless; fascinated especially by his dad's extraordinary equine features, which, as he fielded questions, managed simultaneously to convey utter conviction and a certain wounded vulnerability.

In the media, David Pinner's appearance was frequently compared to that of an English film star, not any film star in particular but different ones by different journalists at different times, suggesting there was something archetypal about him.

He was granted epithets like 'elegant' or 'dashing', presumably because he was tall and slender and allowed his thick mane to grow long. Preston, who was shortish and thickset and cropped his hair to zero, couldn't see it, perhaps because any genes he and his father shared seemed to be concentrated in their faces.

When Preston considered his old man's long, thin nose, therefore, he saw something preposterous that only supported his reservations about his own appearance. He had once read that a man's nose kept growing into adulthood and he was terrified that this was the monstrosity he might soon expect. More than that, though, he was worried that he'd inherited his dad's mouth, with those peculiarly motile lips and tombstone teeth. As far as Preston was concerned, the minister resembled a horse, and not some noble beast like Red Rum or Black Bess but a nag that poked his head dopily over a five-bar gate: his dad was Mister Ed.

'Tupps! *Tupps!*'

'What?' Preston looked at Errol.

'What do we do?'

'About what?'

'About The Game, man. The winners ain't urban enough. The winners is too urban. Like I said, man, it's racist bullshit.'

'Yeah, Errol,' Jodie interjected. 'That's great. But the point is, what do we tell the man? What are we supposed to say? "That's racist bullshit"? They're fronting the money, blood. So what do we tell them?'

Preston blinked at Jodie. Her use of the word 'blood' wasn't working and she knew it. She was trying it out like a little girl tries her mum's lipstick or a mum tries a Top Shop mini. Its failure was only compounded by her evident embarrassment. He glanced around the table at his employees. Apart from DJ Jonny Swift™, the laptop (an in-joke) that sat in the place on his right, they were carefully selected personifications of cool, graduates from some of the best universities, and he liked every one of them. Thinking for themselves, however, had not been one of his prime recruitment requirements. They were all watching him. He let the moment hang. Eventually he said, 'Who's got the power here?'

The team looked confused.

Juice, a scrawny twenty-two-year-old Scouser and the latest addition to the company (bringing vital expertise in skinny jeans and nu rave), spoke up: 'What do you mean?'

'I mean who's got the power.'

'Well,' Jodie said. 'It's their money . . .'

This was what Preston had been waiting for. 'Money? Who gives a shit about money? Everyone's got *money*. Haven't you been following the slump? Money isn't worth shit. It's our kudos they're paying for and if we pull out they're fucked. And we go to the press and tell them why we've pulled out and then they're more fucked and we've got more kudos than ever. Urban? We *own* "urban"! We delivered our side of the bargain, Jodie. We lent them our name, fulfilled our contract and got them more publicity than they know what to do with. Shit! You know what? Errol's suggestion works for me.'

'Which was?' Jodie asked. She looked as if she already knew the answer and she didn't like it.

'Tell them it's racist bullshit,' Preston said. 'Tell them to fuck off.'

The Authenticity™ team exchanged glances before, one by one, they began to look at Preston, to nod and laugh. This was a man at the top of his game. This was why they worked for him. This was why he was who he was.

But the man himself wouldn't meet their eyes. Instead he sat back and contemplated the roof of the yurt and considered, one by one, the reasons he wanted to scream.

4

Of suspicion (1)

Queenstown, Republic of Zambawi, 2008
'My brothers and sisters, today, the anniversary of our independence, is a day of celebration. It is a time to recall the heroic endeavours of those, my father among them, who fought for so many years to secure our freedom from colonial oppression.

'It is also, however, a time for us to reflect soberly on the progress we have made as an independent nation, our current situation and future prospects. It is painful for me to tell you that we face difficult times ahead.'

Even on the ancient television affixed to the wall in the guards' mess at Gwezi prison, Enoch Adini, the recently if controversially re-elected third-term President of Zambawi, cut quite a dash. The image on the screen might have been fuzzy, the lighting unflattering and the flag behind the podium hanging at a distracting angle but Adini had something about him, some quality that made it hard not to watch. He was good-looking, of course – young for a president, tall and slim with broad shoulders – but he'd always been good-looking and the presidential picture that hung on the wall of every hotel in the country was famous for the admiring glances it drew from international visitors. So, this quality was something else: a new gravity that lent intensity to his gaze and determination to his jaw.

Until recently he'd been the popular schoolteacher, perhaps, or the middle manager who flirted with the secretaries, or the affable uncle, but now he was the headmaster, the CEO, the father of the nation. He looked like he meant business. He looked truly presidential. Whether or not this was a welcome development depended on your viewpoint. But it certainly made him watchable and it seemed to have developed in direct response to the challenges of the last few months.

Adini addressed some of those challenges now. He attacked the independent observers ('so-called') who had decried the Zambawian election as 'fundamentally flawed'. He attacked the international community ('so-called'), who had subsequently pressed for a new vote and then imposed sanctions that sent inflation spiralling to a crippling 300 per cent. He attacked his opponent, Joseph Phiri of the Democratic Movement, whose campaign had been, he claimed, entirely funded by the 'white gentlemen's club'.

Increasingly, Adini's speeches were heavy with inverted commas and italics in a way that made them both thoroughly specific to his audience and unfailingly ironic. For example, the United States (Phiri's chief financier) was usually referred to simply as *they*, while Great Britain, the former colonial power, was typically 'that drab little island in the north Atlantic'.

'Who are *they* to tell us about democracy?' Adini asked. '*They* had an election that was neither free nor fair and was ultimately awarded to the loser. And as for that drab little island in the north Atlantic, if the "international media" is to be believed, the Prime Minister may soon subject himself to his people's will. If so, in the spirit of reciprocity, I will happily despatch a team of Zambawian independent monitors to ensure their election is subject to the most rigorous democratic standards. In fact, I have sent exactly such a missive to my counterpart and have yet to hear a response. But the offer stands.'

At this point Adini paused for a moment, pursed his lips, and raised an interrogative eyebrow. This was to signify that he was making a joke, but it was hard to know whether the joke was that he might consider sending such a scandalous message or that he had actually done so. Certainly, in the households of his supporters nationwide, they assumed the latter and laughed wholeheartedly at his bravado, while in opposition homes they shook their heads at this further sign that the President had lost it and the country was going to hell in a handcart.

In the mess at Gwezi, however, the four guards awaiting the imminent end of their shift hardly reacted at all. Captain Makuvitse and Officers Vumba and Masinga simply stared up at the screen, motionless and transfixed, as if watching the landing of an alien spacecraft. Only Officer Matete, the new recruit, showed any sign of life, his eyes flitting between his colleagues as he wondered whether it would be appropriate for him to make a comment. He decided not.

The mess television was of uncertain provenance. Securely attached to the wall with four heavy metal bolts, it had been there longer than any serving guard and, ancient as it was, appeared intent on outlasting them all. It was large and solid, and the impression it gave of obdurate permanence was only increased by the lack of much in the way of furniture. There was a battered row of a dozen metal lockers along one wall, but just one still had a door and boasted the lone coat hook. There was nowhere to sit, just two seat cushions against the opposite wall that hinted at the former luxury of armchairs. There was a rusty water fountain plumbed into thin air. And the great television watched over the room, a memento, one could only assume, of more prosperous days when smart, optimistic, well-remunerated prison guards hung their coats in the lockers and drank from the water fountain before settling back in those armchairs to catch the latest news or maybe a football match.

Simeon Matete checked his watch. He realized that their shift had in fact ended five minutes ago and he considered whether it was OK to leave. After all, he was eager to get home to his wife and newborn son and it didn't seem like the President would be finished any time soon.

Adini was currently attacking the IMF, the World Bank and the policy of 'Structural Adjustment' (so-called) that the 'white gentlemen's club' had imposed upon the nation: '*Their* development, historically speaking, was founded on the principles of protectionism. And yet *they* insist we must prostrate ourselves on the altar of private enterprise and the so-called free market. No!'

Simeon didn't quite know what 'Structural Adjustment' was, only that it had once been trumpeted as the answer to all Zambawi's problems, but was now considered the problem on which every answer foundered.

The new recruit cleared his throat noisily. It wasn't that he had no interest in what the President was saying and he certainly made for an impressive spectacle. But, independence day or not, it wasn't as if this speech was covering much in the way of new ground; neither was it unusual for Adini to appear on television. In fact, these days, it seemed like the President was rarely *not* on TV.

After his re-election, the President had introduced the policy of 'localization', which decreed that 75 per cent of programming on national radio and television had to be locally produced and the rest sourced from countries beyond the 'white gentlemen's club' that did not seek to 'pollute' the Zambawian mind.

The repercussions of this policy were various. The music industry, for example, was flourishing as radio DJs desperately sought out any homegrown tune to fill their airtime. However, filling the television schedules proved more problematic, especially when sanctions bit and the foreign-currency reserve was depleted as never before. The one terrestrial TV channel began to broadcast several new soap operas on patriotic themes, with shaky camerawork and even shakier dialogue, and a string of South American wildlife documentaries that ran back to back, without subtitles, as primetime viewing. Not only could many Zambawian schoolchildren now give a reasonable account of Amazonian biodiversity, but they could do so in Portuguese.

And most nights, after these documentaries, before the nightly news, Adini addressed the nation for anything from ten minutes to two hours. The President described these spots as his 'contribution to the decolonization of Zambawian culture', while opposition supporters considered them an indicator of the nation's slide into totalitarianism. Most people, however, regarded them as signifying nothing more than the ongoing shortage of cheap programming.

Now Simeon began to look between the faces of his colleagues with increasing bewilderment. For all the President's charisma, it didn't explain the mesmerized reaction of his fellow guards. In the recruit's experience, politics was a matter of passionate debate between friends and family, neighbours and colleagues. Occasionally such discussions might overheat but most disagreements could be defused with a good joke.

Certainly such passion had been evident during the election campaign, with everywhere from neighbourhood bottle stores to the university's lecture halls humming with argument and counter-argument. Whether Adini had ultimately rigged the count or not, everyone could agree it had been a close contest between the 'staunch nationalist' and the 'western puppet', or the 'would-be dictator' and the 'progressive liberal' (depending on your viewpoint). Of course there had been occasional violent clashes but, for the most part, they had been quickly contained. And wasn't that just the nature of meaningful politics?

Simeon wanted to go home. Again he cleared his throat, louder than before, and this time, at last, he received brief recognition from one of his colleagues. Officer Vumba's eyes darted towards him and they were full of a mixture of resentment and fear. The look lasted no more than an instant, but it told Simeon all he needed to know and he felt his heart quicken and sudden perspiration at his temples. Dear God, Simeon thought. They suspect I'm CIS!

In the last fortnight of the election campaign, a Democratic Movement parliamentary candidate called Precious Kampampa had been found gunned down in her home. A week later, DM party leader Joseph Phiri was arrested on some jumped-up corruption charge and beaten black and blue in a cell at Queenstown Central police station. More recently, a teenager, Alice Chipinge, had been battered to death by the cops (allegedly) when university students attempted to march on State House.

Each of these events was shocking, of course, but, viewed in isolation, might have been dismissed as an aberration: a tragic consequence of difficult times. Considered together, however, they added up to something altogether more sinister, symptomatic, perhaps, of a state-sponsored descent into lawlessness and oppression. The policy of 'localization', which was quickly followed by the expulsion of all foreign journalists, only fuelled the rumours. Now that nobody knew what the international media were saying, they could only assume the worst. And those who did manage to track down reports on CNN or the BBC (on satellite television or the Internet) found that the international media, in their ignorance, were assuming the worst too.

Key among these rumours was that those who spoke out against the government were disappearing at the hands of the Central Intelligence Service, including a white British businessman, who'd been holidaying in the country, and a celebrated spirit medium, who was a vital figurehead in the coup that had brought President Adini to power more than a decade before. Like all the most successful rumours, this one's strength lay in the fact it suited various agenda. The government liked it, of course, because it discouraged opposition. But the opposition liked it too as it seemed to confirm everything they'd been saying about the government. Indeed, some now claimed that Phiri's own son Benjamin was one of those who'd disappeared, an assertion that added a welcome glint of steel to the image of the Democratic Movement leader.

There were even more personal reasons why individual citizens might keep the rumour alive – the father whose son had forsaken the family homestead to find a job in the city, a wife whose husband had left her for another woman. After all, it was better to be a victim of political intrigue than social disgrace.

What was more, as the rumour propagated so its symptoms mutated. Where initially the supposed disappearances were openly discussed, soon such discussions themselves seemed to carry a risk. What if mentioning the disappearances actually constituted anti-government talk? What if the person you mentioned them to was actually a member of the CIS? Everyone knew the rumour therefore, but could only ever raise it with those closest to them; and there were now further stories – unsubstantiated and, of course, impossible to substantiate – of fathers turning in their sons and wives their husbands.

In the mess at Gwezi, it was these new symptoms of the rumour that were being played out as Simeon wondered if he could say something to allay the other guards' suspicions. After all, in the presidential election, he had, in fact, voted for Phiri so if, for example, he now made a joke at the President's expense, his colleagues would know he was trustworthy. He considered this and was about to give it a try when he realized what a dangerous tactic it might prove to be.

For starters, in his new job Simeon had discovered that the white Brit and the celebrated *zakulu* had indeed been arrested. And while a joke might demonstrate that *he* wasn't CIS, what of the others? What if he'd misread the situation and it was Masinga, say, who was the government agent? What if he said something and, before he knew it, found himself on the other side of the prison bars? Would Sibongile guess what had happened, or think he'd abandoned her and his son?

Instead, therefore, Simeon took the only safe option available to him: he said nothing and adopted the exact same pose as his fellows, staring up at the large television as if it held every answer. He quickly refocused his attention on the President's words. Fortunately, to judge by the tone and subject matter, the speech was building towards its climax. Adini's rhetoric was more forthright than ever as he navigated a route to what had lately become his favourite subject – his decision to default on all Zambawi's debts ('so-called').

'"No" is the key word of my third presidency,' Adini announced, thrusting an index finger skywards. 'We say no to unfair loans, to aid with strings attached, to the Western politicians who treat us like fools and the Western media that describe us as such. We say no to the fruits of those "cultures" (so-called) that boost their egos, pollute their bodies and delude their minds. And when the World Bank and the IMF cry to the "white gentlemen's club" that we are failing to service our so-called "debts", we will look them squarely in the eye and say: "No. It is you who owe us. Return the natural resources that you stole. Return the gold, oil, diamonds, platinum, uranium, copper and rubber that you plundered. Return the bodies of our ancestors whom you kidnapped and enslaved and, if their descendants want to bring them home, they will be welcomed with open arms." We say no, no and no again.'

The President paused and shook his head, as if what he had to say next were almost too troubling to address. Momentarily, he looked away from the camera, then, directly back into it. 'My brothers and sisters, we are involved in a new independence struggle. We are fighting for the independence of our very minds, because the alternative is a mental slavery every bit as pernicious as the apartheid our fathers and mothers, uncles and aunts, grandfathers and grandmothers struggled to overcome.

'The war has already begun. I have increasing evidence that

I cannot share with you now that our former oppressors, that drab little island marooned in the north Atlantic, are already engaged in a clandestine attempt to restore a new form of imperial rule. We must, therefore, be vigilant and resolute. When a pack of jackals circles the village every night ready to steal the children, no man sleeps until it has moved on. We must be the same.

'I will leave you with something that the Traveller, the Child of the Horizon, our founding ancestor, Tuloko, is said to have told his sons just before his death: "A true leader must be as many things as the people require." And this is what I intend to be. I will be strong, my brothers and sisters of Zambawi, and I ask that you are strong too: our independence demands it.'

Adini nodded abruptly and stepped back from the podium. The camera trained in on the crooked flag hanging at the back and the national anthem began to play. Instinctively the four guards stiffened to attention.

For his part, Simeon had quite forgotten any worries about the CIS, even his hurry to return home to his family. In fact, he'd have been more than happy for the speech to continue. After all, there is something about political conviction eloquently expressed, about playing the underdog on the moral high ground, about the adoption of negatives as philosophical principles, about building the facts into a mythological narrative, something that chimes with the uncertain majority who are used to injustice, familiar with taking 'no' for an answer and simply long to be part of the story. Right now, therefore, Simeon felt an affinity with his president like never before, if not with what he stood for then certainly with what he stood against.

It was Captain Makuvitse who broke the spell. The giant of a man sniffed voraciously before growling, 'Right, then, I'll see you lot tomorrow, six a.m. sharp.' With that, he retrieved his coat from the single coat hook in the only locker with a door and left without a further word. The others followed. As they processed out, Simeon cast a furtive glance at Officer Masinga, only to find Masinga glancing equally furtively back at him. Whatever vague suspicions each might have had of the other were thus immediately confirmed and it was guaranteed that the President's speeches would continue to be watched in uneasy, frozen silence for the foreseeable future.

5

```
Insert document
'Preface', The Book of Zamba Mythology (OUP,
2005), Edison Burrows III
```

The career path of an academic is frequently a journey of specialization and, as such, inherently esoteric. The eager student who begins by asking universal questions that matter to everyone slowly evolves into a careworn professor answering questions so specific they interest nobody, not even that same poor professor.

In my experience, there are three ways this gradual narrowing process is avoided. They are as follows: you may address yourself to a fashionable branch of your subject. If successful, you will then be allowed to generalize. In the case of anthropology, this typically means first conducting fieldwork in especially remote, peculiar or savage human societies. You may also be determinedly populist, attacking broad issues with a scattergun while simultaneously developing some kind of 'media profile'. Or you may achieve a level of such academic brilliance that your every word on any subject is thought worthy of consideration, no matter how little you actually know about it.

In my case, however, I hadn't the stomach for the remote, peculiar or savage, I wasn't blessed with the looks prerequisite for the populist, and I am not brilliant. Thus, I specialized and, after thirty years' teaching in six universities, scores of published papers, six books, five bouts of fieldwork and three of malaria, I am the world's leading expert in the mythology of the Zamba, the sub-Saharan African tribal grouping almost exclusively contained within the borders of present-day Zambawi. I say this without arrogance, for I am also the world's only expert in Zamba mythology (except, of course, the eight million or so Zamba people who may have cause to dispute such a claim).

For the majority of my career, Zambawi has been an unremarkable place – a former British colony struggling with the challenges of independence, much like many other African nations – and my work of limited appeal even to my academic brethren, let alone the wider public. My undergraduates have been known to quote myths I recorded as abstruse exemplars of other anthropologists' ideas and I have occasionally been invited to chair panels at various obscure conferences around the world. But, for the most part, my books have grown dusty in the dustiest corners of the dustiest university libraries.

How my life changed, therefore, with the coup in Zambawi a decade ago that saw Enoch Adini succeed his father to the presidency and the subsequent republication of my 1965 ethnography, *The Zamba*. Much to my and, without doubt, my publisher's surprise, this humble field study developed something of a cult following and sold in unprecedented numbers. Through no skill on my part, therefore, my life's work was suddenly fashionable. Thereafter, I became popular, even considered brilliant. It has been quite a ride and I cannot deny enjoying it. Even so, my work has remained unchanged.

In the intervening years, my editor has inevitably pressed me for a new book, but until now I have resisted. I find it hard to explain my reluctance beyond my distrust of fashion and populism and, perhaps, a desire not to upset the perception of brilliance. However, as I near retirement, I have felt a growing urge to set down what I know.

I am not interested in my own ideas – I have spent quite enough time with them over the years and, in truth, I'm not sure I ever found them all that intriguing. But I remain fascinated by the data I have recorded and I want it to have a life beyond the hundreds of cassette tapes that litter my office floor. This is one reason why I present the collection of Zamba myths that follow herein without analysis.

The second reason is that I have come to believe that the anthropological dissection of mythology, however erudite, is a fundamentally flawed practice. All these years spent extrapolating function, interpreting signifiers and investigating variability have arguably taught me more about the politics, religion and socialization of anthropologists than about the Zamba people.

Mythology is the work of the collective subconscious, its purpose always nuanced and mystical, aesthetic and arcane. To say that a particular myth has this or that particular meaning is, therefore, typically an exercise in wilful incomprehension. For example, the origin myth, included here, details what may be termed the 'separation of powers' in traditional Zamba society between the chiefs (the executive), the descendants of the sun, and the *zakulu** (the judiciary), the descendants of the moon. Indeed, this myth was the keystone of my original ethnography and many commentators picked up on it to explain the manner in which Enoch Adini garnered popular support against his father through the legitimization of the powerful *zakulu*, Musa Musa. Such an argument is not without reason (indeed I have made the same on several occasions myself), but to say it is the function of the myth is mistaken and ignores the subtlety of power relations implicit in the narrative.

Having said that this collection of mythology contains no anthropological analysis, I will not now contradict myself here

---

* I do not intend this text to be overloaded with footnotes. Allow me this exception to prove the rule. In the past, *zakulu* has been variously translated as 'shaman', 'witchdoctor', 'spirit medium' and 'traditional healer'. The most accurate of these is probably 'spirit medium' since that highlights the *zakulu*'s prime role as intermediary between the physical and spiritual realms. However, the full role of the *zakulu* encompasses all these terms but outstrips any one. We prefer, therefore, to leave the term untranslated.

any further. However, I hope my point is clear: the meaning of any myth is the myth itself.

Zamba society may not be especially remote, peculiar or savage, but it does boast an unusually coherent and discrete mythological structure. This is the third reason I have chosen to present these myths alone: I genuinely believe that an open-minded reading of this collection offers an understanding of Zamba society superior to any historical, political or, God forbid, anthropological analysis.

Finally, I consider the collective subconscious as expressed in these myths of some universal significance. In the contemporary West, our actions and morality are shaped at a societal level by law and at an interpersonal level by custom, while any remaining mythologies are fragmented and typically regarded as archaic remnants of little current significance. But law is inherently inflexible and custom inherently instinctive. Increasingly, therefore, I suspect that the absence of a coherent mythological structure disables our capacity to truly understand ourselves.

Freedom, democracy, nationality – indeed, all our social constructions – are legally enshrined and customarily expressed. However, the lack of a coherent mythology of freedom, democracy, nationality and the rest, created by the collective subconscious, has fostered a disconnect between who we are and who we claim to be.

Of course, I am all too aware that mythology, by definition, is transmitted orally. The act of recording it is to turn it into something else (a more accurate title for this book, therefore, may be *The Book of Zamba Folk Tales*). To record a myth is to cage it, to limit its range and its opportunities to feed and reproduce. Some contemporary thinkers even consider it an inherently political act of academic neo-imperialism. I take this criticism and I certainly recognize the ironies of my undertaking. Perhaps my motivations for publishing this book are, therefore, somewhat selfish, whether the desire for my life's work to live on or the last hurrah of a vainglorious old man.

However, I still believe in the value of this record. Read on with an open mind and I hope that you will see for yourself the ways in which mythology can bridge the gap between agreed principle and individual choice and thereby represent, I believe, the most accurate manifestation of social truth.

Edison Burrows III, July 2005

6

Paid in full

If his politician father was to be believed, Preston Pinner came
from a long line of distinguished Pinners whose West Country
heritage stretched way into the dim and distant. His grandfather had been a respected Bristol solicitor and former lord
mayor, his great-grandfather a war hero who had died at the
Somme, and his great-great-grandfather a successful tobacco
trader and Worshipful Master of the Bristol Masonic Lodge.
The line extended all the way back to the first Preston Pinner,
who'd made a fortune in the slave trade before a presumed
Damascene moment (or acute political instinct, depending on
whom you believed) saw him take a role at the forefront of
abolitionism.

David Pinner adopted a pious tone when he pointed out
that their ancestors were noted for their public service as much
as their success. Nevertheless, his son and the latest heir to
both the family names – 'Preston' as well as 'Pinner' – rarely
used either of them. He was known to the world as '2P' and
to his friends as 'Tuppence'. Names and associated fonts were
registered trademarks of Authenticity™.

Preston was twenty-eight years old and a millionaire several
times over, but he dressed, as Errol put it, 'like some teenage
ASBO on the rob'. He was raised in Clifton and he'd boarded
at a major public school, but his accent now worked a distinct,
cultivated London twang. He never tried to hide his background but once, after a broadsheet journalist writing a feature
about Authenticity™ had described him as 'the worst kind of
disingenuous Sloane', Preston had tracked him down at an
album launch and broken his nose. The paparazzi were there

and captured him standing over the prone hack snarling viciously. The pictures were all over the newspapers. Preston was slapped with a restraining order, a £2000 fine and a three-month suspended jail term. Passing sentence, the judge said she found it hard to believe that someone of Preston's upbringing could have behaved with 'such recklessness, lack of judgement and plain stupidity'. David Pinner MP was doorstepped a few times over the next couple of days and was not best pleased with his son and heir.

But the truth was that Preston was far from reckless and his judgement was sound. As for stupid, Preston had another motto: 'Deal with stupid people stupidly to get what you want.'

The truth was that, upon reading the journalist's comments, he'd thought long and hard about the appropriate response and, in the end, figured that, for the sake of his growing empire, he'd best keep it 'really real'. He researched the man's background (height, weight, reach) and even consulted a lawyer before attending the launch. The punch had repositioned Preston's brand at least as successfully as it had repositioned the guy's nose and two grand was a small price to pay. Certainly he'd have charged any third party fifty times that for the work.

You see, Preston had a rare talent. He had a bizarre and intuitive grasp of what was cool, and he knew it. He wasn't arrogant about this. He was smart enough to know that he was simply fortunate to live in a place and time in human history where such talent had value – commercial value.

Like any prodigy, Preston had recognized his own talent early. At school in the mid-nineties, for example, he was listening to hip-hop when all his contemporaries were still knee-deep in rave, grunge or, God forbid, Britpop. But Preston knew he was on to something. He bought a CD burner (when such things were still rare enough to cost a packet) and within a year he was selling bootlegs to the boarding house.

Preston wasn't a particularly popular pupil; neither was

he especially clever, rebellious, sporty or any other singular stereotype that typically gives meaning to adolescence. However, while the other boys locked horns on the rugby pitch or in the classroom or dormitory, fighting for their places in the various social pecking orders, Preston watched and listened and, thanks to his unusual detachment, gradually became the sole trusted arbiter of who'd won and lost. So, he stood back as his fellows slapped and gouged and kicked and wrestled themselves into some kind of pile, stepping forward only to shake the hand of the bloody-nosed victor who teetered on the·summit, and lift the face of the crushed loser from a puddle before he drowned. Of course, if his removed position made it hard to be Preston's friend, the general acceptance of his authority made it harder still to be his enemy. He became ubiquitous, the first invited to every party, confidant to prefects and suicidal tendencies alike. And his CD sales took off throughout the school.

His experience at Cambridge was similar. Not much of a student, still less of a joiner, he preferred to spend his time buying music and clothes and magazines about music and clothes. And at weekends he headed to London and hooked himself into club culture. He soon discovered he had an instinctive rapport with the cutting-edge promoters, venues and DJs and quickly founded his second lucrative business: Preston started booking his new DJ contacts to play at the Cambridge May balls whose committees were desperate for vicarious London glamour. On top of his percentage, he raked in a fortune selling class-A drugs to students eager to experiment on their big night of the year. Though he never indulged, this was not cynicism on Preston's part. To suggest as much would imply a quality of moral analysis that was no more in him than it was in his customers. In fact, he viewed them with a kind of detached, uninflected gratitude.

Thanks to his music connections, he got in with the African-Caribbean Society and started to organize the majority of their events (this being Cambridge, the African-Caribbean Society was necessarily a broad church). In his final year, he was elected the society's first (and, to date, only) white president. The story – 'White the Power' – was even picked up by the national press.

By the time he left university, two things had happened. One: hip-hop and its hybrid offspring had been lazily lumped together by record companies, retail outlets and the media into a catch-all category called 'urban', which had become the planet's best-selling musical genre. Two: Preston, the mirror image of his peers, graduated a relatively wealthy man with more than £20,000 in his current account. He founded Authenticity™ with a bank loan he matched from his own savings.

Authenticity™ opened for business in 2001 and was initially run from a bedroom in the Barbican flat his old man had bought following his election to Parliament. As much practical sense as this made, however, it soon became clear that it wouldn't last as Preston and his dad struggled to get along. Despite Pinner's initial enthusiasm for the arrangement, they hadn't lived together for any significant period since Preston was first sent to boarding school at the age of nine; each had little understanding of the other's temperament and, more to the point, ambitions. Although Pinner didn't disapprove of Authenticity™ per se and was quietly (perhaps too quietly) impressed by his son's entrepreneurial spirit, he certainly didn't regard the fledgling business as any kind of career and set about encouraging Preston to consider other options with what he called 'long-term prospects'. He did this in a fashion tried and tested by English fathers over many generations: talking up the choices made by Preston's peers and deflecting any mention of Authenticity™ with knowing sarcasm. Unfortunately Preston seemed incapable (on occasion, wilfully so) of attuning himself to his old man's best intentions and so adopted a sullen and increasingly monosyllabic defensiveness. The atmosphere in the flat was already fractious, therefore, when, little more than a month into their cohabitation, Pinner announced that he was divorcing Preston's mum.

In retrospect, Preston had to admit that this had been on the cards for some time. After all, with Pinner more or less ensconced in London and his mum at the Bristol family home, they were effectively living separate lives anyway. However, his dad's announcement still came as a shock. As long as Preston could remember, his parents' union had been something of a rollercoaster, though a childhood boarding had spared him the extreme peaks and troughs. Indeed, the marriage had probably only survived the nineties because Pinner, then making his name as an immigration lawyer with particular expertise in the Balkans conflict, had spent so much time away from home at long, drawn-out asylum hearings. With hindsight, therefore, the roots of the relationship's eventual collapse could reasonably be traced to his decision to seek election as an MP – partly because it required him to spend more time at home and partly because he had to attend an endless round of cocktail parties, for which he required his wife at his side.

One thing – in the end, perhaps the only thing – that David and Fiona Pinner had in common was the kind of social alcoholism that never quite crosses the boundaries of acceptability. For Pinner this meant that a drink to celebrate a victorious case turned into a marathon at the hotel bar with some paralegal, desperate to impress, who would wake with a hangover and the conviction that their boss was a 'good bloke'; while for Fiona, it was a bottle of red with a plate of spag bol before waking on the sofa at three a.m., dry-mouthed and disoriented. Together, it was G-and-Ts at six, wine with every meal, whisky macs for the road, and dry, drunken sex that seemed only to emphasize the deep-rooted friction between them.

However, with Pinner's bid for selection and subsequent campaign for Parliament, something tipped in Fiona. Perhaps it was simply all those meet-and-greets, the opportunities to drink, the need of a stiffener for self-confidence, or perhaps it was just standing in the shadow of someone she now realized she no longer loved, hour after hour, day after day. Either way, during the process, she developed a drinking problem of increasing visibility.

On the mantelpiece of his Barbican flat, Pinner kept a photograph of his election night triumph. He is standing centre stage, left arm aloft, right arm around his wife, a broad smile on his horsy face. Closer examination reveals the tension in that smile as he supports her full bodyweight, desperate to keep her on the vertical.

By the time Pinner announced his intention to divorce his wife – on the phone to Fiona, in person to Preston later that day – he'd had several meetings with the constituency party and parliamentary colleagues, who universally expressed sympathy and, indeed, admiration for the way he'd handled what must have been a challenging set of circumstances. Pinner, therefore, had already spun himself a workable story in which he was the long-suffering husband who'd finally reached his wits' end and had no support left to give. So, when he told Preston that he didn't expect him to 'take sides', he was being, at least subconsciously, disingenuous: he definitely expected his son to take sides and he was astonished by the side he took.

Preston spent the best part of the next month with his mother in Bristol before he had cajoled her into a drying-out clinic. When he finally got back to London, Pinner listened earnestly and with, he thought, impressive calm as his son detailed the horrors Fiona was going through. At this point, she was still his wife, after all, even though he knew he had to rein in the pain, the awful pain, for Preston's sake.

As Preston finished his report, Pinner watched his son shake his head, as though he were trying to loosen the memories of what he'd been forced to see and do. Pinner didn't know how best to react, so he reacted in the way he knew best and went to the kitchen to fetch a bottle of Scotch. 'You look like you could use a drink,' he said, as he slurped himself a large measure. He caught his son staring at him. He said, 'Oh, come on!' Then, 'I'm sorry, but . . .' Then, 'Really, it doesn't mean . . .'

Preston went to his bedroom without a further word and hadn't touched a drop of alcohol since.

Within three months, Authenticity™'s cash flow was such that Preston could move the business to the Old Street office. Within six, he himself had followed suit, first to a one-bedroom flat near Hackney Central, soon after to a Shoreditch penthouse. He was already making serious money. Thereafter, father and son met sporadically, initially for dinner, latterly for coffee. These meetings were more or less uncomfortable and both men were generally, albeit regretfully, relieved when either had to cancel because of another commitment. Both were increasingly busy.

Pinner was a rare success in a troubled government. He had a facility for shaking people's hands and remembering their names. He looked good in a suit and excellent on camera. He had the easy charm of one to whom everything had come easily. He had the concern for social justice combined with an instinctive belief in meritocracy that is a privilege of the privileged, and made him consistently popular with the press and the upper echelons of the party, if not wholly consistent. As one opposition lag put it, the new MP for Montpelier and St Paul's may have talked to the left, but he dressed to the right. When a member of the Commons press corps remarked, 'It's hard not to like him,' a government backbencher was overhead to mutter, 'Sure, but it's still important to try.'

Pinner was quickly co-opted onto various important committees and appointed a Home Office minister in time to front changes to the asylum system. Though most refugee groups considered the new statutes abhorrent, Pinner's background in immigration law and known commitment to Bosnian asylum-seekers granted him almost untouchable status, even among those who opposed the legislation. Or perhaps it was his hair. Pinner's hair was unruly, giving the impression of Bohemianism barely tamed by pragmatic requirement. And if that were true of his hair, must it not also be true of the man himself?

However, if Pinner's ascent into the public consciousness was stellar by the standards of the House of Commons, his son's was meteoric by anybody else's. And by the time Pinner moved to the Foreign and Commonwealth Office in 2007, Preston was already a full-blown celebrity and Authenticity™ one of the nation's most recognizable brands. Preston described Authenticity™ as a 'contemporary cultural consultancy and production house'. It was known as the 'hip hub' for short.

7

Insert document
'Wherefore cool?' Draft internal memo
(Authenticity™), 2003, Preston Pinner

By definition, cool is and always has been outside the mainstream. It may describe production or consumption but its vital characteristic is that it's not available to the majority.

That said, of course, if something is really cool, the chances are that it will enter mainstream culture and in doing so become 'uncool'. At the moment of said assimilation, anyone associated with the cool thing runs the risk of becoming 'uncool'. They will most likely, however, make a large amount of money.

Until recently, cool could be relatively long-lived and relatively easy to spot. Its unavailability to the mainstream was expressed in one or more of several ways. Cool might have been specifically located and therefore beyond the reach of the majority. Cool might have been expensive and therefore beyond the means of the majority. Cool might have required particular talents and was therefore beyond the abilities of the majority. Cool might have required certain knowledge and was therefore beyond the ken of the majority.

Now, however, we have entered a period when cool is increasingly accessible. This has come about for several connected reasons and circumstances but two stand out. One: the democratization of the production, distribution and consumption of cool. Two: the recognition by big business of the final death of function and primacy of cool as brand attribute. It is a pattern replicated throughout our culture.

The democratization of cool might have produced a disparate, exciting, fractured culture of niche interests. Instead, the combination of the recognition of the value of cool by big business and the mainstream aspirations of independent artists has ensured this hasn't happened. Put simply, no independent artist (whatever their politics) will turn down the opportunity for their work to reach the widest possible audience. Put simply, big business has tried to appropriate cool and in doing so has killed it. Put simply, there is a 'long tail' . . . of crap.

Cool as we used to know it is dead. We have too much access, money, technology and information: as soon as we want something we have it; as soon as something is experienced as cool it is simultaneously experienced as uncool. We are still, though, in thrall to cool. So wherefore cool?

I would suggest the following: cool is now increasingly associated with things that cannot be assimilated into the mainstream (typically people since it is possible to assimilate any 'thing', with the exception of taboo objects such as, say, guns or pornography – although this, of course, is changing). At a general level this means that cool has become associated with minority races and cultures. This has, of course, been true for five hundred years but only now has it established absolute primacy. At a particular level it means that cool has become associated with otherness, alienation, disenfranchisement, anger and, especially (since surely nobody would choose to identify themselves with such attributes), authenticity.

The upshot of all this is that cool has become increasingly antisocial and therefore harder for big business to manage. A company may, for example, wish to associate itself with otherness by using an alienated, disenfranchised, angry person in its advertising. However, it runs the considerable risk of one of three possible outcomes. One: said person ceases to be alienated, disenfranchised, angry and therefore cool. Two: said person remains alienated, disenfranchised and angry and therefore brings negative publicity to the company. Negative publicity is not inherently 'uncool'. But it's not inherently cool either. Three: said person remains alienated, disenfranchised and angry and the corporate brand is accidentally 'overcooled' and thereby ghettoized.

More to the point, however, even big companies (notoriously arrogant institutions) have been forced to admit that, if they know about it, it can't be cool. And yet they need cool.

This is where Authenticity™ comes in. With unparalleled contacts and relationships in the world of contemporary cool, we will provide laterally thought-out associative marketing relationships for any company wishing to 'cool up' its brand. Furthermore, we don't just source cool, we manage it too, providing our clients with an interface they can understand to a world they cannot. We are cool. We own cool. We speak the same language as cool. If you Google 'cool', it's our website that comes up first. That's why we say to our clients: 'We engage so you don't have to.'

[There is a handwritten addendum, presumably addressed to Jodie Sherski, at the time Preston Pinner's assistant. It reads, 'J! Does this make sense? Or do I sound like a cunt? And if I sound like a cunt do I sound like a cool cunt?']

8

Don't believe the hype

London, England, 2008
The Authenticity™ Hummer was dawdling through city traffic on its way to the West London studio. Preston was slouched in the back, his eyes hidden by a pair of 1950s Aviators he'd bought off American eBay. He had a sworn affidavit that said they were the very pair worn by James Dean on the set of *Giant*.

Opposite sat Errol on one of the fold-down seats, fiddling with the controls on his iPhone, which was streaming to the vehicle's bespoke sound system. He was sucking skunk enthusiastically and, to Preston's vague, unspoken irritation, making only a half-hearted effort to blow the smoke out of the open window. About five minutes ago, Preston had exclaimed, 'Errol!' and Errol had said, 'Sorry, man,' and, for a couple of puffs, made exaggerated attempts to ensure not a single wisp remained in the vehicle. But now the Hummer was fugged again.

The Hummer had been Errol's idea, but Preston hadn't taken much persuading. It realized everything he liked best about hip-hop – the blunt honesty of conspicuous consumerism mingling with vain, self-mythologizing bullshit. This was the language Preston used to explain it to himself, but Errol had identified much the same with more panache and less pomposity on the day the vehicle was delivered to the Authenticity™ office and the whole team had circled it, slack-jawed and stupefied by its grotesque magnificence. 'Women will talk shit about it,' he'd said knowingly. 'But, you wait, open the back door and they is wet, you get me?'

The Hummer had a custom paint job (featuring gaudy

graffiti incorporating the Authenticity™ logo), calfskin interior, souped-up engine and signature alloys. When he was ferried around in it, Preston felt like a late entrant to the Wacky Races. It even featured bullet-proof tinted windows on the recommendation of a multi-platinum Queensbridge rapper who knew a thing or two about being shot at. Preston had agreed to this detail partly because, he having spent more than a hundred grand on a car, it seemed churlish to quibble over an extra five K, and partly because he secretly hoped that one day some jealous rudeboy might take an optimistic pot-shot *à la* Westwood (free publicity waiting to happen).

Lethargically, Preston wondered whether getting popped through an open window on account of Errol's reefer could be classed 'ironic'. Exhausted and ever more passively stoned, he couldn't be bothered to think it through.

AuthenTV™, the company's weekly urban-music show, had only been running six months but Preston, who exec'd the production and co-presented alongside an absurdly pro-portioned supermodel called Thandi, was already feeling the stress. Television had always been a key part of Authen-ticity™'s five-year plan and he knew that burgeoning brand recognition was always easier to achieve with a face to put to the name – and that face had best be his.

Nonetheless, though fond of the spotlight, Preston hadn't been prepared for the impact genuine fame would have on his private life – he no longer had one. More to the point, he was finding it increasingly difficult to make time for fundamental elements of Authenticity™'s business.

One example of this was being played out right now. A couple of years ago, Preston had hit upon an idea for a very simple revenue stream and founded The Authenticity™ List ('The A-List™'). The A-List™ was a music networking site that allowed unsigned 'urban' artists from around the world (every sub-genre from hip-hop to hip life, drum 'n' bass to kwaito) to upload songs and videos for free distribution. In this respect it was no different from MySpace or Bebo. How-ever, the USP of The A-List™ was that, while anyone could visit the site and listen to the music, uploading work was a privilege of the chosen – you had to apply to join and your demo was vetted by the company.

As a start-up model, it relied on Preston's intuitive belief that Authenticity™ had already established adequate brand value to attract applications. He was proved right. He had projected a sign-up rate of three hundred artists per year. The A-List™ now had more than two thousand artists posting to the site. In return for the brand association, each A-List™ artist completed a *pro forma* contract granting Authenticity™ five points on any song posted. There had been some buzz on forums and bulletin boards (later picked up by the national press) that this was inherently exploitative. Preston, however, believed that most independent musicians wanted to sell their music a lot more than they wanted to hold on to five per cent of its value – 'Five per cent of nothing is nothing,' he said. Again, he was proved right.

So far, approximately fifteen per cent of A-List artists sold on their music (whether to majors, advertising agencies, libraries or as independent releases) and, whatever the sums involved, it was all money for nothing for Authenticity™. The A-List™ effectively acted as a dummy record company with a roster stretching to three hundred artists and growing. Preston had even toyed with the idea of starting a genuine label (i.e. bankrolling production, marketing and infrastruc-ture himself), but that would have to wait for a sure-fire commercial hit.

The only downside of The A-List™ model was that it required endless ploughing through a great ocean of musical slurry. As Authenticity™'s reputation solidified and The A-List™'s stock soared, so the number of submissions rose exponentially. Currently they were running at about three thousand per week. What was more, Preston knew that while

Authenticity™'s brand lent kudos to the music on the site so that music reflected on Authenticity™, with the potential to scupper its reputation if not of adequate standard. The A-List™, therefore, had to maintain an uneasy balance between the impulse to grow and the preservation of quality. Such tension is, of course, 'uneasy' for any potentially successful business, but for The A-List™ it was particularly problematic since (a) its only value lay in the belief of its customers (producers and consumers alike) that it had one, and (b) the arbitration of quality in the field of 'urban' music is absolutely time specific and lacking any objective criteria.

Preston's solution to this dilemma was simplicity itself – 'I know what's cool. In fact, I define what's cool. So, if I say it's cool, it's cool' – but it was more than a little labour intensive. Of course he didn't listen to every submission himself, but he did insist that he passed final judgement after his team had winnowed the chaff. And the only opportunity he ever had to do this was in the back of the Hummer on the way to the studio.

Preston slumped lower into his seat, partly to avoid any incoming gunfire and partly because he was currently undergoing trial by *tabla*. The tune on offer was Indian electronica, complete with wailing traditional vocal – it sounded, Preston thought, like a fat guy being run over very slowly by a Smart car. He flicked a finger at Errol to skip to the next track, and some wannabe started to yelp in a painful falsetto about what he was going to do to an unsuspecting honey over a generic R&B break. Preston gave it sixteen bars before flicking his finger again. And so it continued.

His phone buzzed in his pocket. He pulled it out and examined the screen. It said 'Dad' and began to flash the unflattering picture he'd assigned to his father's number. He stared at it for a moment or two before reluctantly answering. 'Dad.'

'What's that racket?'

'I think it's carioca funk.' Preston flicked his finger at Errol. The next tune kicked in, some God-forsaken jungle.

'Where are you?'

'In the car. Look, I'm on my way to the studio. Can I call you back?'

'Call me back? I need to see you, Preston.'

'Why? What's happened?'

'Nothing. We need a meeting. We need to talk about what we talked about. Something's come up.'

'I saw. I caught you on TV. What's going on?'

'It's difficult. I'll tell you when I see you.' Preston heard Pinner sigh. It was rare for his dad to be so reticent. 'When can we meet?'

'I'm not sure. Look, I don't have my diary. Can I get Jodie to give you a call?' No sooner had he said this than he regretted it. In the brief silence that followed, he could picture his dad's wounded expression all too clearly.

'Right, then,' Pinner said shortly. 'I'll wait to hear from your secretary.'

'It's not like that,' Preston insisted, but Pinner was already gone.

Preston sucked his teeth irritably and switched the phone to silent. He sat back, shut his eyes and tried to concentrate on the music. But he couldn't stop thinking about the exchange he'd just had with his dad and their impending meeting. It was a prospect that caused him even more trepidation than usual.

With frequent unattributed quotes and off-the-record briefings emerging from Downing Street, it was widely accepted that the UK was on the verge of a general election; also that the government was likely to lose. Of all majority MPs, Pinner had less reason to worry than most. His was a historically safe seat and, though he'd shown little interest in constituency issues, his burgeoning national reputation looked sure to stand him in good stead. However, Pinner was already thinking beyond the election and was determined to position himself for the Shadow Cabinet. In fact, if results went as badly as some predicted, all kinds of senior figures might fall on their swords and – who knows? – he might even take a shot at the top job.

Pinner had explained this to his son on the last occasion they'd spoken, though he'd done so in such high-falutin' style that it had taken Preston a while to catch his drift. At one point, he had asked rhetorically, 'If Fate comes knocking, will I feel its hand on my shoulder?' And Preston was so distracted by the logistics of the image that he missed everything that followed until Pinner concluded, 'When history asks the question, I must be sure I have an answer.'

Preston hadn't known what to say, so he'd just said, 'Right.' He'd had the distinct impression his old man was testing untried soundbites for possible use in future speeches and he wasn't sure he was the target audience. He wondered where the hell this was going.

He soon found out. And he didn't much like it.

Pinner had decided, presumably because some aide had told him as much, that he needed a plan if he was to make the most of the expected ructions within the party. However, since he was only a junior minister and it was not yet certain the government would lose the election anyway, he also needed to avoid raising his head too far above the political parapet. He hadn't the background or experience to have accumulated much political mass and now wasn't the time for ideas anyway, so he would have to capitalize on his public profile. He should appear on daytime TV or a light-hearted news quiz. He should write a memoir, a column or, at the very least, a blog. He should attempt a marathon, half-marathon, or fun run. He should align himself with some uncontroversial, non-partisan issue that captured the public imagination, the only problem being that there weren't many of those to go round – 'I need something to believe in,' he'd mused, without apparent irony. He needed name recognition, face recognition, *brand* recognition.

Pinner – or, more likely, the same witless aide – had thought it through and come up with Preston. After all, Preston made things cool for a living, right? So the very least he could do was the same for his old man.

Now, in the back of the Hummer, Preston adjusted his shades and pinched the bridge of his nose. He didn't know how he was going to get out of this. He didn't even know quite why he wanted to get out of it. He just knew he had to get out of it. It wasn't that he didn't like his dad. It wasn't that he considered making 'Brand Pinner' mission impossible. It wasn't even that he didn't like Pinner's politics. So what was it?

Preston found himself slowly overwhelmed by a profound insight. He realized that at some fundamental, instinctive level he didn't trust his own dad. He didn't trust this urge to become something by saying nothing, to get ahead on the whims of desire, to become – to call a spade a spade – famous. And, consequently, he didn't trust his politics or, more accurately, that his dad had any meaningful politics in which to trust.

With a peculiar vertiginous feeling, Preston ransacked his memory for everything he'd ever heard his old man speak for or against. Pinner championed family values but didn't seem to place much value on his own. He attacked binge-drinking but was drunk six nights out of seven. He supported the minimum wage but paid his Brazilian cleaner cash in hand. The ideas came thick and fast: comprehensive education, the NHS, carbon offsetting, public transport, pornography, MPs' expenses, five-a-day, the local high street . . . now he thought about it, Preston couldn't think of one subject Pinner had pronounced upon that wasn't in some small, uncontroversial, thoroughly predictable way contradicted by his own lifestyle.

What about asylum? Hadn't Pinner spent a decade campaigning selflessly for refugees' rights? Yes, he had. But even that now seemed at best an anomaly and at worst a contrivance. Besides, he'd ended up fronting the draconian new asylum legislation.

In fact, as far as Preston could see, his old man believed in nothing except himself and, possibly, the social order that had allowed him to prosper. Maybe this was true of all politicians. Maybe hypocrisy was the nature of the business and this was precisely what people meant when they talked about the mistake of holding politicians to higher standards than one's own. But Preston didn't know any other politicians.

Preston ruminated. He considered his own hypocrisy. After all, if he was honest, he didn't really believe in anything (except, possibly, 'trends' – the moral equivalent of believing in the weather) but, then, he'd never claimed to and he wasn't trying to run the country, was he?

In spite of himself, Preston's eyes snapped open. For a moment, he couldn't figure out why. But then he found his attention locked on the tune that was currently blaring from the speakers and his mind started to double time. It was basic at best, little more than a thick, spongy bassline, snapping drum pattern and rough acoustic guitar. But the vocalist had something: an insistent tone that seemed undercut by a soulful, mesmeric vulnerability and an indisputable flow that transformed seamlessly from singing to rapping and back again. Preston started to zone into what turned out to be a new take on a very familiar tune – 'And did those feet in ancient time/ Walk upon England's mountains green'. He gestured frantically at Errol to turn the sound down a little. Errol was taken aback. He'd never seen his boss so enthused. 'What's this?' Preston asked.

'I think it's "Jerusalem", innit?'

'I know *that*. I mean, what is it? Who is it?'

Errol checked his iPhone. He shrugged. 'Geezer calls himself Nobody.'

Preston leant forward and started to nod to the music as

the vocal dissolved into an MC's rhymes. He took off his sunglasses. He said, 'Track him down, would you?'

Errol said, 'Sure, Tupps.'

'Don't call me illegal, I'm making my plans / In this bleak, unpleasant land,' Nobody spat, while Preston forgot about his dad and began to make plans of his own.

9

Insert document
'Tuloko and the totems', *The Book of Zamba
Mythology*, (OUP, 2005), Edison Burrows III

The Great Chief Tuloko (the Traveller, the Child of the Horizon) was the founder of the Zamba nation. He led the Zamba people (under the authority of Father Sun, with the guidance of Cousin Moon) for more than ten generations. Throughout his reign, Tuloko married only once, to Mudiwa, but they had many sons. The names of these sons have been passed down through the generations and they are now the totem ancestors of each Zamba clan.

When Tuloko was very old, his sons began to argue over who should succeed him. Lion claimed that he should succeed his father because no one could disagree that he was the greatest warrior. Elephant claimed the right was his because he was as strong as fifty men. Eagle said that he should be the chief because he could fly high into the sky and see what lay in store. Every one of Tuloko's sons defended the value of their own totem and soon it seemed that the nation might descend into civil war. Tuloko was worried and he called his sons together on the plains of Zimindo in front of all the Zamba people.

'My sons,' Tuloko announced, 'my time draws closer. A successor must be chosen who will lead our people with a strong arm and a gentle voice. Yet all you do is argue like arrogant saplings who stand tall in a powerful wind. I tell you that my love is equal and, for all your differences, my heart beats inside each one of you. But there can only be one chief.

Lion: in time of war, you would lead us bravely into battle. Baboon: in a time of negotiation, you would argue well. Goat: in time of surplus, you would recognize the need for temperance. But I tell you this, a true chief must be as many things as the people require. So I have decided to set you a test to determine my successor.

'I am Tuloko. I am the Traveller and the Child of the Horizon. The test for you, my sons, is to journey to the horizon, my birthplace, and tell me what you find there. Whoever does this will succeed me and all of you will accept his judgement.'

When Tuloko finished speaking, the brothers looked at one another in some confusion for none knew exactly where the horizon might be. Lion stretched himself to his full height and looked off into the distance. He said to himself: 'I see the horizon! It is right there. At the base of that baobab.' And he set off quickly to get a head start on his brothers.

Before he began his quest, Baboon climbed a tree and shielded his eyes with his hand so that he could look far to the west. 'There it is!' he exclaimed. 'The earth meets the sky at that hill beyond the river.' And he was sure that he would be the first to complete his father's test.

Of course, Eagle had the best view and he saw beyond the baobab and the river and the hill; beyond even the great lake to the west. 'There is the horizon!' he whispered. 'Where Father Sun rests his head for the night.'

Soon all of Tuloko's sons were racing across the plains of Zimindo, eager to fulfil their father's wish. But the chief watched their shrinking backs with a heavy heart.

One of his sons had not moved. This was Ant, the youngest of all Tuloko's children.

'Do you not wish to complete my test?' Tuloko asked.

'Father,' Ant replied, 'you are a great chief and I have nothing but respect for you. However, I am the smallest and most humble of all your sons and I was named for the smallest and most humble creature. I am hardly worthy to call myself your descendant. I cannot see the distant horizons, like Lion, Baboon or Eagle, and there's no point in searching for something I can never see. I am so small that I live for ever on the horizon. The horizon, my father, is here.'

Tuloko looked at his youngest son and a smile spread across his face. 'And what do you find on the horizon?' Tuloko asked.

Ant thought for a moment and looked around. 'I find only myself and I am not worthy to be called your descendant. I find the people in need of a chief. I find Tuloko in need of a successor.'

'My son!' Tuloko exclaimed. 'You are the first to complete my test and you shall be my successor. For, as Father Sun himself once said to me, who is your descendant but the man whom you trust?'

This was how Tuloko's youngest son succeeded his father as the chief of the Zamba. It is why Zamba chiefs are ratified by the *zakulu* (under the authority of the sun, with the guidance of the moon) on the basis of both age and totem but, above all, character. It is also the source of the Zamba proverb, 'A strong chief stands permanently on the horizon; a wise *zakulu* takes up position everywhere else.'

10

The end of dreams

Queenstown, Republic of Zambawi, 2008
Prisoner 118 dreamt about being the white man again and woke up in tears.

In the dream, he was lying on a thin bunk in darkness. The pain was below the knee of his left leg and it was, curiously, somehow numb and yet agonizing. He had his teeth clenched and his eyes wide. He could sense the rats scrabbling on the floor beside him but he determined not to look at them. He could hear distant noises – occasional voices, gulls cawing and the constant drone of a mighty engine – but he blanked them out. His nostrils were thick with the mingling smells of wet timber and burning oil, but he ignored them. Instead he concentrated on his breathing – short gasps, in and out. He was trying to induce a trance.

Occasionally, however, his bunk would suddenly lurch one way or the other, as if the world had been taken by a rolling wave. Was he at sea? When this happened, his breathing would be disrupted and the pain surged up his leg, filling his midriff until he couldn't breathe at all. He'd feel his mouth dry and sweat begin to bead on his forehead. It took a huge effort of will not to retch. As the bunk settled and the nausea receded, he slowly relaxed the muscles in his back and neck and tried to let his weight sink as deeply as possible into the mattress.

In the dream, the *musungu*'s whole febrile mind was focused only on time passing and staying alive. The desire for time to pass was comprehensible, because the pain would surely, little by little, dissipate. The urge to live, however, was much more nebulous. He had people to live for, reasons too, but mostly

60

he was trying to stay alive only because it was a challenge that could fully occupy him and there was nothing else to do.

Prisoner 118 came to sobbing, huge, desperate, hopeless sobs that convulsed his whole body. He, too, was lying on his back on a thin bunk in the pitch dark, with his left leg some-how numb and agonizing all at once, and rats scrabbling on the floor nearby. So, for a moment, he struggled to establish whether he was, in fact, awake. As the dreams had intensified, this had become a growing problem, not just distinguishing between the reveries and reality, but between the white man's consciousness and his own. Even now, for example, he needed to identify whether they were really his tears. He took his time to trace their tracks up his cheeks, back into his eyes and through the narrow conduits of his being before he lost them in the heavy traffic of his heart.

It was only experience, therefore, that made him guess it was shame at their source. This made sense, as shame had set the tone for all these dreams. But did it belong to him, to the man in the dream or someone else altogether?

In his mind's eye, he slowly picked his way to the source so that he could examine it more closely. Unfortunately what he found was dense, fibrous and wet with those tears so that every time he pulled on a loose end the knots just tightened. The only thing he could say with any certainty, therefore, was that the shame was male – the shame that all men who are conflicted between love and dishonesty confront when alone. But as to the question of ownership, that hardly narrowed it down.

Prisoner 118 sat up and reached beneath the bunk for his painkillers, the bottle of iodine and the paintbrush. He swallowed two ibuprofen and began gently to smear the iodine across the tender stubs of his missing toes. He stopped. Was it his imagination or were the stubs actually receding fur-ther? As he became accustomed to the dark, he lifted his foot towards his face and attempted an examination. He couldn't be sure, but closer inspection seemed to reveal that the small bumps where his toes had been were smaller than ever. In fact, the wound seemed to be progressing further into his foot. There wasn't any sign of infection, just the gradual disappearance of his flesh. Surely that was impossible.

He shook his head and thought he glimpsed a pair of eyes staring up at him from the floor. 'Is that you, Louis?'

There was a squeak and the eyes vanished.

'Billie!' he exclaimed. 'Billie! I'm sorry. I'm almost blind in here and you know you two look alike.' He paused. Then, 'Oh, come on! Don't be so touchy.'

He listened. Nothing. He returned to his careful ministrations.

He had christened the two rats who were his most regular companions Billie and Louis. He didn't know if they'd given him a nickname in return. They rarely addressed him directly, preferring, for the most part, to chat between themselves.

Prisoner 118 had little idea of how long he'd been incarcerated; it could have been anywhere from three weeks to three months. One reason for this was that it was, in fact, closer to three months and he had, as anyone would, lost track. At first, he'd tried to stay on top of it by noting the four hours of electric lighting that his cell was granted each day from the single bare bulb in the ceiling. Within a fortnight, though, these regular spells of illumination had become irregular – 'Cutbacks,' Captain Makuvitse explained, embarrassed and apologetic – and he now went for days, maybe even weeks, in almost total darkness.

He had then tried to keep count of his weekly stints in the exercise yard. But these too had become increasingly sporadic and now, it seemed, had stopped altogether. Makuvitse had offered no explanation for this turn of events, but 118 assumed it was because, as a category-one inmate, he was considered highly dangerous, forbidden to mingle with the wider population, and required half a dozen guards to keep an eye on him for his hour's fresh air. Prisoner 118 didn't regret the loss of his weekly exercise too much – the dreams were so taxing he rarely had the energy to drag his poor injured foot behind him for more than five minutes. Besides, the yard was a miserable place, a dead square of dust surrounded by high walls with no flora or fauna to be seen (even the birds seemed to give it a knowingly wide berth).

Also, apart from the largely laconic guards, his lone companion on this trying perambulation was the preposterous *musungu* (the only other category-one inmate) who had rejected his only attempt at conversation with a dismissive sniff. The *musungu* was clearly the kind of man who'd rather soil himself than shit behind a tree, an option that not only left you in some discomfort, but precluded the experience, the pleasure even, of shitting behind a tree.

The second reason Prisoner 118 didn't know how long he'd been locked up came back, of course, to the dreams. As the white man's dreams had impinged upon his conscious mind, so his own thoughts and memories had developed a dream-like quality that left them opaque, ephemeral and inconsistent. At a simple level, he couldn't seem to picture his house without the maize crop next to it ripening, chin-high, even though he knew – or thought he knew – that he'd left home no more than a fortnight after planting. More troublingly, when he remembered his old friends, some alive, some dead, it took him several minutes to remember who was who, a heartrending process that lurched between all-consuming loss and desperate relief.

Worst of all, however, was that he now couldn't recall the sequence of events that had led to his incarceration. In the place where his memory should have constructed a linear chain of cause and effect, there was just a shoebox of images, all-too-brief reels of action and snatched impressions of emotion that didn't seem to add up to much. He had an inkling, for example, of what he assumed was the day of his arrest. He appeared to be in an ornate office and there, behind the desk, was the President, his dear old friend, regarding him impassively. He could hear his own voice spitting fury: 'What have we become? What have we *become*?' But he had no idea how he'd got there or why he was so angry.

This brief episode then seemed to lurch to another. He was standing in the same spot, the President seated as before, but it must have been later as his hands were manacled behind his back. Adini's eyes were now like stones. He was sitting back, his arms folded across his chest. 'So?'

'I came to tell you I have been dreaming, old friend.'

A muscle in the President's cheek twitched. 'So you want to offer me advice? Come on, then, *old friend*, let's hear it.'

'I have no advice. I have never dreamt like this before. They are a white man's dreams.'

The suggestion of a smile played on the President's mouth, but it wasn't reflected in his eyes. 'Even you are now dreaming as a *musungu*?' he asked bitterly.

Prisoner 118 knew, therefore, that the dreams were at least one reason he was in prison, but he didn't know if that reason was past or future – were the dreams simply the grounds of his imprisonment or might they also be, as he suspected, the reason *for which* he was imprisoned?

It was this question that he felt he had to answer, so he'd spent the last few weeks trying to use that shoebox, those reels and snatched impressions, to build some kind of coherent narrative. But, in a state of consistent confusion, it was painstaking work. In fact, at this precise moment, 118 had been sitting stock still, lost in thought, paintbrush poised above his tortured toeless foot for quite some minutes. But he was now jolted back to the cell by the sound of a whispered conversation unfolding in the darkness.

'What's he doing?'

'Dunno. But he's a funny sort, this one, not the usual type at all.'

'He looks like a statue.'

As if on cue, Prisoner 118 blinked and shook his head. 'Billie? Louis? Is that you?' he murmured. 'Come closer, my murine companions. I want to try and tell you a story.'

II

Insert document
'The diary of a local gentleman', 3 February
1901 (Empire Museum, Bristol), anon.

Kitty visited today. She arrived with her sister, Gertrude, just
after three and found me, as ever, in the library. Although
the weather was brisk, she'd chosen, typically, to walk all the
way from Clifton and she radiated good health as though
she'd just taken a fresh dose of life itself. I heard the two of
them giggling over some joke in the hall, but by the time
Weston showed them in she had composed herself.
Nonetheless, I could see the last vestiges of that laughter still
tugging at the corners of her mouth and eyes. She stood and
looked out of the window so as not to cause embarrassment
to the cripple as he extricated himself from his armchair to
greet her.

   Her soft curls shimmered golden in the spring sunlight. It
would take a poet to express how my heart felt in my chest
at that moment and I have no pretensions in that regard.
Even so, I surely wish I had enough poetry in my soul to
relax my expression, smooth my brow and allow a
suggestion of those feelings to soften my face for her.

   Kitty has taken to making fun of my new studiousness.
I understand that this is a safe way for her to mourn the
carefree young man with whom, perhaps, she fell in love.
If I *were* a poet, I would tell her that, though I may have
become a little bookish, I study nothing so keenly as her
every gesture; indeed her every breath.

   We took tea beneath the window. My stump has given

me terrible gyp the whole day and, for all my efforts, my only expression was one of pain. I know Kitty recognized this and, at one point, she covered my hand with her own soft palm. I quickly withdrew it.

I struggle to explain why I should recoil from such well-intended sympathy. Perhaps it was because it only underscored the reality of my circumstance, perhaps it was because it did not help, or perhaps because I knew that, were the ladies not there, I would already have taken a tot or two of gin, my only source of genuine respite. Kitty's look of hurt and rejection left me wretched.

Gertrude, a young woman who matches her sister in vivacity if little else, was full of a meeting she lately attended that was concerned with the advancement of women's rights. She announced herself a 'suffragist' and proclaimed that she would commit her life to this cause. I regarded this, with amusement, as significant of nothing more than youthful enthusiasm – admirable in its own way – but such talk clearly irritated Kitty. She told her sister that she was too young to understand these ideas and she should be more careful of the company she kept.

If this put-down was meant to quell Gertrude's passion, however, it had quite the opposite effect. Her temper rose and she retorted with some forcefulness that Mrs Fawcett, the leader of these suffragists, had famously made just such a declaration herself at the age of only thirteen.

Though I care little about the issue (which is, after all, an inevitable consequence of the choice too many men make to overeducate their daughters), I felt compelled to step in to pour oil on troubled waters. I told them, therefore, of Bachofen's theory of 'original matriarchy', of which I had lately read. I outlined the principle of general promiscuity (to much blushing and general laughter) that gave way, through natural selection, to a form of social organization in which women held political power. Although it no longer exists, its shadow may still be seen in 'cultural survivals', such as matrilineal kinship systems where inheritance is passed through the mother's line. In fact, it is only in progressive societies like our own that men hold unquestionable political sway.

Each sister found some satisfaction in my diversion – Gertrude that women might be understood as society's natural leaders, Kitty that the current opposite situation could be regarded as the height of progress. For myself, I concluded instead that women, for all their heralded sensitivity, appear only to hear what suits them.

With airy finality, Kitty said, 'I have often considered that the roles of men and women in England – strictly defined and generally understood – are a beacon of sophistication for the civilized world.'

No doubt her sister would have taken issue with such an assertion had she not been so evidently awestruck by my apparent erudition. She addressed me earnestly: 'Kitty tells me that you have a new fascination with anthropology. What is that exactly?'

I explained that anthropology is the science of culture and my fascination was nothing grander than a fascination with people.

At this point, Kitty turned to her sister and interjected with an acidity I'd not previously witnessed. 'But it's a vicarious fascination, Gertie,' she said. 'His interest is in Hottentots, peasants and savages from the four corners of the globe. These days, he shows little interest in anyone closer to home.'

Naturally, I understood the import of her words immediately. But she spoke with just enough lightness that poor Gertrude was uncertain and embarrassed and we sat a moment or two in uncomfortable silence. I confess that Kitty's impropriety made my hackles rise, and, eventually, I couldn't resist a rejoinder. 'On the contrary, my dear,' I said at last. 'My interest in the savage is only to throw light upon the otherwise incomprehensible behaviour of those in my own society.'

I fear I overstepped the mark. Kitty was distressed by my comment and excused herself. Our jolly little tea party had quickly broken up.

When Kitty was composed enough to return, she told me quietly that she and Gertrude had actually dropped by in order to invite me to the new melodrama at the Theatre Royal this very evening. All the 'old gang' were going, she said – Freddy Marks, Teddy Jameson and that sort; as if *that* could prove the final, clinching incentive. Truthfully, I might have accepted (though I loathe melodrama – the most vacuous form of idle entertainment) but the turn of our conversation had left me fearful at the thought of company. So I demurred.

Kitty left me with a forlorn but tender kiss on the cheek. I can still feel its imprint.

There is little more awful than the disappointment of those one would do anything to avoid disappointing. It is a feeling with which I am increasingly familiar but to which I cannot become accustomed. In my present state of mind and body, I have nothing if not the time to think. Much of that time is devoted to Kitty – my dearest Kitty! I wonder if our future together is moribund. But I do so with detachment.

I imagine myself the surgeon who amputated my leg. He must have looked down on my mutilated, comatose body and wondered if I'd survive. Certainly, I believe he hoped for the best. But, in my imagination, his chief interest was in the processes of my body that would ultimately dictate my prospects. So it is with Kitty and me. What is done is done and still I hope for the best. But it is now the process, something beyond the control of either one of us, that most fascinates me.

Our families and friends still expect us to marry. They

expected us to marry before I sailed and, as far as they're concerned, nothing has changed. Therefore, though the dilemmas remain unspoken, it is only Kitty and I who know their number and full extent. But I fear that even mutual comprehension offers no guarantee of reconciliation.

Kitty fears that war has changed me. Her fears are justified. I have seen death in all its terrible drama and all its eviscerating mundanity and I would wish that on no one. She fears that I feel less than a full man. Her fears are justified. I am precisely fourteen inches less than the man I was. She fears that I consider her interests, particularly in fashion and the intrigues of local society, trivial. Her fears are justified. I do, as I always have. However, for my part, I am more concerned with the awful sapping process in which we are now engaged than the reasons it began. I do not require Kitty to understand my experiences, feelings or judgements and I certainly have no desire to discuss them. But I do expect her acceptance.

In so far as a reason may be of interest, I believe that the division between us was first cracked open on the day of my return and the cause was altogether prosaic. When I alighted at Temple Meads station, it was something of a surprise to find Kitty waiting on the platform with Father and David. I had a small suitcase in one hand and my cane in the other, having only lately learnt to hobble on my prosthesis. Kitty, adversely affected by too many melodramas and penny romances, ran towards me weeping tears of joy and threw her arms around my neck.

It is true that I dislike such displays, and it was a shock to be suddenly close to my beloved after so long. However, I had spent much of the preceding weeks imagining the moment we would be reunited. Indeed, on the voyage home, when I had fought the infection well enough to be allowed on deck to take the ozone, I thought of little else. The only reason I did not return Kitty's embrace, therefore, was that it required all my strength to stay upright beneath the weight of her and the very last thing I wanted was to crumple to the floor like an invalid.

Even as she pulled back from me, tears streaking her cheeks, I could see the first signs of hurt incomprehension and the first seeds of resentment in her expression. Thus the fissure was opened and it has widened and it is now a mighty canyon and, when we talk to one another, it is as if we are calling across a great distance and the meaning, if not the words themselves, is too often lost on the wind.

Perhaps it is not surprising that I consider this problem as the soldier I am. When you reach the edge of a canyon, you do not consider what freakish geological or metaphysical event might have brought it into existence, you simply formulate a plan that will allow you to reach the other side. At the moment, I am a lone cripple. I haven't the tools, materials or manpower to construct a bridge. The only resources at my disposal, therefore, are my fortitude and my faith, and my only option is to circumvent the abyss. It seems that I must leave that I might come back – both to Kitty and also, I suspect, to myself.

12
All change

Musa Musa, the most eminent *zakulu* in Zimindo Province if
not the whole of Zambawi, had already been having the white
man's dreams for several months, on and off, before they
finally migrated to his sleep. He could be standing at the
counter in the bottle store, bent over the stove or chatting to
Mrs Chiponda from the Grain Marketing Co-operative when
he would unexpectedly find himself transported to the peculiar
and specific world of these reveries without a by-your-leave.

On some occasions, the power of these sudden visions left
him crumpled on the floor, twitching as though he were
suffering a convulsion or, more accurately, squashed beneath
the weight of his own imagination; on others, he would be
rooted to the spot, eyes wide and fixed mid-distance. Though
all the locals knew him as a man of unconventional talents
necessarily accompanied by certain behavioural eccentricities,
this was somewhat embarrassing.

It might have been a relief, therefore, when the dreams at
last accepted their proper time and place. However, when
this happened, such was their viscosity that they kept him
stuck fast in sleep for almost two solid weeks – thrashing
about at first, later resigned like an ass sinking mournfully
into quicksand. And when he did finally come to it was with
the desperate gasp of the almost drowned, and the profound
conviction, recognizable among both newly lost and born
again (a coincidence that's frequently responsible, one suspects, for the confusion of one with the other), that everything
had changed.

One thing that had certainly changed was his appearance.

Although he didn't know how long he'd been asleep, he could hazard a guess from the state of his face reflected in the small shaving mirror he kept at his bedside. His haunted eyes, patchy beard and dreadlocks that sprouted every which way had always given him a somewhat wild look (and, truth be told, had been cultivated to do so); now, however, he looked positively feral. His eyes were not haunted but vacant, his beard was spotted grey and stained with streaks of crisp snot and spittle, and his locks had coalesced into a dozen great knots that hung over his face like willow branches.

On top of that, once his nervous system began to reboot and every part of his body ran its own series of checks and tests, his brain was assaulted by so many messages of pain that it couldn't possibly hope to process them all simultaneously. His joints screamed like the hinges on doors of rooms that contain only antiquities of no interest to anyone. His limbs had the give and spring of petrified tree-trunks at the business end of an ice age. His muscles felt like sugar cane chewed to string by the teeth of a thousand ravenous schoolkids. His back and buttocks were covered with fetid pressure sores so ghastly that when he sat up he left behind mementoes of necrotic flesh on his sleeping mat. Worst of all, however, were the signals of agony being manically dispatched from the vicinity of his left foot. Some years previously the *zakulu* had lost a toe in an unfortunate incident of near betrayal so this pain was familiar. Now, however, it was a hundred times magnified, which made him fearful to look down and examine the evidence.

He raised himself gingerly to his elbows, then awkwardly eased over onto all fours. Then, pressing his palms into the wall, he pushed himself up into something like a standing position. The required exertion – physical, mental and emotional – left him short of breath and he held himself there for a moment, a crumbling arch, his eyes at the level of his bookshelf.

He read the authors' names – Tennyson, Shaw, Words-worth, Shelley – enjoyed their poetry and gathered his will. The books were relics of another time, not the time of their writing but when he'd purloined them from St Oswald's, the local school. It wasn't so long ago. This was when shortage of reading material (as opposed to the chances of a square meal) was the students' main worry, when parish councils in English shire towns made well intentioned if misguided attempts to address the problem with collections of ancient books that nobody wanted – books that might as well have been written in Martian for all the sense they made to the average local student.

Musa Musa gulped and blinked and finally, hopefully, shoved off from the wall's safe bank and attempted verticality. He could feel the soles of his feet trying to negotiate stability but something was awry. He overbalanced and, reaching out with his right hand, trying to steady himself, took three or four tomes with him as he crashed to the floor. Clearly whatever was wrong with his left foot was worse than he'd wanted to admit. He still chose not to look at it. Instead he looked at the Kipling that had fallen open next to him and he read what he saw there – 'A people always ends by resembling its shadow.'

Musa Musa had always felt an unlikely affinity with Kipling, that great champion of imperialism, and he momentarily considered the horrid relevance of those words before he began the process of standing up again.

This time, when he was upright, Musa Musa kept hold of the wall and, thankful for its support, hobbled towards the door. He pushed it open and was hit by a broadside of heat and light that made him feel as if he must surely be incinerated on the spot. But he wasn't.

The *zakulu* looked out at the world and decided that it had changed too. He couldn't quite establish exactly what he thought was different – was the breeze gusting a little harder?

Did the bushes look more parched? Was the light remarkably clear? – but he immediately had a word for it and that word disturbed him. It was 'unnatural'.

He blinked a couple of times. He didn't want to use this word with its portentous implications and he wished it hadn't popped into his head. He tried, therefore, to imagine that it wasn't the world that had changed at all but his view of it. And, seeing as he'd been asleep for a fortnight until about half an hour ago, that didn't seem an unreasonable position to adopt.

If this thought seemed hardly more reassuring, at least it deflected his ruminations into the past, which seemed like a more comfortable place to be right now. He remembered a conversation he'd had more than a decade ago, before even the Second Revolution. He'd been in the bottle store sharing a drink with P. K. Kunashe, the headmaster of St Oswald's, and James Tulloh, a young Englishman who'd arrived to teach on one of those volunteer programmes the former colonial power seemed to value so highly (like their books, the Brits dispersed their youth in the name of charity with an alacrity proximate to carelessness). They'd all been somewhat drunk and talking loudly about something, now forgotten, which had seemed quite important at the time.

The *musungu*, in particular, had been excitable. 'It's like that philosophical problem,' he'd announced. 'If a bear shits in the woods and there's no one there to hear it, does it actually make a sound?'

PK belched into his hand. 'Presumably it depends what kind of shit it was. Maybe it was a quiet one.'

'No,' said the animated Englishman. 'It was a loud one. That's the point.'

'*That*'s the point?' PK said blurrily.

'The question,' James insisted, unperturbed, 'is whether the shit actually makes a noise or whether the noise only exists because it is heard.'

Musa Musa remembered that the Englishman had looked briefly pleased with himself until PK had shaken his head and muttered, 'There aren't any bears in Africa.'

At this, the *zakulu* had burst out laughing and patted the young man on the shoulder. 'You're asking *musungu* questions,' he observed. 'Try them on your white friends.'

Musa Musa smiled at the memory. But no sooner had he done so than he felt impossibly sad. P. K. Kunashe was dead just a few weeks later, shot and killed with the first bullet of what turned into the presidential coup that had seen Adini replace his father. And now the young *musungu*, who'd grown into a decent man and a good friend, was dying too . . .

Musa Musa was jolted from his reminiscences by the approaching sounds of Garikai Vambe – at twelve, the eldest Vambe son – pretending to be an aeroplane. The little jet soared into view from behind a ridge and commenced a slow descent towards the house. The *zakulu* raised a hand in greeting but the pilot, deep in concentration, didn't look up. Only as the jet approached the landing strip of the front path did Captain Vambe allow himself a glance. But no sooner had he done so than his face locked in fear and he pulled out of the descent. He banked steeply right and the engines screamed as the jet disappeared behind a tree and away. Musa Musa was shocked; shocked enough to finally look down and consider what might have so terrified an aeroplane.

His appearance might have changed, but what had not changed was his clothing, which now hung from his spare frame in rancid strips – some of which were apparently amalgamated with his rotten flesh, others flapping in the breeze. His trousers, gaping at the bottom, were piss-starched at the crotch, which hung like a flap of tarpaulin over his genitals. The backs of his thighs were the crusty moonscape of a fortnight's defecation. Slowly, incredulously, he allowed his eyes to fall for the first time to the excruciatingly painful place that was his left foot. He promptly gagged and retched.

Where his toes should have been was a seething microcosm of the animal kingdom's lowest strata. Through his tears, he saw hundreds of ants and counted three species of fly, four kinds of chewing lice and at least half a dozen varieties of larvae having some kind of diabolical orgy on his foot – fucking and shitting and spawning as if their lives depended upon it (which, of course, they did). There was even a large hornet, perched on his instep, watching the carnage like some kind of indulgent emperor, general or pimp.

Musa Musa, nauseated to a near faint, saw the ground rush up to meet his face with unseemly opportunism. But even the impact of earth on temple failed to knock him cold. Instead, he had to drag himself inside with the determination of his instincts until he came to rest – his breath heaving, his mouth salivating ominously – by the bucket of water he'd put out for his morning ablutions some fourteen nights previously. The water was, of course, now stagnant and smelly, but it would have to do.

Feverishly he reached for the litre of Septox he kept for cleaning the toilet and upturned what was left into the bucket. He easily tore a strip from the sleeve of his T-shirt, stuffed it into his mouth and bit down. It tasted extraordinary, a mixture of salt and death. He plunged his foot into the bucket, watched in wonder at the extraordinary variety of things that floated to the surface, and waited for the pain to hit. Now it hit. And now – finally, blissfully, dreamlessly – he passed out.

13
The chief is dying

It was two days before Musa Musa could do what he had to do next. He dressed gingerly in his best shirt, jacket and trousers (because even a man of his powers struggled to tend wounds on his own back), pulled on a clean pair of socks (the left stuffed with another clean sock) and winced as he eased his feet into his safari boots. Then, gripping the traditional staff, which, for the first time, had a practical rather than ritual purpose, he hobbled outside and set off for Zimindo village.

Although the short walk was one he'd done ten thousand times before, it now seemed totally unfamiliar, and not simply because his eyesight was blurred with tears. Where once every dip, pothole and stone on the path had been a reassurance, a signpost that told you with absolute accuracy where you were in relation to absolutely everything else, now they were just dips, potholes and stones, attempting in their boredom to make you stumble, trip or, worst of all, stub the excruciatingly painful spot where your toes used to be. Everything was different.

He skirted the Mhute homestead. There were no sounds of the women working and no sight of the children haring around, getting under their feet, no animals that shrieked and yapped and lowed and no cooking smells. Where had everybody gone? Where had they run to? This was the nature of hunger: people vanished quietly. Those who remained did so in silence.

Even when he reached the township, the only people he saw were two adolescent boys waiting for White Lightning, the Queenstown bus service. One he recognized as James Murufu, the other he didn't know. They were sitting on the ground, examining the dust between their legs, and neither looked up at the sound of his approach. There was a kind of naïve but sullen defiance to their body language, as if they were saying, 'You don't expect us to acknowledge you, do you? Not when things are so desperate!' And yet when James finally allowed himself a glance from beneath his lazily hooded eyelids, he immediately leapt to his feet and said, 'Good afternoon, Uncle, sir!' His companion, the stranger, promptly did likewise. Musa Musa waved them indulgently to sit down.

He passed the bottle store on his left. It was, as it had been for some weeks, boarded up, but the sight of it, walls still peeling 'Vote Adini', stopped the *zakulu* in his tracks. It was as though he had to run through the chain of events in his head in order to explain exactly what he was looking at and permit himself to walk on.

After President Adini's third election victory, inflation had skyrocketed like never before. For Mrs Mupandawanda, who ran the bottle store as an adjunct to her husband's bus company, this had meant buying fewer goods and charging more for them. Within six weeks, the bottle store sold only beer. Within two months, each beer cost the equivalent of the average weekly wage. Within four months, the bottle store's only customers were the Kenyan engineers who were damming the river at Muzondo on behalf of a Dutch NGO contracted for the purpose by the World Bank.

Four months ago the World Bank had recalled all its foreign personnel and, with the contemporaneous collapse of the local Grain Marketing Co-operative, Zimindo Province was, within a week, recast as a cashless economy in which desperate mothers bartered their last eggs and cups of ground maize. Two months ago, a quantity of rice had fallen from the back of a government relief truck onto the tar road some ten miles east. Most families sent their elder children on a day's mission to collect every last grain from the spill. It was six weeks since Mrs Mupandawanda had last locked the bottle store before returning to the family's other house, in the high-density suburb of Mutengwazi on the outskirts of Queenstown. She'd abandoned her homeland of Zimindo for the time being.

This was what had happened. This was what he was looking at.

Musa Musa kept walking through the township to the village where he stopped at the largest homestead, half a dozen huts with a breezeblock concrete house, once a symbol of aspiration, standing in the middle. Kudzai was hanging out the washing, Tongo Junior buzzing around her skirts, chasing chickens and butting through the damp, flapping sheets. The *zakulu* lifted the gate, calling, 'Knock knock knock!'

Kudzai turned round. Although her cheeks were heavy with exhaustion, they now stretched upwards into a wide and genuine smile. 'Musa Musa!' she exclaimed. 'Welcome, *zakulu*! Where have you been? We haven't seen you in weeks.'

'Asleep,' Musa Musa said, ignoring the minor reprimand and vague disappointment in her tone. 'How is he?'

Her smile melted away and her face fell and she shrugged. 'Can I see him?'

'Of course.' She gestured vaguely towards the concrete house. He nodded. They held each other's gaze a moment. Her expression suddenly brightened. 'You look terrible. I must bring you some food.'

'Only what you can spare, my dear.'

Musa Musa stepped into the house. It was dark and hot, a blanket used as a curtain over the single small window. It took his eyes a second or two to adjust but he knew the layout of the room well enough. The bed was in the right-hand corner, there was a wicker chair under the window and a small table to the left of the door, which held the chief's ancient cassette recorder. The machine was, as ever, playing Billie Holiday – the poor-quality ancient recording of a poor-quality ancient recording somehow granting the impression of verisimilitude, as though Lady Day were actually in the room: 'Sunday is gloomy/My hours are slumberless/Dearest, the shadows I live with are numberless'.

The *zakulu* pressed the stop button.

Now he could hear the chief's breathing. It sounded like an old engine choking on soot, hard to tell the in breath from the out. 'How are you, brother Tongo?' he asked quietly. There was no reply. 'I'm going to pull the curtain. You should get some light in here. If one of his chiefs is sick, Father Sun needs to know about it.'

Musa Musa did as he said he would and, as the day flooded in, turned to peer at the bed. 'Let me look at you,' he said unnecessarily, for he already was – looking at the shallow bag of bones that lay on top of the bed in just a pair of jeans, looking at the torso that was covered in telltale rashes and purple swellings, looking at the fixed wide eyes of his old friend Tongo Kalulu, which looked right back at him.

He sighed and sat himself down in the chair beneath the window. His foot was hurting and, inside its makeshift bandages, it had begun to weep. Still the chief hadn't acknowledged him. The *zakulu* watched the growling chest rise and fall, rise and fall, rise and fall, then stop. He licked his lips. Silence. He looked at the eyes. Not a flicker. He listened for a breath. Not a whisper. Thirty seconds. More. Urgently, he hoisted himself to his feet.

Immediately the chief's ghostly, ghastly face cracked into a broad smile and a deep, pained breath inflated his lungs. He chuckled. Both that sound and, then, the voice that followed seemed to emanate from somewhere far back in his head. 'Ha!' he said. Then, 'Ha ha! I had you going!'

Musa Musa settled back into his seat and, holding his staff upright on the floor, rolled it between his palms. 'What are you doing, old friend?'

'There are not many jokes a dying man can play,' Tongo

said. 'Trust me, that's the best of them. I had you going, didn't I?'

'You did.'

'Good! I cannot play that one on Kuku any more. She doesn't find it very hilarious.'

'I can imagine that,' Musa Musa said.

The two men contemplated one another in silence. Eventually Kudzai entered the house, carrying a tray that held a small bowl of maize porridge and greens and a glass of water. With a token bow, she offered it to the *zakulu*, who accepted it with a gracious nod. She then fussed around her husband for a minute or two, placing a hand on his forehead, attempting to cover him with a blanket, clucking and cooing. Turning back to the *zakulu*, she asked if his food tasted good. He said it did. She told him she usually liked to sweeten the rape with a little tomato but she had none. He said it tasted good as it was. She said she knew the old friends would have much to discuss and she didn't want to interrupt. She left the room.

Again, the two men contemplated one another in silence. Now, Tongo asked, 'What happened to your leg?'

'My foot.'

'What happened to your foot?'

'I don't know. I woke up and . . . well . . . it was a disaster.'

'You look terrible.'

'Not so bad as you.'

'That's true.' Tongo stuck out his bottom lip as if contemplating the weight of this wisdom. Then he said, 'Your bedside manner remains very unsympathetic.'

The *zakulu* shrugged. The chief nodded.

'It has a been a long time, old friend,' Tongo said. 'Where have you been?'

'Sleeping.'

'And you come to see me now? You're lucky you caught me.'

'You're not ready to die just yet.'

'Almost.'

'That's true. Almost.' Musa Musa paused. 'I want to tell you something.'

The chief watched him a second, then shook his head, lay back and regarded the ceiling. 'The worst is for Kuku,' he said quietly. 'She has looked after me but soon I'll be gone. When she is sick like me, who will look after her? When she is gone, who will look after Tongo Junior? I suppose he must go to my brother but it is not the best solution. And who will look after the people? Zimindo is almost deserted. The healthy run to the city while the sick bury the starved before hiding in their houses. I tell you, brother *zakulu*, the same thing that has happened to me is happening to us all.'

'My brother, I want to tell you something,' Musa Musa repeated.

'What I mean to say is this,' the chief continued, again ignoring his friend. 'The trouble with our people is that we suffer too well. We exist in limbo; we live moment to moment; we cope. We are so adaptable to changing circumstances we don't even notice the changes. We can adapt to anything, even to death, without complaint. It is for you, *zakulu*, my brother, to see the changes and to tell us what to do.'

Musa Musa sighed. These were the very thoughts he'd been doing his best to avoid ever since he'd woken up. 'But, my friend, situations are always changing. What changes are you talking about exactly?'

The chief's eyes darted towards him. He raised himself to his elbows and his voice came urgently. 'Are you crazy? When the jackal kills your chickens, you build a stronger coop. When the jackal gnaws through the wood of your new coop, you reinforce it with barbed wire. But if the jackal still gets into your chicken coop? You take your gun and you sit up for as long as it takes and you kill the jackal. What I mean to say is this: you cannot simply react to every new circumstance as if it were the inevitable way of things.'

83

Musa Musa could see the shadows of his friend's biceps straining to support what was left of him, lights dancing fleetingly in his eyes.

'We are dying, my friend,' the chief announced. 'We are sick. We are starving. I am dying. What are *you* going to do?'

'I said I had something to tell you,' the *zakulu* said. 'I am going to see the President.'

Where Tongo's eyes had burnt, now those bulbs were switched off, their heat fading quickly to nothing. He lay down again. He coughed. He tried turning the cough into a laugh but it sounded more like a sob. 'Ha ha! Ha ha ha! The President. That's a good one. There are not many jokes a dying man can play but there are plenty to be played on a dying man. The President . . .'

'That's what I came to tell you,' the *zakulu* said. He was puzzled. He didn't understand what was tickling his friend so mercilessly. 'The President will see me. You know he will. He will listen to me.'

'The President!' Tongo exclaimed again. 'Ha ha! Grain for everyone! Africa for the Africans! Antiretrovirals for all! That's a really good one, old friend! I'm glad you left me with a good joke, brother *zakulu*!'

'We'll see,' Musa Musa said. 'By the time we meet again, maybe everything will be better.'

Chief Tongo Kalulu of Zimindo allowed his face to fall to the side just enough for him to watch the *zakulu*, Musa Musa, from the corners of his eyes. He smiled thinly. 'Let us at least be straight with each other, old friend,' he said, 'because we both know we will not meet again on this earth.'

14

Insert document
'Eddy Kotto: The Voice of Independence for
20 years', *Gazette*, 3 May 2008, Eddy Kotto

So, my fellow citizens, after years in the international hinter-land it seems we have finally *made it*. I read in yesterday's London *Times* (online edition) that we are now a 'pariah state'. It is the culmination of a process that has been going on at least some months (since the presidential election), probably some years (since independence). Let us pat ourselves on the back.

I doubt that many of us have noticed that we have been suspended from the Commonwealth, that our exports have been frozen and that our foreign-currency reserve has dipped to an all-time low. I imagine most of us are similarly unbothered that the foreign superpowers have withdrawn their diplomatic missions one by one. But we have certainly noticed the petrol shortages that force each and every one of us to walk to our place of work (in the West, of course, they do this in expensive shoes and call it 'exercise'). And we are surely bothered that a toilet roll now costs such a vast amount of money that it saves us time and money to simply use our money.

It is undoubtedly these and other aspects of our current situation that lead *The Times* to report a 'state of crisis'. I have myself written freelance articles for this august publication in the past and it does not throw such terms around lightly. Why, then, as I strolled to the office this morning did I feel a melancholic but unmistakable sense of achievement? I will tell you: we should not worry if we are irritating the neo-colonial powers, we should worry if we were not. Let us be clear about these nations' motivation towards us – it is, as it has always been, self-interest masquerading as a higher purpose.

I fully support President Adini, therefore, in his scathing rebuttal of external pressure for a new election. We are a sovereign democracy and must be allowed to function as such. Yes, there was widespread corruption in the electoral process and, yes, Joseph Phiri, the leader of the Democratic Movement, was correct in his demand for a 'full and thorough investigation'. But there is no doubt that the voters saw Phiri's rallying call for greater liberalization and rampant privatization for exactly what it was: the yap of a lapdog.

I also fully support Adini's (long overdue) refusal to service our debts. It is a masterstroke of both common sense and bravado. The neocons and neocols have lately shown appetite for overseas adventure, but there is no suggestion that they might muster the necessary vim to march into the very Heart of Darkness. Therefore, as presidential aide Solomon Mhlanga recently remarked to me: 'They [the West] can do nothing.'

However, I am afraid that these reflections do not add up to a ringing endorsement of the President, who is increasingly paranoid and showing worrying symptoms of African Leadership Syndrome (that notorious condition continent-wide). Allow me, therefore, to make some brief observations.

1. When Adini succeeded his father following the unusual events of the Second Revolution, he quickly passed a statute limiting presidential office to three consecutive terms. Why, then, straight after his third election victory no less, do we hear that he is seeking to repeal this law? Adini claims his country 'needs him' and his work is 'not yet complete' – a typical symptom of African Leadership Syndrome, no doubt. I am sure I am

not the only one who struggles to shake the names of Mugabe, Mobutu, Museveni and countless others from his head. We may be in for the long haul.

2. Following Phiri's call for an investigation into the election, the President promised the same. So why has there been no progress to this end?

3. Further examples of Adini's new paranoia include the alleged police murder of Queenstown University (QU) undergraduate Alice Chipinge during last month's student demonstration, and the imprisonment of Musa Musa, the *zakulu* of Zimindo Province and national hero, in Gwezi maximum-security prison.

4. Though I support the President's refusal to service our debts, his subsequent decision to expel numerous aid agencies and reject the resources that have underwritten our healthcare and education structures for more than a decade smacks of petulance and hurts nobody but our own citizens. Adini claims he's developing 'a new set of strategic relationships'. But to run from a Western embrace straight into the arms of the Chinese is surely folly.

5. In the last fortnight the President has ordered the arrest of UK businessman and government apparatchik Gordon Tranter on suspicion of plotting a coup. I find this supposition unlikely, not because I consider the Brits above clandestine plotting, of course, but because I can't imagine they consider us a big enough fish to merit such frying. If the President truly has such evidence, therefore, I call on him to reveal it now.

Last week, during his Independence Day speech, Adini posed the following question: 'For all the strides made since independence, why do our brains remain Anglicized and Americanized and therefore colonized? We must re-establish our own authentic traditions, philosophy and culture before they are lost for ever.'

Many of us sympathize with the President's media localization programme, which has outlawed a variety of material. However, his strident attitude is fraught with danger, for who will arbitrate this authenticity? As a journalist, must I fear censorship and a return to the restrictions imposed by the colonial apartheid regime?

I am a proud nationalist. I was born, raised and educated in this country and I consider myself authentically Zambawian. But I also fear that in expressing the doubts I have, I may be judged a threat. Should my next editorial be written from Gwezi, therefore, you will know the reason why.

Independently yours
Eddy Kotto

15
Of getting things done

Zimindo township, Republic of Zambawi, 2008

When White Lightning finally passed through Zimindo township that afternoon, Musa Musa got on. He hadn't taken the Queenstown bus for almost three years and it wasn't how he remembered it. It was still jammed full, roof dangling all sorts of luggage, every bench spilling infants, but the one-time atmosphere of good-natured chaos had been replaced by something altogether more sombre.

Once, White Lightning had carried schoolchildren to their parents, sisters to their sisters, and husbands back to their wives or away to their mistresses. Once, the very words 'White Lightning' had been a magical incantation, which, when whispered in the classroom, queuing at the borehole or on the bottle store's dusty stoep, conjured whatever delights that speaker imagined the capital city might offer. Once, this journey had been the airlock in which the passengers reacquainted themselves with the heady mores of urban indulgence – eating and drinking, gossip and song and laughter. But now White Lightning generated all the enthusiasm of a cattle truck on its way to the abattoir: voices were low, eyes bored and restive, the air humming with indeterminate but indisputable doubts and fears.

It had only been a couple of days since the *zakulu* had noticed that everything had changed, but he was already worrying that nothing would ever be the same again. The journey from Zimindo to the city should have taken half an hour either side of four hours. Today it took the best part of eighteen. This was for the following reasons.

Unable to source any diesel in Queenstown, but keen not

to disappoint the rural customers who depended on his bus service, Ignatius Mupandawanda had dispatched White Lightning that morning without adequate fuel for a round trip. This wasn't quite as reckless a decision as it might sound, as Sam Gokwe, who owned the petrol station at Two Hundred Clicks and happened to be half-brother to a policy adviser in the energy ministry, rarely ran dry. Unfortunately, however, this was one such occasion. More or less marooned, Barrington, White Lightning's conductor, who'd only been working the Zimindo route a fortnight, promptly tried to call Mupandawanda from his cell-phone. Unfortunately, Barrington's SIM was registered to the AfroNet network.

AfroNet was a subsidiary of a South African company that was itself a subsidiary of a multinational telecoms giant. Though this giant professed itself eager to maintain the AfroNet service in the face of the nation's 'mounting problems', three months ago it had withdrawn all foreign staff as a 'precautionary measure'. Among those withdrawn was Vijay Dasgupta, a network engineer from Bangalore who was responsible for maintenance of the Zimindo mast.

Two months ago, Elias Murufu from Zimindo township had sent his son James to the tar road after a government relief truck spilt its cargo of rice. By the time James reached the scene of the accident, most of the dropped load had already been carefully collected up and spirited away by dozens of other local children. But on his way home James passed the AfroNet mast and noticed that its steel casing was of a size, shape and weight that would make it easily transformed into a plough, a tool the Murufu homestead urgently needed. On removing this casing, James revealed a sheaf of thick, protected wiring – just the stuff for repairing the Murufu chicken coop, which, though currently understocked, needed mending.

Although he was no natural criminal, there wasn't anyone around, and James figured that desperate times called for desperate measures. So, unthinking of the potential danger to himself, he tore out a fistful of these wires. In doing so, he made it impossible for any AfroNet subscriber in a hundred-kilometre radius to make a call. Two months later, Barrington, White Lightning's conductor, was the first to discover this.

James, who was now stuck on the bus himself, had no idea that his predicament was self-inflicted. He did, however, know that his parents now owned a fine hand plough and that their few remaining chickens were securely enclosed.

On discovering that his phone was no use, Barrington asked White Lightning's passengers if any had a phone he could borrow. Jealous Dube, a Queenstown mechanic, did. Unfortunately, his was AfroNet too. The only other belonged to Agnes Matamba, chairperson of the Zimindo Ladies' Foundation, an NGO-funded initiative that taught local women to make ethnic trinkets sold in charity outlets throughout Scandinavia. At least Agnes's SIM was registered to Z-Net (AfroNet's main rival – itself a subsid of a Nigerian subsid of another multi-national telecoms giant). However, Agnes had no airtime. Barrington, therefore, attempted to buy a Z-Net scratch card at Two Hundred Clicks.

Unfortunately, though the petrol station advertised 'Z-Net Top 'n' Go!', it hadn't taken delivery of scratch cards for more than a year, not since Z-Net had introduced the 'precautionary measure' of insisting all outlets paid for airtime in foreign exchange. This action, Z-Net had said, had been forced upon them by the instability of the Zambawian dollar. Sam Gokwe, the proprietor of Two Hundred Clicks, might have been able to finagle more or less regular fuel supplies through his well-positioned half-brother, but forex was another matter entirely.

Barrington then asked the petrol station's cashier if he might use the landline. Unfortunately the landline was down, as it had been for as long as anyone could remember.

One of the recommendations of the Structural Adjustment Programme, imposed on the Adini government by the

World Bank, had been the end of the state monopoly of telecoms provision. Within weeks of this recommendation, both AfroNet and Z-Net were up and running. With the establishment of the cellular networks, it hadn't taken long for most para-statal engineers to realize they'd earn better money working for the brash new companies on the telecoms block. Then, after brief retraining, it had taken only the same time again for the same engineers to realize they'd earn better money still working in Europe for the parent companies of the subsids of the subsids. This was why AfroNet and Z-Net employed Asian contractors, why the para-statal employed ill-qualified school-leavers and why Zamba could frequently be heard spoken in pubs in towns along London's M4 corridor. It was also why the Zambawian landline infrastructure was on the verge of collapse, and why the phone at Two Hundred Clicks was dead.

Barrington tried to flag down passing cars for an hour before the fourth stopped. It was a diplomatic Land Cruiser driven by Lars Larsson, a Dane who worked for one of the few multinational NGOs still active in the country. His former sunny manner and groundless optimism had only lately calcified into a kind of scaly lugubriousness. It was a change that he had noticed in himself even before his wife's comments and he didn't much like it. That was why he stopped for the stranger's frantic waving: because he saw both the opportunity to practise some humanity and that he needed the practice.

When Barrington explained his predicament, Lars offered the use of his cell. Unfortunately he was also on AfroNet and therefore had no signal. He could, however, offer Barrington a lift to the capital. Lars dropped Barrington at the main Mupandawanda bus garage two hours later. Fortunately, Ignatius Mupandawanda happened to be working late. On learning the dilemma, he immediately called Sam Gokwe's half-brother in the energy ministry. Fortunately, Sam Gokwe's half-brother was also working late and said that Mupandawanda could buy eight hundred litres of diesel from the ministry with a direct bank transfer. Unfortunately the banks were now closed and, besides, a direct bank transfer now took three days since the adoption of an IMF Code of Practice designed to target corruption in the financial sector. This Code of Practice had certainly ensured that the informal sector no longer used local banks to process their money. Instead, the informal sector now dealt exclusively in cash and banked in Switzerland or the UK. But this IMF triumph wasn't much help to Mupandawanda, who still needed to find enough diesel to transport White Lightning's stranded passengers to Queenstown.

Lowering his voice to a whisper, a symbolic more than a pragmatic action (since his phone was not being tapped and, if it had been, the tap would simply have recorded his whisper), Sam Gokwe's half-brother suggested Mupandawanda talk to 'Tony Capone', a self-styled energy dealer, lately arrived from the UK.

'Tony Capone' was a Zambawian, born Anthony Kapotwe, formerly a network engineer for the telecoms para-statal. He had worked briefly for AfroNet before emigrating for a job with Vodafone in Newbury. A year after he had joined Vodafone, the first fuel crisis hit Zambawi, and Tony managed to send some petrol to his father through his line manager, Graeme Macintosh. Macintosh was a white South African whose family had fled following the '94 election, but he talked with bottomless nostalgia of the wonders of home and he was only too happy to help a 'fellow African'.

It quickly became apparent, however, that it wasn't just Tony's dad who was desperate for fuel. Within weeks, Tony was supplying every driver in his father's township. Within months, he was supplying much of Queenstown. Within a year, he had moved home, a rich man with a colourful moniker.

Late that night, while White Lightning's passengers were

making the best of it, curled up on the benches of the bus or in the empty storeroom at Two Hundred Clicks, Mupandawanda bought a hundred litres of diesel from Tony Capone at eight times their market value. He paid in local currency, but that wasn't a problem for Tony. Since the introduction of the IMF Code of Practice, Tony had learnt that he could easily launder his money by stumping up local cash, at black-market rates, for expatriate employees of the few NGOs still active in the country; employees who were paid directly into their foreign accounts in foreign currency. They, in turn, paid into Tony's account in the UK. Everybody was at it, Lars Larsson and the like.

The following morning at first light, Mupandawanda and Barrington drove the fuel down to White Lightning. The bus made it to Gwezi bus station by midday. For the most part, White Lightning's passengers accepted the delay with stoic resignation. After all, though many of them had missed appointments or had their plans ruined, they had not been so presumptuous as to promise that the appointments would be kept or the plans fulfilled. One consequence of living in a nation where it was almost impossible to get anything done was that expectations were inevitably low. This made for a relaxed attitude, which was soon so ingrained as to be described by both locals and foreigners alike as significant of the national psyche. This attitude, in turn, made it ever harder to get anything done.

The only person materially inconvenienced by White Lightning's misfortune, therefore, was Agnes Matamba, who'd had a meeting scheduled with the director of the international NGO that provided the Zimindo Ladies' Foundation with its core funding. When she arrived at the NGO's offices the morning after her appointed time, the director refused to see her. He himself had travelled some distance from a field station to make sure he was there for the meeting so Mrs Matamba might at least have done likewise. And if she wasn't able to make the meeting, why hadn't she called? After all, he knew that the NGO had provided the chairperson of the Zimindo Ladies' Foundation with a cell-phone for precisely such eventualities.

Agnes Matamba tried to explain what had happened to the director's secretary, Grace Chiweshe, who listened with apparent sympathy. Unfortunately this young woman was in no position to help and, besides, after several recent trips accompanying her boss to various conferences in the region, her attitude towards her nation had hardened. Grace wasn't sure what had caused this change – whether it was the impress-ive gravitas with which the white men at these conferences spoke or the monogrammed bed linen in the five-star hotels where she slept, but she definitely now believed that her people's problems (and by 'her people' she meant everyone from Agnes Matamba to her parents) were their own fault and that her only hope was to cling gratefully to the coat tails of her kind-hearted and ever-impressive boss.

Behind his office door, however, her boss, Lars Larsson, felt less than kind-hearted and impressive. Whatever good-will he'd conjured towards his fellow men the previous after-noon by giving a lift to that bus conductor had immediately dissipated when his five o'clock, Mrs Matamba from the Zim-indo Ladies' Foundation, hadn't turned up. After her no-show, he had taken Grace to the Sheraton bar where they'd got riotously drunk with an assortment of other NGO directors and employees. These colleagues, locals and expats alike, had agreed that such wanton irresponsibility as that shown by Mrs Matamba was symptomatic of a more general malaise.

Last night, Larsson had finally concluded that he was unwanted here in Zambawi and that he wanted to return home to Copenhagen. He wasn't entirely sure if he was unwanted because he wanted to go home or vice versa but it didn't much matter now. It was hot and the aircon was broken and Larsson could feel thick rivulets of sweat running down the back of his thick, pink neck. He would have opened his office door but he could hear voices outside and he was worried that Mrs Matamba was still there. He took five milligrams of Valium.

He wanted to go home. He wanted to go home where he would write a book about the impossibilities of development in Africa. This book would be witty and sensitive and, thanks to his track record on the continent, indisputable. He would go on book tours around Europe and the United States on which he would tell melancholy anecdotes of injustice and incompetence to audiences who understood and sympathized with him.

He blinked himself out of his reverie and turned to his computer. He knew he should start to compose his resignation email before the Valium kicked in, but the NGO's Internet connection was down again. He sat back in his chair and popped another five milligrams. It could wait.

16

Lift not the painted veil

Queenstown, Republic of Zambawi, 2008
Musa Musa walked from the bus station at Gwezi, a mid-density suburb famous for little but its buses and Queenstown's main prison, all the way to State House on the other side of the city. He walked through the light industrial area of Gone, took a right up Kwame Nkrumah and a left down Central Avenue to the city centre, passing the National Reserve Bank, the Sheraton Hotel, Steers Rib Shack and Price Right supermarket on his way. He might have caught a *matatu*, but he intended to save the few dollars in his pocket and, more to the point, he wanted to see the city up close, to hear its breath and smell its body.

The population of Zimindo had largely drained away and this was where they'd said they were heading. The *zakulu*, therefore, had imagined the capital now heaving with humanity. But the reality could hardly have been more different, the streets almost deserted.

He passed a young couple, their features every bit as local as their clothes were foreign, hurrying to who knew where and sparring in incomprehensible Zamblish – a mixture of the *lingua franca* of black America and local, urban wit. He passed a middle-aged white man, with sandals and unruly hair, who barked understated commands into a mobile phone and wore an expression of earnest confusion that made him look as if he was attempting some especially tricky mental arithmetic. He passed a gaggle of Oriental men in smart business suits who were taking photographs of a dilapidated building. Then that was it for a while. Workshops were padlocked shut, shops dozing.

97

A low-riding Datsun with rusty wheel arches chugged slowly by, billowing sooty exhaust. An imposing Japanese four-by-four sped in the opposite direction, its windows tinted and impenetrable. A gang of street kids emerged from an alley. He was grateful for the company. They semi-circled him and taunted his pained limp – wary baboons around a wounded lion. Clearly they didn't know who he was. They had eyes opaque with solvent abuse and wore T-shirts that screamed American slogans or NGO advice, the one indistinguishable from the other ('Just Do It' alongside 'Winners Wear Protection'). He scattered them with a look. The troop whooped their retreat like a victory.

He passed a veteran of the First Independence War, who wheeled himself on a makeshift trolley cobbled together from a crate and Price Right casters. The vet recognized him at once and his face split into a broad grin that revealed his missing teeth. 'Musa Musa!' he exclaimed. 'Yes, Uncle! I knew you would come. You have come to save us!'

Musa Musa stopped. 'From what can I save you, my brother?'

The vet's smile didn't flicker. 'To help us, then. You have come to help us.'

'And how must I help you?'

The vet cupped his hands and reached up to the famous *zakulu*. 'In any way you can, sir.'

Musa Musa gave the man the little money he had, shook his hand and limped on.

He looked up at the sky that was clear and blue and the sun that burnt an iridescent white, and he shivered. Both sides of the empty street were cold in the dark shadows cast by tall, modern buildings. Musa Musa wondered if those places were where the people were hiding, looking down on him, playing a game of hide and seek. But many of the doors were bolted, reception desks unattended. A security guard stood motionless in a doorway, keeping a close eye on the pavement at his feet.

A poster for the *Gazette* flapped from a lamppost. It read 'Student Demo Cripples Capital'. It was at least half an explanation of the silent streets.

Musa Musa headed out of the city centre on Saddam Hussein to the intersection with Adini. Here he paused, partly because he wanted to enjoy the cherry trees that splashed the avenue pink and partly because the pain of his poor budless foot was now almost unbearable. Every time he lowered his weight onto his left leg, there was an ominous squelching and he could feel his sole sliding around in a puddle of his own blood. He wasn't far from his destination but, hit by a sudden wave of nausea, he knew he had to rest.

There was an ancient, wrought-iron bench set back from the road and the *zakulu* stumbled over to it, sat down and raised his left leg to allow the blood to drain from his foot. He considered examining the wound, but there was no point in distressing himself when there was nothing he could do. Instead, he took a handkerchief from his pocket, shoved his falling locks from his face and mopped his hairline. The pain was making him sweat.

Screwed to the back of the bench was a brass plaque, the inscription almost rubbed away to nothing. It read, 'In mem_____ as Mallory (1885–1961) who, in lat_____, like____ sit at____ corn___ to admire the blossom and to watch the world _____' Then, 'Lift not the _____ed v___ which th___ ___ _____ _____ life – P. B. Shelley'. Musa Musa read and reread the inscription. Then, filling the blanks of the quotation from memory, he spoke it aloud: '"Lift not the painted veil which those who live call life."'

He felt suddenly and notably sad. His sadness was notable because of its suddenness, because he wasn't typically given to such an emotion (although lately that had changed) and because it was cyclical. He felt sorry for himself. He felt sorry for the cherry trees, transplanted from their own earth at the whim of a colonial administrator to decorate an empire that wouldn't see out the century. He felt sorry for Mallory, whose relatives had been moved to such melancholic tribute, sorry too for the relatives who never knew their bench would be their most lasting contribution to a country that wasn't theirs. He felt sorry for the cherry blossom that would be brown mulch in a matter of days and yet, in its own cycle, outlive him still. And then he felt sorry for himself all over again.

When he heard a gunshot somewhere distant, Musa Musa looked up. Some birds squawked and flapped. A wind picked up and, all the way along the avenue, began to lift the blossom off the trees until it swirled in the air like confetti. He had just begun to suspect that the gunshot had been only in his imagination when he heard another. This was now followed by the sound of distant shouting, like thunder beyond the horizon, but it was quickly coming closer.

Musa Musa peered up Adini, and a couple of hundred metres away, a figure appeared from the junction with President's Drive, which led up to the gates of State House, sprinting at full pelt into the eddies of cherry blossom. No sooner had the *zakulu* begun to consider what an extraordinary sight this made than he saw two dozen other people, following the first, running as fast as they could down Adini Avenue. Some were carrying banners and placards but these were soon discarded in their haste.

Behind this two dozen, came about twice as many policemen. It was the police who seemed to be doing most of the shouting and most had their batons drawn, wielding them above their heads.

Musa Musa watched, rendered impassive (he thought later) by surprise. He knew what was going on as surely as he couldn't quite believe it.

It was only a matter of seconds before the backmarker of the fugitives was brought down by a swinging baton that rapped her calves. She tumbled theatrically and was immediately swarmed over by four or five men in uniform, punching and kicking. A couple of her fellows slowed, as if unsure whether to go back for their fallen colleague. Their uncertainty only guaranteed their capture and, within a heartbeat, they too were overrun and rolling on the tarmac, helplessly attempting to fend off the raining blows.

Musa Musa watched as, one by one, the runners were overhauled, all except the very first he'd seen, who sprinted right past him, glancing across as he went by, his nostrils flared, his eyes wide and terrified.

The avenue made for an extraordinary sight: somehow the policemen's fury was softened into slow motion by the gentleness of the churning cherry blossom, the shouts and the screams and the sickening sounds of baton on body somehow muted in the sea of pink. Every time a policeman raised his arm high from the shoulder, he lifted a flurry of flowers upwards, magically against gravity. Every vicious connection was momentarily neutered, sutured and lovingly tended by the delicate pink kisses.

Musa Musa sighed as he heaved himself to his feet and resumed his journey. No sooner had he stepped onto the avenue proper than he felt almost overwhelmed by the blizzard of petals that filled his eyes and nose and caught between his teeth. He fought his way onward through the colourful snowstorm, every now and then catching the blurry glimpse of a dark arm dropping like a club.

He reached the first fallen body. It was little more than twitching now beneath the metronomic beating of two policemen. At first the cops, engrossed in their work, spitting hatred, didn't notice him and he could look on, detached, as if this were a dream. But the *zakulu* knew a thing or two about dreams and this wasn't one of them. Beside the body lay the placard for which its bearer was now suffering. It read simply, 'Adini out!'

Now the cops glanced at him – one, then the other – and first their curses, then their limbs, froze. Musa Musa must have looked quite something, tall and straight and angry, cherry blossom caught in every dreadlock. But he didn't know if it was just his appearance that prompted what followed. Did the policemen recognize him in the context of what they were doing or did they simply recognize themselves? Did it matter? Either way, they turned and ran as if he were pursuing them.

The body in front of him groaned. But Musa Musa didn't stop to check on it. He kept walking and, one by one, without doing anything, he chased the policemen away.

When he reached the last fugitive, the first to have been caught, the *zakulu* stopped. The young woman's banner proclaimed, 'Phiri for President – We Want Change.' She wasn't moving. Blossom fell on her eyes and cheeks and still she didn't move. It was as if she were playing a game or conducting an experiment. Some of her comrades, those not so badly beaten, crouched around her. Musa Musa saw their lips move and the urgency in their faces, but he heard nothing. He kept walking. He turned out of Adini Avenue into President's Drive and approached the gate of State House picking cherry blossom from his hair.

That afternoon, President Enoch Adini and the celebrated *zakulu* Musa Musa met for two hours. Generally, a secretary noted all of the premier's meetings, but for some reason this one went unrecorded. It concluded, however, with Musa Musa's arrest and transfer back across the city to Gwezi where he was taken to the prison's maximum-security block, assigned the number 118 and held on charges of treason by presidential decree.

Insert document
'African Authority?', Political Sketch,
Guardian, 7 May 2008, anon.

Rarely has the Prime Minister looked more uncomfortable during his weekly interrogation than he did yesterday when challenged by Neil McDonald (SNP) about the arest [*sic*] of British businessman Gordon Tranter in Queenstown, Zambawi.

Mr McDonald demanded to be told 'how the government will respond, both to this specific act of provocation and President Adini's continued flouting of the principles of democracy and freedom'. He then asked to know how the situation might affect the African Authority. 'So far, I get the "African" part of the equation,' he commented, 'but I must say I've seen scant evidence of any authority.'

It wasn't much of a joke from Mr McDonald – a notoriously dour politician – so the fact that it provoked raucous laughter from all sides of the House is, in itself, instructive and the PM appeared discomforted. Even David Pinner, the rather dashing Foreign Office minister with responsibility for Africa, who sat to the PM's right, looked as if he'd be rather dashing for the nearest exit.

The PM's answer was indignant. He promised that Mr Tranter's arrest would be addressed 'swiftly, expediently and at the highest level'. If the rumours around Whitehall are to be believed, it seems this may even mean the dispatch of a government delegation to Zambawi within the next few days.

He went on to deny any connection between the Zambawi

situation and the African Authority, which had met for the first time last month. He pointed out that Zambawi was currently suspended from the Commonwealth, in dispute with both the World Bank and the IMF, and had no representation on the Authority. Even for a premier whose government now seems synonymous with pig-headedness, this was a statement of breathtaking muddled thinking, which illustrates all that is most dangerous about his definitive pet project.

At the launch of the African Authority, the PM declared it 'an open forum for Africans and non-Africans to work together towards realistic and, crucially, African-led solutions to the challenges of poverty, AIDS, governance, debt and many more'. Where are these challenges more poignantly felt than Zambawi? Even before the Tranter arrest, the make-up of the African Authority looked disturbingly like a parade of the usual suspects. Now what the PM described as a 'coalition of the willing' seems ever more to resemble only a 'union of the malleable'. And even they may not be as malleable as the PM might like to think.

Of course, the PM's unease must have been compounded by his own connections with Tranter, a material contributor to his leadership campaign.

An Old Etonian and a familiar face in London society, Tranter is, nonetheless, of relatively humble stock, his father a carpet salesman who sacrificed much for the sake of his only son. After he left Oxford, little is known of Tranter's whereabouts in the seventies and eighties. He surfaced in South Africa in the early nineties at the head of a syndicate holding a significant stake in mining interests across the continent. He is currently believed to have amassed a fortune in the region of £350 million.

Although there is no suggestion of any impropriety on his part, photographs of Tranter shaking hands with the likes of Nick du Toit and Charles Taylor have already embarrassed the government. Indeed, it is notable that none of the African leaders who were invited to join the Authority have yet commented on Tranter's arrest. Indeed, only Oscar Mdluli – respected diplomat, former ANC man and the Authority's nominal chair – has made a public statement: 'We regret President Adini's actions and call on him to release Mr Tranter as soon as possible.' This hardly amounts to the unequivocal condemnation for which the British government must have hoped.

What's more, if the rumours are true and government representatives are indeed sent to Zambawi, it will only serve to illustrate the disingenuousness of the PM's comments. Although such a course of action will be defended as expediency, there is no doubt that it would represent an unprecedented diplomatic step and show the importance the beleaguered PM attaches to the preservation of his African vision.

As we approach a general election, the African Authority may yet become an unlikely area of controversy. The PM has attempted to cultivate a position for himself as an 'honest broker for Africa' that counterbalances a rather po-faced image at home and perceived ovine qualities in other areas of foreign policy. The African Authority, therefore, was a grand plan that promised great results with apparently few risks. Now the PM must worry that his fingers are about to be very badly burnt indeed.

It's hard to avoid the suspicion that all the Africans in the 'coalition of the willing' would secretly like to join Adini in sticking two fingers up to their former colonial masters but fear the consequences. If so, they are little more than schoolboys who have chosen to join the playground bully for expedient reasons of their own.

18
The sins of the father

London, England, 2008
Preston Pinner was at the restaurant no more than a few minutes after eight, but his dad still beat him to it. Though Preston was rarely late and his old man no fiend for punctuality, there was something inevitable about this, as if each couldn't help but live down to the other's expectations, of sloppiness on one side and assiduousness on the other.

The restaurant was a Moroccan joint in Mayfair. Preston had heard of the place but never been there, and as soon as he stepped out of the cab, he knew why – it wasn't his style. Set back from the side-street, the place had three distinct eating areas: a café at the front, a restaurant behind and a private members' club below. The café fed Moroccan 'tapas' to a range of wealthy young people – Arab old money, Russian new money and an assortment of blond, mostly female, Eurotrash. They spilled out over the pavement and in front of the neighbouring couture boutiques, now shut up for the night. They smoked hookahs beneath industrial gas heaters and draped themselves over leather-covered cushions around low, darkwood tables. Chatter was loud to be heard over the insistent *chaabi* that blared from the wall-mounted speakers. Long pale arms emerged horizontally from pashminas to end in long pale fingers that wrapped around tall glasses spewing fresh mint. If you had taken a photograph and then glanced at it too quickly, the dark, cavernous doorway and prone bodies might have given you the impression of the moment after a bomb blast. It looked as if the building had choked and this was what it had spat out.

For Preston, who was not just an expert in reading the

symptoms of contemporary culture but also at passing snap judgement on their merits, the scene smacked of ersatz Bohemia. He pulled his baseball cap a little lower as he negotiated the boisterous cadavers. It was an act of defiance more than disguise. If he knew one thing about fame, it was that it is contextual: even if these people knew his face, they'd never be expecting to see him on their turf. For once he was anonymous.

Inside, through the café, past the bar, the main restaurant was a vast sea of clutter. It was dimly lit and he had to pick his way carefully through the minefield of knick-knacks that littered the floor and every available surface – statuettes, candlesticks and lovingly arranged clusters of brass. Some interior designer had clearly gone mad in a Rabat bazaar. Here, middle-aged oil wearing slick smiles and perfectly groomed moustaches dined with young Ivy League lawyers who had names that ended with numerals to signify their authentic heritage. But David Pinner wasn't in the main restaurant.

Pinner was downstairs in the small private members' club, a bijou grotto where tea-lights twinkled in the multicoloured glass of ornate lampshades. Only here, Preston thought, did you find the born-and-bred white Englishmen – for the most part single-breasted, double-chinned and three sheets to the wind. Their superior expressions suggested self-selecting exclusivity, but it wasn't just the subterranean situation that gave the place a somewhat sepulchral atmosphere. He imagined the assembled members as an expedition of Victorian archaeologists who found themselves in a pyramid's sumptuous vaults and had yet to grasp that there was no way out.

He spotted his dad in a corner booth at the back. He had his right leg crossed over the left, so that his foot hung limp, protruding from both booth and pinstriped trouser-leg to reveal a monogrammed sock. He had his elbow on the table and his chin resting thoughtfully on his fist. Every now and then he sipped his Scotch, ran a hand through his mane or speared an olive with a toothpick. Crouching next to him was Gerald, the minister's brand new personal secretary.

Pinner had a poor record when it came to secretaries. The last had developed stress-related shingles; the one before had suffered a full-blown breakdown. Preston didn't know if his dad was a particularly exacting boss or simply a poor judge of character, but he wondered if Gerald was made of sterner stuff.

Gerald was a tall, slim young man with an earring, a shock of dirty brown hair and an incongruously broad and low-slung behind. Seen, on occasion, jacketless, he resembled nothing more than a mop standing upside-down in a bucket. Preston had been mildly intrigued by Gerald ever since he had discovered they had been exact contemporaries at Cambridge. He hadn't known Gerald but, inevitably, Gerald knew him (because everybody did), and tried to picture the mop and bucket's extraordinary proportions aboard a bike, college scarf flapping, cycling down King's Parade to first lecture amid the shoal of like-minded.

Gerald was, Preston considered, typical of a certain kind of Oxbridge product that he'd only identified in retrospect: a being whose swollen intellect appeared to have left no room for personality, passion or credo. It wasn't so different an opinion from that Preston held of some of his team at Authenticity™ – Gerald was like the cool junkies, only square. Preston imagined that, in another life, he would have been as happy scaling the career ladder at B&Q as at Westminster. Preston imagined Gerald suffering a single moment of existential angst, which had been resolved with an earring. Preston imagined Gerald one day running the country in the same way that a shoe runs a race. For some reason he couldn't quite identify, he found Gerald a little scary.

Preston approached the table. Pinner was signing a document at the point Gerald marked with his finger. Reverentially squatting, the secretary's jacket rode up and his backside strained the seam of his trousers.

Preston stood there for a full five seconds before his dad noticed him. But when he did he leapt to his feet, almost knocking Gerald onto his back like a beetle. 'Preston!' he exclaimed, as if this was the most delightful surprise and they hadn't, in fact, arranged to meet. He grabbed his son by the shoulders and contemplated him for a second, as though he were a miracle.

Preston shrugged off his attention, said, 'All right, Dad,' then slid into the booth.

Reluctantly, Pinner sat down again, sieved the Scotch through his teeth and nodded at Gerald. 'You know Jeremy, don't you?'

Jeremy? Oh, *Jeremy*. Right. 'Sure,' Preston said. 'Hi.'

They shook hands. Jeremy's was warm and damp and his smile curious and sycophantic. Momentarily, Preston assumed the flattery was aimed at him – he was, after all, the brightest of London's bright young things. But when his old man said, 'Are we done?' and the secretary seemed to blush in the light of ministerial attention, he saw his mistake.

'Yes, sir,' Jeremy confirmed.

'Good stuff. Really. Excellent stuff.'

Jeremy stood up. He said, 'Right, sir,' and backed away. He flashed Preston a glance that could only be described as envious. Envious of what? Pinner as parent? Preston watched him leave, somewhat confused. He'd have assumed Jeremy was in some way acting if he'd been able to guess the purpose, let alone imagine him capable of such performance.

'Good fellow,' Pinner remarked fondly. 'Bright spark. Typical grammar-school boy. Doesn't think the world owes him a living.'

Preston stared at his dad. Previous experience told him he was supposed to consider himself the butt of this comment.

But, if so, it made no sense. After all, Preston had worked hard for his money since he'd sold his first CD aged fourteen. In fact, if anybody thought the world owed him a living, wasn't it David Pinner MP?

This was why Preston avoided these meetings: when he picked up on his old man's criticism, he was told he was imagining it, but ignoring it left him open to more of the same. He took off his baseball cap and ran a hand over his number-one. It was growing out and needed a cut.

Pinner scanned a menu. 'Are you hungry?'

Preston shook his head. 'Like I said, I can't stay.'

'Can't stay? Really? What a shame. I thought it would be good. You know – dinner; just the two of us.'

'Dad, Jodie told you. I just don't have time.'

This was, of course, both truth and lie – a lie that he hadn't the time, true that Jodie had been briefed to say as much. And they both knew it.

Pinner nodded. He looked hurt. He said, 'A drink, then,' and waved over a pretty, olive-skinned waitress.

Preston smiled at her. 'I'll just have water, please,' he said. 'Still water.' He could tell she recognized him because she wouldn't meet his eye. He enjoyed her shyness.

'Still off the sauce?' This was Pinner.

'Yeah.'

'That's good. Good for you.' Pinner tapped his Scotch glass at the pretty waitress, signalling another, then uncrossed his legs, sat round and leant into the table. 'So . . .' he said. He contemplated his son and took in the limited-edition Japanese designer T, the diamond ear-stud, and the platinum replica two-pence piece that hung on a thick platinum chain at his neck. He allowed himself an indulgent smile. 'So . . .' he said again.

'So . . .'

'How's your mother?'

'She's a fiend for needlepoint.'

'Dry?'

'As far as I know.'

'Terrific!' And then, as if assuming his son doubted his sincerity, 'Really, that's terrific. Would you tell her I said so?'

'Why don't you tell her yourself?'

Pinner raised a thin smile. 'I don't think there could be anything much more likely to prompt a fall from the wagon, do you?'

Preston grunted and, without thinking, sat forward too; an unconscious lowering of his guard. 'Yeah,' he said. 'I guess so.'

Pinner clasped his hands on the table in front of him. His smile evolved into an expression almost worthy of the word. It was a truce. 'And how are you?'

'Fine. Yeah, fine.'

'And how's your . . . your company?'

Truce or no truce, Preston knew Pinner could never deign to call Authenticity™ by its name, as if to do so would grant it a legitimacy it didn't deserve. 'Good,' he said. 'It's going good.'

'Well.'

'Well what?'

'It's going *well*.'

'Whatever.'

Their gazes locked. They sighed in unison. They were both prepared to let this one go.

'Well,' Pinner said again. 'Well, you're certainly in the papers often enough, quite the man about town.'

'Visibility's a big part of what I do.'

The MP sniffed. 'And that is?'

Preston considered the question. He knew it wasn't really a question at all, just an extension of the same sentiment that made his dad refuse to reference Authenticity™ by name. But he decided it wasn't badly meant, simply a triggered response rendered inevitable by years of practice, and again he chose not to rise to it. 'Lots of things,' he said. Then, unable to resist the temptation to make his dad feel out of touch, he added, 'At the moment a lot of it's about UGC. We're an aggregator but, unlike most of our rivals, we have sufficient brand attributes to act as a trusted arbitrator too.'

'Right.' Pinner managed a humble chuckle. If he felt out of touch, he clearly didn't feel badly about it. 'And what does *that* mean?'

'It means we tell people what to like and they believe us.'

'Right. And you get paid for this?'

Now it was Preston's turn to chuckle. 'I do OK.'

'Good. That's good.' Pinner took another sip of Scotch and swirled the ice in the glass. 'Not so different from politics.'

'Not different at all,' Preston said sharply, without thinking. 'It *is* politics. Only difference is, we're better at it than you lot.' He immediately regretted his aggressive reflex. It was another enduring response to another enduring dynamic but, in this instance, it had not only led him to the point of their meeting but also potentially undermined his argument as to why the meeting was, in fact, pointless.

'I suspect you're right,' Pinner murmured.

But Preston was already talking over him. 'Look,' he began quickly. 'Look, Dad, I hope you won't take this the wrong way but I really can't get involved with your campaign. I mean, I've thought it through and I've realized it won't do either of us any good, know what I mean? Like, in the first place, I'm totally over-committed. And, in the second place . . . well, like I say, I hope you won't take this the wrong way, but it's a big risk of brand association for both of us. I mean, I guess you want to associate with something contemporary, something street, something cool but, look, these things have a horrible tendency to backfire – remember Hague at the Notting Hill Carnival? Remember the baseball cap? It didn't just fuck him up, it fucked up the fucking baseball cap, you get me?'

Pinner regarded his son with a raised eyebrow. Preston

couldn't read the expression and he found himself chewing the insides of his cheeks.

'I get you,' Pinner said eventually. Then, 'Actually, I couldn't agree with you more. It was the party who thought you might be able to help my profile. But, I ask you, is that really what a government minister should be worrying about? Their *profile*? I tell you, Preston, that's not why I got into politics.' He paused and pulled a troubled face, as if considering whether to continue the revelation. 'I got into this to do something, to make a difference, a substantive difference. I suppose you won't believe it and I know it sounds corny, but it's true. I'm just sorry I allowed myself to be seduced by the idea of some kind of superficial beauty contest. So, you know, thanks for the offer – it was good of you even to consider it. But you're off the hook.' He sniffed, sipped his Scotch and shook his head, as if he'd just negotiated a narrow escape.

Preston narrowed his eyes. Although this was precisely what he'd wanted, he couldn't help feeling he'd been outmanoeuvred, perhaps even insulted. Was his dad serious? It was almost impossible to tell. Besides, as far as Preston was concerned, even if Pinner believed what he was saying, that didn't stop it being a lie. He searched his old man's face for a chink in the sentiments. 'What about Fate?' he asked.

'I'm sorry?'

'What about Fate? Do you remember? 'The hand of Fate on your shoulder', that's what you said. Maybe a shot at the shadow cabinet?'

'Aah!' Pinner breathed contentedly as if this was the very question he'd wanted to hear. 'Well. *Que sera sera*, et cetera. That's the thing about Fate, after all.'

At that moment, a young blonde woman approached the table. Slim and gamine, she was packaged in a fitted suit that showed off her lack of hips and bust. Her hair was cropped short and she wore no makeup but bright red lipstick. It was only when she spoke that Preston remembered he'd met her before – when she said, 'David,' turning the *v* into something closer to a *w*. This was his old man's latest squeeze. She was Russian. She drank neat vodka over ice. She was a high flyer in Millhouse Capital. Her name was –

'Eva!' Pinner said warmly. He stood up and kissed her on both cheeks. 'Preston, you remember Eva. Eva, I'm sure you remember my son Preston.'

The woman turned her eyes to Preston. Now that she was looking at him, she appeared older than before – older than him, certainly, which was something. She had the mildly sardonic air that Preston assumed was mandatory for Eastern European women. She seemed essentially bored, but there was a glimmer in her eye as if she'd just noticed something amusing that she would only share with you for cash payment. She looked like the kind of woman who'd smoke while having sex.

Preston said, 'Hello.'

She said, 'Yes, Preston,' as though that would suffice as a greeting. Then she turned back to Pinner and said, 'Excuse me one moment,' before she walked off in the direction of the ladies'.

Pinner watched her go and said, 'You remember her, don't you?'

'Vaguely,' Preston said, then asked, 'Is she the one from Refugee Concern?' Even though he knew she wasn't.

'What? No! You're thinking of – what was her name? – Mila. I think you mean Mila. Or Elnura, perhaps. She worked for Action on Asylum. I'm afraid we rather fell out. Inevitable, I suppose.'

If Preston had intended to shame his dad by drawing attention to his list of recent girlfriends, it clearly wasn't working. In fact, if anything, the length of the list seemed something of a source of pride. Preston changed tack. 'I thought you wanted us to have dinner. Just the two of us.'

'I did!'

'But you invited –'

'So? I didn't think you'd mind.'

'Well, it's not just the two of us, is it?'

'Press!' Pinner exclaimed, puzzled and frowning. 'You said you didn't have time for dinner.'

'I don't. But that's not the point.'

'Oh.' Pinner nodded. 'So, what *is* the point?'

Preston shook his head. This was why he didn't like seeing his dad: they had these childish exchanges and he always ended up sounding like an idiot. He drained his water and shook his head again. 'Why did you want to meet me?'

'I'm sorry?'

'You said you wanted to see me. In fact, you said you *needed* to see me. If it's not about working on your *profile*, what is it about? Like I said, Dad, I've got stuff to do. I ought to go in a minute.'

Pinner stared at his son. He drummed his fingers on the table and adopted his wounded expression. 'Do you *really* have such a low opinion of me?'

Now it was Preston's turn to look puzzled. 'What?'

'No matter.' He drained his drink. The ice chimed in the glass. 'I wanted to see you, Preston . . . I just wanted to let you know . . . It looks like I'm going on a trip.' His son didn't respond, so he pressed on: 'I'll most likely be flying to Zambawi within the next fortnight. Some chap called Tranter's been arrested by Adini, the res pres. Adini says he's MI6, been plotting a coup. We say release him in a fortnight or else.' He smiled ruefully. 'Apparently I'm the "or else". We emptied the embassy six months ago so, in the absence of the grunts, the PM has asked yours truly to sort out the sorry shit.'

'And is he?'

'Is he what?'

'MI6?'

Pinner sneered. He couldn't help himself. 'Oh, for God's sake, Preston, grow up.'

From the corner of his eye, Preston spotted the Russian woman returning. He picked up his baseball cap and fingered the peak. 'That's why you wanted to meet me? To tell me you were going away?'

'That's right. And to tell you what I'd decided about the campaign.' He leant forward and covered Preston's hand with his own. His son instinctively pulled away. 'This is a great opportunity for me, Preston, a chance for me to really do something. This Adini fucker's trying to disrupt the African Authority, knock it off the rails. And I can't let that happen. You know how important this is. The African Authority can be a catalyst – initiatives on democracy, good governance, debt relief, the rule of law. We can actually do something to make a lasting change.'

Preston looked at his old man in surprise. 'You really care about this?'

'I really do,' Pinner said. 'This is what I got into politics for. This is what I wanted – something I can get my teeth into.'

The Russian woman was back at the table. She was procrastinating about where to sit. The nature of the booth meant she'd have to slide in next to either Pinner or his son. Neither seemed to appeal.

Preston made it easy for her. He shimmied out. 'Please. Sit here. I gotta go anyway.'

She took his place without even looking at him.

Pinner stood up again, his face a picture of earnestness. He embraced his son and said, pointlessly, 'Are you sure you won't stay?'

Preston said, 'Have a good trip, Dad.' On his way out, he caught sight of Pinner in a mirror by the door. The dim light and long shadows seemed to stretch his features ghoulishly. He laughed and his huge front teeth shone white against the dark abyss of the rest of his mouth.

Preston thought about what his old man had said he wanted – something to get his teeth into. He wondered if Eva qualified.

Briefly, accidentally, he imagined the two of them having sex, Pinner bucking like an ageing bronco, the Russian smoking placidly.

Since his divorce, his dad had dated an unbroken string of Eastern European women. At first they'd been mostly exhausted-looking Bosnians, and Preston had assumed this was, at worst, an extension of his dad's previous work with Balkan refugees. However, as Eastern Europe had opened up so had his old man's taste and, in the last couple of years, he'd been rattling through elfin Ukrainians, statuesque Czechs, intimidating Russians and several depressed Poles. In fact, now Preston joined the dots, he questioned Pinner's willingness, at the Home Office, to push through the new asylum legislation that seemed to contradict everything he'd previously stood for. Was it possible that his father saw no need to defend the rights of refugees now that there were so many delightful potential girlfriends with legal residency?

Preston tutted to himself. But then he felt obliged to work out what the tut meant. Initially he assumed it was aimed at his own cynicism. He'd spent his career spinning motivations into saleable stories so he could pick apart shaky narratives for fun. But did he really believe government policy could come to fruition, at least in part, thanks to the sexual predilections of its ministers?

Or perhaps the tut was aimed at his dad. Preston thought back to the conclusion he'd come to the last time he and Pinner had spoken – that the MP didn't believe in anything – and realized that was wrong. In fact, he was starting to think the opposite: that Pinner could believe in absolutely anything at all. For when Pinner said that he was going to Africa for democracy and good governance, debt relief and the rule of law, he wasn't *lying*. Rather, Preston reckoned, his dad's lack of conviction had now achieved such extraordinary velocity that it had gone full circle, arrived before it had left, and transformed into something else – a naïve quality, no less, that enabled him to believe whatever came out of his own mouth with absolute certainty purely on the basis that it had emerged from the aforementioned orifice.

Shit! As his father's son, with his father's nose, wasn't this precisely the kind of conviction of which he himself was guilty?

Preston thought all these things in the three strides it took him to pass the mirror, but by the time he'd made it up the stairs, through the restaurant and outside into the street, all these suppositions seemed to have dispersed. Left in their place was nothing but a gaping melancholy, because he had suddenly seen that he understood too much.

Whether they admit it or not, most young men like to believe that someone knows better. They acknowledge their own capriciousness and look to bigger, heavier, older men for the moral gravity that will ultimately and necessarily ground them. And, secretly, they hope that this gravity might be provided by their father. But Preston now appreciated that nobody knew better. Worse still, he was coming to suspect that his dad knew no better most of all.

19
Everything is everything

London, England, 2008

Preston stopped at another club on his way home, this time one where he was a member. Called The Asylum, it was tucked into Noho in the angle of Oxford Street and Tottenham Court Road, a Tardis-like building in which three bars, two restaurants, a reading lounge and a games room were arranged over five floors, with not enough space on any of them.

Fame attracted fame, success, success, and money, money. Broadcasters and podcasters, journalists and bloggers, publishers and book-burners, pop stars and musicians, cineastes and movie-makers rubbed shoulders, buttocks and groins in this institution of the new establishment. This was where the real power was, among these wannabes and has-beens, all in denial about their status, which was at least partly defined by their denial. They were all on their way up or on their way down – so it goes. Such vertical mobility, however, doesn't mean that many moved in or out. The new establishment remained a more or less closed system and The Asylum a bucketful of crabs.

Preston took a seat at the first-floor bar and ordered a J2O. He didn't know what he was doing there. He didn't much like the joint (no one did, that was part of its appeal, its packed rooms teeming with people not much liking it in loud voices) but, after seeing his family, he always felt he needed to be around something familiar.

A few people raised their eyes at him, a couple clapped his shoulder with the words '2P! Yes, mate!' One even shook his hand. A few of these people vaguely knew him, a couple only recognized him from television; one thought she vaguely knew him but, in fact, only recognized him from television.

Thandi, his co-presenter on AuthenTV™, appeared, a blonde sidekick at her elbow. She was fucked up on the junk she'd been smoking on the terrace by way of an evening meal. Preston knew the routine and he could see it in her movements. He was going to have to fire her. It was a shame because he liked her, more or less, and she scored well with every one of their key demographics.

Thandi's eyes snapped one way and then the other before locking on Preston. She pulled a face and began to lurch towards him. Her long limbs uncoordinated, she was an animated music stand. 'Well, look who's here!' she announced, smiling gummily. Her words were slurred. 'If it isn't 2P! You all right, Tuppence?'

'Hey, Thandi. How are you?'

'Me? I'm just *great*! I'm totally fucking great.' She turned and dragged her blonde friend forward for an introduction. 'Tuppence, this is Becki. Becki, this is the *amazing* 2P. He's not just an amazing man, but an amazing boss and an amazing friend too.' She touched her chest as though overcome by the emotion she'd just emoted.

Preston wondered whether her insincerity might work like Pinner's cynicism: whether it might reach a level so bogus that it actually became sincerity again. 'Thanks, Thandi,' Preston said. 'You're . . . umm . . . yeah. Nice to see you too.'

She peered down at him from behind slowly batting lashes. 'Will you do her, Tuppence?'

'Sorry?'

'Becki – will you do her?'

'Oh,' Preston said. 'Sure.' He looked the young woman up and down. He narrowed his eyes. He cocked his head. He hummed and haaed. Though he'd assessed her in an instant, he'd lately added these theatrical touches to his act. 'Your shoes are Jimmy Choo's,' he began, 'only I don't think they're yours. They're half a size too big. Thandi's, right? You turned up wearing something else, Converse perhaps, and she told you to make more of an effort and, since she's the celebrity, you thought you'd better play along.

'Your jeans are D&G, obviously. Belt is model's own. By which I mean you bought it somewhere cheap and nasty. I'm guessing you say it's from Spitalfields but it's actually from Camden. For future reference, you should say it's from Shepherd's Bush – that's where the real kudos is. Your T-shirt's vintage. It's from a line made by Chelsea Girl. You most likely got it in Second Youth or one of those other jumped-up jumble sales. You probably paid fifty-odd quid for it – the usual thousand per cent mark-up.'

'Actually, I got it on eBay,' Becki said. Then, turning to Thandi, 'I'm an open book. Don't you think anyone could do that? I'm not that impressed.'

Preston continued, undaunted: 'Your lipstick's Rimmel, powder and eye shadow are Mac, your eyeliner – somewhat overdone, by the way – is Boots No 7. Your necklace is your mum's. You say she gave it to you, but you never wear it in front of her because she's been wondering where it got to. Your earrings are cheap and nasty. You probably bought them on the same visit to Camden, possibly even from the same stall. You bleached your hair at home but then had to go to a salon to sort out the bleached-your-hair-at-home look. I don't know the salon, but it wasn't expensive.' He sipped his juice.

Thandi burst out laughing. Becki looked embarrassed, but like she was trying to front it out. Preston felt guilty and smiled at her, but that didn't seem to make her feel much more comfortable.

Thandi said, 'And her motivation?'

'Motivation?'

'What's Becki's motivation for the outfit?'

Preston wrinkled his nose. 'Very eighties – Debbie Harry meets Robert Smith,' he said.

Now Becki smiled too. She was pleased with that. 'Yeah,' she said. 'Yeah. Exactly.'

Thandi took a step forward and stood to attention, arms rigid at her sides. 'Now do me!'

Preston shook his head. 'That's old news. Too easy.'

'Don't be boring, Tuppence. Do me.'

Preston sighed and reeled it off: 'Ballet shoes from Office, leggings from Primark – nicked, I'm guessing, from a job lot bought by Wardrobe. Your dress is a unique piece made for you and you alone by Stella – but I only know because you told me. Twice. You never wear makeup socially, your necklace is from a little jeweller off the Old Kent Road – you didn't know that but I do because I bought it – and your earrings, though you have been known to claim otherwise, are from a kiosk at Johannesburg airport. You shaved your head yourself a couple of weeks ago, much to the consternation of your agent, my producer and your shrink. But, personally, I think it suits you.'

'Thanks.' Thandi smiled. 'And my motivation?'

Preston considered her, then shook his head again and peered into his juice bottle as if trying to calculate how much was left. 'No idea,' he said.

'You can do better than that.'

Preston sniffed, shrugged, then said, 'Non-specific despair.'

For an instant hardly visible to the human eye, the smile locked on the model's face like a mask. Then it cracked and widened and became fully flexible again as Thandi let loose a thoroughly convincing laugh. 'You're *evil!*' she exclaimed.

'Yeah,' Preston said. He made his excuses and left.

He was home before eleven. Home was a converted warehouse apartment in Shoreditch Heights, a 'gated community' just off the Hoxton end of Hackney Road, within spitting distance of the Authenticity™ office. Frankly, the Heights wasn't much of a 'community'. Residents may have shopped organically, but any relationships they shared were pure chemistry. It wasn't unknown for a neighbour with whom you'd never exchanged a word to knock on your door at midnight and ask to borrow a gram or 'whatever you can spare'. Certainly, the only local business that was frequented by one and all belonged to Pablo, the ubiquitous but possibly mythological cocaine-dealer.

Pablo was possibly mythological because no one could agree on what he looked like, let alone how he sounded on the phone. Even allowing for the fact that most residents only met him in a state of near-vegetation, this took some explaining.

Preston, who was no cokehead and therefore, perhaps, capable of a longer view than most, suspected that Pablo didn't actually exist. He imagined that a phone call to the man in fact connected you to a switchboard of Pablos who then dispatched another Pablo to deliver Pablo's finest product on one of Pablo's fleet of mopeds. Pablo, he thought, personified an amalgam of value judgements, stereotypes and assumptions. In fact, mythological or not, Pablo was really a *brand*, like Tony the Tiger, the man from Del Monte or Mr Kipling. And Preston considered Pablo smarter than all of them. He wasn't a tiger, he didn't wear a linen suit and he didn't come across as part vicar, part pederast – he was, therefore, just a name and the rest was up to you. Pablo was a drug-dealer constructed from the building blocks of his clients' imaginations. Preston understood this as the epitome of modern branding excellence – a brand just solid enough to remain distinct, otherwise utterly amorphous and imaginative. Preston had even used what he called 'the Pablo model' to enhance the A-List™ website.

From its launch, A-List™ users had always been able to fill in a 'User Profile Form' that would allow Authenticity™'s back-end software to match new music to their taste. If not fun, it was certainly functional. Initially, however, the take-up of this facility had been almost nil. Research suggested that, while A-List™ users were happy to send their credit-card details over the Internet, most were unwilling to divulge the definitive nuances of their taste for fear that it might in some way compromise their individuality and freedom of choice. Indeed, such was the general antipathy to the User Profile Form that Preston had briefly considered scrapping the facility altogether – until he thought of Pablo.

Authenticity™ had lost the form but committed the same software engine to clandestinely characterizing every registered user on the basis of purchases and click-throughs. When that was done, according to 'the Pablo model' (or, to give it its full title, 'the Pablo model of user-generated brand substance'), all they had to do was christen their engine and set it to work.

Errol suggested Preston put his own name to it – '2P'. But Preston knew his personal brand already had too many associations. Instead, therefore, ignoring all focus groups, he pulled a name out of thin air – Authenticity™'s back-end software engine would henceforth be called 'DJ Jonny Swift™'.

Once a week every A-List™ user received a personal email from DJ Jonny Swift™ that recommended new music they might like on the basis of their previous choices. The language of these emails was unusually flat, lacking any accent, hyperbole or idiom, but that proved remarkably effective. A-List™ users, it seemed, enjoyed colouring in DJ Jonny Swift™ in whatever shades they saw fit – it was 'the Pablo model', and DJ Jonny Swift™ was a runaway success.

The runaway success of DJ Jonny Swift™ had three consequences in particular:

1. Traffic to the A-List™ site soared as users enjoyed the latest illusion of individuality and free choice.

2. Authenticity™ recognized that DJ Jonny Swift™'s recommendations were commodities that could be

sold on to record companies in a new interpretation of payola.

3. DJ Jonny Swift™ became a celebrity in his own right.

It was the last of these consequences that was perhaps the most surprising. DJ Jonny Swift™ was soon receiving fanmail and requests for appearances in other media – there was a thirst, it seemed, for a critic who had no taste of his own. The only such request to which Authenticity™ agreed was for DJ Jonny Swift™ to review new urban releases for a cutting-edge magazine called *Musik Muzic*. Even this was a tricky decision for Preston, because how could DJ Jonny Swift™, whose computer-generated opinions were as numerous as his followers, offer an opinion acceptable to enough of them? Quite easily, as it turned out.

Ghost-written by various members of the Authenticity™ core team in the same uniquely bland English, DJ Jonny Swift™ said exactly what people wanted to hear. Before long, the column was widely regarded as the very pinnacle of criticism and DJ Jonny Swift™ as a man who 'tells it like it is'. The fictional DJ was even as popular in Shoreditch Heights as his progenitor, Pablo, the possibly mythological coke-dealer, and outside, more so.

When Preston pushed open the door of his flat, he knew immediately that Pablo had beaten him to it. He could hear Jodie in the kitchen and Errol in the TV lounge and had a fair idea of how the evening had unfolded in his absence. Although Preston nominally lived alone, for some reason he couldn't remember he'd given sets of keys to Authenticity™'s two longest-serving employees and they'd each, quite separately, got into the habit of coming round most nights and letting themselves in. As far as Preston could tell, Jodie wanted to mother him, albeit typically nose-deep in charlie. And Errol? Errol wanted to brother him.

This mothering and brothering seemed to have a competitive edge: Jodie was always clearly irritated to find Errol ensconced, Errol vice versa likewise. So Errol would spread-eagle himself possessively across the leather sofa and switch on the TV, and Jodie would pour herself a glass of wine, tut and call Pablo. These days, Preston often thought he'd rather be left on his own. But he hadn't yet said anything and that made him worry he must be secretly glad of the company.

Preston stood behind the sofa while Errol channel-hopped. He'd kicked off his Jordan Retros and had his socked feet on the coffee-table. The air was thick with dope. Next to him, open face down on the leather, was *The Selected Speeches of Marcus Garvey*.

Preston couldn't think of the last time he'd seen Errol without a book, just as surely as he couldn't think of the last time he'd seen him reading one.

'Yes, Tupps,' Errol said, still flicking the remote.

'All right, Ez, what you up to?'

'Just kicking back, innit? My boy hit me up some crazy nugs and I scored a couple of DVDs from the Chinaman round my ends. Pull up a pew, bruv.'

'What movies you got?'

'Ain't checked them yet but they better be some serious shit, though.' He looked up at Preston. His eyes were swollen and bloodshot. 'Where you been anyway?'

'Hooked up with the old man.'

'Yes, bruv? He still want you working the campaign trail?'

Preston shook his head. 'Uh-uh. He's off somewhere to sort something.'

'Eh?'

'I dunno. That businessman who got himself arrested in Africa. Dad's going out there. Seems to think it's his higher purpose.'

Errol kissed his teeth juicily and sneered. 'Babylon, bruv.'

'What's that?'

'Your old man. It's all Babylon politrix, innit? If you look at it straight on, it's gotta be just another way for a rich white guy to fuck up niggers – that's the history of the world right there. "Do not remove the kinks from your hair, remove them from your brain." Marcus Garvey, innit?'

Preston found himself staring at Errol. He made a noise that was intended to express some kind of agreement but came out only as 'nnnnnnnggggg'. He was beginning to wonder if Errol was too black and, as his friend (rather than his boss), he wondered if he should tell him. Of course, Preston didn't think Errol was too black for Authenticity™ (that was quite possibly impossible) but he did consider he might be too black for his own good. And he seemed to be getting blacker.

Preston worried that such professional blackness might hinder Errol's future career should he ever choose to move elsewhere; and he acknowledged, without irony or regret, that he might even have played a contributory role in Errol's burgeoning negrification. After all, when Errol had first joined the company, six months out of Oxford, he'd sat in the corner at meetings and hardly said a word, just a looming shadow that effectively confirmed Authenticity™ as everything it claimed to be. Lately, however, he'd become more vocal – such as when he'd accused the mobile-phone network of racism – and this had been effective too, sending palpable currents of thrilled fear up corporate spines to dissipate across padded shoulders.

Nonetheless Preston had begun to wonder if Errol realized that to quote Marcus Garvey or Stokely Carmichael or Patrice Lumumba only had value in the specific, peculiar context of his job. What if Errol started to believe that the mobile-phone network actually cared whether he thought they were racist as opposed to caring whether he thought they appeared racist to people *like him*? In such an aggrandized position, was it not possible that Errol might begin to believe that the signified blackness he'd evolved as part of his professional role was, in fact, true? And, if he believed in the truth of this signified blackness, did he actually believe in the significance or just the significance of the signifiers? Was *The Selected Speeches of Marcus Garvey* to be studied and understood or parroted and worn like a badge?

Preston feared he should have seen the signs: the weed, the books, the soundbites, the clothes, the scowl. But these developments had been tricky to spot as Errol had always had those tendencies anyway. After all, *he was a black guy* – and who was to say at what point he'd tumbled over from being a black guy into being too black (or whether he had, or what that meant, or who, indeed, was allowed to make that judgement).

Sometimes, as his friend, Preston imagined he might say to Errol something like this: 'Look, Ez, there's a saying, right? "If it looks like a dog and it barks like a dog, chances are it's a dog." I mean, that sounds true, right? But maybe it's not true. I mean, if you were clever and you wanted people to think you were a dog, you'd make sure you looked like a dog and you barked like a dog, wouldn't you?' But he wasn't sure Errol would appreciate this metaphor in all its subtlety. In fact, he wasn't entirely sure he did himself.

Preston suspected that Errol could slide out of his new blackness any time he chose. But what if the blackness wasn't actually new but newly revealed to Preston? And, new or not, what if this blackness was like a tattoo, something that could never be removed without the risk of terrible scarring? In fact, what if it went deeper even than that?

Put simply, in the name of Authenticity™ (certainly) and authenticity (probably), Errol had begun to express a black credo that, ironically, Preston thought fake. However, he couldn't trust his own opinion since he was neither a believer nor black. Preston had built a career on trusting his own opinions. Little wonder, then, that it was increasingly commonplace for Errol to reduce him to mild, wordless expressions of affirmation, uncertainty or interrogation.

'Everything is everything,' Errol continued, as Preston

backed out of the room. 'It's all politics. And all politics is politrix.'

'Right,' Preston said, finally finding a meaningful word, which he could utter without meaning. 'Everything is everything,' he added. That was his other option – to repeat Errol's phrases straight back at him.

He found Jodie watching a couple of pots simmer on the hob while chopping out a line on the chrome-surface protector. She looked up as he walked in and smiled awkwardly, 'You want some?'

'What is it?'

'Carbonara. I thought you'd be hungry.'

'Thanks.'

Preston watched as Jodie bent to snort the blow. A lock of her thick dark hair kept falling over her face and getting in the way. Eventually she stood up and retied her ponytail, her chin slightly dipped, biting her tongue in concentration. There was something revealing about the way she looked – a bit like a pious little girl readying herself for lessons after swimming, a bit like a desiccated maiden aunt pruning herself for church on Sunday. In fact, Jodie looked almost any age but her own and Preston was somewhat saddened by that observation.

Jodie was one of the few members of Authenticity™'s core team who hadn't been to Oxbridge. She'd left a vaunted girls' grammar in north London with a fistful of top-graded A levels, but was turned down by Cambridge, her sixth-form tutor informed her tearfully, for not having a 'sufficient breadth of interest'.

When she'd told Preston about this, he exclaimed, 'Jesus! You should have seen some of the people they let in!'

And she trilled, 'I know!' grateful for his camaraderie.

Preston didn't tell her that his comment expressed less righteous indignation on her behalf than genuine astonishment at the thought of what the young Jodie must have been like. She had left Manchester University with a top first in some subject or other. As far as he was concerned, she could have turned her hand to pretty much anything – she was capable, clever and thoroughly diligent. But, instead, she came to work for Authenticity™ and threw herself wholeheartedly into the one area for which she had absolutely no talent – the pursuit, development and marketing of cool.

Of course Preston hadn't known this when he'd hired her as his assistant (and very first employee). She had by far the most impressive CV he was sent and, at her interview, wore the right clothes and talked the right language (albeit, with the benefit of hindsight, like a second-language speaker). Besides, Preston knew that cool was aspirational and she evidently aspired. It was only later, therefore, that he began to see she lacked any intuition of popular culture, any of the sensitivity necessary to grasp its ephemeral essence, any appreciation of its irony or, indeed, of irony.

Preston found this terrible – not her failure to understand cool but her dogged refusal to stop trying. And, as with Errol being 'too black', he worried that Jodie's undoubtedly mistaken career path was somehow his fault; first, as her employer and, second, as someone whose considerable wealth was built on convincing people of the importance of cool. These feelings of responsibility, however, didn't seem to stop him abusing his position every now and then.

As he shovelled pasta, Preston told her about his evening, particularly his arrangement to meet his dad, specifically his dad's arrangement to meet Eva. As he described the Russian (which he did, for some reason, in a way that made her sound younger than she actually was) and outlined his old man's apparent East European preoccupation, his tone lurched between moral indignation and amused mockery. This must have been a narrative rather than emotional decision, because he was neither indignant nor amused: his feelings towards his dad were far muddier. However, Jodie had now rested her hand on his arm and he responded to the human contact and expanded his diatribe to take in his mother's alcoholism before concluding, 'My family's so fucked up!'

He didn't really believe that his family *was* all that fucked up, but when you listened to the bare facts of it, it sounded true on any Oprah scale and, besides, it excused what he was going to do next, even though he hadn't yet admitted to himself precisely what that was.

He drained a glass of water while Jodie chopped out and snorted another line of cocaine. Then they went to his bedroom and had sex. This was perhaps the sixth time it had happened. Neither of them was counting.

Preston understood – or, at least, believed he understood – Jodie's various reasons for sleeping with him: there was certainly admiration in there, ambition and pity too, possibly even a teaspoon of genuine affection. But in so far as he was able to grasp his own motivations he did his best not to as they left him feeling forlorn. The sex, like the conversation before it, expressed not openness, intimacy and desire, only the longing for such things. In his business Preston represented passable versions of authenticity. It seemed the same was true in his personal life.

Afterwards, Jodie fetched wine to take the edge off her high, she said. She brought through two glasses, but Preston didn't want to stay in bed. He pulled on a T-shirt and a pair of shorts and went into the kitchen. He picked leftover pasta from a saucepan. He could smell Jodie on his fingers. He rinsed them under the tap. Looking down the corridor to the living room, he could see light flickering from the TV. He couldn't hear anything, though. If Errol was still here, he was watching on mute. Something occurred to him and he wandered through.

Errol was sitting in exactly the same position as he had been an hour or so earlier. On the TV an advertisement showed a statuesque blonde woman in a bikini strutting silently along the side of a swimming-pool. To Preston, there was something grotesquely sexual in her stride and he wondered if this was somehow accentuated by the muting or, indeed, by his post-coital state. Either way, he thought, not for the first time, how advertising looked ever closer to pornography.

'Ez?'

'Yes, mate,' Errol said, his eyes not leaving the screen.

'You ever get hold of that kid?'

'What kid?'

'That MC. Called himself Nobody. He sent in that "Jerusalem" tune for The A-List.'

'Sure. I mailed you about it.'

Still Errol didn't look at him. Preston wondered if he was sulking because he knew he'd fucked Jodie. If so, what was that about? Such an abuse of his position hardly amounted to preferential treatment, did it?

'Ez?' Preston said. Then, when there was no response, 'Can't you just tell me?'

'I can't remember. You're gonna meet him tomorrow. Can't remember the time. I mailed you. I spoke to his manager.'

'His manager?'

'Some bird called Lorraine,' Errol said, then howled with a delight that sounded almost painful. 'Yow!' He started laughing. 'Fuck! Look at that! I love face fucking!'

Preston automatically looked at the screen. The blonde from the advertisement was now on her knees in front of a naked, muscular black man who was holding her by the back of the head and repeatedly thrusting his penis into her open mouth. Clearly, this wasn't an advertisement. As advertising looked like pornography so it seemed the reverse was true. Now he noticed the DVD cover lying next to Errol on the sofa: the same woman again, her naked torso covered with a bouncy, lurid pink typeface that read, *Girls Who Gag 4!*. Errol couldn't stop giggling. 'That Chinaman got some skanky shit, man,' he said. 'He got everything.'

Preston said, 'Nnnnnnngggg.' Then, 'Everything is everything.'

20

The real Africa

Heathrow, England, 2008

It was little more than a week after he'd caught up with his son in a Mayfair restaurant that David Pinner MP sat in the British Airways executive lounge at Heathrow. He smiled at the young woman who brought his Scotch, nibbled complimentary nuts and considered his feelings of apprehension. His mission to Zambawi was a vital one, of course. He wasn't just charged with securing the freedom of Gordon Tranter, the British citizen currently languishing in jail accused of espionage, but also, by extension, securing the future of the African Authority project; possibly, therefore, the future of the British government, perhaps even the future of the African continent. Or was that a presumption too far?

Either way, it was certainly a step into the unknown. Diplomatic relations with Zambawi had been broken off months ago and this wasn't an official visit. So, Pinner was travelling on the hush-hush with none of the usual entourage of advisers and media; no one for support, in fact, but his assistant, Jeremy Shorter.

However, it was neither the importance of the mission nor its nature that made Pinner apprehensive. No. It was the fact that he was going to Zambawi. Or, rather, that he was going to Africa. Or, specifically, that he was going to the 'real Africa'. It was ironic, Pinner thought wryly, that organizations like the African Union, SADC, COMESA and ECOWAS should still struggle with Kwame Nkrumah's vision of a united Africa when outsiders struggled to envisage anything else.

How quickly the Eastern Bloc had broken up into the sum of its parts: nation states with cultural identities and, particularly, fledgling democracies to be respected and protected. But what of Africa? It might have been Britain, France, Belgium, Portugal and Germany who had originally and arbitrarily carved up the continent into fictional territories with made-up names and make-believe borders, but it remained *Africa*, the idea – that wonderful, exotic, unspecific but somehow so utterly meaningful idea – that most successfully impinged on the Western collective imagination.

Of course, nobody in Pinner's social circle, let alone in the FCO, actually regarded Africa as one country. Nonetheless, they frequently talked about it – consumed and regurgitated it, half digested, as if it were – and as if they were ideally placed, even as they humbly acknowledged their ignorance in doing so, to comment.

– My secretary? She's African.

– Went to see this African dance troupe the other week. Fantastic show. Just fantastic.

– What's this music we're listening to? Is it African?

– It's a WFP alert, Minister. They're predicting famine. In Africa.

Pinner knew that, when pushed, one was obliged to attempt some degree of geographic particularity. However, even then you could get away with a breezy tone and careless inflection of the kind a housewife might use when recounting from which supermarket chain she'd bought a particularly well-received cheesecake – 'I think it was Zambia. Or maybe Mozambique. No, I tell a lie, it was definitely Zambia.'

As the minister with specific portfolio for the continent, naturally Pinner had been to Africa several times before – to important meetings in Cape Town and Cairo, to associated jollies in the Kruger and a beach resort near Mombasa, to visit successful British-funded projects outside Dodoma or in a Kampala slum. But even he had never been to the 'real Africa'.

It was a term he used with surprising frequency, though he'd never taken the time to try to define its meaning. There was no need to define the 'real Africa' in the FCO, because it was common parlance; everybody knew what everybody else meant, even if there was no consensus as to precisely what it was they were meaning. At least part of the reason for this lack of consensus was that the key component of the 'real Africa' was that the person talking about it had never been there. Therefore to define it was either to say what it was not, or necessarily a further step of the imagination – and some of those politicians, civil servants and wonks had unspeakable imaginations!

If Africa was wonderful and exotic, then the 'real Africa' must be so colourful, so noisy, so smelly, so damn *alive* that, if you went there, you would most likely suffer sensory overload and go mad or, arguably scarier still, go native. It was the heart of darkness where people who were black, like the negatives of British wedding photographs, lived and died and hunted and danced and fucked and killed with an abandon that any bureaucrat with an office in Whitehall and a semi in Cheam could only imagine. So they did.

And Pinner? In fact, Pinner had little imagination. He suspected he'd been close to the 'real Africa' once or twice – in that Kampala slum, for example, or on a visit to the Shimelba refugee camp in Ethiopia. However, on each occasion he'd felt as if he were being slightly deceived, as if the slum had been cleared for his visit and the refugee camp scrubbed clean. Then half of him had felt frustrated that he couldn't get a true sense of how awful it was to live in that slum or that camp, and the other half of him was relieved.

But Zambawi would be different, wouldn't it? He'd have no armed guard, no air-conditioned convoy, no earnest aid workers to protect and reassure him. There'd have been no clearing and no cleaning. This was the 'real Africa' and in all likelihood he'd catch the Africans at it – being African, that is. And this was why he was apprehensive.

The minister stood up, took a deep breath, and momentarily

allocated the little imagination he did have to picturing his triumphant return from Zambawi. For some reason, this picture had no place for sky bridges and the other attributes of modern airports. Instead it showed him emerging from the aeroplane on to the top step with the liberated Tranter next to him. He imagined old-fashioned hacks wearing old-fashioned macs and old-fashioned hats with old-fashioned press cards poking from their hat bands. They would say old-fashioned things as they pointed at him with their pencils, things like 'That's a man who knows how to get things done.'

Pinner boarded late and directly from the BA lounge. Consequently he didn't even see Jeremy who was floundering back in economy and had presumably already got on. Instead, he found himself seated top to tail across the fanned business-class partition from a large black man who wore a business suit and thick, black-framed spectacles. This man had kicked off a pair of black, tasselled loafers and his socks, and was waggling his toes enthusiastically.

Pinner smiled thinly at his neighbour, offering just enough enthusiasm to signify good manners but no commitment to anything further. To his surprise, the man grinned, extended a chubby hand and announced something incomprehensible that Pinner assumed must have been his name. He then began to talk at Pinner in a loud voice, with a presumptuous and bumptious bonhomie that the minister found galling.

The man said that he was a senior VP at Z-Net, a Zambawian mobile-phone network that was a subsidiary of a multinational telecoms giant. He'd been in London to attend a strategy meeting with 'the Americans'. The way he said 'the Americans' made them sound like a street gang.

Z-Net, he went on, intended to have more than two million mobile phones in circulation in Zambawi within five years. He leant forward and raised his eyebrows and spoke in a way that managed to be simultaneously conspiratorial and jovial. He said that the plans would be much simpler, of course, once

President Adini was out of the way. He said that Africa was the coming telecoms market and everybody wanted a piece of the action.

As if to support his hypothesis, the man's mobile phone now rang and, despite the protests of stewardesses signalling that he should really turn it off, he answered it in a loud voice. This was apparently his only mode of speech. Pinner sat back, relieved, and pulled on his sleeping mask. His mind, however, was racing. He was more than a little confused. Every briefing document he'd read had described Zambawi as a state on the brink of total collapse. In his imagination 'total collapse' made no allowances for mobile-phone networks, let alone mobile-phone-network executives travelling internationally in business class for strategy meetings with 'the Americans'. Wasn't this a nation suffering the rigours of multilateral sanctions? It was something he'd have to look into.

In fact, now he thought about it, he'd barely considered the 'real Africa' as a place of mobile phones at all. Who owned them? How did they afford them? Where did they plug them in to recharge?

The minister was also confused by the man's attitude to President Adini. Although he appeared to be looking forward to the President's impending fall, he spoke of him with an undoubted note of admiration, as though this were some mischievous scamp harmlessly poking fun at the international community – hardly the bloodthirsty despot Pinner had read about.

He caught the snatches of his neighbour's phone conversation that were conducted in English. He appeared to be detailing the difficulties he'd encountered in buying a Harrods teapot. Although the man had succeeded in obtaining a teapot from Harrods, it seemed this was not the same as a 'Harrods teapot', which needed to be Harrods green in colour and say 'Harrods' on it in Harrods gold. Apparently, Mrs Chingarandi (whoever she might be) had a Harrods teapot. But since when was Mrs Chingarandi judge and jury of all things stylish? And, more to the point, who needed a teapot if they didn't drink tea?

After asking these presumably rhetorical questions, Pinner's neighbour fell silent for some time; long enough, in fact, for the minister to fall asleep. He was stirred, however, by an abrupt 'Right! Goodbye!' and woken completely when a thick index finger jabbed insistently at his upper arm.

Pinner pushed back his sleeping mask and raised an interrogative eyebrow. The man was shaking his head and began to make a strange noise, somewhere between a puff and a whistle. 'The old lady,' he said meaningfully. Then, when Pinner remained silent, 'These women, hey?'

The man's expression, Pinner thought, was somewhat childlike in its desire for a response, and he felt he had no choice but to oblige, so he said, 'Quite.' He regretted this immediately because his neighbour clearly regarded even such a terse gambit as an invitation to conversation. Indeed, Pinner was still regretting it more than four hours later, when the plane was somewhere high over Chad and the man was still engaged in a ceaseless stream of cheerful verbiage.

At take-off, the talk was all family. The man had two sons, both at American universities, one completing a master's in computer science, the other on a track scholarship. He produced a picture of his wife. They'd been married twenty-five years. They were very happy. When Pinner made a reflexive congratulatory noise, the man nodded complacently and unleashed a stream of affirmative aphorisms of the kind teenage girls send each other in round-robin emails, several beginning 'You know it's love when . . .'. Then he showed Pinner a picture of his mistress.

As they flew over Paris's western suburbs and Pinner sank a mini-bottle of Shiraz Cabernet and a Valium to his neighbour's three beers, this led to a dissection of the relative merits of Zambawian women from different parts of the country. The man told Pinner proudly that his wife and mistress came from some or other province where the women were famously well trained. At this point, feeling the liberation that often accompanies flight and therefore eschewing any sensible discretion (as if airspace somehow 'didn't count'), Pinner attempted to join in by detailing his own fondness for Eastern European women. When questioned, however, he struggled to identify their merits beyond a general level of phlegmatic compliance.

Across the rest of France, the man ate his dinner, downed two more beers and launched a tirade against the prohibitive expense of the UK: from hotels to cabs, from the price of beer to the price of a cup of coffee – 'Three pounds!' the man exclaimed. 'For some coffee and a little foam!' He shook his head. 'You are a minister of the Crown, isn't it? Explain that to me. Is it not capitalism at its most mercenary and, therefore, absurd?'

'Well, yes . . .' Pinner began.

But the man wasn't interested in any justifications of the unjustifiable and he ploughed blithely on. 'Of course I still love the old country,' he declared. 'The "old country" – that is what I call it! It is our colonial evil stepmother, as it were, and thus retains a place in my heart, if only archetypally. Besides, I do love to shop. And how I *love* to leave!'

By the time they were over the Mediterranean, Pinner found he'd been drawn into a conversation he didn't want to be having. His neighbour persistently mocked Britain and all things British but, whenever the minister tried to reply, the man just shook his head and chuckled indulgently. What was more, when Pinner decided attack was the best form of defence and began to list many of Zambawi's more obvious faults (a tyrannical president, a collapsing economy and so forth), his neighbour was no less self-satisfied and dismissive. According to him, every problem Pinner identified could be traced to the West's neo-colonialism (shake of the head), the nation's colonial heritage (shake of the head) or, simply, 'Africans' (indulgent chuckle). The minister was shocked to think he'd enjoyed more progressive and, in some ways, 'progressive' arguments within the FCO.

It was only when he was utterly exasperated and doped up on fifty milligrams of Vicodine, twenty of Valium and three mini-bottles of red, however, that Pinner finally spat out what indisputably needed to be spat out: 'So, if your country's so great and mine's so terrible, how come all you people are so desperate to leave the former and get to the latter?' He asked this with, he hoped, a lightness of tone that he wasn't feeling.

The man regarded him blearily over his beer glass. Although there was no turbulence to speak of, the amber liquid was slurping dangerously close to the brim. He was drunk.

'That,' the man said slowly, 'is a question that reflects a typical neo-colonial attitude. In so far as my compatriots seek entrance to the UK, it is symptomatic only of the degree to which they have been brainwashed by colonial history into regarding Her Majesty's sceptred isle as their *alma mater*, as it were. And, speaking for myself – as I already have and continue to do, because that is the kind of man I am – I visit your country to shop. In fact, I often say to my wife, "The UK is like a supermarket: you might think it tacky and despise its ethos but a regular visit is probably a practical necessity."' The man shook his head and chuckled deeply. 'Africans!' he announced cheerily, put his glass into the provided slot in his armrest and promptly fell asleep.

Pinner stared at his neighbour incredulously. Despite the booze, Vikes and V, he was now wide-awake and energized for an argument. Unfortunately his would-be opponent was out cold. Irritably, he drained his wine and signalled to the stewardess for another mini-bottle. He turned on his personal screen and flicked to the games menu. He played a couple of minutes of Patience before his ran out. He switched to movies. He began watching a Hollywood blockbuster about an ordinary cop who has to put his neck on the line to save a complete stranger and, in doing so, reveals an unforeseen level of heroism. Experiencing the momentary clarity that can sometimes be chanced upon on the bumpy road to epic intoxication, Pinner realized this wasn't far from how he envisaged his mission to free Tranter. For all his daring, however, the ordinary cop in the movie was having an extraordinarily tough time. And, as Pinner watched the extraordinary way the ordinary cop seemed to bounce off walls, dodge bullets and get up from punches, he began to wonder if he was similarly hardy. Sensing that his brief clarity was about to outstay its welcome, he downed the next bottle of wine in three quick gulps and chose to go for a walk.

Any desire for a fight drained out of him with verticality. Pinner now felt heavily tranquillized and extremely drunk. One consequence of this was that later, when he tried to recall what followed, he found it impossible to distinguish what had actually occurred from the feverish dreams he subsequently suffered in his business-class seat. But as far as he remembered what happened was this.

He pulled back the curtain between business class and economy to reveal a seething jungle of black people. The lights were dim but every now and then he'd see a tooth or the white of an eye illuminated by a shimmering video screen. Then, as his vision got used to the dark, he saw that all these black people were endlessly moving – standing up and sitting down, repeatedly heaving things into and lugging things out of the overhead lockers, roaring to one another across seatbacks over the hum of the engines, passing infants like parcels, laughing and shouting and gesticulating with unnecessary and unseemly vigour.

At the sight of such mayhem, Pinner missed his footing and stumbled forward. A strong black arm went round his shoulders and helped him upright. He snatched a glimpse of flashing teeth. He courageously shrugged off the assistance.

Way off in a back row, he spotted his faithful aide, Jeremy. Trapped in a middle seat between two large women, their heads swathed in Java print, he had his blanket tucked up around his neck and his headphones pressed down on his ears. He looked like a trussed turkey.

Now, beneath the engine noise, Pinner began to make out another sound, a low repetitive thump. What could that be? It only took a glance across to the next aisle of the aircraft to locate its source. Believe it or not, one of the stewards, a chubby young man with an orange complexion and blond highlights in his hair, had stripped to the waist and was beating out a regular tattoo on a large bass drum held tightly between his thighs. Pinner narrowed his eyes to peer more closely through the gloom. To his astonishment, he saw that each and every row of passengers was similarly half naked and heaving on mighty oars that poked out through the aeroplane's windows. All the passengers were singing. The drone of the engines resolved into a dirge of great beauty and no little threat.

His eyes sought out the scattered white faces back in economy. They all appeared to be sleeping. But were they really? He looked from one to another and there was not the smallest movement among them. He began to panic. These black people were rowing the aeroplane back to Africa and they weren't taking any prisoners!

His eyes shot to Jeremy. He had to warn his trusty sidekick – the Mandy to his Tony, the Cheeta to his Tarzan, doomed partner to his ordinary cop. But too late! To his horror, he saw the large ladies on Jeremy's either side tucking in with their plastic cutlery, their fleshy African lips parting around great gory mouthfuls of neck and shoulder.

Pinner didn't know what to do. Of course, as the hero of the piece, he wanted to help but all common sense told him that Jeremy was already lost and discretion the better part of valour. He backed off.

Approaching him down the aisle were two young men with dreadlocks. They were chatting cheerfully and swigging from beer cans. Pinner had to get out of there. In one athletic movement, he ducked back behind the partition curtain between the classes and fastened it with the Velcro tags – that would hold them for a while. His heart was racing and he was sweating profusely as he dragged himself back to his seat.

Pinner slept through breakfast and didn't wake up until the captain announced half an hour to landing. He had a blinding headache and he'd dribbled over the collar of his shirt. His neighbour, Mr Whateverhisname, was beaming at him through a mouthful of scrambled egg and looked primed to resume their conversation. Pinner shut his eyes again. Not only did he not want to talk to Mr Ooger-Booger, but he found his mind, sick and flabby as it felt, enmeshed in a knotty moral problem of isms and semantics. The problem concerned prejudice and the nub of it was this: was a bigoted judgement one based on incorrect information or one that, despite correct information to the contrary, remained instinctively pejorative?

The minister twisted and turned, tugged and picked at the question for some minutes until he hit upon this helpful precedent: a man who thinks women are more stupid than men is sexist. But a man who thinks men every bit as stupid as women and hates women nonetheless is a misogynist. His headache began to recede and his ears popped as if the pressure of the problem had been released just like that – thank God! He was not a racist!

He knew that he believed fundamentally in the equality of all races as surely as he now knew he didn't much like Africans, and the fact that there was no word for this state was secretly rather comforting. Indeed, he even began to wonder if this admission to himself might be a marker of his moral courage, significant of a singular honesty that was all too rare these days. Of course, it was arguably unfortunate that he'd only hit upon this discovery while on an aeroplane to Africa, also that he was the government minister with specific portfolio for a continent whose inhabitants he instinctively (although presumably not exclusively, since he wouldn't want to generalize) disliked. However, wasn't it plausible to assume that it had taken just such a plane journey – a journey alone with no protection but his own wit and cunning – to teach him this aspect of himself? And wasn't it more than reasonable (correct, even) to think that his psychological position, now acknowledged, would enable him to carry out his ministerial offices with impartiality and common sense – more so than his predecessors anyway, woolly-thinking Afrophiles one and all?

When Pinner finally opened his eyes, therefore, as the pilot began his final approach into Queenstown International Airport, any previous apprehension had dissipated to be replaced by a new certainty as to both his mission in the 'real Africa' and his suitability to accomplish it. This was the right place and the right time and he was the right man to do the right thing.

The descent was somewhat turbulent and, as the plane bounced and shook, Pinner noticed his neighbour gripping the armrests of his seat tightly. The minister smiled at the man with a sincerity he found empowering. It was a sincerity that expressed reassurance and disdain in equal measure.

21

Insert document
'The diary of a local gentleman', date unknown
(Empire Museum, Bristol), anon.

[Fire damage has rendered the date and the opening section of this entry illegible. The preceding and subsequent entries suggest it is from spring 1901]

– hardly the send-off I had planned.' She smiled at me a little sheepishly, her eyes full of sorrow and hope.

At any previous time, the sight of my dear Kitty in a state of such heightened anxiety would surely have flooded my heart with sympathy and tenderness. On this occasion, however, I remained so motionless that it was as if my spine were braced and my expression numb with anaesthetic. My response (or lack thereof) at least confirmed the decision to leave as a judicious one.

I didn't want Kitty to see my eyes turn to stone, so I looked away instead. Imagine my dismay when I saw that popinjay, Jameson, approaching from the door. Kitty followed my eyes and may as well have read my mind. She took a quick breath and said, 'Teddy wanted to wish you well,' by way of explanation.

Jameson and I shook hands. He smiled chummily. 'Catherine tells me you're leaving us for a little while,' he said. 'Not just stalling, are we, old man? You'll make us other fellows think we're in with a chance!' He then laughed in that unpleasant and mechanical way of his.

I wanted to say something, make some witty retort that

would put the fool in his place. But no words would come out of my mouth and in my frustration my hands started to shake uncontrollably until I let my glass fall and it smashed on the floor.

Jameson said, 'Steady on!' Then, 'Are you quite all right?' feigning concern.

Kitty fussed around me, which made me feel more idiotic than ever. When Jameson stepped away, I challenged her about his motives. She protested, of course, but the truth is that I am even beginning to doubt her innocence. For isn't such innocence the very essence of a woman's wiles and therefore, one must conclude, not innocent at all?

Listen to me! You can imagine the awareness of my rising cynicism only compounded the desire to leave. My better nature feels too much for Kitty to condemn her to a life with this bitter cripple. What kind of husband would I make in my current humour? The foolish kind whose heart is so twisted with jealousy that, when finally cuckolded by his poor, miserable wife, declares with relish, 'I knew it all along!'

I caught the noon train for Cheltenham the following day. I would have liked to stride right out of Bristol, cane in hand and kit-bag on shoulder, but I knew that Mother would kick up a stink about my fitness to do so. Besides, there will be plenty of time for hiking in the days to come and the train ride lifted my spirits.

As we raced through the green fields, lush with recent showers, I imagined myself Henry Morton Stanley thirty years ago, setting out from the Spice Island into the African interior. The children who cheered as we passed, waving their coats above their heads, were pikanins brandishing pelts, trophies of the morning's hunt. The yeomen playing a cricket match on the village green, their womenfolk arranged at intervals around the boundary, were Bantu elders enacting a mysterious ritual to summon rain. Such fantasies amused me.

I truly think myself an explorer. I may not be seeking the Nile's source but somewhere in this country there is, shall we say?, the 'spring of Albion' that has nourished the whole of our great nation throughout history and I intend to find it. I lately read a quotation from Hume: 'The English, of any people in the universe, have the least of a national character, unless this very singularity may pass for such.' I assume this is the carping of a Scotsman and may thus be understood. However, I have learnt from my time at Standmere (and, indeed, from observing the idle dandyism of the likes of Teddy Jameson) that character cannot be taken for granted, but requires regular care. A wealthy gent may buy the finest Walsall saddle but, if his lad doesn't clean, oil and polish it, won't it perish as quickly as a cheap Indian copy? It is the gentleman's duty to keep his lad honest. If not, and a strap breaks and the fellow comes a cropper, he has no one to blame but himself.

But I am allowing my thoughts to run away with me. As with my experiences, I must explain the progression of my thinking chronologically.

On arrival in Cheltenham, I lunched simply. I had considered staying a night but, fortified by a fine local ale and my new sense of adventure, I instead shouldered my pack and set out.

I have no map to follow, only my own nose and the mores of Fate and Circumstance. This is all well and good, but it also explains why I soon found myself on the edge of town quite confounded by a crossroads! Still, I was only there a minute or two before a milk cart stopped next to me, its ruddy-faced driver enquiring if I were lost.

I asked where he was heading. Prestbury, he said. On a whim, I told him I was going there too and attempted to cadge a lift. He seemed uncertain. He was a timid sort. The farmer forbade it, he said, and the cart was a single seater so where might I sit? I informed him that the farmer would surely expect charity to be shown to a convalescing officer of His Majesty's Army and that I was quite happy to perch among the churns. He reluctantly agreed to take me along with him and I clambered aboard.

His name was George Burt. He was my age with four children and a wife called, if memory serves, Rachel. Our conversation was limited. Even for a farmhand, George's curiosity for the weather was unusual and matched only by his lack of curiosity for much else. No matter: sitting back in the cart, mesmerized by the gentle crunch of the wheels beneath and the occasional neigh ahead, I felt a glow of contented insularity. I enjoyed the blossoming elders at the roadside, decked out from head to toe like brides at a bucolic and medieval wedding. I was surprised to spot a nuthatch busy in the hedgerow.

We arrived in Prestbury at dusk. I found a room in the only hostelry. The landlord was taciturn to the point of rudeness but his lady did me proud with a hearty supper of cured ham and boiled potatoes. The pickles were quite something. I turned in early and woke with the lark.

It was today that I confirmed the specific nature of my adventure, and it happened like this.

This morning I had no inkling of what was to come as I set out from Prestbury to Longborough, a distance of at least fifteen miles. However, in my solitude, I found a clarity of mind that suggested a corresponding clarity of purpose might not be far away. My poor stump has never taken such punishment and was soon weeping, but I did not care about that. In fact, to see it raw and painful felt like some kind of relief – a blessed return to reality after all the weeks of sympathy. I hardly stopped the whole day, only briefly to sketch and to picnic on bread and cheese and some more of those excellent pickles. I spoke to no one and enjoyed the silence.

Here in Longborough I am lodged at the Coach and

Horses, a fine pub in the English tradition. My room is tastefully decorated in the rustic style (how Kitty would laugh at every quaint detail!), meals are simple but hearty, and the landlord is a jovial chap called Briggs who can barely construct a sentence without some amusement diverting him. At one point this evening, I watched the fellow pack his pipe and I swear he had to stop and lay it aside for his helpless laughter at some private joke known only to himself.

I supped with a fellow traveller, an Oxford medic by the name of Seymour. He is engaged in a fascinating study, attempting to correlate the relatively low incidence of consumption in these parts with the quality of local milk. Frankly, his theorizing was all Greek to me. To listen to him talk of this or that advance in inoculation, diagnosis and treatment was to hear a future described that seemed incredible. But he spoke with such passion and commitment that it was hard not to be carried along.

He was, of course, an evolutionist and an agnostic after Huxley. I explained to him some of the ideas I have been developing of an essential, historic Englishness and he was quick to dismiss them as 'romantic'. He asked what form I thought this Englishness might take. I told him I did not know. But I added that not to know of a thing cannot be regarded as proof that it does not exist. He laughed and claimed this to be an insuperable divide between us. He was, he said, a man of evidence, and I a man of faith.

Naturally, I bridled at his attempt to construct such an opposition. I said I was indeed a man of faith and proud to be so. But I also told him of the evidence I'd witnessed as a soldier, how the absence of goodness and attendant sense of loss was surely proof enough of its existence. A man who denied the evidence of his own heart, I suggested, was hardly a man at all. I became quite heated and perhaps went too far, but he listened with apparent interest and good humour.

It is only now, however, bent over this journal alone, in the light of what followed and the thunderous silence of midnight, that I understand the true difference between Seymour and me. The doctor, like many of his kind who have studied much and lived only little, seeks to understand man by what he might become; while I, from the contrary position, remain convinced that to grasp what man is one must know what he was once. There is surely merit in both arguments. However, I humbly submit that the latter is too often ignored by those with a linear view of progress, be it scientific, social or moral.

Seymour retired shortly after supper. I remained in the saloon to smoke a cigarette. There were still a few locals propping up the bar and sharing jokes with the effervescent Briggs, but none with whom I wanted to begin a conversation. I was on the verge of retiring when there was a knock at the door. Thank goodness I stayed up that extra minute or two.

Briggs answered the door and stepped back to allow entry to half a dozen of the strangest characters you could wish to see, their faces painted black and each sporting a different costume. One, a stout man with a fulsome beard who was dressed like a mockery of an ancient knight, stepped forward and asked, 'Would you be wanting the guisers, sir?' My fellows clearly understood what this question meant because, to a man, they cheered.

Briggs permitted these 'guisers' entry and in they came, one ringing a small bell, two more clacking their wooden swords together. Another now took the lead. He wore the queerest get-up of them all, a pink woman's nightgown and a straw hat decorated with flowers. This was, it seemed, the character of the narrator and he threw his arms wide and announced with great ceremony: 'Room! O Room! Brave gallants all/'Tis but once that on thee I call/A room, a room! A mouse, a mouse!/I've brought my broom to sweep thy house!' Then the whole company launched into a comic drama the like of which I'd never seen before.

I noted it in my book as follows: St George (the fellow dressed as a knight) engaged in combat with 'Bold Slasher' (who was also, apparently, the King of Egypt). St George was struck down. However, at death's door, a doctor appeared in the company of a fool by the name of 'Jack Finney'. Amid much farce, this doctor then extracted the patron saint's tooth and he made a full recovery. Finally, several other characters appeared, one of whom was 'Beelzebub'. These latter characters performed a comic song about the peculiar subject matter we had lately witnessed, before offering around their hats for contributions. I estimate the whole performance lasted no longer than fifteen minutes in total.

I do, of course, know something of England's folk plays from my anthropological study. Still, it was quite thrilling to witness such a performance for myself.

Afterwards I bought drinks for the whole company and asked them to indulge my curiosity a moment. I asked about their play's heritage. They seemed bemused by the question. It was passed down from father to son, they said. I told them of some of the current theories espoused by various scholars – that these plays were 'survivals' of ancient fertility rites connected to the changing seasons. The Longborough guisers thought this quite a joke, I tell you! In fact, they said they had heard similar from a London gentleman who had insisted on noting down every word of their 'script'.

The narrator, far the most loquacious of the bunch, claimed that this same gentleman had written a detailed description of his bold pink costume. 'He told me he considered it symbolic and he was right peeved to hear I just took it from Mother's line!' he finished, with a chuckle.

This fellow was named Hoople and, when refreshed, he was quite the orator. 'Mother makes the finest jam from here to Swindon!' he announced. 'Thee can ask anybody and they will tell thee likewise. Her blackberry especially is famous round these parts – never too thick and never too runny because, as she boils up the fruit and sugar, she do test it every minute or so on a plate. She drops a spoonful and, as soon as it sets, she knows it's ready. But the real trick is that she uses a little pummy, which makes it set lovely! Now, when Mother's done, she do always say to me something like, "Taste my blackberry, Hoople! Taste nature's bounty!" And I do always say to her, "It's not just nature, Mother, and it's not just blackberry neither: it's a preserve!"

'That's the same for the gentleman who writes in his notebook. He writes it down and he do watch to see if it sets and, his being a gentleman of the kind most folk listen to, it likely will. But what he writes is a preserve, not the thing itself – just like Mother's blackberry jam!'

Although his hypothesis lacked some clarity, I think it's fair to say that Hoople and I were almost at one on this point. Indeed, I believe I said as much – tradition, in and of itself, I explained, would never be enough to sustain itself, and the guisers, therefore, needed present reasons to continue their practice. The company regarded me, uniformly nonplussed.

'This is a social activity,' I continued, undaunted. 'The play is just that, a *play* that enables you to interact with your friends and neighbours.'

'That's right, sir!' agreed St George. 'And to stay away from the wife!'

They all laughed at that and I laughed too.

But I pressed on: 'However, the subject of your story remains the subject, does it not? Why, St George, England's hero, is struck down by the King of Egypt – what opinion of our great nation do you fellows hold?'

'I don't know what you mean, sir,' said St George, humbly. 'The story has always been like that.'

'I am sure you are right,' I said. I had no desire to labour the point and confuse these honest men with confusions of my own. 'I am merely intrigued by the particulars of your tale – why the extraction of a tooth? Why blacken your faces like Negroes from Africa?'

The Longborough guisers looked between each other silently and I feared I had caused offence, though it was hard to tell with all their features obscured by the coal dust.

Hoople spoke up. 'The gentleman is intrigued and that is all!' he said, as if presenting a bill before Parliament. His fellow guisers all nodded sagely. Then, Hoople had a further thought: 'Should he not go to Fry Norton?'

'Right you are, Hoople,' said Beelzebub. 'Right you are.' The others similarly agreed.

'Fry Norton?' I asked.

'Round thirty miles north of here. Boasts the most celebrated morris men in all the West Country. Do go back centuries, they say. And this year Fry Norton be hosting the Whitsun Ale, so there be mummers and morris men from all round.' Hoople looked at me with such a steady intensity that it brooked no argument. 'If you do be intrigued, that is.'

In the last months, I have pored over Frazer until my eyes have ached and I have found much food for thought in his comparative approach. However, as with Seymour the Oxford doctor, I must now query his faith in progress and his apparent assertion of the infallibility of a 'scientific' analysis. Frazer is a scholar, but in his studies of other men's books is he not, as Hoople might have it, studying the blackberry jam rather than the blackberry? Frazer is an academician who studies the human being as if he were no more than a collection of cells on a Petri dish, but from a position of relative luxury, is it not easy to declare oneself (if only by implication) to be the man who stands at the summit of the highest mountain of the loftiest range yet discovered, the lord of all he surveys?

My point is this: what if you fear, as I do, that mistakes have been made and we are not, in fact, at the summit at all? Human advancement is not a singular process – we know that. We know, too, that great empires have fallen to be replaced by great savagery. And yet had Diocletian been able to see beyond the immediate rewards of the Tetrarchy, might he not have recognized what was lost in the replacement of a single, unifying emperor? We will never know, but we may guess.

I do not believe the British Empire to be on the verge of collapse, nor do I deny the merits of scientific process. I merely point out that the former was in no way built upon the latter. If the Empire is to persist, therefore, is it not a worthwhile exercise to establish the attributes of the national character upon which it is founded? And for this one must look back. In the absence of a time machine, what else is there to reflect upon but surviving ritual, which may aid the distillation of an Englishman? What else is there but the likes of the Longborough guisers and the Fry Norton morris men? Tomorrow, therefore, I go north.

Part two: O clouds, unfold!

22

Musungu Jim

Queenstown, Republic of Zambawi, 2008
Jim Tulloh had got the call the previous week. It came from Tony Stafford, who'd been an under-secretary at the High Commission before the High Commission had packed its bags. This was a smart move from whichever Foreign Office mandarin was masterminding an otherwise harebrained scheme – Stafford had been a long-standing supporter of Mama's House, securing various grants and chunks of discretionary funding for the orphanage over his three years in Queenstown, and Jim liked him.

Jim was on the veranda when the call came. While Stafford soft-pedalled and prevaricated, he watched his wife through the window. Beyond the fly screens, in the pale light of a weak bulb, he could see Sylvia wagging her finger at Tinashe while a couple of the other kids cavorted in the background. The little girl pressed her cheek into her shoulder and fidgeted shyly on the spot, the shadow of a smile playing on her lips. Sylvia held the child's face between her hands for a second and examined it, then wrapped the small body in fleshy bare arms that shimmered. Jim heard Tinashe giggle delightedly.

Suddenly, Jim wasn't listening to the man on the other end of the phone. Instead he was thinking of how his wife had gained so much weight, physically and metaphorically, in the years they'd been here and how, conversely, he'd shrunk. He thought about her upper arms and remembered the way her body smelt in this heat and that made him nostalgic. He knew she wouldn't hold him like that again.

Jim interrupted Stafford. He said, 'You really can't find

anyone else? I mean, for me, it's hardly politic, is it? You know we rely on presidential patronage.'

'And that's why you're the only guy to do this,' Stafford said. 'It'll be fine. Adini's got to come round. What else can he do?'

Jim turned away from the window. He lit a cigarette and looked out over the garden, over Sylvia's rows of rape, maize and runner beans. Sylvia cultivated anything – vegetables from seeds, children from cuttings, hope from death. He made a mental note that the runners needed harvesting in the next couple of days. He marvelled, as he always did, at how everything grew in this soil with, as far as he could tell, no more encouragement than a drop of water and kind words from the likes of his wife. So why were so many people so hungry so much of the time? 'OK,' he said decisively.

'OK what?'

'OK, I'll do it.'

There was silence at the other end of the phone. Stafford was taken aback. Jim licked his lips. The civil servant had spent the last ten minutes trying to convince him it wasn't a big deal, but had clearly never expected him to agree.

'That's great, Jim,' Stafford said at last. 'That's great.'

'No problem.'

'I'll mail you the details when I've got them, OK?'

'OK. Do it soon, though. The connection's dodgy over here right now.'

'Sure. Will do. That's great, Jim. Really. Great.'

'Good.'

There was more silence. Now that the reason for Stafford's phone call had been met, there wasn't much else to say and they each began to feel the thousands of miles between the Whitehall office and the tumbledown Cape Dutch townhouse. These two were friendly acquaintances at best.

Stafford tried, 'So how is it over there?'

Jim didn't answer. He just shrugged.

But it was as if the other man heard the gesture and assumed it merited sympathy: 'It can't be easy.'

'For who?' Jim said, his voice sounding snappier than he felt.

'Right. Quite. Exactly.' Stafford was backtracking, uncertain. Then he sighed. 'I heard they arrested the witch-doctor.'

'I heard that.'

'He's a friend of yours, right?'

'Yeah, he is. But I haven't seen him.'

'I can't believe they arrested him. Isn't he *the* national hero? Why would they arrest him? Do you think he's still alive?'

'I don't know. I haven't seen him.'

'You haven't seen him?'

'No. I haven't seen him.'

'But isn't it . . .' Stafford stumbled over his words, as if thrown by a sudden urgency he'd not previously felt. 'But isn't it just a fucking waste, Jim? Isn't it all just a fucking tragedy?'

Jim sucked on his cigarette. In spite of himself, he laughed. He wasn't interested in this kind of conversation. He didn't know its purpose. It didn't go anywhere. 'For who?' he said again. 'Tragedy's a big word. A waste for who? For me? For you?'

'For everyone,' Stafford declared testily, any uncertainty upended under challenge. 'Don't be so fucking facetious, Jim. No one wins out of this.'

'That's right,' Jim agreed. 'No one wins.' He flicked his butt into the vegetable garden. He could see its cherry still glowing as he and Stafford gently extracted themselves from any possible awkwardness with small-talk that was meaningless and soothing.

A week later, Jim took the minibus because the Laser was out of petrol. Diesel was easier to come by right now. If he'd thought it through, he'd have headed into town and picked up a courtesy car from the Sheraton, but he hadn't thought it through.

He tried to leave the house before Sylvia heard him up and about, but when he picked up the keys from the bowl beneath the mirror, he turned round to find her standing in front of him, blocking the corridor and his route to the door. Without a word, she examined him, her expression playing a mixture of compassion, contempt and disgust. She held his face between her hands, exactly as she did with the kids, exactly as she had with Tinashe the night of Stafford's phone call. 'Open your mouth,' she said.

Reluctantly he did as he was told. He knew what she'd see inside – the yellow bumps on his tongue, his gums thick with white mucus.

She wrinkled her nose at him. 'That's gross, Jim.'

'I'm out of peroxide.'

She made a small snorting noise as though this was no excuse. But then she softened her response by brushing her thumb almost lovingly around his eye socket. 'And how's . . .' she began.

'It's good. I feel better than for ages,' he said. He wouldn't let her finish. He'd started a new fixed-dose combination the previous month and he did, indeed, feel better. But he didn't want to talk about it.

Sylvia nodded curtly. 'What time will you be back? We've got –'

'I know. James's funeral. I'll see you at the –'

'Sure. Don't be –'

'Of course I won't.'

Jim nodded briskly and left. He clambered behind the wheel of the minibus. He found his chest heaving and a familiar thickening in his throat and knew what was coming. Some of the boys were playing football in the yard – Heston, Tefadzwa, Presley and that new kid whose name he could never remember – and he didn't want them to see. Sylvia already had them brushed and scrubbed in their Sunday best ready for the funeral. Jim wound down the window and told them to get inside the house. 'You know if you guys mess up your clothes Mama will take out her paddle,' he said, and pulled a face that made them all laugh.

He told Tefadzwa to open the gate and shut it behind him. He was struggling to control himself. He felt as if he might burst. He eased out of the drive and checked the closing gate in his rear-view mirror. Then he rested his head on the steering-wheel and began to cry.

23
Mama's House

Sylvia and Jim had moved to Queenstown more than seven years previously. At that point, she was a decade shy of twice his age. She was from London, more or less, and hadn't travelled much. Jim was from the Home Counties, but had lived in Zambawi for fourteen months some years previously. He'd taught English at a rural school and been caught up in the whirlwind of the coup, during which time he'd befriended Musa Musa, the spirit medium, and Enoch Adini, the future president.

Sylvia was black and Jim was white. When they'd met, Sylvia described herself as a prostitute (retired), while Jim still hadn't worked out a description of himself that made any sense. They were an odd couple and Queenstown had seemed like a place where that might be OK, not because it was particularly liberal but rather the opposite. On their arrival, Jim explained it to Sylvia like this: 'It's post-colonial, isn't it? If you're British, most people think you're Godless and the rest think you're God. So, you can pretty much do what you want.'

Jim and Sylvia hadn't specifically planned to marry, or to stay, but that was what happened.

At first, Jim didn't really work. Occasionally he wrote press releases for international NGOs for which he was paid in foreign currency. And that was enough to get by. Otherwise he hung out in downtown bars with friends, old and new, and talked football and politics and women. At first Sylvia accompanied him and was happy to do so. But she needed to make her own life so she began volunteering for a local AIDS charity that provided hot meals on home visits and the most basic medical care. Sylvia had read Zambawi's national AIDS statistics. But, until now, she hadn't been able to turn them into anything visual, meaningful, comprehensible. This wasn't her fault, but the fault of the statistics themselves – their breadth, their shamelessness, their vulgar absurdity.

Picture an individual dying of an AIDS-related illness. Place her in a room as quiet as a library, her family around her to hold her hand and mop her brow, a scene of warm colours and heady atmosphere worthy of Titian. But can you really picture two million people infected with the virus, a quarter of the adult population nationwide, one in three in the city? Surely the lens of your mind's eye is not wide enough to record that reality and the resolution of your imagination not sharp enough to capture its consequences.

You can't imagine the despair upon despair upon despair, or the desperate and ultimately risible human will, which learns to accept that despair almost as if it were normal and somehow carries on. You can't imagine the dying begging to die; you can't imagine the vacant expressions of those waiting, hollowed out and collapsing, like desiccated pumpkin heads gawping at the sun; you can't imagine the fear of that first dry cough as necks snap round and scared eyes seek out the culprit. You can't imagine the wailing and you can't imagine the silence. Some take that silence as outright secrecy or, at least, complicity with the secret, but for the most part it's not: it's the silence of those who know there's nothing to be said.

Most of all, though, you can't imagine the children, their sheer weight of numbers, in the city especially where they spill from every nook and cranny, swarming like ants over roadkill. They are wide-eyed and terrified and confident and conflicted all at once. They have seen more than any child should, and nothing too. They are infected, or not. And they know, or they don't. They are cared for by grandparents clinging to transferred dreams, aunts and uncles clinging to memories, or sometimes they just cling to one another. You can imagine none of this until you've seen it. And this was what Sylvia saw.

Sylvia had never considered having children. She'd been a prostitute her whole adult life and a couple of years on top of that. It had never been the right time and now it never would be. In moments of honesty, she acknowledged that she'd never felt capable. Sylvia's womb had never been a nest lodged high in her branches, secure and out of the way. It wasn't a seedbed waiting to be sown, or a blank canvas anticipating the divine artist. Rather, it was a simple receptacle and no more fertile than a coffee cup. Her breasts were not designed for function but with admirers in mind. They symbolized fecundity perfectly but were not fecund. They were as ripe and tempting as a bowl of wax fruit.

Most importantly, though, Sylvia believed that she had no maternal instinct. She believed that a young woman as temptress was a trap that, once sprung by a batch of passing DNA, metamorphosed, psychologically as much as physically, into a mother. She believed that a woman who tempted too long began variously to calcify, congeal and corrupt. She believed that such was the smell of a single woman in her forties – seduction stagnated – and, Jim or no Jim, she was scared that she stank of it.

At least, this was what she believed before she began to foster the orphans.

The first was Tefadzwa. At the time he was five years old. His mother had died, then his younger sister and finally his father. The decimation of the family had taken slightly less than six months. His dad had been called Tefadzwa too. Once, towards the end, Sylvia found the little boy trying to drag his semi-comatose father out of bed. He'd pulled the man's stringbean arm until his shoulder was on the very edge of the mattress and his head lolling off, eyes rolled back, pallid tongue hanging out. The little boy was tenderly stroking his father's shoulder. 'It's time to get up, Daddy,' he kept saying. 'It's time to get up.'

There was an adult cousin, but she didn't want to know. Apparently there was an uncle too, but nobody knew where he was. There were, of course, other orphanages, but they had no room. So one day Jim had got home from the expatriate bar where he'd been watching the English Premier League on the big-screen TV to find Tefadzwa sitting at the kitchen table eating a mango. At this point, Sylvia's feelings about her suitability for motherhood hadn't changed, but in the context of AIDS orphans they'd been put into perspective – because she was surely better than nothing.

Within a year, Sylvia and Jim had moved to a larger house in Riverdean in the western suburbs and she was looking after half a dozen kids. In two years the numbers had swelled to almost twenty. Through Jim's connections, the President's office supported Sylvia's application for local charitable status and the British High Commission provided a small grant. It was Jim's idea to name the newly founded orphanage 'Mama's House', because 'Mama' was what she'd been called by Edwin, a ten-year-old she'd taken in who died just six months later, the first to do so in her care. Mama's House now had thirty-five permanent residents and gave twenty older children a daily hot meal. It had moved again two years previously, this time to the ramshackle Cape Dutch mansion on the fringes of the city centre. Once upon a time this must have been quite a colonial residence, housing a district commissioner or a gentleman merchant, perhaps, but now it was home to some children who were waiting to die and others waiting to live. Every six months Jim whitewashed the house from top to bottom. Several coats eventually concealed the mildew stains but never their smell.

Everything had changed for Jim on the day that his wife brought Tefadzwa home. Later that night, in bed, after he'd told her that she'd done the right thing and promised they'd look after the child together, he'd kissed her neck and cupped her breasts and slid one hand gently into the waistband of her underwear. She hadn't stopped him as she had done in the past, when tired, irritable or plain not in the mood, but she began to tell him about her worries for the boy in a tone that suggested she couldn't even feel that his hand was where it was.

Over the following months, Sylvia transformed into a mother. But she was never a new mother, charmingly flustered with responsibility and prone to the tearful uncertainty that might be comforted by a solid, male shoulder. Rather, she leapt straight into battle-hardened maternity that was self-sufficient, self-possessed and suffered no fool, least of all her husband. Her body went through an equivalent metamorphosis. Parts thickened and drooped, puffed up and deflated. It was, no doubt, down to changes of lifestyle and diet. Where once Sylvia had been rigorous about exercise and fastidious about what she ate, now she was just too busy and picked at whatever came to hand.

Nonetheless, Jim believed, or at least fantasized, something quite different. He imagined that his wife had held her breath for thirty years, that her breasts had kept their position propped up by swelling lungs, that her buttocks had remained so tight while tensed, the muscles deprived of oxygen, that her neck had remained so long and slender to maintain her chin's position above the endless pairs of lascivious eyes. And now, at last, she'd relaxed and breathed out.

Jim was sincerely proud of his wife's achievements and genuinely happy to watch this exhalation. He thought her new shape was womanly and beautiful, and she seemed thoroughly fulfilled and confident for the first time since he'd known her. He couldn't help but be aware, though, that these achievements and this fulfilment had nothing to do with him. He thought it might have been different if the child (and later children) had been his because, whatever he said and whatever he did, he never felt truly involved. But how could he complain when his wife was finding satisfaction in doing such a manifestly good thing?

With hindsight, Jim sometimes told himself that it was this gap between them that had so profoundly affected their sex life; it was as if Sylvia had reached for him one evening and he'd chastely denied her carnal intimacy on the grounds of her ongoing emotional detachment. He felt that such an explanation at least granted him an excuse for what had followed so he chose to bury the memory of the night of Tefadzwa's arrival. Because the truth was that Sylvia had been the first to lose sexual enthusiasm and presumably, at some point, it would have returned. But then Jim had begun his string of infidelities and, either while she was pretending not to know or after she'd been forced to confront them, Sylvia had decided she wasn't going to fuck him again.

She threw him out for a while. She only allowed him to move back in when he became ill. In fact, she nursed him back to something like health.

When he was well enough to sit upright and the doctor removed his throat tube, she sat on the edge of his bed and held his hand. He was still finding it difficult to breathe but he muttered that he was sorry and that he still loved her very much. His hand in hers felt bony and brittle, like a bunch of dry twigs. She squeezed it a little too hard and then she told him she still loved him too. 'But you could have killed me, Jim,' she said. There was no reproach in her voice. It was just a statement of fact and, bald like that, contained a mild interrogative that held a scream in the bulb of the question mark.

Now, some two years later, sitting in the driving seat of the minibus, Jim lifted his head off the steering-wheel and wiped his eyes on his sleeve. He lit a cigarette and wound down the window. He didn't know quite why he was weeping like this and he told himself, 'There's no use crying over spilt milk.' But then he thought, bitterly, that there was no use crying over *anything* – no situation at all that would be resolved by tears. Whatever the trigger, Jim realized, the root motivation for crying was always wholly selfish. This thought felt like an epiphany.

He was crying because that afternoon they were burying James, a six-year-old who'd been desperately sick when he arrived with them and had lived less than two months. He was crying because this would be the forty-third Mama's House funeral and he was tired of it and he felt sorry for himself. He was crying because his wife treated him like one of her orphans, albeit without the same physical tenderness, and that was nobody's fault but his own. He was crying because this was the third James who'd died in the orphanage and he himself would most likely be the fourth. He was crying because it seemed as good a response as any.

Jim looked at his watch. He was running late. He sniffed, started the minibus and pulled out. The traffic through the city centre was surprisingly light; a result, presumably, of the petrol shortage. He made good time. He was thankful for small mercies.

At the airport, in Arrivals, David Pinner and Jeremy Shorter stood back to back, each gripping the handle of a luggage trolley as if it were an attack dog on a short leash. Pinner was exhausted. After his rough night on the plane, he wanted nothing but to get to his hotel and sleep. Instead he was standing in Shitsville, Dystopia, batting off the chancers, hawkers and thieves and wearing an expression that mixed, he hoped, distaste at the lip with steel in the eye. This was, indeed, the 'real Africa' and he suspected that the quicker he was out of it the better.

All the other white people from the flight had been met on arrival by more white people with pinched expressions or black people with wide smiles and crisply ironed shirts, then whisked away in high vehicles with tinted windows and air-conditioning. But Pinner and Jeremy were still waiting for their local contact, someone who, according to their briefing, had connections at the very top of the Adini government. So they now formed a lone white archipelago in the arrivals lounge, while around them returning Africans emerged from Customs, looking flustered but relieved and pushing trolleys that carried a household's worth of electrical appliances. Here, they were enthusiastically greeted by what must have been, as far as Pinner could judge, everyone they'd ever met. Pinner's feelings of distaste were getting stronger and his steel steelier with every passing minute.

In fact, the only other white guy in the whole airport now seemed to be the bizarre creature who'd just shuffled through the broken automatic doors that were stuck half open or half closed, depending on your outlook. He was an ageless rake of a man whose loose white shirt and baggy long shorts billowed off him like the sails of an abandoned schooner above pipe-cleaner legs that ended in dusty bare feet. His features were long and thin, as if they'd been stretched over his skull as an afterthought. What hair he had was sandy blond and dotted in asymmetrical patches as if carelessly glued there by a bored child. Frankly, he would have resembled nothing so much as a corpse were it not for his extraordinary skin tone, which was a deep, shiny and somewhat unnatural rusty brown. He looked like a polished peanut.

As he got closer, Pinner realized, with some horror, that he appeared to be foaming at the mouth and resolved that, when the FCO contact finally arrived, he'd give him hell for keeping them waiting in such a place. The slobbering corpse-peanut was now standing in front of him, much too close for comfort. Pinner turned towards him, manoeuvring his trolley so that it was positioned protectively between them. The peanut had taken a handkerchief from the pocket of his shorts and was dabbing at the froth on his lips. 'I'm sorry. It's a yeast infection,' he explained, with an unmistakable English accent. 'It's an unfortunate by-product of my condition.'

Pinner raised an eyebrow. Who was he talking to? The poor creature was evidently deranged.

The man pocketed his handkerchief again and thrust out his right hand. 'David Pinner?' he asked. His pronunciation of the capital P popped bubbles on his lips. Pinner's other eyebrow shot up. 'Tony Stafford asked me to collect you. I'm Jim Tulloh. Shall we get going?'

24

The road to hell is lined with post-war housing

London, England, 2008

Preston didn't want to be recognized so he went in disguise. He imagined that for most celebrities this would mean wearing a wig or donning a pair of dark glasses – at the very least *putting something on*. But for Preston it meant the opposite. He took off his trademark baseball cap, removed the diamond stud from his ear, the thick chain from his neck and the rings from his fingers. He shed the labels emblazoned across his chest and stitched into his seams, and he pulled up his jeans and belted them an inch below his navel. And there he was in the mirror of the en-suite bathroom of his Authenticity™ office: utterly nondescript.

Brad Pitt could grow a beard, wear a dress, book himself into a hotel under a hilarious name like 'Ivor Biggun', but he was still Brad Pitt. Preston Pinner, a.k.a. 2P, a.k.a. Tuppence, was nothing more than a hat, jewellery and a couple of trade-marked nicknames. He wasn't sure how it would feel to find significance in this so he chose not to try.

He'd spoken to Lorraine, Nobody's manager, that morning. Although Errol had scheduled a meeting, he hadn't actually agreed a location and, besides, Preston thought it was worth adding the personal touch – it often made people feel pretty special to get a call from 2P himself. But on this occasion it hadn't gone well. If an unsigned musician had some kind of representation, it was typically a parent, boyfriend or best mate. Sometimes these 'representatives' were so flattered to be speaking to *the* 2P that they'd do anything to be helpful –

drag the artist out of his day job at the local Carphone Ware-house and jump on the first bus to the Old Street office. Others, they'd read some idiot's guide to the music industry and would be clumsily distrusting and defensive in a way that was easily sidestepped with a little light flattery, ending with 'But I can't make any promises.' Lorraine, however, though most likely friend or girlfriend (to judge by her voice – smart and confident but, most of all, young), was unusually obstructive; so much so that at one point Preston thought he'd lost the meeting altogether.

He'd started by saying how Nobody's music had made him sit up and listen, how he really thought the guy had something, and did she know how much music was submitted for the A-List™ and how rare that was? Whether she knew or not, she didn't respond to Preston's gushing. Instead there was an uncomfortable silence. She suspected he was selling her a line. Ironically he'd meant every word.

He ploughed on. He said, 'I mean, it's quirky and original, but it's commercial too, you know? Like, he's got that musi-cality, but he's also got the headnod – like Stevie meets Kanye and shit. You know, he's got that flow, that charisma, like he's a laidback motherfucker but righteous, know what I mean?'

Still she said nothing, but was it his imagination or had he heard a stifled laugh? He was thrown. He felt like he'd been caught talking shit. Of course, he was always talking shit and sometimes someone caught him, but they never dared show it. He stumbled. He tried to shrug it off. He tried, 'So who is this geezer?'

At last she spoke. She said, 'What do you mean, who is he? He's Nobody.'

'No. I know that. I mean, I know he's Nobody – great name by the way. What I'm saying is, who *is* he? Who *is* Nobody?'

Again, she was silent. Then she sniffed.

Preston asked her if they could come into the office. She said they couldn't. He said he had a busy day but he might come and meet them if that was more convenient. She sniffed again and told him she wasn't sure that was a good idea.

He got frustrated. He said, 'Look, you know who I am. If your guy wants to get his music on the radio or TV or whatever, if he wants to get it heard by the maximum number of people, if he wants to get paid, be a star, whatever the fuck he wants – you know who I am and you know I'm the man who can make it happen.'

She said, 'I'm not sure he wants anything.' He could hear a smile in her voice.

Preston got more frustrated. He said, 'Are you fucking me about?'

'Are you fucking swearing at me?'

'No!' he backtracked. 'I'm not swearing at you, Lorraine. Really. Sorry. Look: what I'm saying is, why did you send me his music if you don't want to meet me?'

She sighed. 'I dunno. Maybe it was a mistake.'

'Look, I'll come and meet you guys . . .'

'No. I don't think he wants that.'

'OK. I'll come and meet *you*. You can see what I'm about . . .'

'I think I know what you're about.'

'You can see what I'm about,' he continued, 'and we'll take it from there.'

Another sigh. 'OK,' she said. 'But I can't make any promises.'

He felt like he'd been snookered.

She said she'd meet him in an hour. She gave him directions to a pub, just past Dagenham off the A12.

It was because he was meeting her in a pub that he'd decided to go in disguise. He didn't want any hassle. When he finally found the place, driving Errol's clapped-out Beamer rather than the Authenticity™ Hummer, he was glad of his decision. Preston prided himself on knowing London like the back of his hand. But this wasn't London and it wasn't the back of his hand. It wasn't the back of anyone's hand. It was an armpit.

Errol had scored a copy of Nobody's six-track demo and Preston blasted it from the Beamer's stereo. The music was hard to pin down, a kind of folk with a hip-hop engine and Nobody's unmistakable blues vocal. Turned up to full volume on the car's cheap system, it sounded rough and tinny, but that only added to Preston's sense that it might be the perfect soundtrack to his journey. The songs were simultaneously nostalgic and angry, funny and desperate.

Turning off the main road, he was immediately lost in a loose cobweb of identical suburban streets of mid-twentieth-century semis, strung out like a shaggy-dog story at the residents' expense by post-war town planning. Most of the houses were in varying states of disrepair – peeling painted façades, rusting grilles, and gardens so small and so overgrown that you had to assume an active, bloody-minded, almost political neglect. Some of the houses were actually burnt-out, their blackened windows like junkies' eyes, as if the houses themselves had overdosed. Others were pristinely kept, their doors freshly painted and their flowerbeds military. But such vain aspiration only added to the overall sense of hopelessness.

There seemed to be hardly any public spaces in this neighbourhood. There were a few shops: identical, grey, concrete constructions, all of which had their shutters half closed as though primed for a quick getaway, Coca-Cola red the only splash of colour. There was a modern mosque that might have been converted from a modern church. A poster flapped from the noticeboard outside. There was a small, concrete playground with a single basketball hoop, swings, a round-about and a slide that was twisted and almost on its side, as though it had been trodden on by a passing monster, escaped from a nearby cinema. But there weren't any cinemas nearby. Three teenage girls wearing thick overcoats and veils were sitting on the roundabout, propelling themselves in slow circles with the tips of their toes.

There weren't many people on the streets and Preston thought there was something strange about those he saw but he couldn't put his finger on what it was. It might have been that they were all young, it might have been that they appeared to move in packs, or it might have been the vague but definite impression that they had no specific destination.

On the car stereo, Nobody's demo clicked over to 'Jerusalem', the track that had first been submitted to The A-List™. Preston nodded along to it, more convinced than ever that he could turn it into a hit record – 'And was Jerusalem builded here / Among these dark, satanic mills.'

Preston needed to stop and ask directions.

Sitting at a set of traffic-lights, he saw a gang of young men lounging in a bus shelter on the other side of the road. There were half a dozen of them, all dressed in identical jeans and T-shirts, faces like mug-shots, tugging on cigarettes pinched between thumbs and forefingers. They had a couple of thick, squat dogs with them, straining at short leads. When the lights turned green, Preston drove on.

A little further on, he pulled into a garage. He could ask inside or one of the clutch of boys sitting on the low wall behind the pumps. They were long and skinny with thin, East African faces half hidden by ubiquitous hoods. They weren't talking or doing anything, just sitting like statues, their expressions blank.

He was getting out of the car when he noticed a bright yellow police sign erected on the pavement behind them. It was an appeal for witnesses to a knife murder on that very spot a couple of weeks before. Now that he looked closer, he saw half a dozen tatty bunches of flowers propped up against the base, the browning petals slowly turning to mulch: it was a modern war memorial. He hesitated. He closed the car door again and restarted the engine. As he edged back into the road, he saw the boys had turned to watch him. Their expressions were still blank but held now, he thought, a degree of scorn. Preston felt ridiculous and the sensation briefly invigorated him and he told himself that he'd ask the very next person he saw, whoever they were. But no sooner had he thought this than he recognized a street name from Lorraine's directions. He took a left, then the first right and there, on the right, was the Admiral Nelson, an unprepossessing carbuncle of a pub.

25
Of somebody and nobody

London, England, 2008

Preston parked in the large car park and pulled out his briefcase from behind the passenger seat. It was lunchtime empty, only half a dozen other vehicles and a couple of industrial bins choking on black bags that, in turn, coughed up their contents. On the wall, a large sign advertised various alcopops at two for the price of one. Several of the brands were clients of Authenticity™. Beneath this sign a smaller wooden one read 'The landlord reserves the right to refuse –' The end was broken off and the wood at the break was clean and light as if, just the previous night, someone had taken violent exception to the landlord's intentions. Apparently the landlord could refuse nothing.

Preston pushed open the door. The handle was sticky. Inside, the carpets were reddy-brown and the seating browny-red. There were about a dozen men arranged at even intervals around the bar. Two were playing pool and the balls clacked. Every one of the rest appeared to be on his own and, with varying degrees of curiosity, each turned to look at him. They were all white.

Preston noticed a cross of St George, cut out from a news-paper, presumably published to commemorate some failed footballing armada, Sellotaped to the inside of a window that might have been frosted or might have been plain filthy. Next to the flag, a fruit machine was talking to itself, its mechanical voice chirruping false jollity. Then, on the banquette behind the fruit machine, he spotted the only woman in the place. She was young and pale with what looked like russet-coloured hair – it was hard to tell because it was brutally scraped back in a Croydon facelift. She had high cheekbones that spoke less of good bone structure than bad eating, and a thin, somewhat unkind-looking mouth. She was wearing a black bomber jacket of the sort that was fashionable twenty years ago, and she had both hands wrapped around an electric pink bottle as if it was the joystick of a plane she was trying to land. He went over to her, avoiding the men's eyes. 'Lorraine?'

She looked up at him. He'd been wrong about her mouth. It wasn't unkind so much as pinched, as if her lips had shrivelled against the cold or in reflex against a lifetime's biting.

He said, 'I'm Preston Pinner. Most people call me Tupps.' He held out his hand. She didn't say anything, but regarded him curiously, her chin raised and tilted slightly to the side. He noticed her eyes. They were pale blue, pretty and somewhat mischievous. She took his hand. Hers was small, warm and dry. 'You want another drink?'

She held up her bottle, weighing the contents. 'OK.'

Preston went to the bar. He ordered Lorraine the same again and got two for the price of one. He ordered mineral water for himself. He paid with a twenty. The landlord stared at him. Preston said, 'Something for you?'

The landlord shook his head, but didn't stop staring. 'It's a bit early for me, son.'

Preston took the drinks back to the table and sat down. Lorraine showed no surprise at getting two drinks and took a sip from one. She said, 'Thanks.'

'No problem.' Preston looked around as though he were assessing the pub for the first time. 'This is a funny joint.'

'Why?'

Preston sipped his own drink to give himself a second to think. He shook his head. 'I dunno. Just is.'

'Guess it depends what you're used to.' She pinned him with a look not unlike the landlord's. 'So, *you*'re Preston Pinner. You look different on telly.'

Preston laughed. 'Better or worse?'

She laughed back at him. She said, 'What do you want?'

'What do I want?'

'Yeah. What do you want?'

He nodded. He'd thought this through and planned every word so he spoke carefully and clearly, without flannel or the smallest inflection of enthusiasm. He told her how Authenticity™, AuthenTV™, The A-List™ and DJ Jonny Swift™ worked hand in hand to create, cultivate and sell the brand value of affiliated artists. He used the example of The Undertakers, a south London grime collective. They'd been signed to The A-List™, then placed by Authenticity™ in a successful viral campaign for the new Ford sports coupé that had been across the Internet in a matter of days (achieving 70 per cent recog among all UK under-twenties).

'Do you know The Undertakers?' he asked, and she shook her head. 'You never heard of them, right? But I guarantee you know that tune and they got paid six figures for that.'

He told her that, up to now, Authenticity™ (the parent company) had not dealt with licences or publishing. It was essentially an aggregator and arbitrator and was, therefore, predominantly a volume business. On the other hand, he was increasingly interested in owning a few key artists and he suspected that Nobody could be the very first.

He told her he didn't want to put a deal on the table at this stage, but he'd listened to the tracks Nobody had submitted to the A-List™ and he believed they had strong commercial potential. He said he couldn't make any promises, but how about they put Nobody in the studio with a name producer and they assembled a single and video package? He said he couldn't make any promises, but with Nobody's talent and the support of Authenticity™, The A-List™, AuthenTV™, DJ Jonny Swift™ and, of course, himself (a.k.a. 2P™, a.k.a. Tuppence™), they would have a better chance of cracking the market than most. He said he couldn't make any promises, but now he came to think of it, Authenticity™ were programming the 'urban' stage at the forthcoming African Authority-sponsored 'Africa Unite' festival, which would be broadcast on terrestrial, satellite, radio, web and 3G, and that might be an ideal opportunity to launch Nobody as a live artist. He concluded that it went without saying that all this was dependent on meeting the man himself, because without meeting Nobody, obviously he couldn't make anybody any promises. While he talked, Lorraine said hardly a word. Occasionally she stopped him to make sure she'd understood something, but mostly she kept her thoughts to herself. The longer he went on, the more Preston liked her. She had poise, she listened, she *engaged*. And he didn't know anybody else who really engaged except him. He found himself wondering idly what she was about, her exact age and how her hair might look if released from its current architectural responsibilities.

When he'd finished, Lorraine excused herself briefly and made a phone call. When she returned, she said, 'OK, he'll be here in a minute.' Then, 'That sounds OK – the video and single, I mean. It's important he gets out there, starts earning some money, innit? I mean, I don't think he cares but I care.'

Preston raised his eyebrows. 'As his manager?'

She raised hers back. 'He's my man.'

My man – there was something ridiculous about that phrase. It had too much weight. How could this girl have a 'man' unless he was away at war (probably the American Civil War, at that). It sounded archaic and naïve, but Preston found that somehow charming. 'Right,' he said. 'Of course he is.'

The door at the far end of the bar, the same door Preston had entered by, squealed on its hinges. A black guy came in. He was tall and rangy, in a way that lent an inevitable lack of co-ordination to his gait, but he moved with self-confidence too, greeting everyone in the place and pausing at the bar for a second to shake the landlord's hand. He was curiously dressed. He looked as though he'd left the house naked and begged a piece of clothing from each of the first half-dozen people he'd passed in the street. He wore a scruffy pair of once-white trainers with thick, sponge tongues that poked out from each instep cheekily. A tight pair of marble-wash jeans was fastened at the waist with a silver-studded black leather belt. A faded rugby shirt with yellow and purple horizontal stripes was visible beneath a long, charcoal grey overcoat that would have looked snappy on a city lawyer. On his head sat a broad-brimmed brown leather rancher's hat that might have been an original from the Australian outback. This was pulled down over his loosely twisted hair, which looked as if it might shoot off the hat at any moment.

As he stood talking to the landlord, Preston tried to size him up with his expert eye. But no single item of the man's clothing fitted with another in any meaningful way. In fact, the outfit was so apparently random that Preston wondered if it must actually be the product of thoughtful curation. Maybe Nobody was in disguise too.

Preston looked at Lorraine sitting opposite him. Something had changed in her face – there was a softening. And, as Nobody approached them, he thought he saw her shoulders rise and fall as if with an involuntary sigh.

Lorraine said, 'Ben, this is 2P.'

Nobody shot her an irritated glance as he sat down next to her. She'd clearly said the wrong thing and Preston jumped in. He did this a little too quickly, as if he thought he was rescuing her. He thrust his hand towards the man and said, 'Call me Tupps. You must be Nobody.'

'Yeah,' Nobody said, and took his hand.

Up close, he looked younger than he had across the bar; younger than Preston, probably around the same age as Lorraine. He also seemed somehow slighter, as if his shoulders couldn't quite fill the overcoat, or his neck the collar of the rugby shirt. But there was something imposing about him, a self-possession that skirted surliness, a physicality that might be born of arrogance. Certainly, and surprisingly for Preston, he'd reduced the previously confident Lorraine to nervous girlishness.

Somewhere in the wordless part of his brain, Preston was making his own instinctive assessment. Had he been asked to label it in that instant, he'd most likely have said 'loathing', but that wouldn't have been wholly accurate. Like most people, Preston tended to confuse discomfort about the way he felt with dislike for whomsoever he blamed for it.

Nobody glanced lazily to where the landlord was emptying spill trays. He said, 'Lorraine's dad ain't feeling you, king.'

Preston looked from Nobody to the landlord to Lorraine. 'That your dad?'

'Yeah.'

Nobody chuckled to himself. 'He was all, like, "Who's that jumped-up little prick with Lolly?"' He shook his head, then murmured the phrase again under his breath, as if he was trying it out – 'jumped-up little prick'.

'So, what did you tell him?' Preston asked.

'Tell him? I told him you were with me, king, innit?'

Preston stared at the musician. There was something peculiar about his accent. Buried within the usual London cocktail, he identified an off-the-boat flavour, but he couldn't pin it down more exactly than that.

'Jumped-up little prick,' Nobody said again. With every repetition the phrase sounded more exotic, every vowel lengthening or shortening, every stress slipping a little further from its correct position. Then, 'You know, I only been hanging with poor white people since I knew Lorraine. It's very interesting from a Marxist point of view. They exactly like black people. I never knew that. Only difference is poor white people kill themselves with alcohol and junk food and cigarettes and television whereas poor black people from Africa to America always had a taste for the dramatic, know what I mean? It's very interesting. I suspect the difference must come in relationship to power. Perhaps this is something you and I can talk about, Tupps. For sure we have a different perspective, innit?'

Preston stared at him. He couldn't read this guy. He couldn't work out if this was a genuine statement in a genuine, if peculiar, hybrid accent, or that kind of performative racial consciousness that Errol had lately begun to employ. Initially he assumed it must be the latter, but then he realized that, in so far as he'd experienced any black politics, he'd done so second hand, so he probably wouldn't recognize sincerity anyway. In fact, if Malcolm X had walked through the door right then and there and started preaching, he'd have assumed he was pitching for a talk-show. Preston didn't know how he was expected to respond so he just licked his lips and said nothing.

There was a moment's silence between them. The guy grinned. Preston noticed that Lorraine had rested her hand on Nobody's forearm. It could have been a gesture of encouragement or restraint, he couldn't tell.

Preston finished his water. He figured Lorraine was onside, so he wanted to give her a minute to talk to her 'man'. He stood up and made a gesture offering drinks. Nobody declined. Lorraine had begun her second for the price of the first. He went to the bar. Lorraine's dad was still looking at him strangely. He tried a smile, but it had no effect. He was clearly still a jumped-up little prick. He swigged water in a manner that he hoped was disparaging and returned to the table.

Nobody had taken off his hat. It had left a circular dent embedded in his hair that slowly disappeared as his twists unfurled like new shoots sprouting in time-lapse photography. He said, 'Lolly says you wanna shoot a video.'

'Yeah.'

'Which tune?'

'I was thinking "Jerusalem". It's got that hook, that attitude. It's an easy sell. And that makes it a good introduction to your stuff.'

Nobody nodded to himself, so Preston ploughed on, précising exactly what he'd told Lorraine. Nobody nodded some more. When Preston was done, he said, 'So, what's in it for you, king?'

'For me?'

'Yes, blood, for *you*.'

Preston smiled. 'Money.'

Nobody dropped his eyes to the table. He picked up a beer mat and tapped it a couple of times. Then he looked sideways at Lorraine and cracked a smile. He said, 'I was all set to agree with Mr Jones's assessment of you, Tupps, but I like someone straightforward, innit? I thought you were gonna tell me you love my music or some rubbish like this. Instead you tell the truth. Because money, that's all people care about in the Western world.

'As for me? I is an artist, king. And here in London, there ain't no room for no artist. There is no art in this city, only commerce. Some people say that art and business are not mutually exclusive, understand? That's only because they don't know what art is. I don't give a shit about no money. Course I gotta get paid, but that's totally separate from my music, you get me?

'Which came first, music or money? Which is it, music or money?' Nobody's eyes were wide. He said, 'I is actually asking!'

Preston shrugged.

'Wherever you come from, it's music, innit? So, I's like a *griot*. I's a minstrel, a *jali*. I's like a historian, king. And you can't trust no historian what's paid by the rich man. It's a conflict of interests, innit?

'I know you looking at me like I is a nutter, but think about it: you interested in my music because I say something different and I say something different because I's not concerned with money. There's no originality in this city. Everything gets swallowed and spat out and swallowed again until you don't

184

remember who it belonged to or what it was in the first place. It's the creative Catch-22, know what I mean? As soon as you try and sell it, it stops being art.' Nobody sat back and fingered the brim of his hat. 'That's just the way it is,' he concluded.

Preston sipped his water and bought himself a second or two. Lately he'd been having reservations about Authenticity™; strange, inexpressible reservations about its purpose, about *his* purpose. Now his doubts seemed to crystallize, to form edges that he could trace with his finger and planes that reflected the light.

Preston was a bullshitter who created monetary value from thin – or hot – air but he'd known that about himself from the start. So, it wasn't the bullshit *per se* that was bothering him. Rather, his misgivings stemmed from the extent of the bullshit. People no longer bullshitted *about* a thing because there was nothing to bullshit about – the bullshit was the thing itself. The bullshit had become so all-pervasive that even anti-bullshit sounded like bullshit. Therefore either Nobody was talking shit or Preston was now so chock full of it that he couldn't tell. And, either way, it couldn't be described as a healthy situation.

In a sudden panic, he snatched a glance at Lorraine, hoping for some rational acknowledgement of his situation, possibly even some guidance either way. But she met his eyes levelly, nodding slightly, the look of an unquestioning disciple. Eventually, therefore, when he turned back to Nobody, he found himself high on cynicism and resentment. Fortunately those turned out to be the ideal energies with which to inspire the musician. 'So?' Preston sneered.

'What do you mean, "so?"'

'I mean, so what?'

'So what?'

'Yeah. I mean, so what do you want to do? What do you want *me* to do? All that stuff you just said – who were you talking to? I mean, you do know who I am, right? Because I tell you, I don't know shit about art. In fact, don't tell anyone, but I don't know shit about music either. The only thing I know is the curious alchemy that allows me to turn music – and I increasingly think it could be any music at all, you could give me a fucking skiffle record and I'd sell it – into gold.'

Preston wiped his mouth with the back of his hand. He was just warming up. 'The stuff you're talking about? You may as well talk to a painter about the quality of a fucking picture hook. He'd be, like, "Does the hook hang my painting? Then it's fine." I can do one thing for you, just one thing. I can make sure a lot of people hear your music. Or I can not do that. All the rest? I'm sorry, *king*, but I don't give a fuck.'

Nobody stared at him and he stared right back. The musician took hold of Lorraine's hand again and gave it a squeeze on the table top. Then he snorted, and a half-chuckle escaped. He said: 'I think we might be good friends, Tupps.'

'I think we might do good business together,' Preston corrected him.

Now Nobody seemed to relax and he laughed aloud, throwing back his hands and slapping them down. Then he forced his face into a serious expression. 'I don't believe you believe some of the things you said.'

'No? I could say the same of you. The question is, so . . .'

'So?'

'So, what do you want me to do?'

Nobody glanced at Lorraine, then back to Preston. 'I want a lot of people to hear my music,' he said. 'I want a single and a video. I don't wanna talk about the video, bruh. I don't wanna be in it and I don't wanna be famous. I just wanna do what I do and you can do what you do. Any talk about money? Any talk about business and plans and such? You can talk to Lolly, OK?'

Now Preston looked at Lorraine steadily. She looked away. 'OK,' he said.

Nobody stood up and thrust his hand at Preston again. He

said, 'All right, 2P, shake on it!' Then, 'I can't believe I is sleeping with the enemy! How many ways you gonna fuck me over, Tupps?'

Preston laughed. 'It doesn't work like that.'

'Ha! Are you sure, king? Don't make promises you can't keep.' He bent and kissed Lorraine's cheek before jamming his hat back on his head. 'Gonna leave you two to talk business. I is already feeling too dirty, innit?'

With that, Nobody slid out from behind the table. Preston and Lorraine watched him leave. He waved to Lorraine's dad and a couple of the other guys at the bar.

Preston said, 'Right, then.'

It was a moment before Lorraine turned to him. He noticed that her neck was flushed pink, as if she were blushing. He reached for his briefcase and pulled out a thin document wallet. 'This is a standard contract for you to have a look at,' he said. 'Do you guys have a lawyer?'

26

Insert document
'The diary of a local gentleman', 10 May 1901
(Empire Museum, Bristol), anon.

I sometimes think of Ackerman, my CO at Standmere.

Even leaving aside the horrors of the camp, for which he must take the lion's share of the responsibility, I would not have cared for the man. He had a cynicism about him. This is often characteristic of those who have gone too long without leave, but in Ackerman's case I came to conclude that it was thoroughly self-serving, giving justification to his actions.

Thirty years of age, he had been a career soldier since schooling at a minor establishment on the south coast (I forget its name). So, from our first meeting, he made it quite clear that he regarded me as a type of innocent abroad – as if I were some naïve dilettante just arrived in Paris on the first stop of the most tedious Grand Tour. He took no account of my service record, and I can only assume that he felt threatened by the presence of a fellow of superior education; though, of course, I made no attempt to draw attention to this.

I remember the first occasion upon which I complained of the living conditions of the 'refugees'. I told him that an English gentleman simply could not condone such treatment of women and children, whatever their race or creed.

He replied pointedly that he could not trust a man who espoused too many principles since, in his experience, these were the worst kind of liars and hypocrites.

What was I to make of that? Certainly, it set the tenor of all our future conversations.

In fact, I have met few greater hypocrites than Ackerman, for while he was happy that the Boers should be treated like savages and talked about them as such, he frequently behaved towards the natives in the camp in an altogether different fashion. On occasion, for example, he would talk to the old men around their fire, adopting a corruption of their tongue and squatting on his haunches as they did. What was more, he refused to curb their singing even though it disquieted the men and put the wind up the Dutch. However, it was only after I had been at Standmere a full month that I came to see the full extent of his tastelessness: Ackerman, a married man and father of two daughters, had taken Mary, the young Zulu girl charged with his laundry, as his mistress.

Since first putting ashore at the Cape of Good Hope, I had all too often witnessed the consequences of such miscegenation and, truly, it was there for all to see in the features of most Trekboers. Furthermore, I had heard all sorts of ribald chatter in many a mess about the peculiar proclivities of the natives. My opinion of Ackerman as it was, therefore, I was not so foolish as to be entirely shocked by his behaviour. However, that he should carry on in such a manner in full view of the men in his command was intolerable.

On one occasion, I felt I had no choice but to remonstrate with him. It was dusk (or at least what passes for it in that miserable place where night follows day with all the ceremony of a slamming door) and he was sitting on his veranda in shirt sleeves and the O/R khaki helmet he'd taken to wearing – an affectation, I believe, to signify his close bond with his men (I have seen such pettiness before and can say from experience that it generally signifies the opposite). He smoked a cigarette as Mary busied herself around him. But for her colour, they might have looked every bit the married couple in some rustic fantasy – her sweeping beneath the resting husband's feet while he enjoys his baccy and chats idly about the trials of his working day.

Ackerman's house was built on a shallow incline that gave it an excellent view of the whole camp. At that point, I was standing at the base of this hillock, approximately fifteen yards away, giving a Tommy a fearful dressing-down for some now forgotten misdemeanour (he was an Irishman, as I recall. They make fine soldiers, the Irish, but you must break their will as you would a colt). I suddenly realized, however, that this young swaddy was not paying me the blindest notice and his gaze was instead fixed on what was occurring over my shoulder.

I turned to follow his line of sight and saw the native girl standing behind Ackerman, quite still. She had put down her brush and her left hand rested on his left shoulder. He, in turn, held his right arm across his chest and his hand covered hers. Neither Ackerman nor the kaffir seemed in any way aware of what they were doing. They were each looking to mid-distance as if they hadn't a care in the world. They presented an image of extraordinary and grotesque intimacy.

Embarrassed, and with my authority as an officer in no small measure undermined, I promptly dismissed the soldier and marched over to Ackerman (in so far as I could 'march' anywhere – even before the infection my wound had left me horribly lame). I was livid and no mistake, but I felt that this situation must be immediately addressed.

As I climbed the wooden steps to Ackerman's veranda, the girl removed her hand from his shoulder, but remained standing behind him and greeted me with a look I fancied sullen. I had, of course, feared precisely such a reaction, so this hardly improved my humour.

I told Ackerman that I needed to speak to him urgently. He didn't reply, merely raised an eyebrow as if amused and dismissed the girl from our presence with a nonchalant inclination of his head.

I informed him of exactly where I stood on the matter. Of course, I was speaking to a superior officer, so I tempered my anger. Nonetheless, there can be no doubt that I made him fully aware of my position.

His response was quite extraordinary. He lit a cigarette and offered one to me. I accepted. Then he shook his head and bent forward, his forearms on his knees. His manner was neither defensive nor ashamed. If anything he seemed bored and a little weary. Had he been able to dismiss me with the same petty gesture with which he had dismissed his kaffir mistress, I believe he would have done so.

'Frankly, old chap, I don't give a *fig* what you think,' he muttered. 'In fact, I recommend you find some female company of your own – would do you the power of good. To what, precisely, do you object? Is it that I have a mistress, or that she is a native?'

I tried to explain myself. I began, 'As a God-fearing Englishman –'

But he interrupted me, raising his voice in a tone of pronounced bitterness. 'I may be an Englishman, but what God should I fear? We are fallen angels, you and I, mute bodyguards of the great Britannia. We are twin Charons who administer this Hades that she may sit on her island throne in all her silks and jewellery.'

His eyes left mine and he peered down towards the camp. The Boer women had a fire going and were washing the children. The sounds of their mewling were distinct and vexing. I already resented his classical allusions – further affectations! Further justification!

'You think I feel no sympathy with these bastard Dutch? Understand this now – I do not. No one in the Empire cares one jot for their welfare. More blankets? More food? Is that what you want? I charge that your Christianity, your *humanity*, is sham and nothing but a salve to your conscience.

'You think I treat the savages too well? You're mistaken. They are all savages to me – kaffirs, Boers, Indians, wogs, the lot of them. I will take them as porters, cannon fodder, lovers if I wish. If I want to starve them, they will starve. I will fatten them up only if I want to eat them. There can be no barbarism for an Englishman and, even if there were, do you not think I would drink deep from the forgiving Lethe on my voyage home?'

I assumed he mocked me, so I regarded him coldly. 'We are not angels, fallen or otherwise,' I said. 'Learning parrot fashion does not constitute a genuine education and, for all your mythologic allusions, we *are* Christian men of science. It is our calling and our duty to lead others towards spiritual and material progress.'

At this he laughed. He called me a 'damn fool' and several other names besides. He said, 'I'm afraid your principles are getting in the way of clear thinking, old man. What will this progress bring? Who will lay the bricks when every man's an architect? Do you truly imagine there is room for the wogs in Paradise? Now, there's a thought! Wouldn't that frighten the life out of your grandmama!

'What progress do you see? Inferior peoples have learnt to worship at the altar of British engineering. But no empire lasted even one sixteenth as long as its most fervent advocate foresaw. Even as land and men and booty are won, so the roots of failure begin to attack their foundations – success eats away at the victors until they are no more than shells of the men they were. Defeat fortifies the vanquished to withstand any pain.

'Have you witnessed the half-breeds that run like rats through Cape Town's Sixth District? *That* is progress. The English will always be outnumbered – *that* is science. Just as the Ostrogoths once strolled through fallen Rome, so one day the Griquas and Basters will roam freely through every London borough to the horror of men like us. Hang your principles, old chap; they make a fool of you.'

I stood up then. I did not choose to provide an audience for his perverse hypotheses that had no reason but to prop up his vanity and justify his indecency. I told him that principle, attested or abandoned, was neither here nor there and that the sole reason for my concern was pragmatic. I told him that the morale of the men was low, that such circumstance could only be countered by strict adherence to the chain of command, that the chain of command relied upon the unquestionable perception of the integrity of its officers. I reminded him of his responsibilities and left him to his sordid pursuits.

I know that on the battlefield a hero can be made to look a fool and a fool a hero. It is in the administration of war, therefore, that a man's true nature will always be revealed.

Although I rarely dwell now on the specifics of Ackerman's deluded solipsism (an infestation of kaffirs in London? Whatever next?), I confess that some aspects of his ravings still give me pause. As a fellow who aspires to free thinking, I contend that this is as it should be.

Sometimes, when discussing politics around a dinner table, I have known Kitty's sister, Gertrude, to speak up with a point that cuts right to the heart of the issue. Naturally, most of the men (her father and brothers in particular) shout her down or dismiss her opinion out of hand. They tell her, 'Now is not the time,' or make a joke at her expense or suggest she retires to the drawing room and readies her sheet music for a short recital.

However, it is on precisely such occasions that I choose to consider her outburst carefully and, more often than not, find something in it. The men dismiss her because, as a woman, she has not their logic, let alone their grasp of context. I, on the other hand, listen for precisely those self-same reasons.

When hunting, one's mount must be bent to one's will. But a wise rider senses the beast's intentions through his thighs and knows it feels the ground differently. So it is with Gertrude; so too with Ackerman. In the case of Ackerman, I remain fascinated by his contention that the roots of our Empire's downfall are laid in its every victory. I cannot accept that this is a fundamental and inevitable truth. However, nobody is more aware of the deep structural flaws in our venture as Englishmen than I.

I will never forget Standmere – that in taming the savage nature, we adopted savagery ourselves. Nor can I neglect the alienation I have felt at home – it is neither arrogance nor jealousy that leads me to conclude that the likes of Jameson have become inured to the responsibilities of true gentlemen, enfeebled by petty luxury and indulgence.

Seymour, the Oxford doctor I met at the Coach and Horses in Longborough, argued zealously for the benefits of scientific progress. I would certainly not contest his rationale. However, if such progress is built on crumbling foundations, one can only imagine what disasters we might be storing for the future. Is progress a worthwhile goal if it means the relinquishing of our best nature? I will not cling to history or tradition for its own sake, but neither will I dismiss these for some fantastical future. Since Longborough, therefore, I have distilled my position to the following equation – to know what we English were is to know what we are and to know what we may yet become.

I finally reached Fry Norton yesterday. I plan to stay a while. In spite of myself, I must confess that the journey has taken its toll on my wretched stump. It is raw and bloody, and I fear further infection. I need to rest. In any case, I can imagine no finer spot to convalesce. The village is picturesque and the locals thoroughly welcoming. Indeed, if this is the heart of England, we have nothing to fear. These are people at one with the land, their souls sympathetic to the changing seasons, their lives locked into the pleasing circularity that consumes the English attention.

I am lodging with a man named Nott, the schoolteacher. He is a fine fellow and, I think, a kindred spirit. Originally from London, he upped sticks after the loss of his wife to TB, desirous of country air for himself and his daughter, Elizabeth. I told him of Seymour's research and he listened with interest.

Elizabeth seems a delightful girl, vivacious and confident with the sun in her cheeks. I can't imagine how she might fit in with dear Kitty's refined set, who regard laughter as rather infra dig.

Upon my arrival, my first enquiry was naturally of the Whitsun Ale and I was thrilled to discover that it will be held in the village in just a fortnight's time. I will, therefore, stay at least until then.

This evening Nott took me to meet the Fry Norton morris men and watch their practice. At the back of a barn, we found seven in idle conversation. They made us welcome with a tankard of cider each, and I've rarely tasted anything so potent.

Nott and I sat to one side to observe but, for more than an hour, the men did nothing but talk – of Young Mr Codrington at the 'big house', who had discontinued his father's custom of distributing rabbits caught at the manor to the village; of the merits of one fly against another ('blue dun' over 'march brown'); of the colour of the trout this year (not so pink as last); of the number of cubs born at the fox covert and what that would mean for the hounds come October. Only when these subjects were exhausted did their attention turn to the ale and, even then, it was just an argument over who should be 'bagman'.

Thomas, the youngest of the side, complained that the duty always fell to him, something he found especially unjust because he danced a better jig than most. He suggested that Percy Stone, the eldest, should have the role, since it would allow him to take a breather – and folk liked and respected him besides.

The argument went to and fro, but was eventually settled by Jack Chavney, the foreman of the side. He told Thomas that he was the junior member and therefore acted as bagman because that was the tradition. And that was that.

Chavney cuts an intriguing figure. He is a strong and handsome fellow of about my age and speaks with a certain authority that the others seem to accept without question. Throughout the discussions I wrote in my journal and Chavney asked me what it was I found so noteworthy. I told him something of my undertaking and he said, 'Well, you'll find no truer Englishmen than those round here. Isn't that right, lads?'

He then asked where I'd come from and I said Bristol. He told me he'd once been to Cheltenham – as if to have visited one town rendered purposeless a visit to any other. It was quite a comical moment and I struggled to contain a laugh. I believe that Chavney took offence.

At that very instant, Elizabeth appeared from behind the barn to call Nott and me for supper. Chavney said, 'Miss Elizabeth has told me much of life in London and it doesn't sound conducive.'

I looked at her and fancied she blushed, poor thing! Chavney, too, seemed discomforted, knowing that he had spoken out of turn. I attempted to smooth things over. I said, 'Are we not to see you practise this evening, Mr Chavney?'

Elizabeth regarded me gratefully; Chavney too. He told me that they had left it too late for the evening, but I would be most welcome in future.

It was only then that I deduced the truth: the side had felt uneasy with a stranger among them – a gentleman at that with his journal and pencil.

As Kitty has told me often enough, I can sometimes be quite the oaf and, in this case, I had forgotten the concerns and fears of the labouring class. Nonetheless, I believe I made a reasonable impression by the end, and I can now look forward to learning something of the morris men's art over the coming days.

27

Insert document
'Tuloko and the warlord king', *The Book of Zamba Mythology*, (OUP, 2005), Edison Burrows III

In the early days of his leadership of the Zamba nation, Tuloko (the Traveller, the Child of the Horizon) had to drive out the Gotzi from the land around the great lake to the west.

The Gotzi Empire was a powerful one that extended over a month on foot. However, it bordered the Zamba nation only at its easternmost point, and the Gotzi in this area were mostly independent warlords, only loosely affiliated to the true royal house. These warlords had terrorized the western Zamba for many generations, stealing their daughters, beating their sons and taxing their harvest.

At this time, the strongest and most feared warlord was called Munu. It was said that his voice was so deep and resonant that his battle cry could burst a man's heart. Munu's approach was different from that of his predecessors. Not content with robbery, he annexed the best land around the lake as a fiefdom and took many Zamba men as his soldiers. He began to call himself king and built a great citadel with walls taller than trees to signify his new status. He ruled with his three sons who were his generals, each of them almost as terrifying as their father, and his daughter, Tapiwa, who was so beautiful that she didn't need to open her mouth for a man's heart to burst.

From this citadel, Munu could take whatever he wanted whenever he wanted, and the Zamba were driven to the great lake's floodplains where their cattle were decimated by *nagana* and the air was thick with mosquitoes. Soon, the indigenous people were so weakened by hunger and malaria that they could not offer any resistance at all.

No sooner had Tuloko united the Zamba nation, therefore, than a delegation arrived in Zimindo demanding that he confront Munu. Recognizing this as the first challenge of his leadership, Tuloko raised an army and set out for the great lake at once. However, he knew that his raw recruits, despite their enthusiasm for their young chief, would be no match for Munu's battle-hardened warriors, highly organized under the leadership of his three sons. Therefore, Tuloko ordered his men to make camp a day's march from the citadel and announced that he would head into the heart of Munu's fiefdom alone.

The *zakulu* who were Tuloko's closest advisers pleaded with him. 'At least you must disguise yourself,' they said. 'Otherwise Munu will have you killed as soon as he finds out who you are.'

But Tuloko's mind was made up. He said, 'I am the chief of the Zamba and proud to be so. All I need is my honesty, for no one can see through such a disguise.'

Renowned for their wisdom, the *zakulu* nodded and complimented the chief on his good sense. But secretly none of them understood his meaning.

The next morning, Tuloko set out alone. He arrived at Munu's citadel at sunset. He stopped at a well outside its walls to bathe before meeting the warlord king. At that time, Tapiwa was returning after an afternoon collecting herbs for her father's kitchen. When she saw Tuloko, his wet body washed by the low sun, she was transfixed. It looked, she thought, as if it were clad in gold armour. She waited in silence, concealed in the shadows of a tree, until he had finished and then she approached him.

She asked him who he was. When he told her, she said that her father would have him killed without a moment's thought.

Tuloko said, 'If that's true, it's true. But your father, who calls himself king, is a powerful man and I know that power without honour is always short-lived.'

'What else do you know?' Tapiwa asked.

'I know that while I washed you were watching me from that tree,' Tuloko said.

Tapiwa laughed. In her experience, every man she met fell in love with her at once. But Tuloko was different. 'What else do you know?' she asked again.

'I know that many men want you for their wife.'

'And you?'

'I only want what is best for my people,' Tuloko said.

Tapiwa was as impressed as she was taken aback by his honesty.

It was dark by the time Tapiwa led Tuloko into Munu's citadel. She took him to her father. She introduced him, saying, 'This is Tuloko, the chief of the Zamba. His army is camped a day's march from here, but he has come alone because he trusts your honour for his protection.'

Munu nodded. 'What do you want?' he asked, and Tuloko felt his heart quicken.

'I want you to leave my people's land,' he said. 'And I want to marry your daughter.'

Now it was the warlord king who laughed and Tuloko felt a terrible pain in his chest. But he stood upright and looked his enemy directly in the eye.

Munu turned to his daughter. 'Is this what you want, Tapiwa?'

'Yes.'

Then he said, 'I admire your bravery, Chief Tuloko. But I'll never leave this great citadel. As for my daughter? If you want to marry her, we must agree a bride price. You'll have to stay here while we negotiate.'

Later, Munu called his youngest son to him and told him

to put poison in Tuloko's cup. But Tapiwa overheard and warned her intended husband.

When they sat down to eat, therefore, Tuloko cunningly switched cups with his would-be murderer and, by morning, it was Munu's youngest son who lay dead in his sleeping house.

When Munu discovered this, he was distraught and didn't know what had gone wrong with his plan. Although he wanted to kill Tuloko, his daughter had appealed to his honour for the chief's protection. He said to his guest, 'We cannot negotiate today. A disaster has befallen my family. We must wait until after the funeral.'

'Of course,' Tuloko said.

After the funeral, Munu called his second son to him and gave him a dagger. He told him to stab Tuloko while he slept. But Tapiwa overheard and again she warned her intended husband.

When Munu's second son entered his sleeping house, Tuloko was ready for him and, though the son was very strong, Tuloko had the advantage of surprise and killed him with a knife of his own.

Munu was furious and demanded to know what had happened. The sound of his voice made Tuloko's heart echo through his body like a drum. But he stood upright and looked the warlord directly in the eye. He said, 'I was defending myself because your son came to murder me.'

Munu wanted to kill Tuloko right there and then. But the noise of the men's struggle had woken the whole household and they could see exactly what had happened. Besides, his own daughter had appealed to his honour. Again, therefore, Munu insisted the negotiations must wait until after his son's funeral.

'Of course,' Tuloko said.

After the funeral, Munu called his eldest son to him and

gave him a spear. He told him to kill Tuloko while they hunted. This time Tapiwa didn't overhear, but she guessed the plan and warned the Zamba chief of her father's intention.

The eldest son was almost as strong as the warlord king himself and, even though he was ready for him, Tuloko wasn't sure he could defeat him in a fight. When they went out to hunt, therefore, Tuloko was first to throw his spear and it ran the would-be murderer straight through. Tuloko carried the body back to the citadel on his shoulders.

Munu wailed at the sight of his last dead son and the sound made Tuloko nauseous and dizzy. But he stood upright and looked the warlord king directly in the eye. He said, 'I killed your son because he came to murder me on your orders. I know this because your daughter, Tapiwa, told me.'

Munu wanted to finish Tuloko there and then. But his entire army, including many Zamba, had now witnessed his dishonour and, though he was stricken with grief and betrayal, it was his own shame that left him unable to act.

After his eldest son's funeral, Munu called Tuloko to him. He said, 'You have taken my three sons from me and wish to have my daughter as well. Go back to your men and prepare for war. I will defeat your army on the battlefield and I will spare no one. I will take my daughter, who is now nothing to me but her womb, and she will marry one of her own. In time, I will return with my grandsons and we will conquer the entire Zamba nation.'

Tuloko replied, 'Before I came here, I believed your army was stronger than mine, but now I'm not so sure. Many of your army are Zamba and they have witnessed my honesty and your lies. You have lost your three generals. Are you certain your men will follow you into battle? I tell you again to leave this citadel and return to your own land.

'I want nothing but peace and prosperity for my own people. In exchange, therefore, I will let you take Tapiwa with you and she can marry a man of your choosing and give you grandchildren. They will not be of your line but at least they will be Gotzi.'

The warlord king thought about what Tuloko said and reluctantly agreed. The next morning Tuloko left the citadel before dawn.

When Tuloko returned to his army and told of what had happened, the *zakulu* ordered a great celebration to commemorate the chief's achievement – he had driven out the tyrant for the loss of only three lives. The party lasted two weeks and the western Zamba, now free of the warlord king, brought food and drink. But Tuloko didn't join in, preferring to spend his time in lonely regret.

The celebration ended on the fourteenth night when an extraordinary sound rang across the land, which made those who were drunk think they were sober and those who were sober think they were drunk. Every heart quickened. It was only Tuloko who knew that this was the sound of a father who had lost his children through his own fault.

Later, the story spread like wildfire. Munu and the other Gotzi had been crossing the great lake when Tapiwa threw herself into the deep water to drown. When the warlord king discovered this, his cry, which reached Tuloko's army at the distance of a day's march, reduced his vain, deserted citadel to rubble. When the Zamba found this out, many considered it a reason for further revelry. So Tuloko mourned alone.

28

Principles are ridiculous

Queenstown, Republic of Zambawi, 2008

For the second time that day David Pinner's plan was not going to plan. It was frustrating because it was such an excellent plan that it seemed inconceivable anyone could be blind to its merits. Indeed, it was so inconceivable that he had not prepared himself to conceive of it before now. His plan required concession and compromise, consideration and competence, consolidation and commitment. He had already said as much once that day. He had enjoyed the alliteration and been as astonished as he was disappointed by the unenthusiastic response.

Pinner thought back to his previous career and every cell he'd ever walked into in every detention centre or police station around the UK. He remembered the horror stories he'd heard from waif-like young women with cheekbones like scars and dark-eyed young men, defiant and damaged. He'd listened to those stories, he'd taken notes, he'd stood up and said, 'Right. This is the plan.' The gratitude he'd seen on those strained Slavic faces was almost tangible. The refugees had been helpless, they hadn't known what to do. But he had been there to help and knew what to do. He'd had a plan.

And he had a plan now too and it was being frustrated – *he* was being frustrated. It was not a feeling he was used to and it felt like a personal affront. Where was the gratitude? He liked gratitude.

Sitting in the anteroom outside Solomon Mhlanga's office in Zambawi's State House, Pinner's frustration manifested itself mostly in the form of wordless grunts, whinnies and snorts. And the more frustrated Pinner became, the greater volume, regularity and variety of his noises.

When he had first sat down, Mhlanga's secretary had thought the visiting UK minister cut quite a dash with his crazy hair and his Savile Row suit. In fact, she thought he looked rather more like a film star than a politician. However, she'd never before come across someone who expressed frustration in such a way and now assumed he must have some embarrassing digestive complaint. Consequently, she tactfully ignored him and Pinner became more frustrated and his noises grew louder still.

According to Jim Tulloh, the skeletal expat who was Pinner's sole contact in Zambawi, Solomon Mhlanga was one of President Adini's top aides. Frankly, Pinner didn't understand why he wasn't meeting the President himself, but Jim had claimed that wasn't possible.

'Does he know our position?' Pinner had protested. 'Does he know how important this is?'

'Yeah,' Jim said. 'I think he does.'

Pinner was beginning to find Jim's attitude frustrating too. This reluctant gofer appeared to find everything slightly funny. But perhaps this was just a by-product of his being half dead of half a dozen AIDS-related illnesses. Such a condition might, Pinner allowed, give one an unusual perspective.

Mhlanga's office overlooked the croquet lawn where Jim was currently losing the third consecutive game he'd played since Pinner and Jeremy had sat down to wait. Jim's opponent was a tall, broad-shouldered fellow in plaid tropical golfing shorts and a polo shirt. Pinner assumed he must be plainclothes security or similar. Whatever his role, he was giving his British opponent a serious croquet lesson. Every time it was his turn, he would successfully croquet one or other of Jim's balls, then send it way off the lawn and into the adjacent rose garden with a muscular flick of his mallet. Jim would disappear for some minutes among the Crystallines and Elizabeth Taylors before emerging, thrashing at the poor plants with his mallet and looking much like an escapee from a Japanese PoW camp after a year missing in the jungle.

Pinner looked at Jeremy and made another noise, this one involving tongue, teeth, small popping bubbles of saliva and an accompanying pained expression. Jeremy took this as his cue to stand up and approach the desk where the aide's secretary sat affixing small plastic tabs to pieces of paper. He leant forward on his hands so she'd know he meant business. He spoke to her in a peculiar stage whisper, though it was far from clear whom he feared might overhear. 'Excuse me, are we going to have to wait much longer?'

The secretary mirrored his tone: 'I do not think so.'

'Because the minister has a busy schedule.'

'I am sure.'

'Thank you.'

Jeremy straightened up and coughed into his hand, a gesture that strangely but indisputably denoted exactly how pleased he was with the job he'd just done. Then he returned to his seat next to Pinner and, though the minister had heard every word of the previous exchange, employed the same peculiar whisper to say, 'Shouldn't be too long now, sir.'

Pinner whinnied. That morning he had already endured an unproductive meeting with Joseph Phiri, opposition leader of the Democratic Movement. According to his FCO briefing, Phiri was a pluralist and free marketeer with broad support as a presidential alternative in the IMF, the World Bank and the wider international community (including, crucially, SADC and the United States). Within minutes of meeting him, however, Pinner had suspected he was motivated by little but vanity and self-interest (arguably a judgement the Englishman was peculiarly qualified to make).

It had started promisingly enough. Jim had driven Pinner to the Democratic Movement offices in Westgate, a residential neighbourhood not far from his city centre hotel. The offices were in a small compound behind padlocked gates with armed guards prowling in unspecific military garb and holding attack dogs straining at leather leashes. Phiri's assistant had met them in the courtyard and apologized for the show of security. He explained that the building had recently been firebombed by government supporters and pointed to the scorch marks that climbed one wall. He said that since the murders of parliamentary candidate Precious Kampampa and student activist Alice Chipinge everyone in the DM was more than a little on edge.

Phiri had stood in the doorway. He was a thick, squat man who wore spectacles, a serious expression and a bad polyester suit. He said, 'Sir David? I cannot tell you how pleased we are to have a minister of the British government here to support our fight.'

Pinner had shaken his hand and felt a fleeting thrill that had little to do with being mistaken for a knight of the realm. Rather, he was thrilled to find himself thrust into a noble struggle for democracy in which people were dying for their beliefs. He had never before been so close to the sharp edges of conviction politics and he vicariously enjoyed the sense of danger. But his excitement quickly passed.

Before the two men could start talking, Phiri made a great show of offering his guest a drink. It was a little early, even for Pinner, but Phiri insisted and eventually the minister accepted a small Scotch. Phiri explained that the whisky was Johnnie Walker Black Label. It was, he said, his favourite tipple, but he was down to his last bottle. He complained that it was hard to get this particular brand in Queenstown these days. He bemoaned the closure of the British High Commission because the former high commissioner, Sir Trevor Willets, had been accustomed to bring him back a bottle or two after every visit home.

Pinner nodded, but he was thoroughly confused as to his host's meaning. Surely he wasn't angling for some Scotch, was he? Pinner waited for him to go on, but Phiri just contemplated the bottom of his glass morosely. Eventually Pinner said, 'Black Label, you say? Well, I'm sure we can organize something.' And Phiri visibly brightened.

Phiri then told Pinner about his son, Tendai, who had been living in the UK for the last four years. He explained that since the 'farcical' presidential elections and the development of a 'systematic campaign of government-sponsored terrorism' against the Democratic Movement, it was impossible for Benjamin to return.

Pinner was confused. 'Who's Benjamin?'

'My son.'

'I thought his name was –'

'Tendai. It is. His English name is –'

'Benjamin.'

'Exactly,' Phiri confirmed. 'My country is no longer safe for my family,' he said flatly.

Pinner nodded and made some sympathetic noises. But Phiri continued, 'Honestly? For me, it's OK. I was hardly talking to the boy in any case. But for his mother it has been difficult.'

Pinner made more sympathetic noises but this time felt himself on firmer ground. He murmured something about the difficulties of father-son relationships, mentioned Preston, told Phiri they'd had their problems too, especially since his divorce.

Phiri said, 'Is that so?'

Pinner was finding the Democratic Movement leader difficult to read, but he suspected he might have made a connection, so he decided to move to the business at hand.

He explained his mission. He told Phiri he had to get Tranter out of jail and back home and he had to do it quickly. Development policy, with the African Authority at its centre, was a key part of UK government strategy, so the situation here in Zambawi was an embarrassment that needed to be resolved as soon as possible. He was, he said, authorized to offer the Zambawian government various incentives for their co-operation. Chief among these was that the British might broker top-level negotiations between the government and the Democratic Movement, which might in turn lead to the cessation of sanctions and pave the way for exploratory talks to rebuild relationships with international financial institutions, trade organizations and so forth.

Pinner leant forward conspiratorially. 'Of course, the intended outcome of these negotiations is fresh elections. But to achieve that will require concession and compromise, consideration and competence, consolidation and commitment.'

'I see.'

'On all sides,' Pinner added.

'I see.'

Phiri sat back in his chair and rested his chin thoughtfully on one fist. Then, using the index finger of his other hand, he indicated a framed certificate on the wall behind him. 'An honorary doctorate from the Ivy League University of Cornell,' he announced. 'Awarded to me for services to democracy.'

Pinner looked at him. He didn't know what to say to that, so he said, 'Congratulations.'

Phiri thanked him. Then he launched into a long and, frankly, rambling speech that Pinner struggled to follow.

Phiri observed that the majority of Democratic Movement funding was from American institutions with the word 'democracy' in their title. He said that receiving money for democracy from the Americans was a little like receiving money for dentistry from Coca-Cola. He quoted Winston Churchill (the one about democracy being the most serviceable of the unworkable) and pointed out that the great man's words were not, in fact, a ringing endorsement of a political system. He claimed that an updated version of Churchill's maxim might incorporate the idea that democracy had only proved truly workable over any prolonged period in societies of considerable and widespread wealth and comfort; and, indeed, that in no such societies had any other form of government yet been tried. He said that he remained convinced that true multi-party democracy was in the long-term best interests of his nation and that he was the man to deliver it. He also said that he was unconvinced that this intention was best served by holding new democratic elections. In conclusion, he explained that the current situation, in which the President was increasingly isolated and he, Phiri, enjoyed growing international support, was quite the most progressive and most likely to produce a democratic outcome, albeit possibly through undemocratic means, which – he smiled – were perhaps not for discussion at this point.

Pinner stared at him. He was thoroughly bewildered. 'Right,' he said. 'Can I get this straight?'

Phiri crossed his legs and nodded his assent. 'Please.'

'The elections?'

'Yes.'

'They were rigged?'

'Most certainly.'

'But you don't want new elections?'

'No.'

'Because you wouldn't win?'

'No.'

'But you might yet come to power by other means that you currently don't want to discuss?'

'Precisely.'

'Right. Like what?'

Phiri shrugged enigmatically. 'The President is under some pressure.'

'So sanctions are working?'

'If you like.'

Now it was Pinner's turn to nod. He wasn't sure he fully understood what Phiri was on about, but as far as he could see it didn't stand in the way of UK-brokered top-level discussions between the DM and the government.

'Right,' Pinner said again. 'As far as I can see, this doesn't stand in the way of UK-brokered top-level discussions between the DM and the government.'

Phiri sighed and shook his head. 'I'm afraid we can't possibly commit to such talks until the government commits to a date for fresh democratic elections.'

'What?'

'The last presidential elections were not free and fair. How can we possibly engage in dialogue with a government that is not committed to the democratic ideal? To do so would be to grant it a legitimacy that it does not deserve.'

Pinner frowned. 'But you don't want fresh elections?'

'No.'

Pinner's frown deepened. He said, 'What?'

Phiri said, 'What?'

'So . . .' Pinner began '. . . so let me be clear about this. You won't take part in talks – which will have, we may agree, no meaningful outcome – without the government calling fresh elections, which it never will and which you don't want anyway.'

'Exactly.'

'But that's ridiculous.'

Phiri drained his Scotch. 'No, it's principle.'

'Well, it's a ridiculous principle.'

'Come now, Sir David,' Phiri said again. 'All principles are ridiculous but your own – it was the British who taught us that.'

Pinner revisited this conversation with Phiri as he watched the latest game unfold on the presidential croquet lawn, Jim off in the rosebushes, his opponent smoking a lazy cigarette, cross-legged on the grass. Inevitably the meeting had ended in impasse with Phiri expressing gushing gratitude for 'Sir David's' presence, but absolutely no desire to make use of it.

Pinner wondered about Phiri's undiscussed plans to come to power without election. Was he really just referring to sanctions or was he actually planning some kind of coup? He chuckled to himself. If Phiri *was* planning a coup, perhaps the British government *should* have sent Tranter (or similar) to flog him some weapons, after all. Or perhaps not since, as far as Pinner could tell, Phiri was hardly more amenable than President Adini anyway.

In fact, the more Pinner thought about it, the more he realized that the Democratic Movement leader was symptomatic of his recently discovered dislike of Africans and, though his distaste remained instinctive and obtuse, he began to see something of a pattern to its impulses.

The trouble with Africans, Pinner thought, was that they could never look you straight in the eye. Either they fawned with the *faux*-deference of the yes-boss mentality, or they talked down to you as if you were some kind of mug who could never understand them anyway. And this was true of everyone, from Phiri to the waiter at Pinner's hotel who couldn't (or wouldn't) understand that the guest wanted his coffee with cold milk on the side.

Of course, had Pinner had the time to think about it, he might have grasped that no attitude of submission or superiority would have worked without his own attitude of superiority or submission in return. But he didn't have time to think about it because, finally, Solomon Mhlanga emerged from his office and, taking no notice of his British visitors, began speaking to his secretary in a genuine whisper that, despite his best efforts, Pinner couldn't overhear.

Mhlanga was younger than Pinner had expected, late twenties at most, and for some reason that irritated him further. However, it didn't irritate him nearly as much as the fact that the presidential aide stood there, with his back to them, muttering to his secretary who, Pinner could see, was repeatedly, and with growing agitation, flashing her eyes towards himself and Jeremy.

Pinner had intended to project an air of indignation at this first encounter, but now knew that wouldn't do at all and instead wheeled out his most charming, slab-toothed smile.

'Gentlemen,' Mhlanga said, and extended his hand.

Pinner stood up, shook it and simultaneously checked his watch. 'I'm sorry, was our meeting not for three o'clock?' He glanced at Jeremy. 'Or was my assistant mistaken?'

Mhlanga looked at him, assessing the situation. Was there a flicker of anger behind his eyes? If so, it was no match for Pinner's teeth and bounced right off. He dropped his chin. 'I cannot apologize enough,' he said. 'I'm afraid I had no idea of your visit until Mr Jim Tulloh's call. Naturally, in the past, we would have expected initial contact from the High Commission, but of course that is no longer possible. However, as soon as I knew you were coming, Mr Pinner, I cleared my diary as far as was practicable. Unfortunately, as I'm sure you know better than I, the day-to-day business of government waits for no man.'

'Of course,' Pinner said. He looked at Mhlanga but the aide wouldn't meet his eye. There was an uncomfortable pause. Pinner filled it by sniffing and clearing his throat. Then he said, 'Excellent weather you're having. Quite a summer.'

'This is our winter,' Mhlanga said flatly. 'You are on the other side of the world here.'

'Indeed?' Pinner murmured, as if this had come as some surprise. Then, 'I suppose I am. Indeed.'

Finally, Mhlanga reanimated as if someone had pushed a button. He lifted his eyes, tilted his head and gestured towards the open door behind him. 'Would you come into my office?'

Pinner lifted his hand, signalling acquiescence. 'Please. Lead the way.'

Mhlanga expanded his gesture towards the door. 'No, no, sir,' he said. 'After you.'

'No, really,' Pinner said, his smile frozen as though the wind had changed. 'After you.'

Mhlanga headed into his office with Pinner and Jeremy

following, single file. The secretary brought up the rear, holding her notebook in front of her mouth to hide her giggles.

```
Insert document
Transcript: meeting between Solomon Mhlanga and
David Pinner (records of the Presidential
office), 31 May 2008
```

<u>Present: Solomon Mhlanga (SM), David Pinner (DP), Jeremy
Shorter (JS), Nyasha Mombe (NM) Time: 16.17 p.m.</u>

JS: Excuse me? Sir? Do you mind if I record the
       meeting? It's simply for our records.

SM: Is this a microcassette?

JS: Digital. It's very high quality so, if you speak
       normally, it should pick up everything OK.

SM: One day they will invent digital politicians, no
       doubt. But for now, you have your digital
       device and I have Mrs Mombe.

DP: Shall we get down to business?

SM: Of course.

DP: You have arrested a British citizen, Gordon
       Tranter.

SM: He has been detained, yes. Would you like
       some tea?

DP: No. Thank you.

SM: Coffee?

DP: No. Really.

SM: What about you, Mr Shorter? Can we get you
       tea or coffee? Or a cool drink, perhaps?

JS: I'm fine, thanks.

SM: Are you sure?

JS: Well, perhaps some water, then.

SM: Mrs Mombe? Would you fetch our guest some water?

 We will wait for Mrs Mombe's return to continue our conversation.

Time: 16.22 p.m.

SM: Are you quite sure you wouldn't like a drink, Minister?

DP: Quite sure.

SM: Our climate makes it very easy to dehydrate, no?

DP: Gordon Tranter.

SM: He has been detained on suspicion of illegal arms trafficking, espionage and terrorism, pending further investigation.

DP: He hasn't been charged?

SM: No. Our law allows any foreign national suspected of terrorist offences to be detained without charge.

DP: For how long?

SM: Indefinitely at presidential discretion, subject to Supreme Court review every ninety days.

DP: I'm sorry, Mr Mhlanga, but that's simply not acceptable.

SM: Not acceptable? Whatever can you mean? Like many former British colonies, we still look to Westminster for a lead. In this instance, is the ruling of our Internal Security Act, 2003, not similar to Part 4 of the UK's own Anti-terrorism, Crime and Security Act, 2001?

DP: Actually, you'll find that Part 4 was overturned by the House of Lords in 2004.

SM: Is that so, Minister? Well, in our country we believe in strong-arm tactics when it comes to questions of terrorism. The War on Terror will not be won with harsh language, is it not right?

DP: Mr Mhlanga, Gordon Tranter is a high-profile and respected British businessman. Do you really believe such a person would be involved in – well, whatever it is you think he was involved in?

SM: (inaudible)

DP: I'm sorry?

SM: I said, yes. I don't wish to be indelicate, Minister, but the British establishment has something of a record of such behaviour, does it not?

      Look, let us get down to brass tacks, as it were: this Tranter is currently in the Zambawian criminal-justice system and he will at some point be released or he will be charged and stand trial. I cannot believe that you have come all the way here simply for me to tell you something you already know.

DP: No.

SM: So what exactly may I do for you?

DP: Jeremy, could you pass me that file?

JS: (inaudible)

DP: *That* one. Right.

      The British government is eager to secure Gordon Tranter's release as quickly as possible with the minimum of fuss.

      You don't need me to tell you about Zambawi's problems. But having defaulted on your debts, with exports devastated by sanctions and inflation running at –

SM: Excuse me, Minister.

DP: I'm sorry?

SM: Excuse me, but I do not need you to tell me about the problems we face.

DP: Right. Quite. Quite right. Well –

I assume it goes without saying that, thanks to the historical relationship between our two nations and the UK's international standing with regard to development issues in general and in Africa specifically, the British government is ideally placed to ease Zambawi's reintegration into the international community.

In return for your co-operation over this Tranter affair, we will be – how should I phrase this? – a *supportive friend*. And, to exemplify this and to initiate this new kind of relationship, we would like to offer to instigate and broker talks between your government and the Democratic Movement with the intention of overcoming the impasse that has so troubled your international partners. Naturally, it will not be easy. Indeed, any such talks will require concession and compromise, consideration and –

SM: Allow me to stop –

DP: And competence –

SM: I am sorry to interrupt your most eloquent speechifying, Minister, but allow me to stop you there as I have another meeting scheduled and I will have to bring this conversation to a close.

DP: I'm sorry?

SM: Really, do not apologize.

There are many observations I could make, but I will limit myself to just these.

The UK is not a *supportive friend* of my country, nor has it ever been so. From the

colonial era through to the present day, the UK
has never acted towards Zambawi motivated
by anything but self-interest and that is the case
now. Your desire to secure Tranter's release is
presumably for internal political reasons. I don't
know. We in Zambawi are not interested in the
internal politics of a fellow sovereign state.
Perhaps this is a position you should adopt also.

Tranter is in our judicial system and I can
promise you it will treat him fairly. But he will
remain in our system and that is that.

DP: You're really not being very sensible about this.

SM: No? I am a mere functionary, Minister, assigned
to convey to you our government's position.

JS: In which case, do you not think it would be
advisable for us to meet with President Adini
himself?

SM: I can put in the request, Mr Shorter. But, of
course, the President has a very busy schedule.

DP: (inaudible) – unelected official – (inaudible)

SM: Excuse me?

DP: I want to see him. I want to see Gordon
Tranter.

SM: Again, I will put in a request, but that is subject
to presidential approval.

DP: I want to see him, Mr Mhlanga.

SM: Yes, Minister. I heard you the first time.

Now, I do apologize, but I have some other
matters that I must attend –

Are you OK, Minister?

DP: I – (inaudible)

JS: What the Minister is trying to say is that we
hope you will convey our profound
dissatisfaction with this situation to President
Adini.

SM: Your dissatisfaction?

JS: Our *profound* dissatisfaction, Mr Mhlanga.

SM: As you wish, Mr Shorter. Gentlemen? . . . Are
you a football fan, Minister? Mr Shorter?

JS: Yes, I am.

SM: And who is your team?

JS: United.

SM: United? The Red Devils? Me too! You know,
I would do anything for Rooney's autograph.
I could even have your man released.

JS: (inaudible)

SM: I was only joking, Mr Shorter.

Time: 16.31 p.m.
Ends

30

Insert document
'The diary of a local gentleman', 17 May 1901
(Empire Museum, Bristol), anon.

I write this by the Burr, propped in what has already become
my 'usual spot' – the worn crook of an oak where dozens of
men must have found rest over the last century or more.
Rarely have I felt so at ease. There is truly no place on earth
so blessed as the English countryside; and the county of
Gloucestershire during an uncommon warm spell is
assuredly the blessed of the blessed!

Today, I have idled away the afternoon with my
charcoals: first, in attempting to perfect the sunlight that
dapples the water through the leaves of beech and ash;
second, in representing the pretty features of Miss Lizzie
Nott, who has been my constant companion these last few
days. I own that she has been a delight, and the ideal foil for
my habitual cussedness. This is a young woman who knows
her own mind but remains a humble and attentive listener.
She is curious, but innocently so, and speaks plainly, without
affectation or agenda. Most of all, she appears to regard life
in all its variety as a great adventure to be approached head
on, with vigour and good humour.

The only misfortune confronting poor Lizzie (although
she's hardly the sort to complain) is that here in Fry Norton
she is starved of appropriate company. Although it may be
only vanity that allows me to imagine myself any sort of
substitute, it has been my pleasure to attempt to make up
the shortfall.

I have already told Lizzie countless stories of my experiences in Africa. She has listened with interest and, though she knows nothing of warfare, has asked questions that display an uncannily sympathetic spirit. To lift our mood, she in turn has regaled me with terrific fantasies of her future travels, of how she might one day journey to India and write a book, hunt a rogue tiger and be accepted as a daughter by one of the great Moguls!

Though she can't have been more than a child when her father first brought her to live here, I fancy she misses city life for she asks me question after question about Bristol. She wants to know the smallest detail of current fashions – of 'Watteau' backs, 'Pouter Pigeon' blouses and the like – as well as the latest melodramas that are playing in the theatres and the latest songs popular at a tea dance. Of course, I am quite the worst person to ask about such matters, but I have done my best to answer each and every enquiry.

In times past, when my Catherine has attempted to engage me upon similar subjects, I have generally found them tiresome. I admit, however, that I find Lizzie Nott's enthusiasm unusually infectious. She has none of that 'Parisian' world-weariness that the ladies of today mistakenly regard as the height of sophistication. Just now, she said to me, 'Do you know the Talbot? I can quite picture you, with your mama on your arm, strolling down Victoria Street and pausing for tea and cake.' I hardly need to add that Lizzie Nott has never seen Victoria Street, let alone the Talbot Hotel!

Although undoubtedly innocent, I would not wish to paint Miss Lizzie Nott as a silly girl, for nothing could be further from the truth. The other day, while we sat in the very same 'usual spot', we were approached by a young gentleman fresh from shooting. He wore a cap, a thin moustache and a Norfolk coat and I knew at once that this was Codrington from the Manor House. I greeted him warmly, though, truth be told, I cared little for his bearing.

Perhaps it is the soldier in me, but I find my judgement in such matters rarely falters. Suffice it to say that he struck me as a young fellow rather too eager to assert his credentials.

He was polite enough, albeit with a certain mannered unconcern. His handshake was limp and he made a great show of struggling to understand my speech. The wretched stammer from which I've occasionally suffered these last months is certainly compounded in the company of strangers, but the way he reacted to me, with a kind of bewildered disinterest, you might have thought I was speaking Spanish.

I'll wager his indifferent attitude was as genuine towards me, the curious lame stranger, as it was put on for the benefit of my companion. There is no ignoring that Lizzie's a beautiful girl and, in attempting to do so, the fellow looked more than a little foolish. Unable to take his 'indifferent' eyes off her, he told us that he'd enjoyed quite a morning's shooting and had, in fact, bagged a peregrine falcon.

Like an actor awaiting his cue, Codrington's keeper, who stood behind him, promptly swung the sack from his shoulder and produced said bird for our admiration.

'Something of a rara avis,' the young gentleman announced proudly.

Lizzie, however, was less than impressed. 'A rare bird indeed, Mr Codrington,' she said. 'And if we can't rely on our oldest families to protect their numbers, how shall we expect ordinary folk to do likewise?'

Codrington looked thoroughly chastened and begged her forgiveness. She granted it too, but only after securing a promise that he would never again –

[Fire damage has rendered the rest of this page illegible]

– from my observations, have begun to compile a list of essential characteristics and mores. I shall add to these with time in the belief that eventually their sum might equal one true Englishman!

Of course, I recognize this as a somewhat frivolous intention. It is hardly a scientific process and the Fry Norton morris men cannot be regarded as the beginning and end of our nation. But this shouldn't necessarily negate the value of my suppositions. Besides, isn't there scientific precedent in the 'control' element of any experiment and, likewise, philosophic precedent in the 'Platonic form'?

Honesty – these peasants of Fry Norton are as honest as the day is long. They may complain that Young Mr Codrington now keeps the manor's rabbits for the house, but they would sooner swim to France than contemplate a night's poaching. In fact, I don't believe a single man among them would consider killing a pheasant found in his own yard.

As for housebreaking or robbery or any kind of common violence, they simply do not exist.

Song – scarcely a quarter-hour is allowed to pass without someone or other beginning a song. I could not vouch for the men's merit as singers, but the sheer volume of their repertoire is quite extraordinary. Can so many 'ravening lasses' truly have been lost to sickness, soldier or tar?

I confess the enthusiasm with which the men greet each song was lost on me until Stone hit upon one whose simple words chimed with my own feelings. I noted down the final verse as follows:

> Now if the world was of one people
> Every living thing would die
> Or if I prove false unto my jewel
> Or any way my love deny
> The world shall change and be most strange
> If ever I my mind remove
> My heart is with her altogether
> Though I live not where I love.

Of course, I do not for one second suggest any literal interpretation of this song. However, the combination of its sentiments with the melancholic tune and my own search for 'my jewel' of nationhood have certainly given me pause.

The 'natural order' – to hear these fellows talk of the hardships of the winter past and the price paid for coffee or fetched for a pack of Cotswolds coarse wool, one might imagine certain socialistic tendencies and, given the chance, they like to harp on about Cromwell (who passed through every village in the area, if one believes the mythology). Nevertheless, I have rarely come across a bunch so keen to affirm the 'natural order' and their place within it. As an example of this, I shall again return to the question of rabbits trapped at the big house, for I truly believe that had Codrington simply explained his decision to the men they'd have been beside themselves with gratitude that he had even deigned to speak with them.

These fellows appear to bathe in the attention and approval of their betters as if it were some kind of divine light. I have already seen one gentleman stop to picnic in the 'leaze' (as they call it) next to the sign for Fairford. When his groom went looking for water and horse feed, the locals fell over themselves to be ingratiating. More to the point, they later talked of the gent's noble bearing in whispers that were almost awed. Indeed, I have heard breeders discuss their prize stud with less reverence!

The exception to this rule is Chavney, the only one among them with any capitalistic tendencies. The son of labouring stock, he has made himself a business stitching together the odds and ends of sacks and selling them on at a profit. Although sometimes wary in my company, he is a self-evidently impressive young man who might find decent employ in a city trade.

Sense of humour – for all the beauty of the natural world, there is no denying that the life of a labouring man and his family is one of hardship, even that of a fellow in steady work. He sees no meat but bacon, must tend his allotment upon return from the fields, and faces old age with little prospect of any comfort.

However, as insinuated in my previous 'characteristics', these admirable fellows spend little time bemoaning their lot, more making light of it with a quick-wittedness that belies their education (or lack thereof). Indeed, I sometimes fancy that there is some kind of unspoken contest among them to make the best joke.

If this were the case, then there can be no doubt that the champion would again be Chavney, who has a comic skill that would not be out of place on the stage. Just yesterday, Sam Jessop was complaining that his wife was still not able to buy any candles, so I explained that there was a nationwide shortage on account of the war.

Chavney spoke up as fast as a whip. 'I own you military men do know best, sir,' he said, 'but are you quite sure you should be fighting these battles by candlelight?'

We all laughed uproariously.

I believe I have almost achieved the acceptance of the Fry Norton morris men. I have watched them practise and familiarized myself with their figures. Indeed, I would have liked to learn the steps myself were it not for my disability.

My burgeoning friendship with Lizzie has undoubtedly aided my accommodation. She has accompanied me to most practices and she, more than any, has persuaded Chavney to accept my note-taking and even to explain the roots of each song and dance.

I suspect that Chavney would not be able to deny Lizzie the world and I sometimes fear that she encourages him unfairly. I have even considered that I should broach the matter with her, but our relationship is hardly close enough for such a conversation and, besides, I'm not sure I'm possessed of sufficient delicacy. I might, of course, warn her father, but that seems like a step too far and, frankly, I am not inclined to deny what is most likely no more than youthful affection on his part. Indeed, if the truth be told, I long for such carefree passion myself. How the world seems to weigh on my shoulders! How strange to think that Lizzie is probably no more than five years my junior and Chavney most likely my age! How old I feel and what I would give for one drop of Lizzie's vivacity!

31
Of mice and men

Queenstown, Republic of Zambawi, 2008
Upon returning to the State House car park, Jim Tulloh found the UK's junior foreign minister stalking a circle around the Lazer and asking rhetorical questions that began, variously, 'Who the fuck', 'Why the fuck', 'What the fuck' and 'How the fuck': 'Who the fuck does he think he is? Why the fuck do they want this stand-off? What the fuck do they think they'll gain? How the fuck do they think they'll win?'

If Pinner was determined to throw his toys out of the pram, then Jeremy was trotting behind, loyally picking them up: 'He's just playing games. They're buying time, taking a position. They think they're holding a trump card.'

Pinner stopped abruptly in his tracks and Jeremy almost ran into the back of him. 'Do these people know what's good for them?' he asked, and then, seeing the approaching Jim, addressed the same question directly to him: 'Do these people know what's good for them?'

Jim ummed and erred for a second before he said, 'I know I don't.'

He hadn't meant anything much by this, simply to deflect the minister's question. However, his answer seemed to flummox Pinner, who was now lost for words. 'No. Right,' he said eventually.

Jim unlocked the car and they climbed in, Shorter in the passenger seat, Pinner behind. Jim kept an eye on the minister in the rear-view mirror as he slowly eased the car down the drive of State House. 'Your meeting didn't go well, then?'

'You could say that,' Pinner said shortly, and stared fixedly out of the window. He now seemed set on some private seething.

'Bad day for the Brits, then,' Jim said breezily. 'I lost at croquet as well. Zambawi two, England nil.'

Neither the minister nor his assistant seemed receptive to such joviality, so Jim concentrated on the road ahead as he swung the car into Presidential Drive. After a minute or two, however, he couldn't resist turning to Jeremy and asking exactly what had happened.

Jeremy glanced nervously over his shoulder, but Pinner was still staring out of the window at the cherry trees flying by on Enoch Adini Avenue, so he felt able to deliver a detailed précis of the meeting with Mhlanga, from the hour's wait to the final, galling refusal to allow them even to see the prisoner, Gordon Tranter, without presidential approval.

Jim listened. Then he said, 'Well, at least visiting Tranter's not going to be a problem. I asked the President myself. He said it'd be fine.'

Now Pinner's attention snapped back to the front seats. 'You spoke to Adini?'

'Of course.'

'When did you speak to Adini?'

'What do you mean, when did I speak to him? I was playing croquet with him. You saw me. You must have done. You were watching from the window on the first floor.'

'*That* was Adini?' Pinner spluttered, 'In a pair of fucking shorts?' before the words were squashed beneath a kind of primeval growl that rose from the pit of his stomach. At the same time, his features began to twitch, as if each and every muscle were trying to direct his face towards a different expression.

Jim had assumed he'd done the right thing in taking the opportunity proffered by his occasional croquet match with the President to discuss the imprisonment of Tranter and the visit of the British politician. Pinner, however, clearly thought otherwise and now lost any remaining scraps of his temper. It was Jim, therefore, who bore the brunt of waves of barely comprehensible invective from the seat behind. He was, it seemed, stupid, irresponsible, incompetent, unpatriotic and ultimately to blame for any possible downturn in the minister's career, which had, to this point, been on a uniform and indisputable upward trajectory.

Jim listened placidly. He was the ideal target for such a torrent of abuse since he largely agreed with the minister's accusations except, perhaps, the last. However, when he pulled into the dusty sports club off Saddam Hussein Boulevard, he finally cut Pinner off, asking him to watch his language in front of the kids.

'Kids?' Pinner snorted. 'What kids?'

'Tefadzwa and Presley,' Jim explained. 'Football practice. Queenstown Buffaloes under-twelves.'

'Oh, for fuck's sake!' Pinner exclaimed, just as Presley opened the back door. Then, 'Sorry.'

Thereafter, for the rest of the journey back to the hotel, the minister made a valiant effort to adjust his humour. Sandwiched between the two boys, he squashed his anger and listened indulgently to their tales of goals scored and tackles won. If his experience of political campaigning had taught him anything, it was to feign interest in children and, watching from the front, Jim began to warm to him for the first time.

At the hotel, a doorman wearing a magenta cap and a uniform with gold-tasselled epaulettes opened the doors. Jeremy got out and the minister gamely clambered over Tefadzwa, patting him on the head and saying, 'A hat-trick next week, eh?'

Jim signalled to the two boys to stay put, then got out too. He called to Pinner before he reached the revolving doors: 'Minister?'

Pinner turned. His anger seemed to have disappeared without trace. He was wearing a defeated expression.

Jim said, 'I'll arrange to take you to Gwezi.'

'Gwezi?'

'Where Tranter's being held. I can drive there.'

Pinner shrugged. 'OK. Thanks.'

Jim produced a packet of cigarettes from his shirt pocket, removed one and lit it. From the back seat, Presley banged on the window and wagged his finger. Jim ignored him, sucked deeply and blew perfect, indulgent smoke rings. 'Look,' he said, 'I've got a couple of friends coming round for some food. You should come too. They'll give you a different perspective on this place. I'll pick you up around seven.'

Jeremy looked at Pinner. Pinner looked at Jim. He said, 'OK.'

In fact, Jim didn't turn up till almost eight. He found Pinner and Jeremy in the hotel bar. Jeremy was nursing a beer and Pinner, unimpressed with the selection of Scotch (it seemed Phiri had a point), had already sunk three V-and-Ts. His mood had lightened a little more with each one.

Jim apologized. He explained that one of the girls had been late home and, though it wasn't anything to worry about, he'd hung around to help Sylvia relax. Then, when the girl got back, Sylvia had lost her rag, so he'd hung around to help the other kids relax. Then, when Sylvia had finished shouting, he'd hung around to help the girl relax. 'That's the trouble with having eighteen children,' he said ruefully. 'Someone's always tense.'

'You've got eighteen children?' Pinner asked.

'Yeah. Well, they're not mine, obviously.'

'Not yours?' Pinner chuckled to himself, as if something were funny. 'What? Do you run some type of orphanage?'

'Yeah,' Jim said. 'Well, my wife does. Didn't I tell you that? I assumed you knew. I mean, this afternoon, whose boys did you think they were?'

'Right,' the minister muttered. Then, 'I didn't think. Good for you. That must be very . . .' Apparently unable to decide upon an appropriate adjective to complete the sentence, he left it hanging and drained his fourth drink.

They arrived at Mama's House in the middle of junior bathtime, and as soon as Jim opened the front door, a naked child dripping water careered into him leaving wet marks on his thighs.

'Julius!' An older girl stalked around the corner brandishing a large towel, but stopped abruptly at the sight of Jim. 'Sorry,' she said, wrapping Julius up in one smooth movement.

Jim said, 'No problem.' Then, gesturing to Pinner and Jeremy, 'Mercy, these are guests from England – Mr Pinner and Mr Shorter.'

Mercy was too shy to look at the visitors and, eyes locked on the floor, made an awkward little curtsy.

'It's always a bit frenetic at this time of day, isn't it?' Jim said.

'Yes,' Mercy said, still not looking up.

As if to confirm Jim's point, another small boy appeared from a side room. This one was wearing just underpants and holding a plastic sword. As Mercy's hands were full of Julius, the newcomer began to slap at her defenceless legs with the sword, shouting, 'Let go or I kill you! Let go or I kill you!'

Jim turned to his guests. 'Let's go through to the back,' he said, smiling. 'Believe it or not, it'll all quieten down in about half an hour.'

'Sounds great,' Pinner said warmly.

Jim's friends had already arrived. They were sitting out on the veranda overlooking the vegetable garden. Behind them, on a trestle table, plates, cutlery, bread and salad were set out; the meat, keeping warm on the barbecue, smelt good.

Lars Larsson was the chief executive of a Danish NGO that funded community projects throughout the country. He was a big man with big features and big hands. He had thinning blond hair that barely concealed the pink of a sun-scorched head. His blond eyebrows seemed fixed in a position of semi-amusement that was in no way matched by the rest of his demeanour. He was returning home to Copenhagen next week, having lately resigned his position.

Eddy Kotto was the editor of the *Gazette*. Jim introduced him as 'the President's last remaining independent apologist', which was clearly an in-joke but one the journalist no longer found funny. Around forty, he wore spectacles, a sleeveless sweater and his hair in neat, thin dreadlocks that bobbed on the collar of his shirt. He also wore an immobile earnest expression, which made his broad smile, when it came, quite disarming.

Jim introduced Pinner: 'The minister's here to deal with this Tranter business. He's been at State House today, so go easy on him.'

They all laughed.

The minister and his assistant settled into wicker chairs and Jim fixed them drinks. Perhaps it was just the alcohol, but Pinner felt more relaxed than at any point since he'd left the Executive Club lounge at Heathrow. Or perhaps it was the company, because he had the impression that he was with men of at least comparable intellect and manner. Even the African seemed more or less companionable – a thought that, when combined with his rapport with the junior footballers that afternoon, allowed Pinner to grow ever more comfortable with his self-diagnosed phobia.

Returning with Pinner's ice, Jim said, 'Come on! Help yourselves to some food.'

'And your wife?' Pinner asked.

'She's just finishing the kids' bedtime. She'll eat later. Really. Tuck in.'

Over dinner, Pinner told Jim's friends about his meetings with Phiri and Mhlanga.

Of the former, Kotto was scornful. 'He's just an opportunist, that one, a stooge for the Americans and you Brits. No one in this city takes him seriously.'

'Young people do,' Larsson countered. 'The students take him seriously.'

Kotto shook his head. 'There's three things you have to remember about students,' he said, and counted them off on his fingers. 'One, they are too young to remember independence. Two, they always protest against the status quo. Three, they'll take anything seriously. They take rap music seriously, for God's sake.'

As for Mhlanga, Pinner was disappointed to discover that neither had anything but respect for the presidential aide. 'He's a shrewd operator.' Larsson nodded. 'Very capable. Very competent.'

Pinner took a mouthful of *boerewors*. 'If the government's so competent,' he said, spitting meat, 'why the hell are they arresting Tranter? Is it a bargaining chip they want? If so, it's short-term gain. It only damages their international reputation further. Isn't that right, Jeremy?'

'Yes, sir.'

'And if they're playing to a domestic audience, I have to ask: is it really worth it?' He put his fork down and looked between the two men.

Larsson shook his head. 'Who knows what they're thinking? I've given up trying to understand this place. That's why I'm leaving.'

Pinner turned to Eddy Kotto, who sat back in his chair and shrugged. 'Maybe Tranter's guilty,' he said. Pinner let slip one of his trademark snorts and Kotto continued quickly, 'And maybe he isn't. But maybe they think he is. I have three principles for you . . .' He held up three fingers.

To this point, Jim Tulloh hadn't really been listening. After serving himself some food, he'd produced a plastic case with a dozen different compartments from each of which he counted out various pills, then swallowed them in ones and twos with his beer. Now, however, he looked up and said to Pinner, 'Oh, God, here we go. One thing you should know about Eddy is that he loves his numbered lists. You should read his editorials in the *Gazette* – they're full of them.'

'Number one,' Kotto continued, unperturbed and wagging his index finger, 'I call the "Saddam Insane Principle", which holds that when a Western government makes a major foreign-policy fuck-up it promotes the point of view that whatever leader is at the heart of said fuck-up is deranged, deluded or plain doo-lally. As soon as they began to say Adini was mad, therefore, I had my doubts. It is the Saddam Insane Principle. Do you understand?'

Pinner sniffed and clinked the ice cubes in his glass. 'Go on.'

Kotto lifted his middle finger towards the British minister. 'Number two is the "False Rhinoceros Principle".'

'Sounds intriguing,' the minister said drily.

'Indeed it is. Did you know that in the sixteenth century the king of Portugal received the gift of a rhinoceros? It caused quite a stir at court, as you can imagine, and within weeks a sketch of the beast had reached as far as Nuremberg. There, a German artist created a woodcut based on that sketch. The woodcut print was reproduced countless times. Unfortunately the sketch from which the artist worked was anatomically inaccurate, including armour-like plates on the rhinoceros's body and a small additional horn at the animal's throat. How-ever, for almost four hundred years (and despite evidence to the contrary), most people believed this was what a rhinoceros looked like. Indeed, as late as 1956, the artist Salvador Dali created a sculpture of a rhinoceros that still included that false additional horn.'

Kotto paused, and Pinner said, 'That's a fascinating story,' if only because he felt he had to say something.

'Isn't it? It seems people's capacity to believe that with which they are familiar and comfortable is almost limitless.'

'And which people exactly are you talking about?'

'All people!' Kotto made an expansive gesture, but then allowed a certain coyness to play around his eyes. 'Although, naturally I believe that we Africans are more likely to know the real appearance of a rhinoceros. After all, we are not only more likely to have seen one, but also less likely to have seen the erroneous woodcut.'

Pinner smiled and ran a finger around the rim of his glass. 'Very witty, Mr Kotto. I'll certainly try to bear it in mind. But . . .'

Kotto held up a silencing hand, which he then turned into three fingers held aloft. 'I'm sorry, Minister. Allow me briefly to state my third and final principle. It is the "Marry My Sister Principle". Let me ask you this, Mr Pinner. Who would you prefer to marry your sister –'

'I don't have a sister.'

'Use your imagination, then. Who would you prefer to marry your sister: the President of Zambawi or the President of the United States?'

Pinner snorted with amusement. 'Why can't she marry an Englishman?'

'You are making my argument precisely. But just imagine she must marry one of the two presidents.'

'Ha!' Pinner said. 'Then I must plump for our American friend.'

'Exactly!'

'Exactly what?'

'If I were asked the same question, I would choose President Adini every time. Of course, I would have doubts about the marital suitability of either candidate, so I would choose Adini because he is more similar to me and I would feel more comfortable in trusting him with my sister.'

'And what if the Americans elect this black fellow?'

'Exactly! Again, you make my argument.'

Pinner chuckled, expressing an amusement similar to the kind an indulgent parent might display for a child's magic trick. 'You're quite the raconteur, Mr Kotto, but what exactly is your point?'

Kotto cracked one of his warmest smiles. 'Really, Minister, you must try to keep up! My point is obvious. When Gordon Tranter is arrested on charges of espionage, your natural inclination, before any evidence is taken into account, is to trust the Englishman and consider the President a lunatic. My natural inclination is the complete opposite.'

Pinner raised an eyebrow. 'So I'm not capable of objectivity?'

Kotto's smile stretched wider still. 'Of course not. None of us are.'

Pinner would have liked to continue this conversation, to have defended himself as a free thinker capable of weighing a decision and making up his own mind. After all, he was a lawyer by background, a profession that relied upon the rigorous application of abstracted principle irrespective of personal interest. But the discussion was now interrupted by the appearance of a large, coffee-coloured woman wearing a headscarf and an expansive Java print dress. She emerged from the house onto the veranda with a swish of cloth and swing of hip that conveyed unquestionable authority and made it impossible not to look at her.

Jim Tulloh stood up. He said, 'This is my wife, Sylvia, Minister.'

She didn't look at Jim but made a beeline for Pinner, who stood up too and offered her his hand. He said, 'Call me David, Mrs Tulloh.'

'OK, David, I will. And you can call me Sylvia. I don't use Jim's name in any case.'

Pinner shook her hand and smiled mutely. He was, he realized, thrown by how she looked. She wasn't what he'd expected and he found himself mentally reordering his assumptions. In the first place he hadn't known Jim was married to a local, which was what he'd supposed on her appearance. Then, when she'd spoken and he'd heard her accent, he'd had to rethink – she was as English as he was (or however the expression went).

The fact that she was older than her husband, and bigger, and healthier, required some adjustment too. Of course, Pinner had never created a mental picture of Jim Tulloh's wife but had he done so she wouldn't have looked like this: she'd have been a small, downtrodden woman, hardworking but unable to stem the tide of factors massing against her happiness. In the mental picture he'd never made, he wasn't sure if she'd have been ill like Jim, but she'd certainly have appeared sickly and pinched and sad. Instead, Sylvia Not-Tulloh was a model of robust confidence and Pinner instinctively found her rather threatening; his relaxed mood was dissipating accordingly. She exuded the clarity and certainty that told you she had no time for playing games. These were qualities that Pinner rarely saw in Westminster. In fact, they were qualities he associated almost entirely with mothers of a certain make and mileage. Once, when campaigning in his Bristol constituency, he'd been asked about the closure of a local outpatients' clinic. He'd made all the right noises about the letters he'd written to the hospital trust and his meetings with the health minister, concluding, 'I care about this as much as you do.' A woman had stood up and said, 'When will you stop lying to us?' and, in that moment, he'd understood for the first time that he was, indeed, lying. He'd stuttered and stumbled disastrously, astonished that someone could recognize his true motives better than he could. And Sylvia reminded him of that woman.

She sat down and took the beer Jim passed to her. Still she didn't look at him. There was an uncomfortable moment of silence.

Kotto said, 'We were discussing the Tranter story, Sylvia.'

Pinner had the strange feeling that Kotto had somehow betrayed him in mentioning this and suffered a pang of panic that they might return to the subject and he'd have to speak and maybe she'd illuminate his true motives (whatever they were).

But Sylvia seemed barely interested, turning her attention to Larsson instead. 'How's Asne?' she asked.

'She's OK. She left on Thursday,' Larsson replied.

'Couldn't wait to get away.'

'No. She wanted to get the children into school. I had some loose ends to tie up in the office here.'

Sylvia turned to Pinner. 'Lars is leaving us, David. The rats are leaving the sinking ship.'

Jim made a curious exclamation – that wordless elision of 'B' and 'W' that the English typically use to denote shock or disapproval.

Now his wife looked at him for the first time. Her expression registered faint surprise, as if she'd only just realized he was there. 'What? It's just a turn of phrase.'

Larsson addressed Pinner too. His tone was flat and bored so there was no mistaking that he'd heard this before and he wasn't going to rise to it. He said, 'Sylvia thinks I am a traitor because I am leaving, Minister. But I have been here for three years and it is time to go home. I cannot achieve anything here. I have tried, but it just gets harder and harder. You know that yourself, Sylvia, whether you admit it or not.'

Jim now lit a cigarette. His wife turned to him, taking her eyes off Pinner. Briefly, he thought he was off the hook, but then she said, 'My husband's smoking because he knows I hate it and he thinks it'll distract me.' Then, to Jim, 'Am I embarrassing you, Jim?' Then, to Pinner, 'I was here before Lars arrived and I'll be here when he's gone and the one thing I've learnt about Africa is that white people don't belong here.'

Larsson interrupted: 'You don't mean that –'

'Yes, I do. Yes, I fucking do. Don't patronize me. You're no different from the fucking missionaries. You come here with your PhDs and your initiatives and you think you're the only ones who can save the fucking continent. But within six months you're holed up in some hotel bar bitching about everything with your white chums. Aid is just another fucking

239

industry and you're getting paid. And the irony is that the more liberal the white guy and the better his intentions, the more fucking racist he is by the time he leaves. Isn't that right, Eddy?'

Kotto looked at her. Then he took off his glasses and began to clean them on his shirtsleeve. He said, 'You and Jim are my friends, Sylvia. Lars is my friend.'

'So?' Sylvia stared at Kotto angrily. She was breathing heavily now. Larsson was examining his knuckles, Pinner examining Larsson examining his knuckles. Jim smoked with apparent calm, but wouldn't meet anybody's eye.

The only person who seemed oblivious to the tension was the one who'd taken no part in the discussion: Pinner's assistant, Jeremy. But he now spoke up, his tone mild: 'What about Jim? He's not going to leave.'

Sylvia turned to him in surprise. 'No,' she said quickly. 'Jim will die here.'

This was only a statement of fact, and if she'd left it there, that was all it would have been. But she threw her hand up to her mouth as if she were trying to cram the words back in, and the discomfort around the table was almost palpable.

'Well, there you go,' Jim said, and stubbed his cigarette.

Pinner was alarmed by the change in atmosphere and felt desperate for a return to the preceding conviviality. He tried to think of something to say, but all he could come up with was, 'Excellent meat you get here.' His words hung in the air, ludicrous and inappropriate, like bunting at a funeral. And all he could think was that he, for one, wanted to go home, and by 'home' he meant England, his England, with his French cellar, Brazilian cleaner and Russian girlfriend.

32
Savages and fathers

Queenstown, Republic of Zambawi, 2008

In Gwezi prison, Officer Simeon Matete opened the hatch in Prisoner 118's cell door with some trepidation and peered inside. He never knew what to expect. Would 118 be awake or asleep? Would he be himself or the white guy? Would he be lucid or confused?

In fact, increasingly, Prisoner 118 seemed to be all these things at once, but he was still a tricky proposition for those assigned to guard him. He'd been known to berate them, to attack them physically (albeit feebly) and, on occasion, to scream with the fury and intent of a soul wrongly imprisoned for something more like a century than just three months.

Several other officers, including Vumba and Masinga, were now scared of him and would come up with all sorts of excuses to avoid working the maximum-security wing. Simeon Matete, on the other hand, was fascinated by 118 and, for the most part, found him engaging company. But today he had problems of his own and he wasn't in the mood to put up with any shit.

Fortunately, Simeon found the *zakulu* sitting on the small steel-frame bed, beneath the bookshelf Simeon himself had recently erected to hold the prisoner's burgeoning collection of esoteric literature (which included everything from Victorian poetry to contemporary self-help books with titles like *The Dream Cipher*). He was holding the very thickest of these books in the light of a candle stub and absentmindedly stroking one of the two rats he'd befriended. Relieved, the guard turned the heavy lock, unbolted the door, picked up his bucket of water and went in.

Without looking up, Prisoner 118 said, 'Good morning, Simeon Matete. And how are you?'

'I have brought you a letter, 118. And I thought I could change your dressing. Would you like that?'

'That's very good of you,' the *zakulu* replied. 'I wonder if any other political prisoner in the whole world is treated with such kindness.'

'I do not think so,' Simeon said, kneeling in front of him and beginning to unwind the bandages from the wound. 'Certainly I don't wash any other prisoner's feet.'

Prisoner 118 now looked directly at him and spoke ruminatively: 'And do you think such a revelation should make me happy or sad? Should I feel privileged to be treated well or distressed that others are not so fortunate? What I am asking is this: must we always judge our position in relation to other people, or might we all permit ourselves certain expectations?'

The guard said nothing. He immersed the *zakulu*'s foot in the warm water and gingerly swabbed it clean of the brown iodine stains, tiny pieces of gauze and God knew what else.

'This is a vital question, especially for Africans,' Prisoner 118 continued. 'What might we reasonably expect? You should think about it.'

'I *do* think about it,' Simeon snapped. 'Of course I think about it.' And he immediately regretted his tone. He dropped his eyes and concentrated on the job at hand. He picked up the small pair of nail scissors and began to snip away at the dead flesh. The prisoner's wound was most mysterious. No matter how many times Simeon cleaned and snipped, more of the tissue seemed to die and 118 was now left with little more than half a foot.

'I have offended you,' the *zakulu* said.

'No.'

'It was not a question. There is something troubling you. What's the –' He took a sharp breath.

Simeon examined his handiwork and saw he'd drawn fresh red blood. 'I'm sorry for the pain,' he said.

'I'm sure it has its purpose.'

Simeon was relieved to have an opportunity to change the subject, so he said, 'And how are your dreams, 118?'

'They are my own.'

Generally, the more the *zakulu* was himself, the less he was prepared to discuss his extraordinary dreams. But Simeon persisted: 'And have you discovered the identity of the *musungu?*'

'No.'

There was a moment of silence between them. The 'no' was so flat and so final that Simeon felt he could say nothing further. He rinsed 118's foot one last time and began gently to pat it dry.

But then the *zakulu* cleared his throat, lifted the book in his hands and spoke up: 'I believe, however, that I may have made a discovery in this extraordinary book. May I read to you?' Without waiting for a reply, he read aloud: ' "The savages of today are primitive only in a relative, not in an absolute sense . . . Compared with man in his absolutely pristine state, even the lowest savage of today is doubtless a highly developed and cultured being." ' Prisoner 118 lowered the book and contemplated the ceiling. 'You can find answers to the questions that bother you in the most unlikely places, don't you think?'

'I am afraid I don't understand,' Simeon said. Although, in fact, he'd been concentrating on bandaging the foot and had hardly been listening at all.

The *zakulu* ruminated thoughtfully. 'I have been dreaming about a *musungu*. Generally, when I have a significant dream, even if I don't fully understand its meaning, I understand its syntax. I know it is about this lineage or that totem, this tribe or that clan. But the whites? They have a savage view of such things. They think they only exist in the present day, alone

243

and detached from their ancestry. I assumed therefore that my dreams – that is to say, *their* dreams – must be equally incoherent and absent of logical meaning, literal or metaphorical. But Frazer is right: the *musungu* is a highly developed and cultured being, relatively speaking. So there is a savage meaning to be found if only I am patient.'

'I'm sure you are right,' Simeon said. Then, 'Finished.' He gently lowered Prisoner 118's foot to the floor and admired his handiwork. Despite his agreement, he didn't really know what the *zakulu* was talking about. It wasn't that he had no interest in such arcana, but he had real problems of his own that were dominating the same part of his mind that might otherwise be set aside for those things. They were problems he wanted to bring to the *zakulu*'s attention, but he didn't know how and he was worried that, if he did so, he might lose his temper, even though he knew he had no right to.

The rat that had been sitting on Prisoner 118's lap now scurried off and down the bed frame to the floor where it met its partner. The two sniffed around each other for a moment before disappearing into the shadows in the corner of the cell.

'Louis is a fair-weather friend,' 118 morosely observed. 'As soon as his girl shows up, he goes for sex, even though he knows I have not seen a woman for months.' Then he laughed to himself and addressed the guard directly.

Had Simeon not been so overawed by him, he'd have realized the *zakulu* was eager to engage him in conversation and somewhat put out by his unusual reserve.

'But you should see how they fight!' 118 went on chattily. 'Billie has the most terrible temper and sometimes I have even seen her bite him. But still he follows her as if he is stupid. Sometimes I think she is trying to run away from him to protect him. "She knows, because she warns him, and Her instincts never fail / That the Female of Her Species is more deadly than the Male." Isn't it so?' The *zakulu* looked at Simeon hopefully. But, somehow, the more he spoke, the more the young man seemed unable to. In the end he sighed and said, 'I thought you had a letter for me.'

Simeon jerked his head, part nod and part reflex, as if he'd suddenly been jolted into a response. He produced an envelope from the pocket of his uniform and handed it over.

Prisoner 118 read the front. He paused for a moment. He blinked. He carefully opened the envelope and read the contents. Then he looked up at the guard and said, 'I need to be left alone now.'

'What has happened?'

'It is a letter from the wife of my friend Tongo Kalulu, the chief of Zimindo Province. He has died.' The *zakulu* narrowed his eyes and bit the inside of his cheek. He suddenly looked, Simeon thought, very different, although it was hard to say quite why. He seemed vulnerable, perhaps.

'He was sick for a long time,' the *zakulu* went on. 'There are no doctors there any more. I am not there any more. He died. Now I need to be left alone. There are some rituals I must perform, but I must do so alone.'

Simeon turned towards the cell door, but he knew he couldn't leave because, however tied his tongue felt and even if 118 lost his temper, he had to talk to the *zakulu*. After all, he'd promised his wife that he would and he found her more intimidating still.

He stopped and turned back to the prisoner who had shut his eyes and was rocking on the bed, his lips moving silently. '118,' he said. But the *zakulu* was now in another place entirely and didn't respond.

He said it again, more urgently this time – 'Prisoner 118!' – but again, nothing.

'Musa Musa!' Simeon hissed. And this time the prisoner's eyes snapped open, like a lizard's. 'It is my son, John, *zakulu*. He is sick too. Sibongile and I are very worried about him. He has diarrhoea all the time and you know an infant cannot survive like that for long.'

Prisoner 118 regarded him unblinking. 'Have you taken him to the doctor?'

'What doctor? We took him to St Mary's, but they have no space and no medicines any more. And they have no doctors. It is the President's fault, you know, the same President who locked you up in here. All the doctors have left. They are working in Europe. But what about us? Can we not expect for a doctor to see our children?'

'What do you want me to do, Simeon Matete?'

'Do? I don't know what I want you to do.' Simeon shook his head desperately as if that might set loose some solution that was stuck somewhere inside. 'You are the most celebrated and powerful *zakulu* in the whole country –'

'I cannot do anything,' 118 interrupted. 'I am in prison and I cannot see your son. Even if I saw John I don't think I could do anything. Since I started having these dreams, I cannot see anything else, not even our own ancestors.'

'But you told me,' Simeon spat. He could feel his heart racing, he could hear his voice rising, he could see his finger shaking as he pointed, but he no longer cared. 'The first day I was here you told me that, although my son was born early, we would be OK. That is what you said to me. Were you lying?'

'I see,' the *zakulu* said quietly. Then, 'No, I was not lying.' He patted the bed next to him. The guard was breathing heavily but he reluctantly sat down. 'Of course you know the stories of our greatest ancestor, the founder of the Zamba people?'

Simeon nodded. 'Of course. He is Tuloko, the great Traveller, the Child of the Horizon.'

'Exactly. So, you know how he came to be succeeded by his youngest son, Zveko, who went on to become one of our finest leaders?'

'Every child knows that story.'

'Quite. But do you know the name of Tuloko and Mudiwa's first son?'

246

'I thought it was Shumba.'

'A lot of people think that, but it is not right. In fact, their first son was called Bongani.'

'Bongani? I have never heard of Tuloko's son, Bongani.'

The *zakulu* nodded, as if this were confirming everything he'd suspected. Then he said, 'He was born soon after the marriage, when Tuloko was still new to the role of chief. But from the day he was born he was sickly. He would not take his mother's breast and, even after six months, he did not seem to grow at all.

'Of course, Tuloko consulted with a *zakulu*. And the medium told him that he did not know what the problem was, but perhaps a *shamva* spirit had cursed the boy, since it was Tuloko who drove the *shamva* into the rivers.

'The *zakulu* therefore suggested that they travel to the eastern mountains so that they might consult with Cousin Moon for his advice.'

Prisoner 118 paused, causing Simeon to prompt him: 'And did they speak to Cousin Moon?'

The prisoner shrugged. 'I don't know. I only know that before they returned Bongani had passed away. It was before his first birthday.'

Simeon stared at the *zakulu*. A great balloon of sadness was swelling in his chest until he felt as if he couldn't breathe. 'Why are you telling me this? Are you telling me that John will die?'

The *zakulu* returned his gaze levelly because that was the least he deserved. He said, 'I don't know about your son, Simeon Matete. I am telling you this story because it is not one you already know. You know all the stories of Tuloko as a warrior, a general, a politician and a hero. But you don't know of the terrible wound he suffered in the loss of his firstborn, a wound he shared with Mudiwa and then took from her so she could give him more children.'

'I don't understand, *zakulu*.'

247

'On the first occasion I saw you, Simeon, I told you that you must never be afraid to let John go, and I told you that you and your wife would be OK.' Prisoner 118 took the guard's hand in his and held it gently. 'I did not lie. I told you all I knew.'

Simeon started to cry. He said, 'And what should I do?'

'Do? For now, there is nothing to do. But, if the worst happens, you must share the pain with your wife, Mudiwa –'

'My wife is Sibongile.'

'Sibongile! That's right . . . You must share the pain with Sibongile and then, when she is ready, take it from her and hold it safe for as long as she requires. Can you do that?'

'Yes, *zakulu*.'

'Then you will be OK, Simeon Matete.'

Prisoner 118 squeezed the guard's hand and they looked at one another for a moment. Then Simeon pressed the heels of his hands into his eyes before standing up and leaving the cell without saying another word.

33
Shame

Queenstown, Republic of Zambawi, 2008
Musa Musa sat back on his bed and listened to Simeon Matete's key enter the door and the heavy bolt clunk back into place. He raised his hands to his face and placed his index fingers on his temples and his thumbs beneath his ears, lifting his dreadlocks away from his cheeks. He sat like that for a moment.

Never before had the *zakulu* felt so uncertain about the choices he'd made that had led him to where he was now, and he didn't like the feeling. He knew that those of his vocation were typically able to make choices safe in the knowledge that they were the ones making them, which would, therefore, however crazy they had seemed at the time, ultimately render them 'right'. But he was no longer sure this was true – or, at least, not for him.

What comfort had he been to the poor young guard? What help had he been to his dear, dying friend? What use was there in his incarceration in this miserable cell? He told himself that he had left his own people behind in Zimindo and come to Queenstown for the sake of the greater good. But could he really trust this decision? Had he not been bewildered by the provincial suffering, blinded by his own arrogance, confused by the *musungu* dreams?

He reread Kudzai's letter and tried to detect the accusations that he was sure must lie behind her words. But he couldn't find any. She wrote that Tongo had passed away quietly in the end, that she'd been surprised by the size of the funeral (considering the problems in the country), with people travelling from as far south as Lelani and as far west as Maponda, and that she hoped he'd be released to come home soon.

He thought back to the last time he'd seen Tongo, to Lady Day playing on the old cassette recorder – 'Dearest, the shadows I live with are numberless.' Musa Musa considered the shadows concealing the truth behind the white man's dreams. If he couldn't see beyond them, his journey from Zimindo Province to Gwezi prison via the President had been utterly pointless. As he thought this, the feelings of shame that always accompanied the *musungu* dreams surged through him again and, for the first time, he realized that the mysterious shadows were, of course, shameful. But what could possibly have cast them so long and so dark?

Until now, Musa Musa had always regarded the shame as something unspecific. Initially he'd wondered if it was shame of his own, then if it was the broad, embarrassed, somewhat arrogant regret that, in his experience, most white men appeared to feel most of the time (at least, if you took their apologies at face value), latterly that it was the shame of love betrayed. But he had witnessed nothing in the dreams that seemed to merit such extraordinarily powerful sensations of ignominy.

However, the truth was that the *zakulu* had found no logic, literal or metaphorical, in the *musungu* dreams at all, and he now had to wonder if it was the limits of his own imagination that had prevented him seeing it. After all, as he'd intimated to Simeon, these being *musungu* dreams, he'd assumed they had all the eloquence of a child's tantrum. But what if Frazer was right? What if the white savages were primitive only in a relative, not an absolute, sense? If he truly chose to look out of the shadows of shame, what image might be silhouetted there?

No sooner had Musa Musa thought this than he sensed sleep enter the cell, its footfall as quiet as ever, its touch as gentle as breath. Of course, he was quite used to sleep's unwanted intrusion and, typically, he would have surrendered without going through the motions of resistance that were always, inevitably, futile. But on this occasion, as his head lolled and the air in his lungs, throat and nose seemed to thicken, he found himself fighting to stay awake – a sure sign of his fear of what he might see.

He pressed his thumb into his eye, he bit his lip until it hurt. Then, when neither of these tactics worked, he flicked out his freshly bandaged left foot and kicked the wall. But even that pain, though he felt it as acutely as ever, wasn't enough to keep him awake, as sleep gently lowered his head to the thin pillow.

In gathering fog, he heard Louis speaking from the end of the bed: 'He's gone again.'

Then Billie replied, 'So? Why are you so interested in him anyway?'

The rats' voices were a long way away, then vanished altogether. He was dreaming. He was the white man.

He was walking on a dirt road towards a large wooden barn. He found that he was unsteady on his feet and it wasn't just because of the diffuse pain that shimmered up his left leg every time it hit the ground. There were two other reasons besides: the rage, as undeniable as it was unexplained, that coursed through him and seemed to drive him forward too fast, so that every stride was like a stumble, and the assumption of strong alcohol, signified by the state of his tongue, which felt dry and tasted sour.

The sun was out, but it was cold. He looked up at the sky and almost fell over because it seemed so shockingly low that he didn't know whether to duck or reach up and pick the pale orb-like sun like a piece of fruit. He looked around. On his right there was a copse thick with old trees he couldn't name, on his left a lush meadow where tiny blue butterflies danced among nodding yellow flowers. Behind him, he was leaving a village of small squat houses built from heavy grey stone. This was the England of the white man's memory or his own phantasm built from picture books and postcards – did it matter which?

He reached the barn door and pushed it open. Inside, her back to him, was the young woman he'd seen several times before in these *musungu* dreams. Previously, she'd only ever appeared in snatches, brief apparitions that coalesced and quickly evaporated. Now, however, she was here, real and physical, in front of him.

She turned round. She had her hands in her hair, as if she'd been fixing it while waiting for him. Her cheeks were pink and her eyes were bright and blue. His feelings of rage were suddenly competing with others, of sorrow and pity, of fear and desire.

At the sight of him, her eyes softened, her face lit up and she said something. It was only when she spoke and he couldn't hear her that Musa Musa realized the dream was unspooling in total silence. It seemed he said something in return. He must have done because, though her expression was still warm, her brow furrowed and she shook her head.

He approached her and reached for her hand. She gave it to him and he held it gently. He was talking and she was listening. Her face was soft and her eyes were pained. His anger was calming now and he was able to hold it within himself, contained. She squeezed his fingers and he knew this was an apology.

She nodded, and smiled without showing her teeth. He lifted her hand to his chest and held it there. She smiled without showing her teeth and shook her head. He held her hand to his chest and reached for her elbow. She shook her head and the smile disappeared. She pulled away from him and turned her back.

Musa Musa felt the anger return, or something like it – something hotter and more impetuous still. He was standing behind her and he reached for her again and threw an arm round her waist and pulled her towards him. She didn't turn but he caught a flash of her eye. She must have said something, raised her voice, shouted at him, even cursed. But he didn't hear it. Instead, his senses were now overwhelmed by her smell, which was deep and ripe and viscous, and he knew that this new version of his anger was vigorous and lustful. She began to struggle against the strength of his forearm, and she felt so small as he held her; small like an animal. He could feel his penis hot and thickening against his thigh, and the charge of the exact point at which it pressed against her through the material of their clothes.

She pulled at one of his fingers and bent it back until he let her go. She looked round at him and there was fear in her eyes. He felt simultaneously wronged and apologetic, and when she tried to get away from him towards the door at the far end of the barn, he went after her. His lips were moving and he knew that he was pleading.

He caught up with her, his hand on her shoulder. She hurried away and he likewise picked up his pace. Then his painful left leg caught on a root that protruded from the dirt floor and he stumbled forward. He reached for the girl to steady himself, but she couldn't support him and he came down on top of her.

Musa Musa was winded. The girl tried to struggle out from beneath him. He saw her face, the lightning in her eyes, the burn at her ears, and her mouth was wide and he knew she was screaming. He felt a surge of panic and pulled himself up her body so that she was completely pinned to the floor, on her front, one cheek flat in the dirt.

His heart raced. He covered her mouth with his hand and she bucked against him. He heard cloth tearing and, though he didn't know how, he now found that his other hand was holding bare skin at her buttock and hip. For a second, such intimate contact froze them both and they lay like that, quite still.

Musa Musa couldn't process the full spectrum of emotions that now suffused his being. After all, they were not his emotions and it was not his being. Nonetheless, he could distil the anger and lust and sorrow and fear and contempt. He dug his thumb and forefinger deep into the girl's flesh and held her tight against him.

This seemed to spark her back into life. Her whole body convulsed and tensed and then her teeth clamped down on the middle finger of the hand covering her mouth. It may not have been the *zakulu*'s finger, but the pain was as real as any other. As he tried to pull his hand away, she managed to free an elbow and swung it backwards, blindly, as hard as she could. It caught him in the soft of his gut just beneath the ribcage and again he was struggling for breath, this time retching too. But he had no time to think about it because the girl's teeth were sunk deep into his knuckle and he was sure his finger was about to be bitten clean off. His eyes were filling. The vomit rising in his throat tasted alcoholic and noxious. His free hand was scrabbling across the floor until it closed around something small and hard and symmetrical. In desperation, anger and all sorts of other emotions too, he brought the brick down on the back of the girl's head. He couldn't see for tears but her jaw slackened immediately. He rolled off her and lay on his back, out of breath.

Suddenly the *zakulu* found himself elsewhere, jump-cut with the brutal but functional feel for narrative that characterizes a dream (because, contrary to the beliefs of many, Musa Musa knew that no detail gets into a dream without reason). His eyes were still full of tears that took a moment to clear and his chest was heaving, partly with one desperate sob after another and partly because he was short of breath, apparently hopping this way and that on his one good leg.

Though his vision gradually returned, it was now restricted to a narrow window straight ahead. He turned his head this way and that, trying to build some kind of full picture of his surroundings. He must be, he thought, wearing some kind of helmet or mask and peering out through a slit. He was surrounded by children, who clung to his hands and clothes, their upturned faces bright-eyed and smiling, moving with him as he whirled round and round, like a drunk. The absence of any sound now seemed deafening, filled with all kinds of competing suggestions, each of which was more terrible than the last.

His breathing stuttered and tears were streaming from his eyes, mucus pouring from his nose, and the muscles of his face contorted in fear, pain and horror. Who were these children? Were they mocking him?

Despite the pulling and pushing, Musa Musa managed to slow his reeling and tried to get his bearings.

He appeared to be in some kind of immaculately landscaped garden. There were thick, high hedges on two sides, a low wall with a gate in the middle on a third. A path ran from the gate, bisecting a trimmed lawn that was lush, green and punctuated with flowerbeds, some bare, others blooming yellow, blue and purple. The path led to steps and then a small paved terrace in front of an imposing dark house of a design Musa Musa had never seen before.

For reasons that he didn't know, Musa Musa found himself approaching this house and, though he now ignored them, the children followed. Perhaps he was looking for someone. Perhaps this was the young woman's house.

He climbed the steps. A pair of glass double doors over-looked the terrace: three panes in each, top to bottom. They were swinging open and, in the sunlight, the interior was pitch dark and the doorway a gaping mouth. He stood in front of it. Some intuition told him he was about to see who or what he needed to see, presumably emerging from inside.

There was a gust of wind and the double doors swung to. The *zakulu*'s breath caught in his chest as he saw his vague, semi-transparent reflection in the glass. What kind of dream was this? What kind of creature was he?

He appeared to have the body of a man though it was covered with a capacious white smock that concealed most of the details. His head, however, resembled that of a beast with big ears, a long face and large teeth that seemed locked in an eerie grin. Perhaps it was the head of a donkey or a horse; either way it was the most horrifying chimera Musa Musa had ever seen.

He turned on his heels. He wanted to run from his own reflection but he'd quite forgotten about his weak left leg, and as he tried to break into a run, it buckled beneath him and he pitched forward onto the terrace. The children scattered.

Musa Musa woke up to find himself actually falling forward, just as he had in the dream. He must have got to his feet in his sleep and now he was falling head first towards the cell door. Unfortunately he only had time to comprehend this, not to do anything about it, and his head made the thick iron chime sonorously. Though the *zakulu* was probably more used to falling over than most people, it didn't stop it hurting and he pulled himself up against the door somewhat groggily.

He was awake, he was certainly awake, but as he touched the cool metal, his fingers saw the corridor beyond and there, he was sure, was the chimera from the *musungu* dream. The beast was standing at the far end by the barred internal gate. The white smock had been replaced with a smart business suit, but there was no mistaking that face, whether horse or donkey, looking straight down the corridor.

Musa Musa banged on the door with the flats of his palms and made it ring. He shouted, 'I see you! I see you!' at the top of his voice. Then, 'What's your name? I will find out your name! I will find out your name!' He banged again, as hard as he could. But when he touched his fingertips to the door once more, he realized that the chimera was gone.

He sat down with his back to the door and gingerly fingered the rising bump on his temple. He might not have had a name, but now he knew something of the shame and something of its owner. The rest would come. He just had to be patient.

34

Insert document
Press coverage of 'Jerusalem' by Nobody
(Authenticity™ PR department), 4 June 2008

[*Hip Hop Connection*]
'Jerusalem' by Nobody
A-List Recordings
Reviewed by Konfushun

Love or hate him, you gotta give mad props to the ubiquitous 2P. Over the years, he's proved himself tuned in to both crowd-pleasing club bangers and only-for-the-heads underground classics. Little wonder, therefore, that the first release on his very own A-List Recordings is a bit of both, a neck-snapping anthem and mic masterclass from a mysterious masked maestro who calls himself Nobody. 'Jerusalem' takes the classic hymn from the football terraces to the streets and serves up a story of immigration and frustration in our skittish British nation. Very necessary.
Stars (out of five): *****

[*Guardian Guide*]
Pat Gill's new releases review
*PICK OF THE WEEK
Nobody: 'Jerusalem' (A-List)

So let's get this straight: Nobody is signed to The A-List, promoted on The A-List and made his television début last week on AuthenTV. What's more, rumour has it that the previously unheard-of rapper has been signed up to headline the urban section of the 'Africa Unite' festival programmed by – you guessed it – parent company Authenticity. And now Authenticity's own DJ Jonny Swift, the infamous straight-talking critic, has described 'Jerusalem' as the 'best record of the year'. Can Preston Pinner really think we're such sheep? Unfortunately this tune's a killer. All together now: baa!

[*Musik Muzic*]
Review by DJ Jonny Swift
'Jerusalem' (A-List) – Nobody

Here at The A-List, we already know that 'Jerusalem' by Nobody is the best record of the year and it is sure to be one of the most successful.

The first to buy 'Jerusalem' will be cool young people with an extensive knowledge of urban music. Then it will be bought by those who aspire to such knowledge and such cool, then by their younger siblings and so forth. In this way, 'Jerusalem' will delineate society in decreasing circles of cool by the date upon which the song is purchased.

Initially, 'Jerusalem' will be heard only in nightclubs but, within a fortnight, it will be played on apparently continuous rotation on every music television channel. It will be played at too loud a volume from the windows of the following makes of car: BMW, Saab, Lexus, Volkswagen, Audi. It will twitch the lips of young mothers in the supermarket. It will irritate from the ear buds of a neighbouring iPod.

Ironically, 'Jerusalem' will be licensed for use in an advertising campaign by a company intent on establishing its patriotic credentials; possibly a bank or a brand of beer. Ironically, it will be heard for decades to come in the last hour at purpose-built Mediterranean discothèques where drunken young British men will sing along enthusiastically.

You will buy 'Jerusalem' by Nobody; the only question is when.

35
Of balaclava and other masks

London, England, 2008
'This is fucking dark, bruv! This is just plain wrong. This is some serious fucking dark shit.' Errol was grinning broadly as, on the director's monitor, he watched the Queen propelled across the bonnet of a car to drop painfully onto the tarmac street, her crown bouncing into the gutter.

Preston laughed, tugged down the peak of his baseball cap, put his arm round Lorraine and squeezed her shoulders. She laughed too. She was, Preston thought, smaller than you might expect; small and strong like a gymnast.

'Jerusalem' by Nobody, the first release on the newly formed A-List Recordings™, was going better than Preston had dared hope. And it hadn't even been released yet.

It had been distributed as an MP3 and limited-edition dub-plate to various key DJs and it was already getting play on the necessary dance-floors and radio stations (both digital and terrestrial). Authenticity™'s in-house designers had already mocked up a flash video with 'Jerusalem' as the soundtrack – seminal patriotic imagery (Winston Churchill, the Spice Girls, Chris Waddle missing that penalty) interspersed with pictures of Nobody in his balaclava. Preston had successfully finessed a 'featured' spot on YouTube. So far, it had attracted half a million views.

The Authenticity™ guerrilla unit had been fluffing hard on networking sites, forums and message boards across the web, while a Google search for 'Nobody' and 'Jerusalem' now turned up five million pages. The Nobody Wiki had been edited 2,500 times, though nobody could yet claim to know who Nobody was. The Authenticity™ street team had carpet-bombed every public surface in every major UK city with the Nobody stencil, a simple outline of that trademark balaclava above the question, 'Who is he?' and the release date, '01.06.08'.

DJ Jonny Swift™ (in this case in the person of Preston himself) had written his most effusive review to date (on both The A-List™ website and his column in *Musik Muzic* magazine). When Jodie read it, she said, 'Isn't it just too post-modern actually to exploit, forecast and take the piss out of the whole commercial process as if it were a *fait accompli?*'

'Of course not,' Preston replied, and shook his head. He sometimes wondered if Jodie had any idea of the business she was in.

And inevitably Preston was proved right as his Jonny Swift™ review had been quoted, paraphrased and plagiarized across the mainstream press.

But 'Jerusalem' by Nobody hadn't even been released yet.

They were working to a tight schedule. The official release date was a week away. That same day Nobody would make his first television appearance on AuthenTV™. The following day his proper video – the one they were currently shooting – would be the most requested across the music TV networks. The day after that 'Jerusalem' would go into the UK singles chart at number one. There was no doubt about this: the presales into the major chains alone guaranteed it. They had ordered such volume that they couldn't afford any other outcome.

The Authenticity™ team was pushing so hard and working so fast because Preston was determined that Nobody should headline the urban section at the 'Africa Unite' festival in three weeks' time. By his calculations, the schedule should ensure that Nobody made his live début as the UK's number-one artist, broadcasting round the world to half a billion people. It would shift some units.

Preston had been working closely with Lorraine on the

'Jerusalem' campaign and had been consistently impressed with her input. In fact, if she hadn't been Nobody's manager-cum-girlfriend, he'd certainly have offered her a job on Authenticity™'s core team since she seemed to have an intuitive grasp of brand identity that almost matched his own. What was more, she was vital when it came to dealing with her boyfriend's moods, which, to Preston, seemed like a more or less full-time job.

In fact, the single largest cloud on the horizon for label and artist alike was that they couldn't seem to see eye to eye. There were various reasons for this that might be unpicked in terms of personality, profession or politics, but one key division informed most of the rest. For all his sincere admiration of Nobody's music, Preston secretly considered that he could have taken any Tom, Dick or Harry and turned them into a pop star. And they wouldn't have insisted on being addressed by their pop-star moniker either – it irritated Preston that he had to call Nobody 'Nobody', especially since it had no obvious contraction (except, Preston thought, 'Nob').

Conversely, for all his apparent acknowledgement of Authenticity™'s commercial nous, Nobody couldn't bring himself to play ball when his record company seemed to reduce his music to stats and jargon – of such and such a spike in such and such a demographic, and X per cent recognition among Y per cent of teens.

What this rift meant in practice was that Preston hardly listened to Nobody, no matter what his first and only artist said, assuming it was, at best, creatively whimsical, at worst, deliberately obstructive. Instead he would positively *not* listen and make small, horsy, snorting noises, which made him resemble his dad (although when Errol made exactly that observation Preston was less than amused). For his part, Nobody didn't listen to Preston much either and, when he spoke, he increasingly enjoyed just how irritating his whimsy and obstruction could be.

A prime example of the rift was the issue of showing Nobody's face – Nobody flatly refused to have his picture taken. It had started with the press shots and images for YouTube: 'People gonna know my music, king. Why they got to know *me*? I am just a channel, a conduit for the sound. My face is just a distraction, innit?'

For a moment Preston was dumbstruck. Then he said, 'But half the people who buy your music don't give a fuck about your music. They only give a fuck about what you look like and the half who *do* give a fuck.'

'You don't know what you're talking about,' Nobody said.

'You're right,' Preston nodded. 'It's more like ninety per cent who don't give a fuck to ten per cent who do.'

Nobody shrugged. 'I don't understand percentages.'

The confrontation was only resolved by Lorraine's input – the balaclava was her idea.

At first Preston was sceptical, but he soon saw the potential of the mask, which, now he considered it, offered a strong and easily replicable image. He discussed it with Jodie and Errol. Errol was enthusiastic: 'I think it's crazy, like some super-hero shit.'

Preston said, 'Think of the merch!'

Jodie said, 'But we gotta know he's black.'

'What you chatting about?' Errol sneered. 'You heard the geezer's voice? You never hear no white boy sound like that.'

'He can't just *sound* black, he's gotta *be* black.' She turned to Preston. 'Am I right, blood?'

Preston winced. Then he nodded. He said, 'I'm with Jodie.'

Consequently Nobody wore the balaclava in every photo, but in each there was just enough of his hands, neck or face on show to ensure his racial identity was not in doubt.

This was probably the last significant conversation Preston had had with Errol and Jodie about the 'Jerusalem' campaign.

For the subsequent two weeks, he'd really only discussed it with Lorraine. This wasn't so much a deliberate decision as recognition of her commitment to the project and flair for its marketing. After all, at street level, Lorraine knew the Barking kids flogging mixtapes, the walls where the Leyton writers left their mark and the lone pirate that broadcast in a half-mile radius of Canning Town. And she knew these things not because she was an expert in the ways of working-class urban youth but because she was one of them. She was, Preston thought, authenticity personified. It appealed to him personally as much as professionally.

Some evenings they worked late at Preston's penthouse. They talked into the small hours about album release dates, alternative revenue streams and international potential. If Lorraine was overawed by the opulence, she didn't show it. Then again, the opulence was deliberately downplayed by all the residents of Shoreditch Heights out of respect for the neighbourhood. Where 'class consciousness' was once signified by a brazen upward stare, it now glanced shyly down.

To Preston's amusement, Jodie and Errol still hung around the flat, for once united in their sudden redundancy. Errol pretended to read *The Souls of Black Folk* and Jodie pretended to cook, while Preston and Lorraine tossed ideas around the kitchen table. Jodie seemed particularly put out and Pablo, the possibly mythological cocaine-dealer, was a frequent visitor.

It was during one of these conversations that Lorraine came up with the concept for the video and they had the whole thing storyboarded in less than three hours. With any luck, it would be controversial and political and funny all at once.

'You are some crazy fucking white people,' Errol exclaimed, to no one in particular, before roaring with laughter as Nobody, hidden beneath his balaclava, knocked together the heads of the Prime Minister and the American President before launching first one and then the other on top of the Queen's prone body. Their prosthetic faces twisted in comic humiliation as Nobody lifted his arms in a victory salute and Prince Charles skulked sheepishly away and round the corner.

The director yelled, 'Cut!' and the kids who'd been gathering to watch behind the crash barriers on the street in Limehouse whooped exuberantly. Nobody turned away from the camera and offered his salute to them instead, provoking more cheers. Lorraine slipped out from beneath Preston's arm and on to the set to congratulate her boyfriend.

The director turned to Preston. He was a New Yorker who went by only one name: Sanchez. He'd been working in Europe for six months and had, in that time, developed an impressive moustache and a peculiar accent that seemed to mix east-coast Hispanic with a little French and a touch of Cockney, and involved stretching vowels in the most unexpected directions before, most bizarrely of all, cutting them off with a quasi-Oriental clip. Although Preston had never before come across anyone who did likewise, he considered the director a 'type'. He was also a 'name', who'd lately won several awards on both sides of the Atlantic. 'Nearly done,' Sanchez said, although he made it sound like 'kneeling down'. Then, 'We cut in the mobile footage to give it the look of happy slapping, and then we drop in the animated fighting noises – kapow! Shazank! Perdunk! We going for that seventies Batman feel. And you know what? If it's funny, we'll get away with kicking the crap out of the Queen.'

'Right.' Preston nodded, but he regarded the director quizzically.

In fact, the happy-slapping thing had been Lorraine's suggestion and the seventies-Batman thing his own; Sanchez had lifted the sentence 'If it's funny, we'll get away with kicking the crap out of the Queen' verbatim from Preston's briefing notes, albeit substituting 'crap' for Preston's 'shit'. Preston wondered how the guy could be so comfortable appropriating someone else's ideas that he actually parroted them back to their originator without hesitation. Then he remembered something Nobody had said to him about London: 'Everything gets swallowed and spat out and swallowed again until you can't remember who it belonged to.' Just because Nobody talked rubbish, Preston thought, that didn't mean rubbish was all he talked, so he kept nodding and let it slide.

'We're only short one shot,' Sanchez said, though it sounded like 'shot one short'. 'We just need the archetypal super-hero ending. So he saved the hot chick from the politicians and royalty. Now she gotta run up, throw her arms around him, rip off his mask and kiss him.' He pointed off into the distance where the Dome was a big grey thumbprint on the big grey skyline. 'We'll saturate the colour, Tupps, romanticize the whole effect,' he enthused, before singing the last line of the song with a curious Mariachi twist. ' "In England's green and pleasant land!" '

'Right,' Preston said. He glanced over to where the 'hot chick' in question – Thandi, his co-presenter from AuthenTV™ – was puffing glumly at a cigarette. She'd been none too keen to play the video honey, but when Preston had offered to sack her as an alternative – which he'd been threatening ever since he'd discovered the full extent of her junk habit – she'd grimly agreed. His attention then wandered to Nobody and Lorraine, locked in an embrace in front of the catering truck. He watched them a moment, waiting for them to break, but they didn't. He turned back to Sanchez. 'Right,' he said again.

These ideas – the unmasking and the final kiss – *were* the director's own and hadn't appeared in any brief or notes or script. But, Preston could quite see Sanchez's line of thinking and figured he may as well give the guy a chance, because what else was he paying him for? So he shrugged and he nodded and he said, 'Cool.'

He watched the argument unfold at a distance. He saw Nobody shake his head vehemently, Lorraine touch his arm, the director's mouth open and palms raised in bemused supplication. He saw Thandi light another I'm-so-bored cigarette,

Jodie lift a placatory hand, Nobody's flashing teeth and tongue. He saw more teeth and tongue, Sanchez wagging a finger, and yet more tongue and teeth.

Professionally, Preston didn't care whether Nobody took off his mask in the final scene or not. On the one hand, it would certainly make a dramatic dénouement to the video, and he knew from personal experience that brand recognition was always easier to achieve with a face to put to the name. On the other, he was convinced by the mystery value of the balaclava, that it could become a commercial identity in its own right. Furthermore, so long as nobody knew who Nobody was, he could turn anybody into Nobody (as it were) when or if the first and only artist signed to A-List Recordings™ developed an unmanageable self-importance.

Preston could, therefore, have stopped the confrontation between Nobody and Sanchez with a word. But he didn't because he was enjoying it too much. He could see the indignation in Nobody's body language and, for some reason he couldn't or didn't want to identify, he thought it funny. At least, if you'd asked him then and there, that was the word he'd have used – 'funny' – but 'satisfying' would have been more accurate.

The argument splintered. Sanchez stormed off to the coffee trolley and poured himself a cup before bumming a cigarette from a runner with a haircut that was all fashionable angles. Then he talked at her, and Preston could see his eyebrows jumping up and down as if he were a cartoon. The runner's expression was one step from terror.

Errol was listening to Thandi and nodding. She was probably telling him what a cunt Preston was. Errol had a thing for her. Then again, most men did and, like most men, Errol wasn't getting anywhere. Thandi didn't have much time for a love life amid all that self-hatred and consequent self-abuse.

Errol held his chin at an angle and his lips locked in an aggressive pout. He had his hands thrust deep in the pockets of his jeans and his legs an inch or so too far apart. He had lately developed this ostentatious masculinity that correlated with his ostentatious blackness. Preston couldn't believe in this new Errol and thought he looked somewhat ridiculous, but Thandi didn't seem to have noticed.

Jodie and Lorraine were with Nobody. Jodie seemed to be doing some straight talking and was using her hand to cut a path for whatever she was saying. Nobody was stony-faced and it was Lorraine, with her hand resting on his elbow, who was shaking her head. Then she said something and Jodie turned sharply to her. Both women looked over at Preston and suddenly were stalking towards him, eyes darting between them as if each was fearful the other might break into a run.

It was Jodie who spoke first: 'He's not gonna take his mask off, Tupps. Sanchez is laying a fucking egg.'

Lorraine said, 'He won't take it off.'

'Well,' Preston murmured, 'at least we're all agreed on that.'

'Sanchez is laying a fucking egg,' Jodie said again. 'He's threatening to walk if he doesn't get the closing shot he wants.'

Preston took off his cap and rubbed a hand ruminatively across his cropped scalp. It was a gesture that smacked of problems and frustration. But he was still enjoying himself.

He furrowed his brow at Lorraine and spoke earnestly: 'We got to see his face, Loll. I know I went with the balaclava thing and I like it, but we got to see his face. People want to put a face to the music.'

'But Sanchez wants –' Lorraine began, but Preston interrupted her.

'This isn't about what Sanchez wants. I can fucking fire Sanchez. This is about what I want.'

'He won't take it off,' she insisted. There was now something slightly desperate in her voice.

Preston shrugged. 'You're his manager, Loll. That's your job – get him to do what he's got to do.'

Lorraine was looking up at him and her eyes were pleading. The give-a-shit confidence she'd displayed in their first conversations had been dissipating ever since, but this was the first time she'd appeared weaker than him, deferential, needy. And he liked it.

He was being an arsehole. He didn't care about seeing Nobody's face on screen. He was being an arsehole and he knew it. But, in so far as he told himself anything, he told himself he was having too much fun. In fact, if he'd stepped back and thought about it a moment, he'd have realized it wasn't fun he was having at all. Rather, he was relishing Lorraine's difficulty, punishing her for what she'd done. And what had she done? What *exactly* had she done? Preston didn't know, because he wasn't thinking about it. He just knew he was being an arsehole and he couldn't help himself. Nonetheless, as he glanced casually from Lorraine's face to where Nobody stood and back to Lorraine, he heard his own voice in his head, sneering, *'That'll teach you'*. But who would be taught and what they would learn, he had no idea.

Then Lorraine said, 'He can't, Press.'

Whether it was the way her voice faltered slightly, or that he intuited some gravity in her tone, his peculiar, unrecognized rage, which had masqueraded as enjoyment, now vanished as quickly as it had appeared, leaving little discernible trace in his heart. When Jodie scoffed, 'What do you mean, he *can't*?' he immediately silenced her with a raised finger.

'What do you mean, he can't?' Preston repeated Jodie's question, albeit with a much gentler tone.

'He can't,' Lorraine said again, her voice now thin and reedy. 'He can't afford to show his face.'

'Why not?'

'Because he ain't got papers. And if he gets caught he'll be deported, innit?'

'Right,' Preston said. Then, 'He's illegal.' Then, 'Fuck.'

For once, Preston didn't know what to say or do, so he

reached for Lorraine and gave her a hug. Over her shoulder he saw Nobody watching them, and lifted his chin to acknowledge him in what he hoped was a gesture of solidarity. He didn't know what to say or do, but a rush of compassion surged through him and washed away any last stains of resentment. He felt warm and strangely pleased with himself. Here was a situation to get his teeth into, a situation that required someone of his position, power and passport. He didn't know what to say or do, but he knew that it was up to him to say or do something. He squeezed Lorraine tight and murmured, 'We'll figure it out.'

She was so small and she didn't feel so strong any more and he felt as if he might snap her in two. So he released her gently and shouted to the director, 'Sanchez! New plan!'

36

Insert document
'The diary of a local gentleman', 21 May 1901
(Empire Museum, Bristol), anon.

I am in a state of some confusion, at war with myself, divided as surely as we were once from Cronjé's troops by the Modder. It is fair to say that it is my better and lesser selves in conflict. However, truly I cannot tell them apart.

In the past, I have always considered that a gentleman intuitively *knows* the right path, and to claim otherwise is to deceive oneself. Indeed, I have vehemently argued as much on many occasions – to Ackerman, to my brother David and to 'Foxy' Wolfe (after his wager with the Irishman), to give just three examples. I upbraided each of them for their apparent uncertainty and proudly dismissed any distress they felt as symptomatic only of a shortfall in moral fibre. Now, how such bullish judgements have returned to haunt me!

Our idiom claims that 'pride comes before a fall'. It must have been a proud man who rewrote it as such, because, according to Proverbs, chapter sixteen, it is in fact 'destruction' that follows hot on pride's heels. I believe this too, for it is no exaggeration to say that I struggle to see anything but destruction, whichever way I look.

My heart is divided in a way I would never have thought possible, but this signifies only my previous lack of preparation. For, surely, pride's comrade in arms is none other than that idle oaf complacency.

My circumstances seem unjust, even ironic, because

surely I have never felt as uncertain as in these last months. If I had attempted to describe myself since returning home, 'complacent' is the very last word I might have chosen.

Indeed, at various points in this period, I have questioned most aspects of my life – my country, my purpose, the devotion of Catherine to me and, by return, my fittingness for her. But, as a gentleman, the one thing I never doubted was my constancy. And yet it is this that now threatens its leave.

Constancy – should I not add this to my list of key national characteristics? Was the Empire not built on the virtue of steadfast predictability? You know where you are with an Englishman. He does what he says he will, as regular as clockwork.

This is not to claim that the English are beyond deceit (though they have far less inherent inclination in that regard than the French or Spanish, say). Rather, it is to say that a true Englishman never allows his judgement to be swayed by some or other petty concern, but fixes his attention on the higher calling.

I fancy this is why some other races have been known to find us 'cold', for our singularity of purpose is not swayed by any transient passion. And yet? And yet . . . In my time at RMC Sandhurst, I had a direct contemporary by the name of Gaspard. Whatever his heritage and however his father may have willed it, this fellow simply wasn't cut out for the soldiering life. Upon my judgement, he was neither weak nor especially cowardly, but at the sharp end of any drill or exercise, you could reasonably hazard that Gaspard would be the first to lose his nerve and make an elementary error.

As I recall, Thomas, the NCO charged with whipping us young bucks into the shape required for command, gave poor Gaspard a tongue-lashing. On one particular occasion, I remember him barking, 'Are you nervous, sir? Of course you are. It's fine to be nervous. We're all "figging" nervous. But you can't show it, sir. Do you hear me? You can't "figging" show it!'

Gaspard knew better than to respond directly. But later, in the mess, he confided in me. 'The trouble is,' he said, 'I have too much imagination.'

At the time, I considered this but an excuse and, frankly, not much of one at that. Right now, however, I wonder if I feel much the same.

My conscious mind has begun to make all kinds of schemes and plots – apparently of its own accord, most of them utterly impossible – that might allow at least half of my heart to follow its deepest desire. My subconscious, meanwhile, churns with fantasies and dreams so vivid and so viscous that they cling to the walls of my head like some kind of treacle. I cannot describe them, for I fear to do so may set them free and strip me of any remaining semblance of self-control.

I must leave. Surely, I must leave, for have I not read enough to know that the pursuit of the forbidden is a tragic flaw so commonplace as to be almost careless? What's more, I know that this *desire* I feel goes against every facet of my character, even the principles by which I have always tried to live. So, why do I find it so difficult to walk away and choose the other, familiar, path for which I have been preparing my whole life?

Unfortunately I know the answer and it is this: I fear to walk away because one half of me suspects that it is not the desire that is wrong at all but my character and those same principles. For was it not this character and those principles that sent me to a war I can no longer support in a place I despised for reasons I could not trust? Was it not them that robbed me of my leg and, worse, any lightness in my person? And was it not them that made me flee my intended on the pompous pretext of some academic pursuit that has, ultimately, led me nowhere but *this very point*? Little wonder that I am, as Thomas put it, *'figging* nervous' and I fear I may show it too.

I still feel a little feverish, so I must retrace the last few hours to be sure that I understand my predicament correctly.

I spent the early part of the evening with the morris men at their usual practice. With Whitsun almost upon us, the tenor of these sessions has changed somewhat, the light-hearted banter and raucousness giving way to serious rehearsal. Today they were attempting what Chavney described as 'Crabfish – a newish kind of figure, similar to Old Jack'. They lined up in two banks of three, with Chavney at one end and Hasted, the fiddler, at the other. Chavney is, I have discovered, not just the 'foreman' of the Fry Norton side, but also their 'fool'. In so far as I have been able to divine the role of 'fool', it is as follows – he wears a marginally different costume from the rest, and is less restricted by the figure. Instead his task is to parody the formality of the dance and to interact with the audience, encouraging them to dance themselves, and cheer and laugh. I have represented Crabfish diagrammatically in my sketch book. It is a lively and somewhat ribald number involving all kind of hops and leaps, and grandiose gestures with the handkerchiefs for comic effect.

Though they repeated the dance again and again over the course of an hour, they could not perform it to Chavney's satisfaction and eventually he called proceedings to a halt. 'Come on, boys! Do you not think Bledington Morris or Badby Stumpers be bringing all kinds of new sticking and complicated jigs? But we be Fry Norton and we have a good name to uphold. Everyone knows that Fry Norton dance the tricksiest, most humorous dances!'

Generally, when Chavney had something to say, all the others stopped and quietly listened. But on this occasion Thomas immediately spoke up: 'That be all well and good,

Jack. But a dance like Crabfish will never look right without a hobin, so.'

Chavney didn't even have a chance to reply before the rest were agreeing; even old Percy –

[Fire damage has rendered the rest of this page illegible]

Although it was against my better judgement to partake in this way, I confess I came to thoroughly enjoy my role as 'Nobbin the hobin'. My remit was simplicity itself: while the morris danced Crabfish, I was to appear from the side and pretend to attack the audience – women and children especially – in a comical fashion. I had no figure to follow, so my lame and somewhat shambling gait was no disadvantage. In fact, quite the contrary, for several of my fellow morris men commented that my limp seemed to make my depiction of the hobin all the more plausible.

My fellow morris men – it seems I am part of this grand old English tradition! 'Nobbin' is simply a heavy mask made of paper, cloth and straw over a wooden frame. One can see out from within – *from the horse's mouth*, as it were.

It felt most strange to be so hidden and, at first, I could not bring myself to move with any great freedom. Since I lost my leg, I have become somewhat ashamed of my appearance, and the very idea of others watching me hobble this way and that quite terrified me. However, beneath the costume, I soon understood that I was utterly anonymous and thus beyond the judgement of myself or anyone else. Such liberation!

In fact, I was so taken with my beastly character – jumping here and there, snapping around the dancers' ankles and the skirts of Lizzie (our only audience), who laughed and shrieked in mock terror – that I quite forgot my weakness until the end of the rehearsal.

It was hot inside that costume and, when I finally took it

off, I was profusely sweating, rather flushed and short of breath. The necessities of the dance meant that I had relinquished my cane and when I looked down at my leg I saw that the material was soaked with blood where my poor stump had rubbed raw from the exertion. I suddenly found myself almost overwhelmed with nausea and not far from a faint. I had to rest for some minutes on a hay bale before, with the praise and encouragement of the side still ringing in my ears, Chavney supported me back to Nott's house.

Nott came to the door and helped me inside. He also helped me to remove my trousers and the prosthetic. Then, Lizzie attended to me. She pressed a cold compress to my forehead to stave off any fever and bathed my stump gently in warm, salted water. She is but a girl, no nurse, and of course she had never seen my horrible disfigurement before. But she did not flinch at the sight of it. Rather, she softly chided me for my enthusiasm. She told me she did not want to see a hero who had survived the horrors of a foreign battlefield cut down by a simple country dance. She told me she found me remarkably brave and stoic in my attitude, but I must be careful of my stump, which was always at risk of infection. She asked to whom she would talk if I keeled over and died.

I told her that, alive or dead, at some point I would always have to take my leave.

She said, 'Yes. I suppose you must.' But her attitude was one of surprise, as if such an eventuality had never previously occurred to her.

I tried to make light of the situation. I said, 'Besides, you're at a frivolous age. You must be with your friends and suitors. What must people think to see you in my company? Me? A battered old cripple who can barely walk unaided.'

She looked away. 'Please!' she whispered. Her one hand was rested upon my thigh, the other fanned across her breast, which rose and fell with every breath. My own heart was beating faster than I'd ever known. She turned back to look at me. She smiled. 'You should rest,' she said, and moved her hand to my forehead, gently pushing away my hair.

I woke up some time later. I do not know the hour. My fever had subsided and I felt a momentary and thrilling clarity. It was dark outside and the light from distant lamps barely crept through the cracks around my bedroom door.

I could hear Nott talking to his daughter. His voice was hushed and his tone faltering but insistent: 'I am not, that is to say . . . I am not . . . but I have seen . . .'

'What have you seen?' There was anger in her voice and she showed no concern for who might hear.

'Lizzie! Don't be like this! Why, you have been to every rehearsal of the morris and I have seen the way you look . . .' The teacher was cut off by a wordless exclamation from his daughter. After a moment, he attempted to continue: 'All I . . .' Then he thought better of it and tried a different tack. 'You must trust that I have more experience than you in these matters and this . . . this . . . well, you are not from the same society and *it* will simply never happen. And it is not fair to him and it is not fair to yourself to pretend otherwise. So it must stop before it has begun, Lizzie, do you hear?'

There was a moment's silence between them. I could hear my own breathing and it sounded loud and intrusive. Then Lizzie spoke again and her voice was defiant. 'As you say, Father, nothing has begun. Therefore there is nothing to stop.'

'Lizzie!' Nott attempted to call her back but the conversation was at an end.

'I am going to my bed. Please let us not talk any more about it.'

I tried to sleep again, but it would not come. Instead I lay awake and turned things over and over in my mind until the sky began to glow indigo with the first suggestions of sunrise. Then I sat up and began to write here in my journal.

It would now seem facetious to refute that I have quite fallen in love with Lizzie Nott. We have spent much time in each other's company over the last week or more, and I believe that my attachment was there almost from the outset. Certainly, it has been strengthening and coalescing for some days. But it is only now she has admitted her own true feelings that I can do likewise.

However, even as this admission gives rise to the warmest sensations in my heart, so I know what I must do. Nott is right when he says that Lizzie and I are not 'of the same society'. How might I seriously consider marriage to the daughter of a country schoolteacher? I cannot – I *will not* – break my promise to Catherine for whom I still feel fondly. I am a gentleman and I mean to behave as one, for what else is there to do? However doubtful his mind, no Englishman ever turned his back on his principles simply to avoid a life of unhappiness.

I mean to leave, therefore, at the conclusion of the Whitsun Ale. Until then, I will pray for God's forgiveness and think only on Pilgrim: 'One here will constant be/Come wind, come weather.'

37
The waiting room

Queenstown, Republic of Zambawi, 2008
It took Jim Tulloh several days to organize Pinner's visit to Gordon Tranter in Gwezi prison. This was partly because the government bureaucrats who would have to ratify such an excursion were being deliberately obstructive, and partly because they were being accidentally so.

When the President's office faxed the Ministry of Justice, the latter was clean out of fax rolls. When the Ministry of Justice tried to telephone the prison governor, it transpired that all lines into Gwezi district were out of order. Such was the state of the nation, where fax paper had to be imported and there was no money for imports and for this reason, among others, telecoms engineers emigrated as soon as they passed their last exam.

That same day the prison also missed a phone call for Officer Simeon Matete from his wife Sibongile who wanted to tell him that their son John's diarrhoea and, therefore, dehydration had worsened and she needed to take him to St Mary's as soon as possible. Consequently Simeon only discovered this when he returned home that evening and found his father-in-law waiting to escort him to the hospital. Fortunately the baby's condition stabilized within a matter of hours, but the episode put enormous strain on the young couple's relationship. Thereafter Sibongile silently felt a little betrayed each time her husband left for work, while for his part Simeon found every moment at the prison a purgatory of fearful imagination.

Western newspapers typically described the Zambawian economy as 'in a state of collapse', but there is of course no such thing – where there's life there's hope, and where there's hope there's trade. However, it was true that, like the Matetes' relationship, the machinery of the economy was in a state of high stress with popping rivets, worn-down tyres and grinding metal.

Curiously, the social consequences of this stress were simultaneously reductive and expanding. The stress reduced IMF policy and international sanctions to one man's failure to visit his critically ill son. It expanded another man's inability to send a fax to a declaration of political intent (with potential international ramifications).

Most significant of all, though, was the effect this economic stress had on the individual psyche, with the pettiest occurrences developing fated significance and major events shrugged off as neither here nor there. Basically, it made everybody super-superstitious; no one more so than Jim Tulloh, who increasingly came to see his own wellbeing as tied to that of the nation.

Jim had thrown in his lot with the country seven years earlier to the extent that he had even contracted its national illness. This meant that he regarded every minor cough as an indisputable portent of doom, but also, contrarily, that the knowledge of his certain, impending, imminent death was sometimes as slippery and forgettable as a shopping list.

However, when the fax went unsent and the phone call unmade and Pinner's visit to Gwezi remained unarranged, the one certainty was that Jim would take it personally. And, in this instance, he developed fluid on his lungs that sent him to bed for forty-eight hours. This caused further delays.

While he was waiting for a green light for his prison visit, Pinner might have ventured out into Queenstown and got to know the city a little. But he didn't. While his assistant, Jeremy, availed himself of the hotel courtesy cars to visit local markets and stock up on authentic African masks, fertility symbols and soapstone chess sets, Pinner increasingly retreated. He told himself it was for his own protection, although from what, exactly, he needed to be protected even he was none too sure.

At first, the day after visiting the orphanage, he had set out into the street with what may be described, considering his fear of the 'real Africa' and his now bravely acknowledged dislike of Africans, as a surprising amount of enthusiasm. He was approached by gaggles of street kids who asked him for money and tried to catch his arm, but there was no need to indulge these orphans so he walked right through the middle of them as if they weren't there, his eyes fixed straight ahead, his mouth locked in a half-smile that conveyed resolution. He saw a high-street bank's familiar sign and headed inside. The queues were preposterous and he almost refused at this first hurdle but, upon asking, he discovered that a specific teller dealt with foreign-exchange transactions; the queue to her counter was much shorter so he waited.

The teller appeared surprised that he wanted to change three hundred pounds, which seemed odd. He wondered if it was a particularly large sum to be changing in the 'real Africa'. Certainly this was what he figured when she handed him six hefty bricks of banknotes, each bound with an elastic band, in exchange for his six crisp fifties.

'That's a lot of money,' Pinner remarked pleasantly.

The teller smiled at him and said, 'It's not so much.'

Pinner stowed the cash in his shoulder bag. It was lucky he'd brought it with him. It was one of a job lot they'd produced for the launch of the African Authority. Made of soft padded leather and large enough to carry a laptop, it had the African Authority logo printed on the side. The bags had been provided for each delegate and their entourage and given away to journalists as part of the press pack. However, a lot of them hadn't been taken and there were now boxes of the things knocking around the Foreign and Commonwealth Office to be picked up by politicians, bureaucrats and wonks every time they needed to go to Tesco and, more often than not, discarded afterwards. The bags' unpopularity was probably the fault of the logo, which was a fashionably impressionistic representation of Africa beneath the letters 'AA' in a strip on a diagonal from bottom left to top right. Unfortunately, the fashionably impressionistic representation rather resembled a pint glass, which made anyone who carried the bag look less like a proponent of African development than Alcoholics Anonymous. Indeed, the logo had been ridiculed in some sections of the media, which was somewhat damaging to the African Authority's brand identity – almost as damaging as the arrest of Gordon Tranter, British citizen, in this nation with its economy 'in a state of collapse'.

The money fitted snugly into the bag and, as he zipped it up, Pinner felt a minor thrill; the same kind of thrill he'd had when he'd first considered the 'real Africa', the same he'd experienced when he met Joseph Phiri and discovered the Democratic Movement headquarters had lately been firebombed. Just as he'd never been to the 'real Africa' and he'd never been firebombed, so he'd never been to a place in the throes of hyperinflation before and it was rather exciting to see. This was precisely the kind of problem that the African Authority, with its branded leather shoulder bags, would address.

Pinner felt energized and mirrored the bank teller's smile. She was a pretty girl with good teeth and bone structure, and he wondered if he should ask her to the hotel later for a drink. Though she looked young and innocent and, frankly, much too good for him, Pinner knew from long experience of Eastern Europeans that economies 'in a state of collapse' brought most women within his price range. But no sooner had he thought this than he recalled his girlfriend, Eva, and, more pertinently, the AIDS-ravaged face of Jim Tulloh. He thanked the girl and walked out of the bank.

He looked left and right, considering which way to go to

continue his daring excursion. Opposite him, on the other side of the road, was a large shopping mall. He decided to go in there, partly because security guards were standing outside and partly because his hotel was only a block away. Figuratively speaking, he might not have been carrying a lot of money, but he was literally carrying a *lot* of money and that made him feel uneasy.

Inside the mall, he appreciated the air-conditioning. Although there were security guards and shop assistants and cleaners, as far as he could tell he was the only customer. He sat at a table outside somewhere called the Italian Coffee House, which had red and white checked tablecloths and a sullen elderly white man – possibly Italian, possibly not – peering from the window. He ordered a *latte* and a Danish pastry from the waiter, who was immaculately turned out in white shirt and black trousers. The coffee was bad and the Danish worse, but he was pleased with how he fitted in. He was almost local. His bill came to seventy-two thousand Zambawi dollars and he paid it expansively, depositing large denomination bills with exaggerated carelessness. He left an eight-thousand-dollar tip and walked back to the hotel.

It was only that evening in the bar that Pinner realized one of his bricks of money was more than a touch light. He was signing for the drinks to his room (it was so much easier for expenses), but the AA bag sat next to him and something made him want to peer at its contents. When he did, he saw that the wad from which he'd paid for his coffee was more than half gone. He quickly counted what was left, attempted some mental arithmetic and, after checking and rechecking, was forced to conclude that his revolting *latte* and pastry had cost him the best part of forty pounds.

A local white businessman, who'd introduced himself when he sat down at the next table (Greg Something-or-other?), noted his disquiet and asked, 'What's the matter?' Something-or-other couldn't have been more than a decade older than

Pinner but he'd spent a lifetime in the sun and a frown dug great canyons in his forehead.

Pinner told him he'd been ripped off by the coffee-shop owner. Something-or-other said he wasn't the first and certainly wouldn't be the last to be ripped off by an Italian, especially since the Italian was, in fact, Lebanese and that was even worse.

Pinner made an uncertain humming noise. When he explained exactly what had happened, Something-or-other laughed. This time the canyons opened into the corners of his rheumy eyes. He claimed it was actually nothing to do with the Lebanese Italian. Rather, the official exchange rate given by the bank was more or less a fiction, imposed by the government precisely to take people like Pinner for every penny of foreign exchange it could squeeze out of them. The real exchange rate, he explained, would have given him something like twenty times as many local dollars for each pound.

'What do you mean the *real* exchange rate?' Pinner asked.

'The rate on the street, the one they deal in day to day. You'll get about forty thousand to the pound.'

The one they deal in day to day? Pinner wondered at Something-or-other's use of the word 'they'.

Something-or-other then used the direction of the conversation to tell his new drinking buddy something of his own circumstances, which mostly took the form of a protracted complaint. He owned property and businesses across the country, he said, but now they were barely worth a bean. His savings too, all local, had been decimated by the crashing currency, and he couldn't even draw a line under his losses by buying pounds or dollars because the government was keeping a tight rein on all forex and there were none to buy.

Something-or-other offered Pinner the 'real' rate for any further sterling he might want to exchange. He said his only desire was to 'go home', by which he meant England, although he'd heard that home was going to the dogs, which was no surprise since 'they' were now all over there. He described the country he remembered, but it wasn't a place that Pinner recognized. It was as though Something-or-other had emigrated in the mid-nineteenth as opposed to the mid-twentieth century. What was more, Something-or-other remembered this place with such misty-eyed love that Pinner couldn't imagine what might have caused him to leave in the first place.

Something-or-other reiterated his offer to change Pinner's money and the minister muttered something encouraging but noncommittal, like 'I'll bear it in mind.'

'Because we've got to stick together,' Something-or-other said. 'I know these buggers and they'll fuck us.'

Pinner suddenly understood the 'they' in all its bluntness. Because Something-or-other was, to put it bluntly, one of 'them'. He was an unreconstructed racist, a white African who longed for a mythological Albion, a man whose entire being was defined by his power and minority status. Gallingly, he clearly thought the minister was cut from the same cloth. Pinner was just about to explain the logic he'd worked out on the aeroplane – that he wasn't a racist, he just didn't like Africans – when he spotted another man at the bar and the man spotted him. It was none other than . . . Whateverhisname, his next-door neighbour from business class on that same flight, and he was coming over.

Pinner had no choice but to introduce Whateverhisname to Something-or-other (an act of judicious mumbling), but he did so with some trepidation, assuming they'd hate each other and, perhaps, act out some kind of independence war / terrorist insurgency (depending on your point of view) right there in the bar. Instead, much to his surprise, they got on like a house on fire.

He'd assumed that the new élite and the colonial old guard could have nothing in common, but it transpired they shared a disdain for modern Britain that was only as remarkable as their deep nostalgia for some past society of their imaginations. They took it in turns, therefore, to rubbish one aspect of the 'old country' (the police, homosexuals, the homosexual police) before reminiscing inaccurately about the former merits of another (the police, public schools, corporal punishment). Frankly, Pinner was more relieved by their camaraderie than offended by their opinions. But he couldn't believe it would last. He sought sanctuary in his bedroom and bolted the door behind him.

It wasn't any of the day's experiences in particular that led Pinner to hole up in his hotel room thereafter; rather, he simply felt safer ordering room service, watching DSTV, and chatting with Eva on Internet Messenger (the Russian's implacable torpor gave him a peculiar frisson). He refused to accept any incoming calls, except the occasional room-to-room from Jeremy, who kept him up to speed with the impatience of the British media and the growing frustrations of Downing Street. And he allowed his imagination to run wild with what was going on outside in Queenstown, where kids with tragic eyes grabbed at your clothes, girls with pretty faces had incurable diseases, shops sold their goods at incalculable prices and bores with boring opinions interrupted you when you were trying to have a quiet drink. Pinner was coming to agree with the assessment of Jim Tulloh's wife – 'White people don't belong here.'

On the second day of his self-imposed retreat, however, he suffered three setbacks in quick succession. First, the hotel's Wi-Fi Internet connection collapsed, putting paid to any entertainment from dear, dull Eva. Then his phone line stopped making outside calls and the engineer who came to fix it took an hour to discover he couldn't and told him, smiling broadly, that there wasn't a free room with a working phone to which he could move. Finally, the waiter who brought his club sandwich attempted to engage him in conversation about his chances of finding employment in the UK. It took Pinner ten minutes to get the man out of the room and he only managed that by taking his email address and promising to contact him if anything came up. Afterwards he thought it safer to order as few meals on room service as possible and began to subsist almost entirely on the contents of the minibar – snacks and alcohol.

Forty-eight hours later, therefore, when Jim had finally obtained clearance from the prison governor for their visit to Gwezi and arrived at the hotel to tell Pinner in person, he encountered a most curious scene: Pinner had finally succumbed to the same temptation as his wife – full-blown alcohol abuse.

The minister hadn't left his hotel room in all that time. He'd just watched back to back Nollywood epics followed by three solid hours of *Africa's Got Talent*; his subconscious had been over-stimulated by startling tales of juju, betrayal and revenge, and the succession of young girls from Johannesburg who thought themselves the next Beyoncé. Also, having long ago consumed all the vodka, gin, crisps and peanuts in the fridge, he was now drunk on local beer and tequila miniatures and had eaten nothing all day but packet after packet of biltong.

When the hotel-room door opened, therefore, Jim was confronted by the unshaven minister wearing nothing but a dressing-gown. He had a leather bag around his neck, out of which poked an open beer sitting on a nest of banknotes and, when he smiled in vague recognition, he revealed strings of dried meat hanging from his teeth at irregular intervals. Behind him, *kwasa kwasa* blared from the TV and a thin shaft of sunlight between the heavy curtains picked out tissues, bottles, underwear and other bits of human detritus. Worst of all, though, was the smell, somewhere between a bar and an abattoir. At first, Jim assumed it was rising from the room behind, but he soon realized it was simply Pinner's breath.

The scene looked, Jim thought, like an outtake from *Apocalypse Now* – or, at least, how an outtake from *Apocalypse Now* might have looked if the whole film had been shot within this five-star hotel and Leslie Phillips cast in the Brando role – 'The horror! The horror! Ding dong!'

Swaying gently in the doorway, Pinner belched and Jim backed off a step.

'Mr Tulloh, you look terrible,' Pinner slurred, as if affronted. 'Your wife tells me you're dying.'

Instinctively, Jim reached for his cigarettes. 'Right,' he said. 'And what's your excuse?'

38
Gwezi

'How are you feeling, sir?'

'I'm fine.'

'Are you sure?'

'I'm fine.'

'Would you like –'

'Please shut up.'

Jeremy Shorter held out his bottle of water towards his boss for a second or two longer, but Pinner took no notice. Eventually, the younger man retracted his arm, unscrewed the cap and took a swig himself.

They were sitting in a waiting room at Gwezi prison. It was bare but for benches on three sides, an open hole in the fourth wall where, presumably, there had once been a window, and a clock. They had been shown in by the governor, a small man with glasses and an air of proud and unshakeable misanthropy. Jim Tulloh wasn't allowed to wait with them; neither, it seemed, was he permitted to visit another inmate of whom the governor claimed to have no knowledge.

As Jim and the governor left and their voices receded, the UK delegation could hear the Englishman asking questions with ever-increasing numbers of caveats – 'Of course I understand that you know the name of every inmate under your care, sir, and it's impossible for you to discuss the location of prisoners of whom you know nothing and for whom I haven't the necessary paperwork to visit in any case. However, if Musa Musa *did* happen to be . . .'

There was now no sound but the clock. To Jeremy, it

seemed to get louder and louder with every tick and tock, while Pinner measured his heartbeat against it and was disturbed by the skittering irregularity in his chest. Then, somewhere a long way off, they heard a strangled scream. Then nothing. Another scream. Nothing again.

In spite of himself, Pinner muttered, 'Oh, fuck!' under his breath.

Jeremy looked at his boss. There was something he needed to address. He cleared his throat. 'Sir?' Pinner didn't respond, so he pressed on: 'Sir, I think I should see Tranter on my own – at least at first.'

Pinner looked up resentfully. He was feeling decidedly shaky and he didn't want to be talking at all, let alone talking about something that required genuine attention. 'What?'

'I believe he's been in solitary for some time. To see us both might be something of a shock. I have the training for such a situation. They call it "Trauma Management". I did a two-day course. I'll be able to calm him down, reassure him, advise him of the circumstances. Then you'll come in, sir, and as you're a member of Her Majesty's government, he'll be able to see just how seriously we're taking this.'

'What are you talking about?'

'I just think . . .'

Pinner sat up and granted his assistant all the attention he had left in him. His heart was now beating so fast he was scared it might jump right out of his ribcage and start hopping around the room. 'Well, don't think . . .'

'Sir, Foreign Office protocol . . .'

Jeremy seemed unnaturally calm, which only confused Pinner further. 'Don't think,' he said. 'Stop thinking. There's too much thinking going on. I've done this before, you know – these interviews – victims from Vukovar, Srebrenica and Kosovo. Women from the rape camps. I don't need a two-day course. Trust me, thinking doesn't help.'

Jeremy stared at him for a moment as if weighing up whether to push his point of view. But eventually he just said, 'Yes, sir.'

They sat in silence for a further ten minutes, until they heard approaching footsteps. The door to the waiting room swung open and a prison guard entered. He was tall and young and wearing a full uniform, including a thick wooden truncheon with a bulbous end that hung at his hip. He had a round face, flawless skin and a gentle air that gave him the appearance of a piece of soft, ripe fruit. He also looked as if he'd just been crying. Pinner found this disturbing. For some reason, it opened his mind to all kinds of horrific possibilities. He tried not to think about them.

'You are here to see the *musungu*?' the guard asked.

Jeremy said, 'I'm sorry?'

'Tranter. You are here to see Gordon Tranter?'

'Yes.'

'Fine.' The guard nodded briskly, as if this knowledge allowed him to collect himself. 'I am Officer Matete. I will take you there.'

Jeremy sprang to his feet. Pinner stood up more gingerly.

The guard led them through the prison, down various corridors, across a miserable strip of dirt that he described as 'the exercise yard', inside again and up a staircase. The guard went first, then Jeremy, with Pinner bringing up the rear.

Officer Matete explained that he was taking them to Tranter's cell in the maximum-security wing. Pinner, who was now sweating profusely, asked why the hell Tranter was being held in maximum security when he hadn't even been convicted of any crime. Matete looked at him as if he were mad and explained that it was for Tranter's protection from the wider population rather than vice versa. Would he rather that the Englishman was the only foreigner in a communal cell?

They stopped at a heavy metal gate in front of a heavy metal door. 'Maximum security,' the guard announced helpfully, unlocking first one and then the other. He led them through into yet another corridor, which appeared to have half-a-dozen or so doors down one side and a single door facing them at the other end. The air in here was particularly thick and fetid. Pinner felt claustrophobic and his breathing was shallow.

The guard stopped by the first door. In its middle was a small steel hatch at head height and he slid it back to peer through. He then barked a command: 'Prisoner 237! Kneel on your bed and place your hands on the wall. Thank you.' When he was satisfied, he stepped back and opened the door. He gestured to his charges. 'Gentlemen.'

Jeremy immediately entered the murky cell and the guard followed him. But Pinner didn't move. He just stood and stared down the corridor.

Some weeks later, in retrospect, Pinner would say that he was transfixed by the door facing him at the far end. He would claim that he was drawn towards it, even that he could picture something – he wasn't sure what but *something* – behind it. But the truth was he just stood there, feeling slightly queasy, and stared for no reason he could identify.

He was given a reason to stare when there was a great clang from behind that very door, as if something or someone had thudded into it. Pinner stiffened, his stomach constricted and he had to swallow back a mouthful of vomit.

Then there was more banging – quieter this time, but rhythmical – and he heard a voice, which was definitely emanating from that last cell. It was deep and rumbling like timpani and, for all the world, it seemed to be addressing him: 'I see you! I see you! What's your name? I will find out your name! I will find out your name!'

Now Pinner was genuinely transfixed and 'What do you want?' formed silently on his lips.

Later, when he related these events as a story, he claimed that he was on the point of going to investigate, and perhaps

291

he really was, but at that moment Officer Matete touched his shoulder and said, 'Excuse me, sir.'

Pinner blinked and gestured down the corridor. 'Who's down there?'

'That is . . .' The guard seemed to catch himself. 'That is Prisoner 118. You don't need to worry about him. He is known to have nightmares. Come, sir.' With a gentle touch at his elbow, the guard manoeuvred Pinner into Gordon Tranter's cell. He said, 'I have been told to leave you alone for ten minutes. I will be outside.' And with that, he left and locked them in.

It took Pinner's eyes a moment to adjust to the dim light. The cell was small with two thin metal beds. Tranter sat on the bed by the wall opposite the door, Jeremy on the bed to the right. They looked as though they'd already been silently communicating with their eyes and Pinner had butted in.

The minister had read Tranter's file, or at least skimmed it with enough attention to feel he had the measure of the man, albeit only when weighed next to himself. Tranter had been to Eton and Oxford. He hadn't. Tranter had ventured to Africa and established mining concerns across the continent. He'd joined the Bristol law firm that carried his father's name. Tranter was a multimillionaire. He wasn't. But Tranter was also the son of an ambitious carpet salesman and locked up in a third-world prison, whereas he was a Pinner and a minister of the realm.

Pinner was familiar with Tranter's appearance from photographs and television footage but he looked thoroughly different in the flesh, and it wasn't just down to the ravages of imprisonment. In the pictures, Tranter was just another wealthy Englishman who wore his money poorly – pricy suits cheapened by an unflattering cut, body abused at great expense over decades – but none of the images or television footage had captured the coldness in his eyes. Here, in person, they barely looked like eyes at all, just two blue lights burning behind two ice cubes. They made Pinner feel decidedly un-comfortable, as if he wasn't uncomfortable enough already. He took out his handkerchief and mopped his brow. Then he tried a smile and said, 'Mr Tranter, I'm –'

But before he could launch into the speech he'd prepared, Jeremy interrupted. 'Roses are reddish,' he hissed. 'And violets are bluish.'

Pinner stared at him. What had he just said? There was a curious intensity in Jeremy's expression and he was sitting forward, eyes wide. Had he just said what Pinner thought he'd said? Pinner said, 'What?'

His assistant turned to look at him, his face locked in a kind of wired sincerity. 'Roses are reddish and violets are bluish,' he said again.

Pinner glanced at Tranter, just to confirm that this was in-deed the blathering of a madman, but the prisoner's ice cubes were fixed on Jeremy as he murmured, 'And if it weren't for Christmas, we'd all be Jewish.'

'Excuse me?' Pinner began to feel most peculiar. What the hell were they talking about? Was he hallucinating? He leant back against the cell door. The metal was warm and wet.

As far as Jeremy and Tranter were concerned, Pinner might as well have stepped out of the room. Their attention was fully fixed, each upon the other. Jeremy said, 'We haven't got long.'

Tranter asked, 'Who are you?'

'I'm family.'

'And who's he?' The prisoner nodded in Pinner's direction.

Pinner tried to collect himself. He said, 'I'm David –'

But his assistant talked over him: 'He's a friend of the family.'

Tranter wasn't satisfied: 'Who *is* he?'

'David Pinner. He's a minister in the FCO.'

'*That's* Pinner? The Africa minister?' Tranter snorted, though he'd certainly found nothing funny. 'They sent a fucking politician?'

Jeremy shrugged. 'That's how family get to visit. Look, I need to know whether you delivered the present?'

'Of course not. Do I look like Father fucking Christmas?'

'Is it on the sleigh?'

'Maybe. But the sleigh . . . well . . . the sleigh hasn't entered local airspace, as it were.'

'Are you sure?'

'Sure.'

'How do you know?'

'Because I spoke to Prancer and Dancer just before I was arrested. They were still sitting with Rudolph on the other side of the border. Still are, far as I know.'

'What about Father Christmas?'

'Father Christmas?' Tranter smiled ruefully. 'I'm not stupid. It's best not to believe in Father Christmas.'

'Hmm,' Jeremy hummed, then thought for a moment. 'So what have they got?'

'Who?'

Jeremy lifted a finger and painted a circle in the air, as if indicating his immediate surroundings. 'The children.'

'The children? They haven't got anything. Look, I've played St Nick before – Sierra Leone, Mozambique, Angola – but here I'm just Santa's little helper. My only job is to make sure that the good little boys have been good enough the whole year to get their presents come Christmas time. My guess is that one of them wasn't nearly as well behaved as we'd hoped.'

Pinner could no longer contain himself. He said, 'What the fuck are you two talking about?'

Again, he was more or less ignored, Jeremy granting him the briefest glance, like a parent with a child seeking attention. 'So who's the naughty boy?' he asked, but it was directed to Tranter.

'Don't know,' Tranter shook his head, 'but it must be someone senior. Maybe even Phiri himself.'

'Joseph Phiri?' Pinner exclaimed, and suddenly he understood.

It was as if this name were a tree-trunk that had fallen from the apparent gobbledegook of what he'd heard over the stream of his physical fragility to the place of what he knew. And now he had no choice but to walk across, whether he wanted to or not.

'Oh, fuck,' Pinner said. So President Adini was right: there had been a coup planned with opposition leader Joseph Phiri, Tranter was dealing arms, the British government (of which he was a part) was implicated. So . . . so . . .

He told himself it couldn't be true and, strangely, the one thing he clung to as evidence of this was the involvement of his assistant, Jeremy. How could Jeremy, that feeble and colourless vessel, that object of obsequiousness, that most toadying of toads have anything to do with such a crazy scheme? He looked at said amphibian for reassurance, but unfortunately Jeremy was wearing an expression he'd never seen before: earnest and eager but, above all, self-confident, as if he'd finally leapt into cool and familiar water.

Jeremy spoke to him in a soft, even voice: 'Stay calm, sir. No point getting us all into trouble, is there?'

'Oh, fuck,' Pinner said again.

39
Prisoner 386

Queenstown, Republic of Zambawi, 2008
Officer Matete returned to Tranter's prison cell after precisely ten minutes. 'Your time is up,' he said, and then, checking the faces of the three men, he frowned. 'Are you guys planning an escape?'

'Of course not,' Pinner spluttered.

The guard smiled sympathetically. 'Don't look so worried, sir. I am only joking.'

Pinner didn't speak again until they got back to the hotel. In the car, Jim, their *de facto* driver, asked how the visit had gone, but Jeremy answered smoothly that he was still confident of Tranter's release and a swift resolution with which everyone would be happy.

The minister was tempted to interject, but Jim started talking about his frustrating confrontation with the prison governor and his concern for his missing friend. Then he had a coughing fit and had to pull over for a couple of minutes until the hacking subsided. Pinner stared daggers at his assistant, who ignored him nonchalantly, his hand resting comfortingly on Jim's heaving back.

The delay only exacerbated Pinner's indignation, and by the time they got out of the car, he was spitting fury. He summoned his assistant to his hotel room, and as soon as the door shut behind him, he let rip. Jeremy listened impassively.

If he hadn't been so angry, Pinner might have understood his own anger (such is the nature of the emotion). Was he angry because of the plot's purpose? Was he angry because of the intervention of the British government (or, at least, some part thereof) in the affairs of a sovereign (albeit failing) state?

Was he angry because some shady cabal of British intelligence and private enterprise had acted independently of any demo-cratically elected representatives? Or was he angry simply because of the dangerous situation in which he'd been put?

He wasn't *really* angry for any of these reasons. But because he was so angry, he claimed that he was, and Jeremy, with a calmness that veered towards patronage, answered him point by point, which made him angrier still.

While he'd been out, Housekeeping had finally gained entrance to Pinner's room, cleaned it and, more to the point, restocked the minibar. While his assistant spoke, Pinner attacked it with gusto.

Jeremy told him that he was naïve. He told him that this was the nature of a modern democracy in a global politi-cal framework. He made some complex points about the practicalities of representation in nations of tens of millions, which concluded with the idea that delegation to an 'unelected executive' was an inevitable and necessary evil. He correlated Suez, Kissinger and Iraq in ways his boss didn't understand. He claimed that intervention in Zambawi had no specific, planned outcome; rather, it was a case of supporting the under-dog in an inherently one-sided scenario, giving the donkey a carrot, putting the cat among the pigeons. The metaphors were tailgating. He said, 'Isn't it arguable that a failure to represent the people negates a claim to sovereign status?'

Pinner was confused and asked to whom, precisely, he was referring.

Jeremy said, 'Adini, of course.' He pointed out that Pinner's ignorance of the precise machinations of the situation was, he could surely now see, the preferable option. He pointed out that the Adini government didn't know anything and, so long as they played it cool, Pinner would surely get his media moment with Tranter on the tarmac at Heathrow. He pointed out that there was no need to worry.

If Pinner's anger had actually been caused by any of the

reasons he claimed and, indeed, believed to be true, Jeremy's cogent bullshit might have stopped it in its tracks. But, in fact, Pinner was angry for another reason entirely: he was angry because of his worldview. Pinner didn't actually care about what he knew and what he didn't, about democracy and sovereignty, but he did care about being in the know and about being one of those who decided what was democratic and who was sovereign. He knew what a rhinoceros looked like and he wasn't about to be told otherwise. Had he been able to understand this about himself, he would surely have avoided the trouble that followed. Unfortunately he couldn't, so he didn't.

Pinner told Jeremy to get out of his sight. Jeremy's parting shot was, 'Don't do anything stupid, sir.'

It was a red rag to a bull. Alone, Pinner drank himself stupid and then acted accordingly. He picked up the hotel phone. He pressed zero and immediately got an outside line. The phone now appeared to be working, a miracle that lent weight to his chosen course of action. He said, 'About fucking time too,' as though someone were there to hear him. He rang Downing Street. It was after eight p.m. London time and he spoke to some minor bureaucrat, but couldn't explain exactly what he wanted them to do. This was partly because he didn't know what he wanted them to do, partly because he was already drunk and partly because he was still possessed of enough prudence to consider the situation might not be best discussed on the phone.

Then he rang Eva. He didn't know what to say to her, so he said that he loved her. She told him not to be so stupid and promptly put the phone down. Her reaction gave him a sudden and uncontrollable impulse to call his ex-wife, so he did. She asked him what he wanted. He said he wanted to tell her something, something important, something he should have said before, in fact something he should have said a lot more over the years of their marriage. She cut him off right there. She informed him that she didn't want to talk to him, but had a piece of advice that she was prepared to share – alcohol was not his friend. Then she put the phone down on him too.

Pinner regarded the receiver blearily and wondered if what his wife had said was true. He struck up a brief conversation with a vodka miniature that swiftly convinced him otherwise.

Finally, when he had no one left to bother, he called the one person he actually wanted to speak to: Preston.

Preston was at the studio for AuthenTV™. He immediately said he couldn't talk. He was too busy. The first signing to A-List Recordings™ was making his TV début. Pinner had no idea what he was talking about. He told him it was important. He said, 'Please.'

Preston sighed. He asked him to hang on a minute while he stepped out of the gallery so he could hear. A couple of minutes later, he returned and said, 'OK. How's . . . Where are you again?'

Pinner found himself speechless. Whether it was because of the drink or a sudden recognition of his own distress, his throat had constricted. It was a second or two before he managed to squeeze out, 'I'm in trouble.'

'What?'

Pinner told him. Or, at least, he told him as best he could. But at the other end of the phone Preston kept having to answer questions from people around him and, what with all Tranter and Jeremy's peculiar Christmas code, nothing he said seemed to make much sense anyway. He tried to break it down but that didn't appear to help. He said that it was true, they had been planning an insurgency. Preston asked what was true and who'd been planning what emergency. Pinner said, *insurgency*. He said that Father Christmas had sent a present but it hadn't arrived in the country. Preston asked who Father Christmas was. Pinner said, 'It's best not to believe in Father Christmas,' aping Tranter. Preston asked what the present was. Pinner realized he had no idea and said as much. Preston asked where the present was and Pinner said, 'I believe it's still with the reindeer.'

There was a pause. Preston made some strange noises. Was he tutting? He said, 'How drunk are you, Dad?'

'I'm not drunk.'

Preston said, 'Look, if you don't know who's passing what to whom for which purpose, I don't think you've got anything to worry about.'

'Really?' He was somehow reassured by his son's indifference. 'But I know that someone's passed something to someone, and you don't just do that for the sake of it.'

'I don't think that's –'

'You don't think that's what?'

'I don't think that's enough reason to start panicking. Look, Dad –'

'Can you hold on? There's someone at the door.' Only as he said this did Pinner grasp it was true: someone was banging insistently on the door of his hotel room.

'Dad, I gotta go.'

'Just one second,' Pinner insisted, and laid the receiver on its back. He stood up and wove across the room. He opened the door and found himself face to face with a man smiling broadly. The minister contemplated him vaguely. Wasn't he familiar? 'I know you,' he said. 'You're the man who couldn't fix the telephone. Well, it's working perfectly now, thank you.'

For a moment, the man's smile remained immobile and inscrutable. Then two other men materialized behind him; one over each shoulder. They were impeccably turned out in dark, buttoned suits, white shirts and ties. They looked, Pinner thought vaguely, rather like those black Muslims he'd occasionally seen on television. Then the telephone engineer who wasn't a telephone engineer said, 'David Pinner? I am Sergeant George Ndlovu of the Central Intelligence

Service. These are my colleagues. We are arresting you on suspicion of espionage.'

Pinner sniffed. He felt suddenly and terribly nauseous. In fact, he felt so suddenly and so terribly nauseous that he couldn't remember what the man had just said. He said, 'What?' And Sergeant George Ndlovu repeated himself. 'Right,' Pinner said weakly. Then, 'I'm just on the phone to my son.' With that he turned on his heels and got back to the phone before anyone could say otherwise. 'Preston?' he said. 'Preston?' But Preston had gone.

Pinner's arrest was surely sobering news, but he didn't sober up. Instead, he stayed drunk, as if his body anticipated what was to come and figured this was the best course of action.

The next few hours, therefore, were a blur of heaped humiliations. He was taken to a police station. He adopted various postures – angry, indignant, desperate, insinuating – but each was as unsuccessful as the last. He demanded to make a phone call. When that didn't work, he pleaded to make a phone call. That didn't work either. He was locked in a communal cell and sat quietly in a corner. The other occupants soon worked out that if they ran up to him and shouted at him in the local language they could frighten the life out of him. So, in the absence of other distractions, they took it in turns to do this. He wailed to make a phone call.

He was desperately thirsty and begged the policeman on duty for some water. The officer pointed to a dirty tap in the corner of the cell. He drank from it greedily, but within minutes he was attacked by the most terrible stomach cramps. There was a seatless toilet in another corner of the cell that was pebbledashed with an epoch of shit. Pinner had no choice but to drop his trousers, squat over it and empty his bowels. This took a lot longer than he'd hoped and his prodigious diarrhoea, combined with the extraordinary accompanying sound effects, gradually attracted the interest of his fellow prisoners, who gathered round to laugh and point. They'd rarely been so royally entertained.

Sweating profusely and guts knotting, Pinner told himself that at least this might discourage any inmate who'd been considering him as some kind of sex object, which was what he feared most. He shut his eyes and couldn't stop a low groan escaping him.

After about an hour, he was dragged out of the cell and fingerprinted. He was led into an interview room where he was met by Sergeant Ndlovu and presidential aide Solomon Mhlanga. Mhlanga greeted him with the words, 'How the mighty have fallen!' Now Pinner started to weep. Had anybody ever spoken more truly?

When he'd calmed down, he made a faltering but determined speech about being a minister of Her Majesty's government and his right to be treated with the respect commensurate to his position. He demanded to make a phone call and said that he wouldn't say anything further until he'd been allowed to do so.

Mhlanga listened to his speech with rising eyebrows. Then he shrugged and nodded at the wall of the cell where there was a telephone. Pinner slowly stood up, walked towards it and lifted the receiver to his ear. He said, 'It's dead.'

Ndlovu, the telephone engineer who wasn't a telephone engineer, said, 'Is it? Unfortunately I'm not a telephone engineer.' He turned to Mhlanga. He said, 'Do you have a cell-phone our guest might use, sir?'

Mhlanga produced a state-of-the-art mobile from his pocket. He offered it to Pinner with the words, 'But I haven't any airtime. The networks in our country are very problematic these days.'

Pinner sat down again. He felt suddenly calm. He said, 'I'll tell you everything I know.' Even as he said this, he remembered he didn't actually know anything.

After half an hour of extreme frustration for all concerned,

Mhlanga and Ndlovu abandoned their interrogation. Pinner was led to a waiting police car and driven to Gwezi prison. Ndlovu sat next to him on the back seat. By now, the Englishman must have been physiologically sober but he felt drunker than ever.

At the prison, Ndlovu handed him over to the misanthropic prison governor, whose face was arranged with a surfeit of happiness that Pinner would never have imagined possible. The governor handed him over to a great beast of a guard, the blackest man Pinner had ever seen, a man so black his complexion seemed to swallow what little light there was from the feeble overhead strips. The guard smiled at him. His mouth was a grotesque horror of misshapen teeth, as if he'd just chewed his way through a brick. How Pinner wished that the gentle Officer Matete he'd met just a few hours earlier was still on duty!

'I am Captain Makuvitse,' this behemoth said. 'You will do what I say, Prisoner 386, and you will come to thank me.' Makuvitse took him to a bare, dark room and told him to strip. He took away Pinner's clothes and possessions and returned with a bucket of cold water and a bar of soap. He said, 'Now you wash.'

Pinner washed and the captain watched. When Makuvitse was satisfied that he was adequately clean, he returned his shirt and trousers. Then he led him barefoot through the prison to the maximum-security wing, the very same journey he'd made earlier that day; or was it the previous day? He couldn't tell.

Pinner found himself standing outside Gordon Tranter's cell once again. The crash of the heavy doors must have woken the other *musungu* prisoner, because Tranter began to call, 'Who's there? I want to see the Englishmen again! Do you hear? I want to see the Englishmen again! I want to get out!'

The captain turned to Pinner and said, 'You will share a

cell. In my experience, it is good for a new inmate to have some company, someone to show him the ropes.'

Pinner swallowed. The very last thing he wanted, he thought, was to share a cell with Tranter. No sooner had he thought this than he discovered it wasn't the very last thing.

There was a bang from the cell at the far end, the sound of a fist beating on the back of a heavy metal door and, as if this was his cue, the captain began to lead his new charge down the corridor. 'I see you!' Pinner heard the same voice from before, but in the echoing silence he wasn't sure if it was only in his imagination. 'I see you! I know your name!' The minister could barely even hear the voice above the thud of his heart.

Makuvitse lifted a key from the heavy bunch at his waist. The lock turned with a scream of metal. He pushed open the door and thrust him forward. Pinner felt a trickle of piss escape down his leg.

It took him a moment to process what he was seeing: the tall bare-chested man in front of him, the bookshelves behind, the shock of dreadlocks, the wild eyes, the paintbrush in his hand, the way he stood stock still on one leg. 'Pinner, son of Pinner, son of Pinner!' Musa Musa said. 'I have been waiting for you a long time.'

Part three: And was Jerusalem builded here?

40

Insert document
'The diary of a local gentleman', 24 May 1901
(Empire Museum, Bristol), anon.

While at Standmere, I did my utmost to cultivate discipline –
among the men under my command, the Dutch and kaffirs
too. I do not believe that Ackerman was a cruel man, but in
so far as he gave not a fig for appropriate regulation, did he
not display terrible cruelty?

It was not because of the flaws in his administration that
the Boers were ravaged by sickness and hunger, or that
soldiers felt able to punish kaffirs with seemingly wanton
violence; rather, it was through the absence of any
administration worthy of the name. However, in that he
failed to impose appropriate discipline, he might as well have
spread infection himself or wielded the sergeant's notorious
stockwhip.

Soon after my arrival, for example, I discovered that the
mess officer had reported the theft of half a dozen tins of
bully beef some weeks previously and no culprit had been
apprehended or a thorough investigation served. However,
one month before a swaddy had done no less than beat a
Negro to death with his rifle butt. If memory serves, the
record showed that, when questioned, the soldier's response
was 'The bugger looked at me queer,' and for this he had
received only a reprimand from his CO. It was because of
incidents like these that I made it my first task to establish
some basic regulations for the entire camp.

I cannot pretend that my efforts were popular.

Nevertheless, soldiering men instinctively appreciate strong leadership, even if they protest otherwise. In time, the Boers, too, came to see the merit in my new rules with regard to hygiene, waste disposal and the like. The Negroes, however, caused me no end of problems.

I have heard some fellows argue that the Negro is genetically unsuited to discipline. I am not one who holds such a position. To my mind, the problem here was that Ackerman had largely left them to organize themselves. I made it my purpose to draw up minimum expectations of conduct and decency to which they must adhere. At first I had little success, not least because so few of them spoke a word of English and those who did found it practical to pretend they did not.

Latterly I hit upon an idea. I approached Mary, the Zulu whom Ackerman had taken as mistress, and told her she would act as my translator and relay my orders to her people. Truly, I was doubtful of such a course of action, but I knew that Ackerman had taught her the language successfully and I felt I might as well put his folly to some use. Initially she was reluctant in the extreme, but she could hardly refuse my request, and if she ever complained to her lover, he was certainly prudent enough not to attempt to counter my intentions. In time our arrangement came to work quite effectively and there was, I believe, a general improvement in Negro behaviour.

I recall all this now on account of one particular incident. I had passed a law ruling that the Africans should light their fires around the southern kitchen. In this way, I ensured that their smoke would blow away from the main camp. It was, I believed, a practical decision. When several young *kaffirs* decided to light fires along the western ridge, therefore, I ordered that they should be flogged.

The redoubtable Mary came to me forthwith and I could see that she could barely contain her anger. I had not told her, she claimed, where they must not light their fires, only where they must. I confess I was almost impressed that this feisty young Negro should attempt to challenge me over a question of semantics! I reminded her again of my regulation and she told me that the southern kitchen was unsuitable for their open fires on account of the wind. Eventually we reached an accommodation, but still she wasn't satisfied. I remember her words exactly. 'These are your rules,' she said. 'These are your rules. What good are they to me?'

What might I have said to that? I might have explained to her that the regulations were devised for the good of all, but I knew that she was quite incapable of seeing beyond her own interest.

At the time, I considered her inability almost childlike. It is, therefore, strange that I now find myself sympathizing with that African girl, Mary Silongo. 'What good are your rules to me?' These last days it has served as my quotidian refrain.

I believe that with every passing moment Lizzie and I grow closer and I am powerless to resist. I think of my Catherine, of course I do, but only to conjure countless ways to justify this new and intimate attachment. I tell myself that I am not the man with whom Catherine fell in love. I tell myself that she will find happiness with another (even reconciling my spirit to the likes of Teddy Jameson!). I tell myself that love by its nature is a fickle creature that chooses its home in spite of any practical concerns. I tell myself that I have suffered terribly and merit happiness of my own. But I return unfailingly to the promise I made: it seems the *rules* tell me to light my fire at the southern kitchen, no matter that the wind will immediately extinguish it. I cannot reconcile myself to this. I will not.

Nott has already recognized Lizzie's affection for me if not that I return it one hundredfold. How long may I honourably keep it secret from the good schoolteacher who has offered me nothing but generosity and kindness? Besides, though the match is an unlikely one, would he not be relieved to know my attachment to his daughter? However, I must ensure that he hears of it from me rather than any wagging tongue, of which there are many in a small village like Fry Norton.

Indeed, it was just this afternoon that I understood the exact nature of my predicament. As Lizzie and I returned home from practice with the morris men, we made our customary stop on the bench beneath the willow by the side of the leaze to allow me to remove my prosthetic and rest my stump a moment. It is a secluded spot and these brief interludes in none but each other's company have become more precious to me than anything, and I believe that Lizzie feels likewise.

Today, as we sat quietly side by side, she observed that I had stopped writing in my notebook so much as before. She wondered if I had lost interest in the morris and questioned how my theories of 'essential Englishness' (of which I have talked so much!) progressed.

Of course I had no plan to make a declaration, but in that moment I found myself quite naturally talking with a freedom like never before. I confessed that I had come to know that my desire to comprehend my nation and its character, my belief that it had somehow taken the wrong path, was in large part a projection of my analysis of myself. I told her that I considered England incomplete because I was incomplete, less than a whole man.

She looked at me with such tenderness then that my heart was almost rent in two. I might almost have thought she pitied me! Instinctively she reached out and touched my arm. She told me that, of all the people she'd met, I had the most reasonable claim to wholeness, no matter my affliction. I cannot express how much these words meant to me.

Emboldened, I said that I was not speaking of my status as

a cripple, but as an Englishman. I said that when I searched for Albion it was simply because I did not know what – or *who* – it was for whom I truly searched. I took her hand and held it tightly between my own.

At this point she sat back. She was flushed at the throat and I feared I had gone too far when she pulled her hand from mine, stood up and told me that we should return to the schoolhouse. Then, however, I saw we were not alone for, across the leaze, who should be watching us but Chavney, the foreman of the morris. Instantaneously I realized Lizzie's propriety and, truly, I loved her all the more.

41
Honesty is not a policy

London, England, 2008
Preston was sitting on his own in the green room. He took a mouthful of his first beer in more than five years and then rolled the cold bottle gently across his swollen lip. It was sore, but not so sore as his pride. He surveyed the carnage – the remnants of half-eaten canapés on the arms of sofas, a champagne stain spattered up the wall, cakes trodden into the carpet, chicken bones and olive stones spat across the floor. He took another swig. It was much the same every week, the liggers and hangers-on trashing the joint because the food and drink were free and they could. But this week it annoyed him because it had been Nobody's entourage who'd done the damage, an army of minor estuary thugs who'd turned up to abuse the perks of their boy's fifteen minutes in the spotlight.

Preston called a halt to that train of thought and the muddle of its middle-class sentiments – the voice in his head was beginning to sound like his old man's.

If he'd been honest with himself, Preston would have admitted that, most weeks, he was at the heart of this destruction; hanging with the stars, laughing at their jokes, fucking up the room, then soberly picking up the tab. But, for once, he was in no mood to be honest because that would have meant acknowledging his feelings of humiliation. Instead, therefore, he told himself he didn't want to turn into his dad.

Lorraine came in. She looked embarrassed, which only made him feel worse. She said, 'Hey, Tupps.' He didn't respond.

She said, 'Look, I'm really sorry. He was bang out of order. I told him that.'

Preston shrugged. She hovered. Then she approached and bent down to kiss his cheek. She smelt of perfume and champagne. 'We're all going out somewhere,' she said. 'You should come. We should squash this before it gets stupid, you know? It's business, innit?'

'Yeah,' Preston said bitterly. 'It's all business. You should tell him that. I can fuck him.'

Lorraine's mouth twitched with a flash of vexation, but she kept it in check. 'Don't talk like that. Come with us.'

'Where you going?'

'Dunno. We're gonna start at the Admiral. Take it from there.'

'What you going there for?'

'What do you mean? It's Dad's place.'

Preston reached into the mini-fridge, took out another beer and cracked it open. 'It's a dump.'

Lorraine stepped back, as if he'd actually knocked her off balance. 'You're being an arsehole,' she said, and left. Preston raised his beer bottle and toasted her departure.

He was feeling sorry for himself. This should have been a day of celebration. 'Jerusalem' by Nobody, the first release by A-List Recordings'™ first signing, had gone straight in at number one and had its first live performance on AuthenTV™. The reviews were great, the word of mouth was great, and the music video was the most embedded on The A-List™, YouTube and MySpace, and the most requested across the music television networks, from MTV to Channel U. Everything was going exactly to plan. So how come he'd been made to feel like shit?

After Nobody's performance, Authenticity™ had arranged his first major interview with *The Times*. Of course, they'd been inundated with requests but the core team had selected the journalist and newspaper carefully. They figured that the street buzz was already on track so a respected writer with a broadsheet publication would guarantee the next wave of interest and sales among the older generation of early adopters, culture vultures and tastemakers.

It had started well. Preston showed the journalist into the green room himself and Nobody was hyped from the stage and surrounded by his crew, who were being noisy and smoking weed and showing off their newly downloaded 'Jerusalem' ring tones. When the journalist asked if it was safe to leave his laptop by the door, Preston knew the atmosphere was perfect, just the right mixture of boisterous good humour and latent threat to give the rock hack a shiver of authenticity. That would get the juices flowing.

Nobody and his interviewer took the comfy chairs. Preston, Errol and Lorraine sat around a table to watch hawkishly – far enough away to let the pair talk, near enough to hear every word. Nobody was still wearing his balaclava, of course, and the baggy orange overalls he'd worn onstage. Lounging back in his chair, he was part hip-hop star, part super-hero and part Guantánamo terrorist.

Errol lit a reefer and nudged Preston. 'He looks crazy, Tupps, man,' he murmured approvingly. 'I told you. Looks crazy.'

The hack started by talking about Nobody's name. Nobody said that names were a distraction, appearances were a distraction, he just wanted people to listen to his music.

The journalist said, 'Sounds like you're not interested in celebrity.'

'What's a celebrity, king?' Nobody replied. 'A celebrity is a commodity, innit? I is not a commodity. Unfortunately my music has to be commodified because, in this society, that's the only way people get to hear it.'

The journalist said, 'So I guess by calling yourself Nobody, you're saying you're the same as everybody else.'

Nobody laughed. 'I *is* the same as everybody else.'

'You don't want to be rich?'

'I don't wanna be poor, bruh. That's different.' Then, when asked about the balaclava, Nobody said, 'Same thing, innit?'

The journalist said, 'The lyrics to "Jerusalem", your video, they're quite confrontational.'

'Says who?'

'Well, in the video, for example, you're shown beating up the Queen.'

Nobody laughed. It was a deep and true sound. 'But I's not beating up the Queen! It's an actress wearing a mask, innit? I don't wanna bother no old woman. I don't have no problem with the Queen so long as she don't bother me. It's just some fun, you know? I thought the British were supposed to have a great sense of humour.'

'Have *you* got a great sense of humour?'

'Of course. But I's not British.'

'No? So where are you from?'

Again, Nobody laughed: 'I's from Super-hero Land, king, down the A12. Eminem's got D12 – the "dirty dozen". I got the A12 – commuters, roadworks and traffic jams. Very British, innit?'

During the last exchange, Preston had held his breath – they really didn't want to get into the whole cloudy area of Nobody's heritage and the legal questions therein. But now he relaxed. His new signing was doing well: he was being cheeky, but bright and witty too.

No sooner had Preston thought this than it started to go wrong.

The journalist said, 'And what about Authenticity? You're lucky to be hooked up with 2P, right?'

'What you mean?'

'I mean, you're signed to his label, you just appeared on his TV show . . .'

'For sure, *someone* is lucky. I explain it to you like this: Tupps – I's only saying this 'cos he's my friend, innit? – he good at making money. And no doubt he thinks I's gonna make him a whole lot of it. So *someone* is lucky. But if you is an artist, king, you just want people to experience your art. And, like I said already, in the divided kingdom that means making a commodity, innit? And if you gonna make a commodity, you need a white man to sell it.

'This is truth old as history. You don't need me to tell you. It's not my job to educate in no interview: we make, you take. Trust me, son, if there was a brother who could do this for me, I'd be talking to him. The fact that there ain't? You could say that it's one among many artistic impulses.

'But don't think I is lucky. Fact is that the slave of a king lives in a palace, innit?'

The journalist thought he could smell a story and he looked over to where Preston was sitting and raised his eyebrows. 'What do you think, 2P?'

At this point, Preston didn't think anything – after all, this was the same shit Nobody had been spouting from their first meeting – so he just laughed indulgently. 'Well, I *am* good at making money,' he said.

But Nobody hadn't finished: 'What you asking him for? If you wanna know, talk to me. I am an educated man. It was Oscar Wilde who said, "An Englishman knows the price of everything and the value of nothing."'

The journalist corrected him self-importantly: 'I think you'll find it was a cynic.'

'What?'

'"A cynic knows the price of everything and the value of nothing."'

Nobody sat forward. The eyeholes in his balaclava were full of his eyes. 'You see now,' he said.

'So you're saying 2P is a cynic?'

'Of course. But it's more than that, king. I's saying that if you go down a mine, you don't want no sculptor standing next to you with his chisel. If you go down Babylon, you don't want no saint for company, you know?' Again, the journalist looked at Preston. Nobody caught the glance between them. 'Course, Tupps knows I's only speaking metaphorically.'

316

After that, the interview passed without incident. The hack seemed pleased and Preston told himself any controversy wouldn't do them any harm – they'd released a controversial record, so they'd have to capitalize on the brickbats.

Once he'd shown the journalist out, however, Lorraine approached him and said, 'He shouldn't have said those things.'

'Don't worry about it.' Preston waved it away.

But the way that Lorraine had brought it up made him feel as if now he had to bring it up himself. In fact, it almost felt like a point of honour to explain to Nobody exactly which side his bread was buttered.

Nobody was still slouched in the armchair, his balaclava now replaced by that strange cowboy hat, reliving his new stardom with some of his mates. It was, Preston thought, typical: you can talk the talk but the spotlight of celebrity is like a drug. 'That went well.'

'Yes, Tupps,' Nobody said. 'It's all good.'

He took a lazy gulp from a bottle of champagne. Preston had never seen him drink before. 'You shouldn't fuck with me, though,' Preston said.

'Fuck with you?'

'Yeah. You shouldn't talk that shit. Neither of us looks good.'

Nobody drank more champagne. He almost gagged on the bubbles. He laughed. 'I didn't talk no shit, king. I's just saying it like it is.'

The junior thugs sitting with him, waiting on that champagne bottle, chimed in: 'Yes, yes, son.' And, 'Tell the man.'

'You need to treat me with respect,' Preston said flatly. He was in danger of losing his temper. He could tell by the lack of emotion in his voice.

'Respect? Respect for what? Let's be serious, Tupps. You just a cuckoo, innit? You, like, sitting on someone else's nest like they your own eggs. You can't make music, but you

317

wanna sell my music. You ain't no nigger, but you wanna sell my blackness. You ain't got no opinions of your own so you gotta sell mine – it's not like I is telling you nothing you don't know. You said it yourself, king. You said you were like the picture hook and I was the picture.'

'I didn't say that.'

Nobody shook his head. 'You said exactly that.'

'You misunderstood me. But even if you're right, it's a symbiotic relationship, isn't it? I deserve respect.'

'Deserve? What do you mean, "deserve"? We are not equal, Tupps. That's no value judgement, it's just the way it is. We are *not* equal. Whether my music's sold or not, it's still my music. Nothing changes. But you, king? Without something to sell, you're out of work, redundant, without purpose.'

'Fuck you!' Suddenly, Preston had lost his temper. He could feel his hand clenching and opening at his side. He didn't know what had made him so angry. It wasn't as if he didn't agree with what Nobody had said, but he couldn't accept the way he'd said it and, more to the point, that it was him saying it. He sensed Errol next to him and he knew he was speaking words and they were meaningless and placatory and patronizing in their placatory meaninglessness. This only made him angrier still. What was this new world order in which even Errol, a man whose whole identity was a fiction authored by aspiration founded in self-doubt, dared to tell him – him! Preston Pinner! Tuppence™! 2P™! – to calm down?

Nobody had now stood up and was standing face to face with him, his head tilted to one side and turned a little, so that he regarded him with one eye from beneath the brim of his hat. He looked like a cowboy. It felt like a gunfight.

'Fuck who?' Nobody asked. 'You need to be careful, king. You need to be careful what you say. I understand this now. You say you just wanna sell shit, but you don't. Fact is, you can't bear someone else take the shine, let alone some black geezer, innit?'

'Don't be so –'

'Don't be so what? Don't matter whether you see it, bruh. You is blind and I see clear enough for both of us. Lolly told me about you and your fancy flat and all that corn you splash around and you and your friends talking about me like I'm a washing powder to be sold and taking that cocaine like you a bunch of crackers. You got everything, Tupps, but you still want what I got. You the exact reason why racial politics so messed up: take black people enough time to get their heads straight and when we do we discover the white man still confused. You wanna make my music, Tupps, you want my life. Being black is heavy, king. And you want some of that weight 'cos you scared you might just float away. But it don't work like that. It's not the vessel that got the weight, it's what's inside, innit? I seen the way you look at Lolly, but she ain't gonna weigh you down, king. You just float away together.

'What? No. Don't start lying to me, Tupps. You know I seen the way you look at her . . .'

Preston raised his fist and lurched forward.

Later, he wasn't sure whether he'd genuinely intended to hit Nobody or not. All things considered, it might have been better if he had, or had taken a swing at least, and missed, and had A-List™ Recordings' first signing take a swing back. At least then he'd have been able to look on it with some sense of his own integrity: that another man had questioned his honour and he'd done what needed doing. If that had happened, then he and Nobody might have made up later over further drinking and, perhaps, some humorous misogyny of the kind that fighting men are known to enjoy; or they might not have made up at all and cultivated a long-standing feud that he could have leaked strategically to the music press.

But instead Errol saw what he thought Preston intended and he caught him by the elbow saying, 'Leave it, Tupps! It's not worth it.'

Errol was bigger and stronger than Preston, but the restraint just provoked him further and he swung round with such force that he pulled Errol forward so that Errol overbalanced and his forehead thudded into Preston's top lip. The blow sent Preston sprawling across a coffee-table and Nobody's crew hooted in delight, saying things like 'Shit shit shit' and 'Fuck fuck fuck', as if they were a troop of curse monkeys swinging down from the trees.

It was Errol and Nobody who helped Preston to his feet. Errol was rubbing his forehead. Nobody's concern was apparently genuine when he asked, 'You OK, Tupps?'

Later, alone, Preston tried to numb his lip with beer and the cold glass that contained it and to numb his ego by retelling the evening's events over and over again in his head until he felt victimized and brimmed with indignation. The alcohol helped because, to ring true, lying to oneself requires persistence and tedious repetition. A willing accomplice with an agenda of their own is also, of course, useful.

Jodie came into the green room to turn off the lights. At the sight of Preston, she said, 'I didn't know you were still here.'

Preston said nothing.

'You're drinking,' she observed. 'I've never seen you drinking.'

Preston shrugged.

She came and sat next to him. 'Great show tonight.' She put her hand on his thigh. 'He's gonna be massive. Nobody, I mean.' Then, 'I heard what happened. You OK?' And, heatedly, 'Arrogant motherfucker. "Nobody" is right. He's just a fucking nobody.'

Preston touched her hand with his own. He'd meant to move it from his leg, but now he was touching it he enjoyed the contact and it was Jodie who took it away.

She picked up a copy of *Musik Muzic* magazine that was lying around, produced a wrap of Pablo's coke and chopped out a line.

Preston said, 'What about me?'

She looked at him, inclined her head a little as if trying to work out whether he was serious; then she cut a second. Preston snorted it, then licked his finger to pick up the stray crumbs. He rubbed them on his lips. They were numb in seconds. His brain was fizzing.

Jodie said, 'You know you could fuck him, right?'

Preston said, 'Sure. I told Lorraine that.'

'Lorraine?' For some reason, Jodie considered that name worthy of a sneer. She thought for a moment. Then she said, 'Would only take a phone call. Wouldn't even hit sales I shouldn't think.'

Preston said nothing. Jodie chopped out a further pair of lines. As she did so, she giggled about nothing in particular.

42

Resurrection

Queenstown, Republic of Zambawi, 2008
Jim Tulloh opened the fly screen and stumbled into Mama's House. His breathing was shallow and his left hand was clamped to his side. He was feeling nauseous. He was worried he might faint. He propped himself against the wall in the hall and gradually the cold sweat on his forehead dried. He could hear the crickets outside and Sylvia bustling around in the kitchen, but the kids were all in bed. That was a relief.

Sylvia emerged from the kitchen carrying a pile of folded clothes. She barely acknowledged him, but said, 'Did you see him?' before going into the laundry. She appeared again a moment later, or at least her face did, round the frame of the door. 'I said, did you see him?'

Jim shook his head.

Again, she was gone, but she kept talking from the laundry: 'How come you didn't see him?'

Jim opened his mouth. He didn't know whether he could speak but, as it transpired, the words came out OK and he sounded like himself, more or less: 'He wouldn't see me. He's isolated, backed into a corner. I guess he thinks I'm the enemy.'

'I *told you*,' Sylvia said, sounding both irritated and pleased with herself. 'He's the President. I'm sure he's got better things to do than see you.'

'He's my friend,' Jim said quietly. Then, louder, 'It's true, though.'

'What's true?'

'Apparently he's in Gwezi.'

Again Sylvia's face appeared. 'Jesus!' she said. 'An MP! A British minister! Does he know what he's doing?'

'Who?'

'Adini.'

Jim tried to shrug but it hurt too much. He could feel the wet warmth beneath the palm of his left hand. He didn't dare look.

Sylvia had started talking to socks in the laundry: 'Tefadzwa grey with Tefadzwa grey, navy with navy, and who do you belong to? What about you, Julius blue? Do you need darning? Or are you past saving?'

Jim felt a sudden, desperate pang of misery, distinct from the pain. He could feel his throat constricting and his eyes filling. He had to keep talking, so he called, 'How was your day?'

'OK. Mercy got her period. She's grown into a young woman. I can't believe it. I don't know who's more scared, her or me.'

'Right.'

Jim realized he couldn't support himself any longer so he turned his back to the wall and allowed himself to slide gently down.

'What the hell have you done?' Sylvia asked.

'What?'

'Sorry. I'm talking to Presley's school trousers. He's through the knees again.'

'Right.'

Sylvia re-emerged from the laundry to show her husband the offending item of clothing. When she found him slumped on the floor, she raised her eyebrows and tutted. 'Are you drunk?'

'No,' Jim said, and for some reason he started to laugh. His vision was blurring. 'I've been stabbed.'

'What did you say?'

'I've been stabbed.'

He finally took his left hand off the wound to show his wife. Now that he looked at it, it wasn't as scary as he'd thought:

just a soaking, spreading patch of red around the small tear in his shirt where the screwdriver had gone through. He was, however, somehow pleased by the amount of blood, as if it showed that he wasn't making a fuss over nothing.

'Jesus!' Sylvia said. 'Oh, Jesus!'

She was frozen to the spot, staring at him, but only for an instant before she sprang into action – Sylvia, his wife, the founder of Mama's House, who'd seen more horror than most and buried forty-three children and survived.

She carried him, semi-conscious, upstairs to the bathroom. It was a peculiar experience for both of them: Jim, detached, astounded by his wife's strength; Sylvia, in the moment, bewildered by her husband's weakness. He was no heavier than a bundle of kindling. He felt no more real than a marionette to either of them.

He meekly allowed her to strip him to the waist. She hadn't seen him so naked for a while and it was a shock – the deathly white of his torso compared to the nut brown of his face, the xylophone ribcage, the blotches and blemishes. She put on her professional front, the same she wore for funerals, because that was the only way she could cope. But Jim inevitably misinterpreted it and he could now feel his misery as if it were something physical, a boiled sweet stuck fast somewhere deep in his oesophagus.

As she tenderly bathed the wound, she asked, 'Have you been looking after yourself?'

In spite of himself, Jim resented her professional tone, which accompanied her professional front, as if she were a nurse and he just another poor dying fool on the production line to the cemetery. 'Apart from being stabbed, you mean?' he said.

He told her what had happened. Driving back from State House, he'd stopped at the expat pharmacy on Machel to collect his drugs. He'd walked out straight into a gang of dusty street kids who'd been rendered feral by death and had no respect for the life that had no respect for them. One of them held a long screwdriver.

He gave them all the money he was carrying without complaint. But when the boy with the screwdriver tried to grab his prescription, he'd attempted to pull it away. 'I knew AIDS would kill me,' he told Sylvia. 'But I never thought it would be like this.'

'Save your jokes,' she muttered. 'You're not going to die just yet.'

He said he didn't think the boy had meant to stab him. He said that, however shocked he'd looked when the screwdriver went in, he couldn't have looked as shocked as the kid who was holding it.

'Didn't they know who you are?' Sylvia whispered indignantly. 'We spent all this time trying to help them and then this happens.'

Jim shook his head. '*You* spent all this time trying to help them. Watch out, beloved, you'll start sounding like Lars if you're not careful.'

Sylvia tutted. But Jim thought it was probably the term of affection that had offended her.

'It's funny,' he said. 'I saw the screwdriver go in. And the last thing I thought was, At least it's clean.'

Sylvia taped gauze and padding over the wound. She told him she didn't think the blade had hit anything essential, but he needed to see a doctor. She was worried about the bleeding.

'Where should I go?' Jim asked. 'St Mary's? These days, I might as well just drive myself to the morgue. Cut out the middle man. I'll be OK.'

Sylvia carried her husband into his bedroom and helped him out of the rest of his clothes. Although she thought she'd felt everything and seen everything, she found herself curiously offended by his penis. It was the only part of him that hadn't changed and, even limp as it was, it looked unjustly healthy between his withered thighs. After all, his errant dick had been responsible for everything that had gone wrong and here it was looking relaxed and smug and as if it had got off scot-free. She felt simultaneously nostalgic and disgusted and quickly covered Jim with a sheet.

Jim made himself comfortable on his right side and Sylvia sat behind him on the edge of the bed. When she thought he was asleep, she stood up. But as she went to turn off the light by the door, he rolled onto his back and said, 'Please stay with me.' He was weeping.

Sylvia hated it when Jim cried. It made her feel weak. She'd married a man and had no time for a tearful bag of bones.

Jim knew that Sylvia hated it when he cried but, for once, he couldn't help it.

'You feeling sorry for yourself?' she asked, with some spite.

'Yeah.' He wiped his eyes with the back of his wrist. 'But don't go. I have to tell you something.' He cleared his throat.

He knew what he wanted to say – sorry. It was all he ever wanted to say. He came at it from many different angles, even shifting the blame to her or refusing to apologize at all, but it always came back to sorry. And he kept trying new angles, because, like many men, he believed that his wife's failure to respond as he wanted was simply because he hadn't found the right words, never acknowledging that she might not have had such a response left in her. His position was wilfully foolish, but at least it gave him a hope he could cling to.

'You get married . . .' he began. 'I . . . I got married because I could see the best in you. And I think you got married because you could see the best in me. And . . . and . . .' He was already stammering and Sylvia wanted to be somewhere else. 'And you became that person and I didn't. But I love you. And there's no point saying sorry because I've tried that and it doesn't change anything. But this is it. This is *it*. I had dreams . . . *we* had dreams of what we could be. Now I only dream that you're next to me when I die. Just stay with me. For a bit. Just stay with me for a bit.'

Sylvia looked down at her bag-of-bones husband and felt utterly exhausted. 'You fucker, Jim,' she said. 'I had dreams too.'

'I know you did.'

'I had dreams too!'

'So tell me about them.'

At that moment, in spite of herself and much to her own surprise, Sylvia gave up. She gave up her defensiveness, anger and contempt, the very substances that had stuck her together for the last couple of years. Certainly, giving them up had nothing to do with Jim's words, but maybe her defensiveness, anger and contempt had run their course, or maybe she was simply too tired to hold on to them any more. And now she found them running out of her like water through her fingers.

She lay down next to Jim and told him about her dreams, things she hadn't said since they were married; simple dreams of passion, kindness and security that, surely, shouldn't have been too much to hope for. Then she told him how it had felt to bring home Tefadzwa, the first orphan to stay at Mama's House. She told him it hadn't been a question of feeling maternal, it was a question of purpose.

She remembered Jim's infidelities. She said she wasn't surprised, but disappointed. She said she wouldn't have expected him to be different from other men if he hadn't said he was different from other men. She understood why he'd lied about the women, but why had he lied about that? She said she'd thought they were in it together; in the marriage together. So why hadn't he told her that wasn't true, instead of demonstrating it and killing himself in the process? She told him she wasn't defensive, angry or contemptuous any more, just tired. Like he said, this was *it*. She knew he was scared, but she was scared too, and she wasn't allowed to be scared because she had eighteen children and a dying husband to look after.

Jim didn't say anything. He just lay on his back and stared

at the ceiling, his breathing coming slow and even. But when he rested his hand on Sylvia's hip, she didn't move it away.

Now she began talking about the future. But she daren't talk about their future or that of the positive kids, so she talked about the other children instead. She told him about Tefadzwa, who said he'd be a doctor. Although he was always bottom of his class with no apparent aptitude for anything much, he had a doggedness about him that she thought would see him blossom in the end. She told him about Chennai who'd developed a curious desire to move to Sweden after a project she'd done at school. 'You know what she said to me?' Sylvia laughed. '"Mama, did you know that in summer the sun can shine for almost twenty-four hours?" And when I asked her about the winter, she said, "It's OK, I'll just sleep."'

She told him about Mary, who was bright and capable if she could only keep her eyes on her books and off those boys. She told him about Mercy, who was so helpful around the house and had a rigid plan mapped out for motherhood and marriage, which involved two boys and two girls and a God-fearing mechanic for a husband. She suspected Mercy had been reading *The No.1 Ladies' Detective Agency*.

Of course, she wasn't really telling Jim anything he didn't already know. But the fact that she was telling him with a softness he hadn't heard for such a long time relaxed him and he shut his eyes and felt almost happy. Her voice began to slow down as she drifted into sleep. But every now and then she'd wake up again and start another anecdote as if she'd just been pausing to think.

Truth be told, after a while, Jim was barely listening anyway. Instead his full concentration was on his right hand where it lay on her thigh. From time to time he moved his fingertips a little, just shifting the thin material of her dress and clarifying in his mind's eye the picture of the soft flesh beneath. Ignoring her words, he imagined her voice was seducing him and his nose was full of her scent, which was both strange and familiar, a cocktail of soap, sweat and the tantalizing essence of Sylvia that had always mesmerized him.

To Jim's astonishment, he felt his penis wake up. It had been so long that, at first, he didn't know quite what it was but he soon realized: he was getting an erection. He immediately tried to think it away, but it was coming whether he liked it or not. He opened his eyes and looked at his wife, but hers were shut so he abandoned himself to it. He could feel it thicken, then slowly begin to rise and press up against the sheet. He struggled not to laugh, hit with a sudden and delightful sense of absurdity.

His wife was now fully asleep next to him. He considered nudging her and, in their new spirit of rapprochement, showing her his erection and saying, 'You see? *This* is what you married,' like a punchline. But he wasn't sure she'd find it funny. Maybe she'd think it was true and maybe she'd be right.

Unfortunately as a small tumbler of Jim's blood filled his penis, a large bottle of the stuff had begun to seep unnoticed from the wound in his side. As quickly as it had appeared, the erection was gone, the blood needed elsewhere. Jim began to feel light-headed and very, very tired. He knew what was coming but there wasn't anything to be done. This was it. He pressed his fingertips into Sylvia's thigh and she made a contented-sounding noise. But she didn't wake up.

He had regrets, perhaps more than most. But in the main, rightly or wrongly, he considered himself fortunate, and that's the most any of us can hope for. He closed his eyes again and slowly bled to death.

Sylvia woke an hour or two later. She knew immediately what had happened. She got up calmly and looked down at her husband's body, the sheet thick with blood. Then she walked out of the room, dropped to her knees in the corridor and screamed. The children emerged in ones and twos and terrified clusters. Sylvia couldn't speak, so it was Mercy who went and saw the body and told them what she'd found. Eighteen children gathered around Sylvia and latched themselves on to whatever part of her they could reach, and they all cried together.

43

Insert document
'UK Official Arrested In Zambawi', *Daily Telegraph*, 10 June 2008, Joseph Barnes

A 'senior figure' in the Foreign and Commonwealth Office has been detained in Zambawi, according to a Whitehall source. The FCO has refused to officially confirm or deny the report.

The figure, believed to be a high-ranking adviser to the FCO board, was making a covert visit to the troubled African state to negotiate the release of British businessman Gordon Tranter. Tranter, the multimillionaire executive director of FTSE-100-listed mining company G&T Holdings, has himself been imprisoned for more than a month since his arrest on suspicion of terrorism.

The UK's diplomatic mission to Zambawi was withdrawn in November 2007 after the re-election of President Enoch Adini for a third term. The withdrawal was in response to widespread electoral corruption, brutal suppression of political opposition and President Adini's subsequent refusal to service Zambawi's international debts.

In January the Zambawian government expelled all foreign media and most international aid agencies. However, remaining NGO sources report widespread food and fuel shortages, crippling power cuts and a crumbling infrastructure.

If confirmed, the arrest of the FCO official would be yet another body blow to the UK government's 'African Authority' initiative. Launched by the Prime Minister in August 2007 to promote 'increased understanding and co-operation between Africa and the West' and 'African solutions to African problems', the Authority has been dogged by problems from the outset. African delegates have bemoaned Western governments' intransigence on debt relief, while Western politicians have been increasingly frustrated in their calls for improved democratization, transparency and governance across the continent.

The latest setback came just last week when the former South African president Nelson Mandela, who famously counts the Spice Girls among his heroes, turned down an invitation to attend the 'Africa Unite Festival' at Wembley Stadium. Planned as a celebration of the African Authority's achievements, the festival is beginning to look like a white elephant that will only cause the Prime Minister further embarrassment.

44

Insert document
'The diary of a local gentleman', 26 May 1901
(Empire Museum, Bristol), anon.

They say, 'There is no fool like an old fool.' If so, what can
I look forward to but half a century of increasing foolishness?
For I am still a young man, but I am guilty of an idiocy as
old as humanity.

I am also quite drunk, though it is barely midday. I have
been conversing with my hip flask for more than an hour,
but even this dear, trusted companion seems determined to
let me down for I feel no comfort from the pain. It seems
that I am an incomplete man after all. I am reduced. I am
reduced by fourteen inches of left leg. I am not convinced
that the reduction in my heart can be subject to such precise
calculation.

Outside all is spring. The festivities are under way and
I can hear the merriment on the green, everyone decked out
in their best, fresh from the service. Several of the other sides
have already arrived for the ale and their fiddlers are playing
to the delight of most. Beneath my window, children are
enjoying a game of hide and seek, but I assume their
laughter is directed at me, the village idiot. How I despise
them, these rural savages! How I despise myself for allowing
them to seduce me with their pagan games and base
sensibilities!

It now seems ridiculous that I entertained the notion that
these uneducated and unquestioning masses might be
representative of my country. In my fancy, I imagined this

the society from which modern men of God and science evolved. Now I know it as the primordial torment from which we fled.

These last few days have been a purgatory of unfulfilled desire, but I own that I was a willing victim, so feeble is my mind. I cherished every moment with Miss Elizabeth Nott, found solace in her laughter, suggestion in her smallest comment and briefest glance. In fact, I now crave such purgatory; better than this hell of knowing her true contempt for me.

This morning I rose early, determined to perfect my role as 'Nobbin' in Crabfish for this afternoon's ale – to think that my desire was not to ridicule myself in front of the village! So I took the grotesque horse costume to the barn that I might practise alone.

As I approached the barn, I saw its door was open and Chavney, the captain of the Fry Norton side, loitering in the doorway. I was about to call out a 'good day' when I realized he was not alone. I recognized Elizabeth's voice at once and simultaneously the circumstances of the situation. I swear I was paralysed with shock. Fortunately I was concealed in shadow and invisible to young love. Though I think I might have stood next to them and still they wouldn't have seen me, so intent was their gaze each upon the other.

Elizabeth emerged into the sunlight and I could see her face quite clearly, the blush of her cheek extending down her long, pale neck. Just the day before yesterday it was I who made her blush with what I must now concede was embarrassment.

I might have shown myself there and then. I might reasonably have taken my stick to the brute Chavney. But, such was my horror, I did not.

It was clear I had arrived at the conclusion of their love-making. Each was now to hurry home to conceal their deception and prepare themselves for church. It was equally clear that I had arrived at the height of an impassioned exchange.

'Are you jealous, my darling?' Elizabeth asked coyly. She reached out for her lover in an attempted caress, but Chavney stepped back. Whatever their subject, evidently Elizabeth wanted to make a joke of it, but Chavney would not concur.

'Not jealous.' He shook his head. 'But I don't like the way he looks at you, so.'

'Come now, Jack, don't be such a dunce. He's just a cripple and a drunk.'

Immediately I grasped their subject and my blood ran cold.

'You don't think I know his kind, Lizzie, the wealthy gent who thinks he's due whatever he can take? I don't know why you give him encouragement.'

'Encouragement, Jack?' Her voice rose in indignation, presumably because I was an object of such disgust to her.

'Codrington at the big house is the same.'

'So it's Codrington, now. What kind of woman do you take me for?'

'No. Not Codrington. I'm just saying he's the same. But it's the other one you need to watch. I saw you in the leaze with him, remember? You're too kind to him, Lizzie. Do you not wonder at everything he writes down in those books of his? Honestly, sometimes I think you like the attention. Don't you think I know what kind of life a man like that might give you?'

For a moment I thought Elizabeth might lose her temper. But she didn't. Instead, she took Chavney's hand and, though he resisted, she wouldn't let it go. 'You *are* jealous, dear Jack,' she said firmly. 'But how little you know of a woman's heart. I am sorry for him is all. Do you honestly believe I could ever want a life in the company of such pompous misery?' Then she laughed. Where once that sound was almost a drug to me, now I heard it for all its unmistakable cruelty. 'You know the only time I've seen him happy was playing Nobbin?'

She moved back from Chavney and began to reel on the spot, laughing all the time, before pretending to stumble and support herself on the doorway. 'Oh, my wretched st-st-stump!' she exclaimed. 'One of you men fetch me a tot! Oh, those B-B-B-Boers! The b-b-b-buggers!'

It took me a moment to comprehend that she was mimicking me. It is true that I occasionally now stammer. I have been so afflicted since the loss of my leg, but I didn't realize it was worthy of mockery.

I have asked for pity from no one, but the complete absence thereof was shocking. Chavney laughed too and they embraced and parted before my shock slowly gave way to anger. No man who has served England as I have should be subjected to such ridicule! What kind of fool am I to have been so taken in by such a silly girl and her ruthless games?

No sooner had I returned to the house than I told Nott what I had seen; not my part, of course, but the intimacy between his daughter and the labouring man. He accepted the news with some resignation, which only increased my feelings of foolishness as it dawned on me that the conversation between the two of them that I had overheard some days ago was about Chavney. It seems that lust, for that was what it was, is the blindest emotion. He vouched that he would talk with her again. But I fear that Nott, for all his generosity to me, is a weak man and incapable of controlling the girl.

I sat with them in church. Chavney was some rows behind but I caught every last glance and smile between the pair. Their contempt for modesty and the good name of the schoolteacher repelled me.

Afterwards I stayed behind on the pretext of speaking to

the vicar. But Elizabeth waited for me outside and asked why I looked so troubled. I told her shortly that I was thinking on the sermon and she might do likewise. The apparent openness of her face only rekindled my anger. She asked if I was worried about my role in the morris and suggested we meet in the barn that I might practise my steps. I agreed. If Nott cannot take his daughter in hand, then it falls to me. Cripple and drunk I may be, but I remain an English gentleman and now, more than ever, I see the virtues therein and thus welcome the responsibility.

[Subsequent pages have been apparently burnt or torn out. The following undated entry is struck through on the inside back cover]

My dearest Kitty
I have already written and discarded this letter a dozen times. I cannot—

[The diary ends]

45

Insert document
'Where Illegals Dare', *Sun*, 12 June 2008, Hamid
Khan

<u>Number one rapper is illegal immigrant – A *Sun* exclusive</u>

New rap star Nobody, currently at number one in the pop
chart with his first single 'Jerusalem', is an ILLEGAL African
immigrant called BEN PHIRI, a *Sun* investigation has revealed.

'We're all in shock,' says a source at Nobody's record
company, A-List Recordings. 'None of us had any idea. I guess
this explains why he insists on wearing a mask.'

In every photograph and television appearance that Nobody
has made so far, he has appeared in a balaclava of the kind
worn by TERRORISTS.

'I don't think anybody knows what he looks like except 2P,'
our horrified source explained. 'It's awful, especially when you
think of the single and video and the way they put the boot
into Britain.'

Nobody's 'Jerusalem' is a mickey-taking version of the
William Blake hit loved by football crowds and sung before
every FA Cup final. In Nobody's version, he actually delivers
the line: 'Don't call us illegal, we're making a stand.' BUT HE
IS ILLEGAL!

What's more, the video shows him apparently 'happy
slapping' the Queen and other members of the royal family.

<u>SICK</u>

'I can't believe I bought this song on the Internet,' says
Joe Tanner, 18, from Kingston. 'At first I thought the video

was funny, like *Double Take*. But now I know he's an illegal immigrant, it's just sick.'

Andy Paddick, 43, a mechanic from Chelmsford, agrees: 'Who does this guy think he is, taking our kids' money under false pretences? I'll give him a happy slapping, I tell you.'

<u>FAVOURITISM?</u>

A-List Recordings is a subsidiary of Authenticity, both companies of popular media tycoon, Preston '2P' Pinner. The son of junior Foreign and Commonwealth Office minister David Pinner, Preston is also booking music acts for next week's Africa Unite Festival at Wembley Stadium, the climax to the Prime Minister's African Authority programme. Preston has booked Nobody to headline one section.

The Africa Unite Festival has promised to review the line-up in the light of our investigation, while a Home Office spokesman says, 'We will look into your claim and thank the *Sun* for its vigilance.'

It is not yet known which country Ben Phiri comes from. His surname is common across sub-Saharan Africa. According to government estimates, there are currently more than 750,000 illegal immigrants in the UK. As many as A QUARTER OF A MILLION may come from Africa.

46
Sometimes shit is just shit

London, England, 2008
Preston wanted to be alone but it was a day of visitors.

Errol had got it right when he'd dropped by in the afternoon. 'It's all the shape of a fucking pear,' he'd said. And Errol didn't even know the half of it.

Errol had come round because Preston was lying low for a second day. Yesterday the *Sun* had broken the Nobody story and Preston rang into Authenticity™ saying he was staying home to avoid the paps. Today, having checked the feeding frenzy online, he hadn't even bothered to call. So Errol came to him.

The first thing Errol had said was, 'What the fuck, Tupps? I mean, what the fuck?' Then, 'It's all the shape of a fucking pear.'

Preston didn't respond.

Errol said he'd had to leave the office by the back door to dodge the scrum. He asked Preston if the tabs knew where he lived. Preston said they didn't; he was careful.

Errol said, 'You sure, Tupps? 'Cos they gunning for you. This ain't just about Nobody, bruv, they want 2P. There's a fucking lynch mob and they're shouting your name – or your brand name anyway.'

'They don't know where I live,' Preston said. 'Unless you told them.'

Errol sneered. 'I didn't tell those fuckers nothing, bruv. The question is, what did *you* tell them?'

'What do you mean?'

' "A source at A-List Recordings",' it said. Who's that source, Tupps? You?'

Preston sighed. He sat down at the long table in the huge kitchen. Errol sat opposite him. Preston thought how strange it was to see Errol in the kitchen. Generally he kept himself busy in the living room with his stash of weed and porn. This was Jodie's domain of cooking and cocaine.

After what he imagined was a long enough pause to disconnect Errol's last question from the next of his own, he asked, 'Jodie been in?'

But he'd misjudged his employee's skills of association. 'Oh, shit!' Errol exclaimed. 'I knew the bitch was dumb, I didn't know she was *that* dumb.'

'Don't . . .' Preston began wearily. But he didn't know where that was going so he left it there.

'Don't what?'

'Just don't, OK?'

They talked numbers. As far as they could tell from the online stats, the sales of 'Jerusalem' were actually going better than ever; amazing considering the bile on the A-List™ message boards. Errol couldn't understand it, but Preston figured people wanted to know what the fuss was about, to understand who it was they were supposed to start hating. 'But it's not about "Jerusalem", is it?' Preston said. 'I mean, sure we'll stay at number one for a couple of weeks, but it's about what we do next. I mean, this will die down, but Joe Public's not gonna buy a Nobody album now, are they?'

'Shit.'

'And what about Africa Unite?'

'It's all fucking pear-shaped,' Errol said again. 'What we gonna do?'

'I don't know.'

'What do you mean, "I don't know"? Who the fuck else gonna know?'

Errol's panicking was making Preston feel jumpy. He produced a wrap of cocaine and cut himself a line on the table. Errol was staring at him. 'You doing charlie now?'

'Just to take the edge off, you know? You want one?'

Errol jerked his head to the side. He looked suddenly uncomfortable. '"Recreational drug use" – that's what they say, innit? White people do that. The only black people what do that shit is junkies.'

Preston hoovered the line, sat back and heaved an exaggerated sigh of satisfaction. 'Black. White. Whatever,' he said.

Errol held his eyes and wiped his mouth with the back of his hand. Preston could see an expression hiding behind his face; it was hard to say for sure, but it looked contemptuous. 'What?'

'Where's our boy?'

'Who?'

'Where's Nobody?'

'No idea.'

Errol stood up and sent his chair skidding backwards. Preston said, 'What's the matter with you?' But Errol didn't reply and instead disappeared into the heart of the flat. He shrugged as though Errol were still there to see him, then chopped himself another line. Errol reappeared a couple of minutes later carrying a pile of DVDs. 'What are you doing?' Preston asked.

'I'm telling you this because I'm your friend, Tupps. You're in serious danger of becoming just another arsehole.'

'Because I'm doing coke?'

'That's just symbolic.'

'So you're taking your porn? You know I hate you keeping that shit here anyway.'

Errol stood up a little straighter and lifted his chin a little. 'That's symbolic too,' he said. 'You need to sort shit out, Tupps. You need to check yourself. Later.' And he was gone.

Preston scrunched his face. He didn't know what that was all about, or if he did he wasn't yet ready to admit it. Instead he puffed out his cheeks and allowed himself a derisory blow at the absurdities of moral relativism. He didn't know whether to laugh or cry. So he did another line.

If Errol's visit left Preston bewildered, it was nothing compared to how he felt when the spooks in suits showed up half an hour later.

They rang the bell at the entrance to Shoreditch Heights and waited to be buzzed in. No one *ever* did that. People were always coming in and out so visitors would just catch the gate and duck inside. Therefore when Preston looked at the grainy image on the security camera – three men, three suits, three collars and ties – he assumed they were making a point and his stomach turned somersaults.

If he hadn't been such an inexperienced cocaine user and hadn't been too high to realize it, he'd have known he was too high for this and pretended he wasn't there. But he was too high so he pushed the intercom and said, 'Yes?'

And when one of the men said, 'Preston Pinner?' he immediately pressed the gate-release button without further enquiry.

He then panicked and spent the two minutes it took the men to reach his front door in a paranoid sweep of the flat, clearing away anything incriminating. He wasn't a criminal so this only meant flushing the remnants of his wrap down the kitchen sink, but he still completed a couple more circuits as if he'd mistaken himself for John Gotti.

He assumed the suits were from Immigration and wanted to talk about Nobody. But they weren't and they didn't.

He opened the door to find himself face to face with Jeremy Shorter, his old man's assistant. 'Gerald?' Preston said. He did actually remember that the guy's name was Jeremy, but he was high and it just slipped out.

'Jeremy,' the suit corrected him. 'Can we come in?'

It was only then that Preston took any notice of the other two men, which was strange because they were thoroughly noticeable: as tall and impassive as mannequins.

343

He led them into the kitchen and they told him to sit down. So he did. Jeremy sat opposite him in Errol's spot.

Jeremy asked him if he'd heard from his dad. Preston told him it had been a few days. 'What's this about?' he asked.

Jeremy nodded and placed his hands flat on the tabletop. He paused for a moment and eyed his two colleagues, who'd sat at the far end of the table. Preston thought there was something different about him; a new confidence, perhaps. Or maybe it was just that he'd got rid of the earring.

Jeremy told him that Pinner had been arrested in Zambawi on suspicion of espionage. He said they believed they knew where he was being held and had no reason to think he wasn't safe and well. He said the whole thing was just grandstanding by the Zambawian government and they were confident of securing Pinner's release very shortly.

Preston said, 'What?'

Jeremy repeated himself.

Preston said, 'Where?'

'Zambawi. It's in Africa.'

'Right,' Preston said, then burst out laughing. It took him a minute or two to rein it in and Jeremy watched him placidly the whole time. 'Sorry,' he said eventually. 'It's the shock.'

Jeremy asked if Preston had any spirits in the house, a drop of brandy, perhaps, or a Scotch. He said it sometimes helped take the edge off bad news. Preston struggled not to laugh at the choice of expression. He said he hadn't any Scotch or brandy. What he didn't say was that he'd had enough bad news and he hadn't any edges left anyway.

Jeremy told him that he'd been in Zambawi with Pinner. But after the arrest, when he'd discovered there was nothing he could do, he'd flown home. He'd only got off the plane that morning but he'd wanted to talk to Preston himself because they'd been at Cambridge together.

'Right,' Preston said. 'Thanks.' He wondered at Jeremy's use of the word 'together'. He might as well have said 'because we both live in London'. He asked how come it wasn't on the news. Jeremy ummed and erred. For the first time his colleagues spoke up. One mannequin said they'd been hoping to keep it quiet, to resolve the situation before it got out, though that was unlikely since there'd already been a minor leak from the FCO. He said this last clause with an intonation of disgust.

The second mannequin said they didn't know why the Zambawians hadn't announced it but he figured that they were bricking it now they'd realized what they'd done.

Preston asked what he thought was a reasonable question: 'If they're "bricking it", why did they do it in the first place? In fact, if they're really "bricking it", why don't they just release him?'

The second mannequin pulled a disdainful expression, engaging his left nostril and eyebrow. 'Who knows why these jokers do anything? The only thing I know for sure is that they're bricking it all right. You'd better believe it.'

Suddenly Preston found himself glad after all that Jeremy was there. The two mannequins were evidently idiots. He looked at Jeremy, who was fingering his pierced, empty ear-lobe. He reached into the inside pocket of his suit and produced a manila envelope. From it, he extracted a single sheet of paper folded in half. He pushed it across the table. Preston read it. It was a transcript of his last conversation with Pinner.

Preston said, 'Where did you get this?'

The second mannequin answered. 'We've got people,' he said. Preston was really starting to hate him.

'Can you tell us about it?' Jeremy asked quietly.

'What do you want to know?'

'Do you know who Father Christmas is?'

'Of course,' Preston said, and Jeremy leant forward. 'He's a fat man who comes down the chimney.'

Jeremy sat back and smiled thinly. 'What does it mean?'

'Mean? It doesn't mean anything. He was drunk. I assumed

he was talking shit. I mean, I know he's my dad, but he's a politician and he talks shit. That's what he does: talk shit.'

Jeremy held out his hand for the paper. Preston returned it. Jeremy said, 'Is there anything you'd like to ask us?'

'Yeah. I saw my old man not long before he left, that night at the Moroccan place in Mayfair. You were there. He told me that he was going on this trip, said there was some English geezer who'd been banged up for plotting a coup.'

'That's right. His name's Gordon Tranter. He's still being held. In fact, we suspect the minister's in the same facility.'

'Right, so what I'm asking is, did they do it? I mean, I know he was talking all this shit about Father Christmas but even shit's got to come from somewhere.'

Jeremy chuckled. 'Like I said, Preston, the Africans are grand-standing. Sometimes shit is just shit.' He stood up. Clearly their meeting was over. He asked Preston if he wanted them to contact his mother. He shook his head. He'd call her himself. Jeremy said, 'We're going to sit on this as long as possible. We think it's best for your father. But we don't know about the Africans. What I'm saying is, it could come out at any time. You should prepare yourself. For the press, I mean.'

'I think I'll cope.'

'Of course.' Jeremy nodded. 'I saw today's papers. Looks like you've got –'

'Yeah,' Preston interrupted. 'Exactly.'

Jeremy handed him his card. 'All I mean is we've got people who handle this sort of thing, so call me if you need anything.'

'You've got a lot of people.'

'Yes,' Jeremy said. 'We have.'

Preston showed them out. At the door, Jeremy said, 'Are you sure you're all right?'

'Me? I'm fine,' Preston said, but when he shut the door he wondered just how fine he really was.

He wasn't sure if it was the mind-numbing drugs or the collision of mind-bending events, but he was starting to feel disturbingly two-dimensional. It wasn't an entirely unfamiliar sensation, since he frequently found that he looked at his life with detachment, as if he were watching an advert for himself. But he'd never before felt quite this cartoonish. He felt as if whatever character he'd once had might have slipped away to be replaced by no more than a catchphrase or soundbite, and he didn't even know what that catchphrase or slogan might be. There was always the Authenticity™ slogan: 'Keeping it really real'. But he was in no state for irony. He began to feel unnerved and he wanted to talk to someone. He meant to call his mum, but for some reason he called another fictional character instead.

Twenty minutes later, he opened the door to his third visit of the day. A pasty-faced white kid stood on his doormat, about fourteen years old and swamped in a hoodie. Preston handed him the cash and accepted the tiny polythene bag. He couldn't resist asking the question: 'Are you Pablo?'

The kid sniffed: 'Yeah, blood. Whatever.'

Preston wondered how long it would take to develop a coke habit. His was four days old and counting.

47
Just another arsehole

London, England, 2008
When Lorraine knocked on the door, Preston was in the shower. It was just before eight. After Pablo's delivery, he'd refreshed his high, thought a little, watched it sink, resurrected it again and finally called his mother.

She'd accepted the news of her ex-husband's incarceration in the deep and dark with such remarkable lack of interest that he might as well have told her he'd bought a new toaster, and he wondered if she was drinking again. The closest she came to an expression of regret was, 'Africa, you say? Oh dear. He won't like that.' Then she changed the subject to some tapestry patterns for cushion covers she'd ordered over the Internet, how they were an Indian design but had arrived from California and wasn't that remarkable?

Preston cut her off, 'Are you all right, Mum?'

'Me? I'm fine. Whatever do you mean?'

'I mean about Dad.'

He heard her sigh. He could almost hear her brain grasping for the right words. 'I know he's your father, Preston,' she said at last. 'And, for that reason, I hope he's OK. I'm not going to blame him for what happened – for his actions, I mean. That's just him. And I'm not going to say, "I gave him the best years of my life," or anything like that. Although I did. But I really hate the man.'

Preston expected her to continue, but she didn't. Apparently that was it. So, eventually, he said, 'Right.'

'What about you, Press? I saw you in the papers today. They wrote some horrid things.'

'Yeah.'

348

'Do you want to talk about it?'

'Not really.'

His mother sighed again. She seemed so distracted. Clearly it wasn't his news and she didn't sound drunk either. Maybe she'd dropped a stitch. 'Well . . .' she said.

'Well . . .'

'I should probably go, darling boy. I'm expecting Mona any minute. Our programme starts at half past.'

'Sure,' Preston said.

He had no idea who Mona was, or what they would be watching together. He didn't ask. Somehow nothing would have surprised him.

Preston took the shower because he wanted to clear his head. His wilful new cocaine habit was, he now decided, absolutely unhelpful. No wonder Thandi was so flaky and Jodie so paranoid.

The hot water didn't exactly straighten him out, but at least it granted him the room to think. He thought about his dad, but he couldn't get his head round it. He couldn't decide whether he felt nothing or his imagination was simply incapable of processing what had happened. He tried to picture his dad's situation, but every image was borrowed from something he'd seen or heard or read. Somehow the second-hand nature of these pictures, with Pinner Photoshopped in their midst, made them funny. He didn't know what to think about that. He began to develop an impressive headache and the taste for another line. He blew his nose down the plughole, first one nostril then the other. Each produced an impressive string of blood, snot and bloody, snotty coke. He decided not to develop a cocaine habit after all. Then he heard the knocking.

At first he tried to ignore it, but it only became more insistent. Whoever was outside could probably hear the shower pump. He hurriedly dried himself and threw on a T-shirt and a pair of jeans. He opened the door to Lorraine.

She looked even more small and pinched than usual, her hair scraped back as if it was being punished for something and was determined to take her face with it. Her taut cheeks were tear-stained.

At the sight of him, she said, 'Fucking arsehole! What the fuck, Press?' Then her shoulders slumped and she started crying again, long, deep, almost silent sobs that seemed to start at her knees, then overtake her whole body. Preston, still feeling curiously detached and now more than a little Groundhog Day, tried to hug her. But she wriggled free, muttered, 'Fuck you,' and dodged past him into the flat.

He made her a cup of tea and sat opposite her at the table. This time she sat in his position and he was in Errol's/Shorter's. The variety was something of a relief.

She held the mug so tightly that her fingernails went white. She stared at the table. Preston wanted to say something but he couldn't think of an opening gambit. Luckily, Lorraine spoke first: 'Ben says it's my fault.'

Preston was confused. He cleared his throat. 'Who's Ben?'

Lorraine looked at him sharply and the hatred in her eyes answered his question. Preston wasn't accustomed to being hated, not properly hated: he was accustomed to being loved, if not properly loved. He wondered if he was going to have to get used to it. 'Right,' he said. 'Ben.'

'It was my idea to send his stuff to The A-List, innit? He said you'd fuck him up, but I was all, like, "They're different", you know? Turns out only difference is you fucked him up quicker.'

'Where is he?'

Again she considered him. The hatred was still right there. She looked as if she were fighting the urge to launch herself across the table and beat him with whatever came to hand. 'Even if I know, you think I'm gonna tell you? They catch him, they gonna send him back, Press. He's fucked. He can't go back.'

'Back where?'

Lorraine started to cry again. 'He embarrassed you at the TV studio, so you decided to fuck him up.'

'That's not what happened,' Preston said quickly, and it was only a lie of one word – 'exactly', 'precisely' or 'quite'. He got to his feet, walked round the table and crouched next to Lorraine. She was leaning forward resting on her elbows. He put his hand on her back. Her bomber jacket had rucked up and his touch accidentally found the exposed skin above the waistband of her jeans. She didn't try to pull away or even, in fact, appear to notice. He made his hand comfortable, flat against the small of her back. On the range of her spine he noticed a thin line of soft silver hair. He blinked. He was struggling to concentrate. 'That's not what happened,' he said again. In Preston's moral universe, which was currently at its most flexible, the role of evil Jodie was growing by the second.

'It wasn't you who called the *Sun*?'

'No,' Preston said, and the truth lent such indignant conviction to that one word that he said it again. 'No, Loll.'

He now put his left hand comfortingly on her knee and, feeling such a sympathetic touch, she twisted herself towards him, put her arms around his shoulders, buried her face in his neck and quietly wept.

'I'm sorry,' he said meaninglessly. 'I'm so sorry.' And he began to rub a soothing thumb across her backbone.

The way she was weeping and the way he was crouching, his thighs were soon cramping and he had to stand up. But he didn't want to let her go, such was his desire to console, so he pulled her up with him and she was so light that he managed it in one swift movement that lifted her to tiptoe, hanging from his neck. He raised the hand that had been on her knee to her hair, but it was stiff with product. He contented himself with whispering sweet, sincere, thoroughly meaningless apologies in her ear.

Unfortunately it was in this moment, at the height of

351

his deception (of Lorraine, of course, but more particularly himself), that Preston suddenly felt truly present and real for the first time in as long as he could remember. And in that surge of reality, he finally understood that this was what he'd wanted all along: to be a hero. He was St George, ready to kill the dragon; Robin Hood primed to rescue Marion; Winston Churchill aboard that tank; Becks lining up that free kick at Old Trafford; Tony urging restraint at Camp David.

Fortunately this comprehension was simultaneously incompatible with the deception (of himself, if not Lorraine). So, no sooner had he understood the reality of what he wished to be than he knew with a certainty even he couldn't deny that he wasn't it. He wasn't a hero. He was hardly real. He was just a salesman of knock-off merchandise, a huckster with a coat full of Rolecks™, a hawker with a case full of Mike™ sportswear, a peddler of brand Tuppence™, brand 2P™, brand Authenticity™. Deep down, he'd always known this, hadn't he? So how had he become just another arsehole?

He let Lorraine go and, gently removing her arms from round his neck, he guided her back to her chair. She wiped her nose and sniffed and said, 'Sorry.'

He didn't know what she was apologizing for; maybe the damp patch of tears on his T-shirt. 'It's OK,' he said, and sat down again too.

'Look,' he said. 'We just need to work out what we're going to do.' Lorraine shook her head, but Preston pressed on. 'Come on, Loll. There's always something to do. So Ben's illegal? So what? People loved him before they knew that and it doesn't make any difference. They've just been told the wrong story. We need to tell them the right story. We just need to make it cool. And that's what I do. I make things cool.'

She looked up at him hopefully. Frankly, Preston wasn't sure what he was talking about, but he continued because he didn't know what else to do. 'So tell me everything about Ben,' he said.

'What do you mean?'

'We want a new story and I need a central character. Who is he? Where's he from? How come he's illegal? I don't know. Tell me everything.'

So she did. And Preston listened with growing incredulity and a slowly solidifying sense of redemption – not just Nobody's but his own. This was going to be easy. Maybe he'd even be a hero. No, that wasn't right. A martyr? No, because a martyr had to be innocent and he certainly wasn't that. He was just going to have to tell the truth and take the blame. But he found he was quite looking forward to it. It might even be fun.

48

Insert document
'Murderer Executed', *News of the World*,
24 November 1901, anon.

Gloucestershire Man Hanged For Killing Teacher's Daughter

Jack Chavney, convicted of murdering Miss Elizabeth Nott at Fry Norton on Whitsunday, was hanged in Stafford gaol this week.

Chavney killed Miss Nott with a single blow to the head in the village barn after she refused his advances. It will be remembered that he then partook in morris dancing in the hours before the discovery of his crime.

A labouring man of little refinement, Chavney protested his innocence to the last. However, several witnesses, including the victim's father, a local schoolteacher, and two other notable gentlemen (Mr Codrington and Mr Pinner), attested to the man's infatuation.

Fully five thousand persons gathered outside the gaol to see the hoisting of the black flag. Two representatives of the press were admitted to witness the execution. The High Sheriff, Sir Robert Crumb, in granting the orders, exacted a promise that 'sensational descriptive writing' would be avoided.

Chavney slept fairly well during the night, and when visited in his cell by Billingham, the hangman, a few minutes before eight o'clock he betrayed no emotion. He walked to the scaffold with a wonderful firmness and deliberation, and repeated after the chaplain the prayer for the dying.

As he stepped on to the drop he put his heels together, and

otherwise seemed anxious to adapt himself to the pinioning arrangement. Unrepentant to the last, he refused the white cap and his face wore an almost cheerful expression. 'I look forward to seeing my dear Lizzie,' he said, and met his fate unflinchingly.

The High Sheriff, Under Sheriff, officials and warders were in attendance. Billingham was assisted by his son.

49

Insert document
'The curse of the namesake', *The Book of Zamba Mythology*, (OUP, 2005), Edison Burrows III

There was a time when a great drought came to the Land of the Moon and for three years hardly any rain fell. Rivers dwindled, crops withered, and animals and people starved.

Even the household of Chief Tuloko (the Traveller, the Child of the Horizon) suffered. The well near his homestead dried out and the girls who fetched his water had to walk an extra hour to fill their containers from the river. Sometimes they were so tired that they fainted in the hot morning sun and spilt their load. Eventually the river was so dry that they could only draw water from its stagnant pools and it wasn't good for drinking. Tuloko called the girls to him and said, 'Do you think this is water fit for a chief?' After that they had to collect water from the river beyond the river.

The vegetables died in the earth and the farmers who produced Tuloko's maize and greens brought offerings of decreasing size and quality. Tuloko called the farmers to him and said, 'Do you think this is food fit for a chief?' After that the farmers gave everything they grew to Tuloko and their own families went hungry, forced to eat nothing but berries that tied their stomachs in knots.

The animals starved in the bush and the hunters who hunted for Tuloko caught only rabbits and fowl whose flesh was tasteless and tough. Tuloko called the hunters to him and said, 'Do you think this is meat fit for a chief?' After that the hunters travelled the length and breadth of the Land of the Moon in search of game to bring to Tuloko's table. Many never returned.

The whole nation was suffering.

Eventually, Tuloko called an assembly of his wisest *zakulus* and asked them the cause of the drought. Was his leadership failing? Had he in some way offended Father Sun or Cousin Moon? The *zakulus* had no answer.

Tuloko became frustrated. He said, 'What should I do? Do you think this is advice fit for a chief?'

Eventually, a young *zakulu* called Musa Musa spoke up. He said, 'I don't know what's wrong, but I will travel to the mountains in the east so that I can speak directly to the moon. I will ask him what to do and if he doesn't know I'll ask him to intercede with the sun. I will discover the cause of the problem or I'll never come back.'

Musa Musa was gone for almost two months and many people assumed he'd failed in his mission. But eventually he returned and he went to see the chief directly. He said, 'I have discovered the cause of the drought.'

Tuloko said, 'Tell me.'

'You have not offended Cousin Moon or Father Sun in any way. Rather, we are under the curse of a powerful man.'

'Who is this man?'

'I don't know. I only know that he has taken the same name as you: he also calls himself Tuloko.'

Tuloko was astonished to hear this and asked, 'Why would another man take my name?'

'Perhaps he plans to replace you as chief of the Zamba when we are too hungry and thirsty to resist.'

'So what must I do?'

Musa Musa told him that he must fight and kill his namesake in order to break the curse. He told him that he'd made a plan with Cousin Moon and Father Sun and, if Tuloko travelled eastwards alone, to the place of the last tree, they would deliver the impostor to him.

'How will I know when I've reached the place of the last tree?' Tuloko asked.

'You will know,' the *zakulu* replied.

Tuloko set out the next morning. He carried with him the clearest water the girls could bring, the farmers' freshest vegetables and the two fattest rabbits the hunters had been able to catch. On the fourth day of his journey, Tuloko reached what he thought must be the last tree. Beyond it there was nothing but desert all the way to the mountains that loomed in the distance. That night, he ate the last of his rabbit and sharpened his knife and spear.

The next day, he waited for the impostor. At nightfall, he ate the last of his vegetables.

By the end of the third day waiting for the impostor, he'd drunk the last of his water. In the darkness, he called out to the moon: 'Where is my namesake who has cursed my people? Send him here quickly. Otherwise I might be too weak to fight him.'

On the fourth morning, even though he feared missing his enemy, Tuloko had no choice but to return to the last watering-hole he'd passed on his journey, or he would die of thirst. The water was stagnant and rancid, but to the chief it was the freshest water he'd ever tasted. He filled his container and carried it back to the last tree. Still there was no sign of the impostor.

On the fifth morning, Tuloko was so hungry that he went picking berries. By midday, he had collected a plateful and he ate them greedily. Afterwards, he suffered a terrible stomach ache. He was glad the impostor didn't show up that afternoon because he was in no condition to fight.

On the sixth morning, Tuloko resolved to go hunting, even though it meant leaving the last tree. It was a tiring and fruitless exercise but, just before sunset, he speared a small bird. Though he ate it in barely two mouthfuls, the meat tasted better than any he'd eaten before. And still there was no sign of the impostor.

On the seventh morning, Tuloko gave up. He called to the sun, 'Where is this man who cursed my people? I have done as you asked, but if I stay out here I shall die waiting.'

He began the long journey home. He arrived four days later, dejected by his failure. He called Musa Musa to him and told him what had happened. At first, Tuloko was angry, because he'd suffered terribly in following the *zakulu*'s instructions and nothing had come of it. Musa Musa listened to the chief's story and concluded that the impostor must have come while Tuloko was at the watering-hole, or collecting berries, or hunting. Tuloko couldn't very well be angry after that.

In the subsequent months, the drought continued and the people continued to suffer. But they also noticed a change in their chief. When the girls who brought Tuloko's water could only carry a small amount, hardly enough for cooking and drinking, he thanked them for their efforts. When the farmers offered him a paltry selection of maize and greens, he accepted a portion and told them to return the rest to their families. When the hunters brought him half a dozen rabbits, he ordered them to be cooked and distributed equally among the local people.

Tuloko's behaviour was so different that some people wondered if their chief had in fact been killed by the impostor who'd then returned in his place. But, despite the hardships, their lives were a little easier so they kept this thought to themselves.

In the fourth year, the rains were good and the drought at last ended. Across the Land of the Moon, streams became rivers again, crops flourished and grew, and the animals and people prospered. The Zamba gave thanks to Father Sun and Cousin Moon for their good fortune, and to their chief, Tuloko, who had led them so wisely through a difficult time.

50

Truth, part truth, and anything but the truth

London, England, 2008
Sitting in his dressing room, Preston was nervous and Errol and Jodie weren't helping.

Every ten minutes or so, Jodie would disappear into the toilet. The first couple of times she'd looked at him as if to say, 'Do you want one?' and been evidently disappointed when he shook his head. No sooner had she cultivated a coke buddy than he'd baled on her.

After each dose, she returned to the room and sat in silence for about thirty seconds, then was unable to resist firing a scattergun of pointless verbiage in Preston's general direction – 'Are you nervous? You don't have to be nervous. You'll be great, Tupps. Really. You'll be great.' That kind of thing.

Errol, on the other hand, was utterly taciturn, but Preston found his silence no less irritating. Whenever Preston refused Jodie's offer, Errol would shake his head with, Preston thought, a certain smugness, as if his moral fortitude as a righteous brother (with the literature, in this case not pornographic, to match) was solely responsible for his employer's newfound abstinence. Otherwise he sat behind Preston and, as the makeup girl brushed away the shine on Preston's forehead for the umpteenth time, looked on with grim disapproval.

Of course, it hardly improved the atmosphere that Errol and Jodie were not just refusing to talk to one another but wouldn't even meet each other's eye, such was the current state of their mutual loathing. Preston had banned talk of the press leak. After all, he'd more or less okayed it. But Errol knew that it was Jodie who'd rung the *Sun* journalist and he despised her for it. And Jodie despised him back because she'd apologized to Preston who was, after all, her boss and who the hell did Errol think he was anyway?

It was something of a relief, therefore, when the assistant floor manager showed him into what was called 'the bar', even though here he had to make polite small-talk with the chat-show's other guests. 'The bar' wasn't really a bar at all, just a small anteroom with a counter set up on one wall, a celebrity standing behind it with a tea-towel draped over his arm. This week, it was an actor Preston didn't recognize from a soap he'd never watched, who appeared to have the catchphrase, 'Hello, pal!'

Around the room, there was a small selection of pub tables and chairs where the guests were supposed to sit, have a drink, or at least pretend to, and have VIP fun, or at least pretend to. The guests were an American stand-up comedian, who talked non-stop about himself, pausing only to laugh at his own hilarity, a supermodel from Basingstoke, who buttonholed Preston for advice on her planned singing career, an Irish emo band with a seemingly limitless fanbase among pre-pubescent girls and an evidently homosexual lead singer, and Preston. The wall by the door was entirely taken up by a huge plasma TV carrying a live feed from the show, and a camera filming the guests' interaction, which was in turn beamed onto two large screens in the studio.

The show's structure allowed the host to 'cross to the bar', every now and then, and engage in some off-the-cuff banter with the celebrity landlord – 'Hello, pal! Hello, pal!' Etc. Occasionally the host would crack a joke at the expense of one of his forthcoming guests and they'd be expected to laugh and raise their glass to him.

The running order had Preston on last, and as the recording started, he began to get seriously nervous. Was it wise to have chosen a light-hearted prime-time chat-show for his confessional? He'd considered approaching more serious programmes – *Newsnight*, perhaps – but they'd have insisted on talking about his dad and he didn't want to do that. Besides, this would hit a far wider audience and that could only be a good thing, unless it backfired.

The studio audience bothered him too. He knew that the Nobody story had cast him as public enemy number one (well, number two, anyway), so he was worried about their reaction and how that would play out on live TV. He was gambling that the news of his dad's incarceration might have generated a balancing sympathy, but he didn't know that for sure and there was no way his grand testimony would convince anyone who simply refused to listen.

When his name was trailed at the top of the show, the studio response was muted, the applause sporadic. He figured that was about the best he could hope for. At one point, between the interviews with the comedian and model, the host 'crossed to the bar' and the camera dipped into Preston's face. Dazzled by the lights, Preston heard him say, 'And still to come we have the founder of Authenticity and London's coolest man, Preston "2P" Pinner. But we'd better get to him quickly because I believe immigration officials are in the building!'

Preston heard the laughter and then felt a hand on his shoulder. He looked up and, through the green and yellow spots of his blindness, saw a man in a uniform with a peaked cap. It took him a second or two to clock that this was a runner in fancy dress, and he must have looked shocked because the studio audience laughed all the harder. Preston gathered himself, pulled a smile and toasted the camera with his mineral water: cheers!

As the show cut back to the studio and the model teetered her way onto the stage, a giraffe in high heels, Preston sat back in his chair and shut his eyes. He was now so nervous he thought he might puke. But no sooner had the nerves overwhelmed him than they drained away: he had realized their true source.

All day, Preston had told himself that he was nervous because there was a lot at stake. But there wasn't – at least, not for him. Ben Phiri might get banged up, deported, thrown off Land's End, but Preston could always find another Nobody to make somebody. Authenticity™ might take a hit on popularity and the business might suffer. So what? It was not a labour of love but work for money, and he'd done plenty of work and he had plenty of money. Joe Public might hate him, but Joe Public had the memory of a toilet bowl, and if he was suddenly less wealthy and influential, he'd still be wealthy and influential.

What about the other people involved? Errol and Jodie would be OK, and if they weren't, it would be down to their own shortcomings. As for Nobody, he'd chosen his own path and Preston was sorry but he could certainly live with the guilt. And Lorraine? Well, he *did* care about Lorraine and he *did* want to do the right thing; after all, that was what he was doing here, sweating buckets and risking ridicule. But, if he was honest (which he was very much trying to be), he didn't even care about Lorraine as much as he'd thought. When he'd imagined himself a hero, he'd imagined her a damsel. When he'd remembered he was a salesman, he'd recognized she was just a pretty girl from Dagenham who had a boyfriend.

So, Preston was nervous because the game plan he'd worked out for this interview, after his conversation with Lorraine, required him to be himself. He would have to walk out there, tell the truth and throw himself on the public mercy.

Strangely, it wasn't the latter part of this equation that terrified him (i.e. the revelation and all the vulnerability inherent therein) but the former. How could he be himself when he had little idea of who the hell he was? The surge of grounded self-possession he'd felt as he held Lorraine in the kitchen at Shoreditch Heights had long since evaporated. It was one thing being 'real' in a ten-minute spell in the safety of his own home, quite another attempting it on live TV. He could do media mogul standing on his head, personify urban cool in his sleep, even front hip-hop roughneck at a pinch. But Preston Pinner? How could he possibly speak truthfully as someone he didn't know?

No sooner had he phrased the question like this than he knew the answer. Just like 2P™ was a brand, just like Tuppence™ was a brand, so was Preston Pinner™. It didn't matter if his character had authenticity, it needed Authenticity™ and that was his trademark.

His nerves were gone. It would be ridiculously easy. He was the personification of confidence. He was the personification of Preston Pinner™. How could he have forgotten his key motto? 'Don't worry about what you think they need, engage with what they think they want.' He could engage, all right. He'd give the British public what they wanted. Fuck honesty: they wanted the *truth*.

The assistant floor manager led him to the stage, holding his elbow, checking his lapel mic, wishing him good luck. He entered the studio. The reception from the audience was cautious, but that was fine. Or it would have been fine if the house band, a Tropicalia-styled ensemble of Brazilian transsexuals, hadn't played him in to a peculiar re-bastardized version of Nobody's already bastardized 'Jerusalem'. Somehow, their bizarre, tuneless falsettos lent the song an even more disrespectful tone and he heard the odd catcall and boo.

Preston dropped his chin a little as if he were ashamed of himself. He knew he couldn't afford to lose the audience so soon.

The host greeted him with a handshake and a matey clap on the shoulder. Preston, however, took the opportunity to embrace him. The host hadn't perhaps planned on such an immediate show of support but he could hardly push him away.

The host sat behind a desk, Preston in an armchair. On previous appearances on other people's TV shows, Preston had lounged back, legs wide apart, hand slightly covering his mouth, a pastiche of rudeboy chic. But this time he sat forward with his elbows on his knees and an earnest expression – this was a man who needed to get his point across.

The host began with a light-hearted anecdote about the first time he'd seen the notorious 2P in the flesh. It had been at the after party of a film première and he'd spied Preston hanging out with Diddy, sipping Cristal, surrounded by fly honeys – was that what he called them, 'fly honeys'? The middle-aged, middle-class man who spoke to and for middle England parodied gang signs and the audience laughed. Preston smiled politely. He couldn't pander to the patter. He needed the conversation to change tack.

'But, seriously . . .' the host began, and Preston breathed a sigh of relief.

Preston agreed that he'd had a tough week. He agreed that he wouldn't talk about his dad because it was an ongoing situation and obviously he didn't want to say anything that would put his father in further danger. He spoke slowly and precisely. He avoided any slang, stripped his accent of its usual London edge, but stopped short of his private education. His tone was blunt and incontrovertible – he sounded like DJ Jonny Swift made flesh.

He was asked how he felt about Pinner's arrest. 'I don't know,' he said. 'He's my dad . . .' He left the word hanging like that, as if he was about to continue so that the host wouldn't interrupt. But he just let it hang and he let it hang. He noted the audience's respectful silence.

Preston confirmed that he'd come here to talk about Nobody. He denied the assertion that he was brave to do so considering how most people now felt about Ben Phiri. 'I'm not brave,' he said flatly. 'That's the last thing I am.' He pointed out that Nobody was still at number one in the singles chart, so clearly he still had his supporters. He knew he was on dangerous ground here. He had to play it carefully.

The host came at him from an angle he hadn't expected, declaring that 'Jerusalem' was only selling because it was all over TV, radio and the web. Basically, he claimed that Authenticity™ had brainwashed the nation.

Preston regarded him earnestly and pretended to give this serious consideration. But, inside, he was thanking the guy for presenting him with such an open goal – this was easier than he'd dared hope. 'I don't think I have that kind of power,' Preston said slowly, eyes wide, face open. 'I don't think anyone has that kind of power.' Then he smiled, humble because he'd been humbled. 'I have too much respect for the intelligence of the British public to think something like that.'

The host thought he heard an accusation here and retaliated sharply, asking Preston about the video for 'Jerusalem' – did he really think it appropriate to show Her Majesty the Queen happy slapped by some hooligan?

Preston shook his head. He said the video had been his idea, nothing to do with Nobody at all. He conceded it was misjudged, but he'd thought it funny. He pleaded naïvety, referenced the cartoons of Muhammad that had caused such a stink across Europe, and said he knew the British public, on the other hand, had a great sense of humour. In his defence (and, indeed, in defence of that proud comic tradition), the video had proved enormously popular until the truth about Nobody's background came out and, in fact, it remained the most requested on YouTube, MySpace and The A-List™.

'So,' the host brimmed with swelling pomposity, 'you understand the reaction when you came out here, when I introduced you? *That* is my question: do you understand the reaction?'

'What reaction?'

'*What* reaction? I mean the fact that you were booed, that people are disgusted by what you and this "Ben Phiri" who, incidentally, has now disappeared, have done – you understand that?'

Preston heard the studio audience grow restive. They were fidgeting in their seats. The host had goaded them and they could barely contain their righteous fury. If they'd had vegetables, they'd have thrown them. If there'd been stocks, Preston would have been in them. If they'd had a noose, they'd have strung him up. It was perfect.

Understand it? Of course Preston understood it. No one had greater respect for the British public than he, he bristled, as his mind raced through his other key motto – 'Deal with stupid people stupidly to get what you want.'

Who did they think had called the newspapers? *He* had. Him, Preston Pinner – Preston Pinner™, proud patriot, man of the people. *They* were disgusted? *He* was disgusted. He'd been bamboozled, hoodwinked, hornswoggled by this fiend, this demon, this *illegal immigrant* who was surely intent on the destruction of all we – *we* – hold dear.

Those weren't the exact words he used, but this was what Preston heard as his tone rose and quivered and he feared he was hamming it too far. Oh, well, there was no turning back now: in for 2P, in for two pounds.

'But . . .' Preston announced grandly, raising a single finger. 'But . . . I didn't know the truth. *We* didn't know the truth.' He lowered his finger and took a deep breath. It was time to lose the man possessed. It was time to play his trump card and he knew it was best to lay it softly.

'The *truth*? What's the truth?' The host's tone was sarcastic, but Preston didn't care. He was in charge.

Preston told them that Ben Phiri had arrived in the UK from the Republic of Zambawi in the summer of 2004. He was on a three-year student visa to study at the Guildhall School of Music and had graduated with a first-class degree. The newspapers hadn't tracked this down because he'd applied under his Zamba name, Tendai. He'd graduated in 2007, just months before the Zambawian presidential elections. His father was Joseph Phiri, leader of the opposition Democratic Movement. Fearing for his safety if he returned home, he'd applied for asylum and been refused. He'd faced a choice: detention, deportation or disappearance. Preston quoted the Independent Asylum Commission report, which described a system 'marred by inhumanity in its treatment of the vulnerable'. He'd done his research.

Preston spoke quietly. His words began to hum with emotion. He didn't know where that came from. He wondered if it was real. He said that obviously he didn't know all the details of the case, but it seemed to him that the British government claimed to support democratization in Africa but couldn't even support those at the forefront of the movement, the Democratic Movement. The Prime Minister had launched the African Authority to foster a new relationship between the continent and the UK. But if Britain could ignore a vulnerable young man in his hour of need, maybe Mr Mandela was right and the great initiative was nothing but tokenism. The Africa Unite festival was supposed to be the Authority's showpiece conclusion. Nobody was billed as one of the headline acts. Indeed, he was the only African artist in the line-up. What sort of message of unity was this – this witch hunt?

'My dad,' Preston said, and his voice cracked pleasingly, 'is currently in a Zambawian jail cell. Look, I'm no politician. But if we, in Britain, the Western world's oldest democracy, can't stand up for what is right, then what do we stand for? Ben . . . *Tendai* . . . has definitely made a mistake, but it was my fault as much as his. And I can tell you that nobody loves this country and respects its principles as much as Nobody. I really believe he deserves our support, don't you? And, like I said, I trust the British public . . .'

Preston saw the floor manager signalling manically to the host to wrap it up.

The host looked shell-shocked. 'That . . .' he said. Then,

'Well, you heard it . . .' Then, 'Quite a show.' He blustered his way through thanking the comedian, the supermodel and, of course, 2P.

Preston heard the applause, but he didn't know what it was for, and it was soon drowned by the opening chords of the emo band's limp anthem, the very record that Nobody was currently keeping off the number-one spot.

Preston suspected there was still a camera on him and, if not, the audience was still watching so he kept his game face – serious and a little pained. But his heart was racing and he was almost bursting with exhilaration. Fuck honesty. Fuck the truth. Preston Pinner™ told The Truth™.

51

Insert document
Letter from Lieutenant Colonel Preston Pinner,
General HQ, St Eloi, 26 May 1916 (Pinner family
archive)

My dear Kitty

Thank you for your letters and parcels. I cannot tell you how much it means to me that you write so often. Even after so long, your constancy is my comfort and redemption. How are David and Gertie? I hope Pandy isn't spoiling them too much! Kiss them both for me. I hold you all in my heart at all times.

I will not write at length. Frenchies arrive tomorrow and I have much prep for H. I cannot tell you how much of a boost his leadership has given us all. H has even promised me a command of my own and I imagine I will at last see action before July is out. I know he values a fellow of my experience, even incapacitated as I am. I have no reservations, only pride. As you know, this is the reason I enlisted: to fight for King and country.

I finally received a reply to my letter from RK. Of course, I was only briefly involved in his son's prelim, but apparently he mentioned me in a card he once sent as 'the finest example of an upstanding English officer'. I was deeply touched by that and, indeed, the whole of RK's letter, although the poor man is clearly racked with grief, guilt and regret.

I am tempted to write again but I wonder if that is seemly. I need your advice on matters such as this! He wrote the following postscript: 'If any question why we died, tell them, because our fathers lied.'

Curiously, this made me think of Robert Ackerman – do you

remember my mentioning him? He was my CO at Standmere, the worst sort of petty pragmatist, the kind you inevitably find hiding in the darkest corners of a war. I recall he said to me once that he considered men of principle the worst kind of liars and hypocrites. At the time, I considered this symptomatic of his stultifying cynicism, but now I find a certain bleak truth in his words. It is strange how one's mind can change, is it not? Nonetheless, I'd still take a fellow who fails to live up to his principles over someone who has none. What is your opinion of this?

In light of a possible posting to the front, I must ask you something, my dearest, and trust, once again, in your fortitude. It concerns the period when I had lately returned from Africa up to and including that frightful business in Gloucestershire in which I was briefly embroiled. I know we agreed never to discuss this again and I would not do so now were it not for what I consider the demands of prudence.

In the bottom drawer of my bureau on the right side, you will find various of my journals, sketchbooks and notebooks; each marked by date. You will see that there are, perhaps, half a dozen covering the first two years of the century. I must ask that you destroy them as soon as possible and suggest you give them to G the next time he bonfires.

I must also ask that you do not succumb to the natural temptation to read my youthful words. I tell you now that there is nothing of any significance contained therein. I trust you to believe me when I say that I make this request only to protect you, my beloved, and our children from any future misinterpretation by persons who do not know me as you do.

I will write again soon. I miss you all very much for I am a lucky man indeed.

Your devoted husband
Preston

52
Of suspicion (2)

Queenstown, Republic of Zambawi, 2008

The entire shift stood in the guards' mess at Gwezi, their eyes upturned to the screen. Generally one of the President's speeches wouldn't have occasioned such interest, but the recent releases from the maximum-security wing, combined with the rumours circulating Queenstown of an impending and significant policy shift, meant that everybody wanted to hear what Adini had to say. As he took his position behind the lectern in front of the Zambawian flag, therefore, the guards stood apparently transfixed. None of them exchanged a glance or word.

'My brothers and sisters of Zambawi, I will keep my remarks brief for I know that many of you are looking forward to the Friday Movie Magic, as am I. I am told that tonight's film is *Kini and Adams* by Idrissa Ouedraogo, a film maker from Burkina Faso. One of the many advantages of our "media localization programme" is the chance to celebrate the work of leading African artists as opposed to the quite brainless fare offered up by their Western contemporaries. Perhaps soon we will be showing features made by Zambawian cineastes. I look forward to that day.

'But I digress, and I have several important points to raise with you tonight.

'I would first like to scotch any rumours by confirming that I have indeed ordered the release and repatriation of the British conspirators Gordon Tranter and David Pinner MP. Please believe me when I say to you that I have in no way succumbed to so-called "international pressure". I am the elected leader of a sovereign state and I answer to nobody but you, my people.

'However, I have lately met with Joseph Phiri, the leader of the Democratic Movement, and he assures me that he had nothing to do with their clandestine plotting. I believe Brother Phiri. Indeed, I cannot even confirm with certainty the complicity of the upper echelons of the UK government in this matter, for I know that not all leaders are able to run so tight a ship as I. Therefore I have released the conspirators as a gesture of goodwill. I grant the UK government the benefit of the doubt. Such generosity is rare indeed in the field of international relations so I hope that my actions may be an example to those who might need such.

'Second, it is my pleasure to tell you that Phiri and I had a most productive meeting. As you know, my people, since the presidential election, we have suffered at the hands of the "white gentlemen's club" because we refused to cede to them our culture, accept their economic strictures or any continuing responsibility for the debts that have crippled us for so long. I cannot promise swift solutions, but I know that we must stand together during such trying times. Phiri feels the same.

'Therefore, I would like to announce that I have invited the DM to join me in forming a Government of National Unity with Brother Phiri acting as Prime Minister. I am delighted to be able to tell you that he has accepted. From now on we will work as one nation for the betterment of all our people. It is with this in mind that I declare the investigation of the Electoral Commission null and void. It will cease with immediate effect.

'I can also tell you that I am currently brokering a deal worth five hundred million US dollars with the Chinese government to assist us in our exploitation of our plentiful mineral deposits. Prime Minister Phiri will fly to the United

States next week to explain our new relationship to his many friends in Washington.

'Third, I hereby announce my intention to make a change to the Zambawian constitution, which currently forbids a president to serve more than three terms. This intention will, of course, be subject to the due process of Parliament and the Supreme Court.

'I say to you only this: I have no present desire myself to apply for re-election for a fourth term. In the new government structure, there are several excellent candidates for a future presidency and I am fully aware of the risks of what my critics describe, with lazy facetiousness, as "African Leadership Syndrome". However, I remain the servant of my people, not a slave to the urban media élite. And I will never refuse my people's call.

'Finally, it has come to my attention that Tendai Phiri, the Prime Minister's son, has caused something of a stir on the UK pop scene. This will come as no surprise to any student of popular music – we Africans are generous with our culture, frequently to our own detriment.

'It seems, however, that the British find the truth in young Tendai's talent a little hard to stomach. In the spirit of reciprocity, therefore, I say: "Return our son to us! He will be greeted with open arms, as will all other Zambawians, including many doctors, lawyers and telecoms engineers, currently plying their skills in the diaspora. You are our future. Come home and let us build it together."

'Thank you for your time. I hope you enjoy the film.'

As the President concluded his speech, there was plenty of celebration in pro-government households around the country, and supporters turned to each other and said things like, 'You see? I knew Adini was the man with a plan!' In opposition households, meanwhile, the response was more muted: they argued over whether the President could be trusted and resolved to wait and see.

In the guards' mess at Gwezi, however, where no one was sure of anybody else's allegiance, the entire shift simply stood to attention until the end of the national anthem, then filed out in silence. It wasn't just that they still feared one of their colleagues might be a member of the Central Intelligence Services and effect their disappearance. Rather, that fear was just the most poignant symbol of what had become true in the months since the presidential election: government propaganda had given people reasons to fear the opposition and the opposition had squared the equation. Zambawi, therefore, was now a divided nation in which people could no longer trust each other.

For all the bellicose rhetoric, the political conflict had ultimately been pragmatically resolved – compromises had been reached, promises made, hands shaken. But the culture of suspicion, so casually created for short-term gain, would take years to unravel – if, in fact, it ever unravelled at all.

53
Lest we forget

Heathrow, England, 2008

Power has no concern but self-preservation. People may fight for it or to defend the little they have, they might use it for good or bad, but power takes the long view. It maintains. Power is realistic. It plays the odds and never loses: history's bookmaker. Power is conservative. It won't jump ship until the last possible moment when it can be certain it will wash up on dry land.

But it's pernicious in its conservatism too. Conspiracy theorists unpick events and identify culprits – MI6 in Africa, Mossad in New York, SIS in London, the CIA just about everywhere – but they miss the giant figure whose shadow covers them all. There goes power, stepping out of the spotlight, leaving heroes to take the plaudits and villains to take the rap.

Take your eyes off the action! Take your eyes off the individuals and step back! Look at the decision-makers, sure, but when you've finished blaming them, look to those who allowed them to make those decisions. Look at the supporters. Look at the opposition. Look at those who don't care either way. Panic a moment. Blame the system. Compose yourself and blame the media. Understand the freedom of the press. Look at the public interest. Look at the public's interest. Look at the readers and listeners and watchers. Watch the shoppers. Scoff at their hunger and obesity. Blame another system. Look at the churches, mosques and synagogues. Blame faith. Blame the lack of faith. Look at the teachers. Look at the teachers' teachers. Blame the curriculum. Blame the kids. Look at the English. Distinguish between the perpetrators and the victims. Blame one, then the other. Look at the Eastern Europeans,

South Asians, East Asians, West Indians, Africans, Palatines, Huguenots, Jews, Normans, Vikings, Celts, Angles, Saxons, Jutes, Frisians and Franks. Blame the immigrants who won't take part but will take us apart. Look at the foreigners. Look at the little they did with the little they had. Blame them. Look at the conspiracy theorists, those oddballs who know everything and nothing, whose protests excuse you from protest. Then, finally, look at yourself. Feel the complicity. Understand. How powerful you are! Look away. Blame your parents. Blame their parents. Blame their parents' parents. Power maintains: the social selfish gene.

And here's the trick, power's greatest deception – the status quo is not the stuff of story. Stories give us hope of progress or caution us against despair. They are how we learn. They miss the point. They are about change. Power maintains.

But in our new position of understanding, when we've blamed everybody but ourselves, then blamed ourselves, then shrugged because what was the use of that, let us at least hold judgement on David Pinner MP for what he did or didn't do. This is his story, after all, so let us cling to the belief that he's changed.

Look at him set behind a lectern in a featureless Heathrow briefing room, Jeremy Shorter to his right, Gordon Tranter to his left. It's standing room only in here as the cameras flash and a live feed is beamed to news networks worldwide. He needs a good meal, a haircut by Stan, the Kosovan barber he likes, the love of a good woman or even just the affection of a bored one. The journalists murmur about his weight loss, how his face looks rather horsy, his haunted eyes, the horrors he may or may not have seen. Some whisper tasteless remarks about dropping soap in a prison shower, their cruelty and cynicism a badge of honour.

He'll take no questions. He'll read a short written statement. Or he won't.

The statement was written by Shorter. It is almost entirely

without truth. The names have not been changed to protect the innocent; rather, everything else has been changed to protect the guilty.

Pinner licks his equine lips. He reads the first few words to himself. He wants to say something different. He *planned* to say something different. The room has fallen silent, waiting.

Let us step back to his journey home: business class on a 747, the middle-aged British Airways stewardess who almost makes him cry with nostalgia for his nanny, the firm hand who taught him right from wrong, who gave him liquorice when he was good. Maybe that's what's been missing from his life all this time: liquorice.

He is again unlucky with his neighbour. This time it's Tranter, his fellow jailbird. The man is grotesque. He orders mini-bottle after mini-bottle of champagne. He eats his meal noisily. Pinner isn't hungry. His stomach has shrunk. Tranter helps himself to the minister's bread roll. He was held five times longer than Pinner but his fingers are still fat. He seems unshaken, even pleased with himself, as if his incarceration was all part of some master plan that has worked out just fine. No sooner has he finished eating than he asks Pinner's nanny for more champagne and an ice cream. He drops a dollop of the white Magnum onto his polo shirt and lifts the material to his mouth to suck it clean.

Pinner gets up. He walks back to economy. He considers the sea of black faces just as he did on the way out. He considers the atmosphere. It seems a little less raucous. Maybe it's because he's sober. Or maybe it's because last time all the black people were going home while now they're all leaving. He considers his dislike of Africans. Has it gone? No, it's still there, but it seems to have lost a little fire. He is momentarily bemused by their number. Where are they going, all these black people? What do they all want?

A young woman wants to get past him on her way to the toilet. They dance an impasse – she steps left, he steps right;

she steps right, he steps left. 'I'm so sorry,' he says, and makes an exaggerated effort to thin himself, lifting his hands above his head. She looks at him as if he's mad. Then her face clicks with recognition and she exclaims, 'You're the *musungu* who was at Gwezi!' She makes a high-pitched noise with her mouth: not quite a hum, not quite a shriek, the whistle of air from a balloon. The people in the surrounding rows look at her. The people in the surrounding rows look at him. Pinner flees for business class and his own people.

Step back again and Prisoner 386, for that's how he still feels, steps into a bath in his room at the Queenstown Sheraton. He's been out of Gwezi three hours, his plane leaves in four. He's gone overboard on the hotel's complimentary bath salts, and the combination of the sweet smell and hot water makes him feel a little faint. He looks down at his body through the rising steam. His chest hair is totally grey. Was it like that before? He can see his ribs. He has an old man's feet, knees and genitals – his balls hang loose and low; his old man looks like an old man. The bath feels like a coffin. He drags himself out of the water in a sudden rush of animating fear. He stands dripping on the mat. He doesn't recognize the face looking back at him from the mirror.

He is dazed, disconnected, discombobulated. He tells himself he's a changed man. He must be a changed man. How could somebody have gone through what he's just gone through and not change? He must be a changed man. But what has he changed into?

His mobile beeps where he left it by the wash-basin. It's a text message. He hopes it's from Eva, but it's not: it's from one of the local mobile networks advertising their new capacity for 3G roaming. He is still staring, bewildered, at the LCD when the room phone rings. He picks it up. It's his assistant, Jeremy. He talks too fast for Pinner to understand. He says it's great news that he's out, great news. He asks how he's holding up and doesn't wait for an answer. He says he'll see him in London tomorrow. He concludes with, 'You'll get your tarmac moment, sir!' Pinner doesn't know what he's talking about. Momentarily he longs for his jail cell. He must be a changed man.

Step back to that jail cell and see Prisoner 386 sit on one bunk and Prisoner 118 sit on the other. The latter talks to the rats, he talks to himself, he talks to his cellmate. He paints iodine onto the stump where his left foot used to be. The electricity cuts and the lights go out again and they're left in darkness.

118 reflects on his disability. He says, 'Do you know how difficult it is to walk with no toes? It is very difficult; very, very difficult. If you have one leg, you always know you have one leg and you are prepared to compensate. But with no toes? I tell you, the number of times I forget and I stand up and immediately fall over.'

118 tells 386 stories that can't be written down here – or, rather, if they were, they wouldn't mean anything. He tells stories for days and slowly they weave into a mythology that is utterly specific in its coherence. 118 has known some of the stories for as long as he can remember: stories of great leaders and the lessons they learnt – they are more or less the hard wiring of his spirit. Others have come to him only lately in his dreams.

Prisoner 386 begins to think of the jail cell as purgatory, a waiting room. But he listens to the stories because he has no choice. In fact, in time he listens like he's never listened before. In fact, he wonders if he's ever listened before. He doesn't understand everything. He has no moment of epiphany. But he listens.

At one point, after he's been sleeping a few hours, 386 wakes up and thinks that he's died and is standing at the gates of heaven. There, in a shaft of celestial light, are Joseph and Mary holding the baby Jesus. He's not a Christian. He's projecting the image from a Christmas card he once received. As his thinking coalesces, he realizes he's simply looking at the open cell door and light from the corridor. 'Joseph' is, in fact, the guard who first showed him into Gwezi when he was still David Pinner MP. The guard's smile is wide and white. Next to him the young woman shyly cradles her child. 386 looks over to his cellmate's bunk. He is sitting up.

'Makuvitse is doing his rounds.' The guard speaks quickly. 'But I wanted to introduce you to my family. This is my wife, Sibongile, and my son John Kipling.'

118 nods and addresses the young woman: 'And how are you, sister?'

'We are all well, thank you, *zakulu*.'

We will step back one last time to an English country garden almost a century ago, where the father of the other John Kipling writes a letter to Lieutenant Colonel Preston Pinner, a soldier he's never met, a soldier who will be dead in less than six months, the letter lost with his passing.

This is an inconsequential-looking man. He is slight, hunched and balding, with spectacles and a moustache. His hand is small and neat. He wears a broken expression. It's hard to believe that this is the great imperial propagandist who wrote of 'The White Man's Burden' and 'lesser breeds without law'. That colonialist! That racist! That apologist!

But let us hold our judgement on him too, the great deceiver, who was so greatly deceived, whose male line died with his only son at the Battle of Loos. Let us remember: 'Judge of the Nations, spare us yet./Lest we forget – lest we forget!'

54

Insert document
'TV Pick of the Week', *Guardian Guide*,
21 June 2008, Pat Gill

'Africa Unite – Live Broadcast' 1 p.m.–11 p.m., BBC3
(Highlights: 11.30 p.m.–12.30 a.m., BBC1)

Oh, for those innocent times of Live Aid, before Bob was knighted and Bono canonized, and pop stars changed the world with a synth anthem! These days, with telethons a dime a dozen, compassion fatigue running at an all-time high and most of us swimming in credit-card bills that give us a new sympathy for Third World debt, it's hard to get excited about yet another benefit gig. But there are still good reasons to turn on to 'Africa Unite', the climax to the PM's pet project, the African Authority.

Besides a top-notch line-up boasting the usual suspects alongside an interesting selection of cutting-edge talent, rumours persist of an appearance by 2P's protégé Nobody, the illegal alien responsible for both the soundtrack to the summer and a brewing international incident.

Should the PM be grateful? After all, ticket sales were sluggish before the *Sun*'s revelations and 2P's extraordinary chat-show appearance. Now a sell-out is guaranteed. Indeed, with the junior Foreign Office minister suffering a bizarre bout of Stockholm Syndrome on live TV, one can reasonably conclude the Pinner family's intention is no less than revolution.

Stay tuned for the after show, if only to witness the moment the PM is forced to shake Nobody's hand. Perhaps the PM had best ask him for advice on an election date. Perhaps Gil Scott-Heron had it wrong and it will be televised after all.

55
Africa Unite

London, England, 2008
Preston was the eye of the storm. The bass was thunderous, the lyrics indecipherable, and a hundred thousand people bayed in delighted incomprehension. Roadies lumbered on and off with mic stands, monitors, drum kits. Technicians scrambled over scaffolding, switching gels and adjusting spots. Pop stars, their publicists and other faceless liggers took every drug known to medical science and a few that were not. A teenage television presenter with gargantuan breasts (All Stars, Diesel denim, Westwood top. Motivation? Unfettered ambition) conducted backstage interviews consisting entirely of giggles. Cameras zoomed in and panned out. A blimp overhead gave the bird's-eye view.

On stage, zonked-out indie combos sang their stoners' anthems for Africa, booty-shaking R&B chicks got freaky for Africa, and ripped boy bands rubbed their waxed chests for Africa. Scary thugs in hoods shouted about gun crime for Africa, the runner-up in a reality TV show danced the Macarena for Africa, and stadium rock bands sang their stadium rock ballads about Africa, for Africa.

Preston had made this happen – not all of it, sure, but a lot of it. This was what he'd worked for. He was top dog, king pin, big cheese, a man at the height of his powers. He was awestruck by the scale of it. This was the apotheosis of contemporary culture. Had so many excellent intellects ever before gone to so much trouble and spent so much money to create such a spectacular festival of shit?

He hoped Africa was grateful because he had a blinding headache.

Someone touched his hand. He looked round to find Lorraine standing next to him. He didn't know how long she'd been there. She was wide-eyed. He smiled. She shouted something, but there was no way he was going to hear. He beckoned her to follow him back through the stage door. It was still loud in the corridor behind, but you could just about hold a conversation.

'What did you say?'

'I said, how's it going?'

'Oh.' Preston nodded. 'It's good.'

This wasn't quite true. In fact, the atmosphere had lulled in the last hour, partly because it was late afternoon and the crowd were sun-beaten, tiring and yet to hit their evening stride and partly because it was the 'urban slot', Authenticity™'s particular area of responsibility. Preston had done his best and booked as many singers as he could get away with and they'd largely held their own. But the various MCs – hip-hop, jungle and grime – had mostly stiffed, shuffling onstage in T-shirts and jeans and expecting to hold a stadium's attention with nothing but the gravity of their arrogance. Still, Preston had a trick up his sleeve, didn't he?

'You sure this will be all right?' Lorraine asked.

'What? Oh. Yeah, it'll be fine.' He took her hand and gave it a light squeeze. 'Look, hardly anyone even knows he's here. And even if they did, they're not going to bust him onstage, are they? Especially now they know who he is and where he's from. Everyone's on his side.'

'Right.' Lorraine seemed reassured. Preston hoped he knew what he was talking about.

She squeezed his hand back. 'Thanks,' she said.

'For what?'

'For the other night. I watched it. You were great.'

Preston shrugged. 'I only said what needed saying.'

'Well, you didn't have to.'

He looked at her closely. 'Yeah, I did.'

She held his eyes. 'Well, yeah,' she said. 'Suppose you did.'

She let go of his hand, briefly distracted by the lead singer of a multi-platinum American band walking past. He was surprisingly short. They all were; once you were used to it, it was no surprise.

She said, 'We should talk.'

'We're talking.'

'No. I mean about an album. He wants to get into the studio. We need to talk about the deal.'

Preston laughed. 'Well, listen to you, Ms Manager Lady, it's all business, for real.'

'Seriously, Press.'

'Seriously?' He looked at her again. He hadn't planned on telling her this today. 'Well, you'll seriously have to talk to Errol about it. I'm taking a step back from The A-List. Errol's your man.'

'What do you mean, you're taking a step back?'

He pretended to check the time. 'Hey,' he said, 'hadn't you better make sure our boy's ready to go?'

He watched Lorraine stalk off down the corridor. He found something endearing about the purpose in her stride. In fact, he liked the way she walked. He liked everything about her. He stopped that thought right there. It was a large part of how he'd got into trouble in the first place.

He retuned his mind to what was going on out front. Onstage was the winner of The Game, the nationwide urban talent competition run by Authenticity™. He was a rapper from Manchester who called himself Poodle. It had been a stitch-up. The kid had only won because the sponsors, a mobile-phone network, considered him the finalist most suited to their specific brand profile. Why the hell a phone network thought they were best personified by a guy called Poodle was beyond Preston but, what with everything else that had been going on, he hadn't felt inclined to argue the toss. Once upon a time, rappers came from the streets and had a grounding in hip-hop; Poodle came from drama school and had an HND in 'urban theatre'. That was the problem.

He could hear the kid trying to enthuse the crowd: 'I say "Afri!", you say "Ca!". Afri! Afri!'

The response was paltry but dutiful.

'I say "Uni!", you say "Ty!". Uni! Uni!'

Preston had to give it to him. He may not have game, but he was certainly game.

Errol approached. He was wearing a headset into which he said, 'No. No. No,' and then, 'Shit.'

Preston raised his eyebrows. 'Problems?'

'We're five minutes down and the director's spitting blood, innit? What does he expect me to do? What does he think I am? Doctor Who?'

His ex-boss shrugged and privately enjoyed the fact it wasn't his problem.

'I could use some help, Tupps,' Errol hissed. 'Where the fuck's Jodie?'

'I sacked her.'

'What?' Errol pulled off his headset. 'What you do that for? You didn't even consult me or nothing.'

'I thought you hated her.'

'No!' Errol exclaimed. 'I don't hate her.' Then, checking Preston's expression, 'I *don't*! I just think she's ridiculous. All that coke. All that "Yeah, blood. Seen. You get me" shit. She's from fucking Hampstead. It's embarrassing. But she's tight on the admin stuff and that. Come on, Tupps, you know it.'

'So give her a call and offer her her job back. That's the point, Ez. You're in charge. Look, I had to put someone in charge and it was either you or Jodie, right? If I hadn't sacked her, she'd have been all resentful and made your life hell. This way, you give her her job back and she's grateful instead. Everyone's happy.'

Errol stared at him, then started to laugh. 'Damn, Tupps. You're good. You're so good, it's scary. In fact, maybe you're just scary. You really wanna give this shit up?'

'Yeah,' Preston said. 'I really do.'

Errol's headset crackled. He examined it ruefully. 'But what am I gonna do right now?'

'Right now, you tell the director to remember who he works for and to calm the fuck down. Tell him to ditch one of the bimbo's interviews, because they're all rubbish anyway. Then tell him not to bother you with this shit again. He's a director. Tell him to direct.'

Errol nodded. He was about to do as Preston said, but he had another thought. He pursed his lips and wiped his nose with the back of his hand.

'What?' Preston asked.

'I just wondered . . . you seen your old man yet?'

'No.'

'You ain't spoken to him?'

'No.'

'I mean, that's some craziness right there. What he been through? And to come back and take down Babylon like that? I just wanted to say . . . I mean, respect, you know? I hope he OK.'

Preston laughed. He couldn't help himself. David Pinner recast as hero to pseudo-Rastafarians and other ostensibly radical black men nationwide: who'd have believed it? 'Thanks. But I'm sure he's all right.'

'Give me a touch on that,' Errol said, and they touched fists.

Authenticity™'s new CEO started to walk away, but then he thought again and turned back, wearing a sly smile. He said, 'You sack Thandi, Tupps?'

'No.'

'But you were gonna, right?'

'Yeah, I thought about it.'

'You should sack her, man. I mean, your plan for Jodie is

all good, but if I want someone to be grateful to me it's Thandi every time, know what I mean?'

Preston pulled a horrified face. 'And you think *I'm* scary?'

Now it was Errol who laughed. He turned away with a spring in his step, put on his headset and began to bark commands into the mouthpiece.

Preston headed back into the wings. Poodle had just finished his prize-winning tune to tepid applause. The crew had five minutes to set up for the next performer, the last of the urban slot, the man whose appearance was still only rumour for most of the stadium.

Preston peered out into the crowd. They looked restive and a little bored. He started to worry. He wondered if he'd judged this right. Maybe he should have put Nobody higher up the bill.

The sun caught his face. Although it was low in the sky, it was still surprisingly hot.

He peered across the stage to where the members of the string quartet were getting ready. The cello was a woman in a long black dress with elegant grey hair. Preston had a sudden urge to play a musical instrument. He wished he had a skill that was measurable in something other than money.

He turned back to the paying punters and gazed high up into the stands. He wondered where the Prime Minister was; probably in a shaded box somewhere, pretending to have a good time with a bunch of other dignitaries all pretending to have a good time. He wondered what the Prime Minister actually made of all this. Did he think he'd done something good? Did he think this was some kind of answer and, if so, to what question?

As the foreign minister with responsibility for Africa, his old man should have been up there with them. But he wasn't. Preston wondered if he should be worried. Because he wasn't. He'd had his phone on silent since his TV appearance, so had missed his dad's only call.

Pinner had left a long, rambling message. He was at the family home in Bristol reading through some ancient letters that his grandfather had sent during the First World War. He read one aloud down the phone. Then he said he was going to a cemetery in some place called Fry Norton because he wanted to know the truth.

Preston had no idea what his dad was talking about, but there'd been a curious lightness in his voice that he found somehow reassuring. Perhaps it was just the lightness of freedom. In fact, if Preston was worried about anyone, it was his mum and how she might be coping with Pinner's sudden reappearance. But she, too, had left a message and sounded surprisingly chipper. So long as there was no booze in the house . . .

The crew was almost done. Preston turned round and saw Tendai Ben Phiri hovering by the doorway. He was holding his acoustic guitar and wearing his trademark overalls and balaclava. He looked nervous – or as nervous as it's possible to look in a balaclava.

Preston went over to him and tried to front confidence. He said, 'That Nobody under there?' He'd hoped to sound cheerful but Nobody just shrugged. There was an awkwardness between them. Then again, there always had been.

Eventually Nobody said, 'You think this is a good idea, king?'

'Yeah,' Preston said. 'Yeah, I do.' And, as he said it, he believed it too.

'All these kids?' Nobody said, and gestured to his left.

For the first time, Preston noticed the hundred primary-school children. Jodie had arranged this. It was her last act as an employee of Authenticity™ (for now, anyway). They were lined up in four banks of twenty-five. They looked terrified. They were being as good as gold. 'Yeah,' he said. 'They're the icing on the cake.'

'OK.' Nobody's left hand was practising chords on the fretboard. He said, 'I saw you on TV. That interview.'

'Yeah, right.'

'You said that nobody loves this country as much as me.'

'Yeah.' Preston laughed. 'I got a bit carried away. But I just said what needed saying.'

'You talked nonsense, king. I don't love this country.'

Preston tried to read his eyes behind the mask. 'You must love something,' he said. 'You've been here four years.'

'But only because I could not go home, innit?'

'So love that,' Preston said resentfully. 'I'm only asking for five minutes of love. Not a lot. And it's for your benefit, not mine. Seems like you got a good deal, *king*.'

Nobody stiffened. But then he nodded smartly and changed the subject. He said, 'Lolly tells me you're leaving The A-List.'

'Not just The A-List. I'm leaving Authenticity. I'm going to do something else. You'll be all right. Errol will look after you. He's a good guy.'

'What you gonna do?'

'I don't know.'

'What else can you do?'

'I don't know.'

Unexpectedly, Nobody laughed. He said, 'Well, I guess you gonna find out, king, innit?'

'I guess so.'

Preston watched from the wings as the PA announced the next star name with the usual hyperbole – 'Give it up for the best-selling recording artist in the UK right now and the most controversial man in music, it's Nobody!'

Preston was standing next to Lorraine again. He tried to smile at her, but he had no reassurance left. He looked out into the crowd instead. They seemed averagely interested, craning their necks, but there were no screams or chants.

When the man himself finally appeared, however, Preston saw the audience stand up as one and surge forward. Their cheers were so loud and so excitable that, though relieved by such an enthusiastic response, Preston did wonder if they knew exactly what they were cheering for.

The main attraction took centre stage alone. He didn't say a word, simply strummed his guitar and the stadium was rapt. But it was when he began to sing, or rap, or whatever the hell it was he did, that Preston knew he was watching something special. It was the quality of Nobody's voice. It had a slight reediness, a hint of vulnerability, but there was no questioning its power, or its truth. Preston thought it was the sound of a broken man put back together.

Nobody's foot hit a pedal and the syncopated drums kicked in. At the same time, the string quartet launched into the melody. Again, the crowd surged. They were now part of the music, heaving forward and back with each snap and snare. In spite of himself, Preston was lifted by the rising swell and thought it really quite beautiful.

Now it was time for the icing and, in a moment of perfect theatre, Nobody ripped off his balaclava as the primary-school kids formed four banks behind him. Here was the faceless face and his child army. The crowd screamed and rushed and broke over the stage. Nobody touched eager hands – one, two, three; his momentary friends.

Nobody's expression was lit up with his own potency. 'My name's Ben Phiri,' he declared. 'And I'm a proud African. I hope you all gonna sing the traditional words with me.'

'"Bring me my bow,"' the kids began. Their voices counterpointed any cynicism and the crowd quickly caught on. '"Of burning gold."' The sound rose, unified and magnificent. '"Bring me my arrows of desire."' Nobody threw his arms out, crucifying himself on English ambition, exposing his chest to the heat of that lusty arrow. '"Bring me my spear! O clouds unfold!"' The audience seemed to look up as one, as if expecting some celestial intervention. There was almost palpable disappointment that the chariot of fire didn't come galloping into view over the great Wembley arch.

Suddenly Preston was singing too and he believed every word and, specifically, their pertinence to him. He wasn't a man to cease from mental fight! His sword would never sleep in his hand! He looked out over the masses and he was one with them. He glanced at Lorraine and she'd joined in as well, though he couldn't hear her over the children's trebles and the crowd's baritone. '"Till we have built Jerusalem,"' he bellowed, '"In England's green and pleasant land."'

Even as he hit that last note, Preston was doubled up laughing at the sight of Nobody, statuesque in ecstasy, martyred on the celebrity altar. But still he couldn't deny the prickle behind his own eyes and how he wished he could hold the moment for ever or until he figured out what he might do next.

56

Freedom

After his release, Musa Musa stayed in Queenstown for his friend Jim Tulloh's funeral. It was more than a week since Jim had died, but Sylvia had waited because she wanted to give mourners a chance to come from England. None did.

Musa Musa didn't know whether Jim's friends and relations were too scared to visit the 'pariah state' they read about in their newspapers or whether he had no friends and relations over there any more. But he thought how strange it would be to be buried so far from home, whether one's soul would find its way back to where it had come from.

The small church was very full. There were all the children from Mama's House, of course, but Musa Musa didn't know many of the rest. Unusually, Sylvia gave the oration. She described her husband as 'a man of flaws and friendships, but no flawed friendships'. The *zakulu* found that a touchingly honest and fitting tribute. Certainly the turnout suggested the *musungu* had been well loved.

President Adini was there, sitting in the front row between two security guards. It was the first time the *zakulu* had seen him since their confrontation in State House, immediately after he'd witnessed the police murder a student called Alice Chipinge amid a storm of cherry blossom.

Musa Musa studied the President from across the aisle. He looked dapper in a dark suit: self-confident, every inch the politician. Musa Musa didn't resent him for his incarceration any more than he felt gratitude for his eventual freedom. But he did resent the loss of a man he'd once considered a friend to the vanities of dark suits and politics.

Afterwards he saw him again on the church steps. He hadn't meant to: he was looking for Sylvia to express his condolences that he might then slip away. But he felt a heavy hand on his elbow. 'You see, *zakulu*?' the President breathed. 'We won.'

Musa Musa looked up at him and now resented his self-confidence too. 'Who is "we"?' he asked. 'And what was it that we won?' He didn't wait for an answer before turning away. The *zakulu* had read once that a people gets the leadership it deserves. He couldn't remember who had written this, but he suspected it wasn't an African.

Musa Musa walked back to Gwezi bus station, not far from the prison. What remained of his foot was now healing, the scar tissue thickening and toughening into something like a hoof, but he was left with a pronounced limp. He caught White Lightning back to Zimindo. After running out of petrol halfway, the bus didn't reach the township until dawn. Clearly White Lightning was yet to suck at victory's teat.

On his way home, the *zakulu* stopped at the chief's homestead where he found Kudzai bent double over her laundry. At the sound of the gate opening, she straightened up and wiped her brow wearily, but when she saw it was Musa Musa her mouth peeled in delight. 'We have missed you!' she exclaimed simply. She invited him into the main concrete house and they sat opposite one another on the same chairs that he'd so often shared with her husband, his dear departed friend. Kudzai saw what he was thinking but she didn't want to discuss her loss just yet, so she asked him to tell her everything.

Musa Musa didn't tell her everything, but he did tell her some things and she listened intently.

When he had finished, she said, 'You left because we were suffering. While you were gone, we suffered. Now you are back and we're still suffering. When will it end?'

The *zakulu*, who always knew what to say, didn't know what to say to that. But he was spared by Kudzai whose face

395

broke into another warm smile. 'Listen to me!' she said. 'Talking like this when you must be hungry. Come. Let me get you some food.'

'Thank you, my dear,' Musa Musa said. 'But only what you can spare.' He followed her outside. While she cooked, they were silent.

As he ate, she asked, 'Is it good?'

'It's very good. Thank you.'

A small boy came into the compound carrying his slingshot in one hand and a dead rabbit in the other. He was stocky and athletic with a broad chest and a steady, purposeful gait. It was a moment or two before the *zakulu* recognized him as the younger Tongo, the chief's son.

Kudzai noted his surprise and laughed. 'I know!' she exclaimed. 'He's grown! And he's a better hunter than his father ever was . . .' Her words tailed away.

'Tongo couldn't hunt a thing,' Musa Musa confirmed.

'No.' Kudzai laughed again. 'Only girls.'

Tongo Junior was shy – nothing like his father, they agreed – and it was only at his mother's prompting that he greeted the *zakulu* and shook his hand.

'He's been looking after your garden,' Kudzai said. 'He says the maize is coming on nicely.'

Musa Musa held the boy's hand and wouldn't let it go. 'Thank you, young Tongo,' he said, and eventually the child cracked a smile.

Musa Musa walked home in a state of undiluted happiness. The distant familiarity of every bush and ridge delighted him. When he reached his house, he could almost have cried with joy. How many times had he painted its outline in the darkness of his jail cell?

His maize was indeed healthy, every plant already up to his waist. He dropped to his haunches and went round each and every one. The boy had done a good job caring for them.

He went to the well and drew some water. It tasted sweet.

He sat in his doorway the whole day. Occasionally locals passed and each one stopped to welcome him home and listen to his stories. He didn't tire of telling them.

He went to bed at sunset and slept a dreamless sleep.

57

Insert document

From Document 001287678 (Zulu Christian
Industrial School - Unclass., 1904, Trans.,
2003 (Translation Initiative [TI], Department
of Arts and Culture, Republic of South Africa),
Bhekisisa Mary Silongo (Trans. Malusi Dube)

*Cishe ngaba kwabanye abesifazane bokuqala abafunda
ukukhuluma, ukufunda nokubhala kahle isiNgisi. Empeleni,
ngakwenza lokho ngaphambi kokuthi ngikwazi ukubhala ngolimi
lwai, okulikhono engisanda nakulifunda kuMnu. John Langalibalele
Dube – umfundisi ophambili. Nakuba kunjalo, angeke ngiphinde
ngikhulume noma ngibhale ngesiNgisi futhi.*

*Ngafundiswa ngumyeni wami, uMnu. Robert Ackerman,
engahlukaniswa naye, ngisese Standmere. Ekuqaleni, wayengafuni
ngikhulume isiNgisi kangcono kunabanye, kodwa ngambonisa
ngokumtshela ukuthi kuzoba wusizo; ngokuthi ukumhumushela
kwami kuyomenza akwazi ukuxhumana ngokucacile naantu
abasenkambini. Ngamtshela lokhu ngoba kwakungukuphela
kombono ayengawamukela. Empeleni, lencazelo yabuye yabuya
ngakimi kanzima lapho sekuyisikhulu esixhugayo, owesilisa
omhlophe u-Robert ayemzonda kunabo bonke, owabe engisebenzisa
ukuchaza imigomo yakhe eminingi kwabamnyama.*

*Iqiniso wukuthi, nakuba, ngangifisa ukufunda isiNgisi ukuze
ngiqonde okwakushiwo ngu-Robert lapho silele ndawonye ebusuku
ethi kimi, 'ngikholwa wukuthi ngiyakuthanda'. Noma yinini uma
esho lokhu kimi, ngokushesha waye landelanisa ngokuthi asho
okunye – njengokuthi, 'angikwazi ukuzibamba'.*

Sasilala sibhekene ikhala ekhaleni kukhanya amakhandlela

I must have been among the first women to learn to speak, read and write fluently in English. In fact, I could do so long before I could write in my own tongue, a skill I learnt only recently from Mr John Langalibalele Dube – a great teacher. But I will never speak or write in English again.

I was taught by my husband, Mr Robert Ackerman, from whom I am now estranged, when I was at Standmere. At first, he did not want me to speak English better than the others, but I convinced him by telling him that it would be useful; that my translation would enable him to communicate more clearly with the people in the camp. I told him this because it was a reason he could accept. In fact, this explanation came back to haunt me when it was the limping officer, the white man Robert hated above all others, who used me to explain his countless regulations to the blacks.

The truth is that I wished to learn English so that I could understand Robert's meaning when we lay together at night and he said to me, 'I believe I love you.' Whenever he said this to me, he immediately followed it with another phrase – for example, 'I cannot help myself.'

We lay nose to nose by candlelight and I could smell

futhi ngangikwazi ukuzwa iphunga le-whisky emphefumulweni wakhe, kodwa ngangingakwazi ukubona ukuthi wayehloseni uma ngimbhekile. Ngathola ukuthi kukhona ukuqhelelana nokuthi kukhona ongakubona okuningi ebusweni bomuntu wesilisa ngale kokudidwa yilokho obuvezwa yibona. Lokhu kuqhelelana budengange ngalo yakho, kanye nobukhulu bengalo yendoda, kanye nobukhulu bengalo yakho futhi, ukuze uqiniseke.

'Ngikholwa wukuthi ngiyakuthanda,' kusho u-Robert kimi. 'Kumele ngibe nokuzenyeza.'

Ngangifuna ukwazi ukuthi kwakusho ukuthini – 'ukuthanda'. Ngangifuna ukwazi ukuthi kwaku ngakholakala kanjani. Okuseqinisweni yikuthi wayengithanda noma wayengangithandi. Mhlawumpe wayekhuluma iqiniso noma amanga. Yikuphi okunye, uma ayengakwazi ukuzibamba, kungani kwakumele abe nokuzenyeza?

Ngambuza u-Robert ukuthi ingabe 'ukuthanda' kwakufana 'nokufuna' noma 'ukudinga' noma 'ukulangazelela'. Wangitshela ukuthi kwakufana nakho konke, kodwa kwakungaphezulu kwakho konke futhi. Lapho engitshela lokho, ngamane ngabona ukuthi wayengayazi incazelo yakho naye.

Ngabe sengikhetha ukufunda isiNgisi ngakho konke ukuze ngizitholele incazelo ngokwami. Ngatshela u-Robert ukuthi ngangifisa 'ukufunda ulimi lothando'. Wakuhleka lokhu wabe esethi ngiyahlekisa. Kodwa ngangingenzi mancoko.

Zikhathi zonke zokuphila kwami njengo nkosikazi omhlophe, ngafunda konke engabe ngikuthanda mayelana noku 'funa' noku 'dinga' noku 'langazelela'. Kodwa, kangikaze ngifunde ngencazelo yothando eyayingangigculisa.

IsiNgisi wulimi lwamagama amaningi futhi kangicabangi ukuthi ukhona umuntu ophilayo owazi wonke; ngisho u-King Edward imbala. Ngakusho lokhu ngelinye ilanga ku-Robert wangitshela ukuthi kwakungenxa yokuthi amaNgisi acabanga ukuthi anobuchwepheshe futhi athanda ukucacisa kunayo yonke into. Wakusho lokhu ngokucasuka, kungathi kwayena wayengakukholwa.

Kangikholwa. Ngikholwa wukuthi isiNgisi sisebenzisa amagama

the whisky on his breath, but I could not tell what intention there was in his face. I have discovered there is an ideal distance from which you can see everything you need in a man's face without becoming confused by its details. This distance is the length of your arm, plus the length of the man's arm, plus the length of your own arm again, to be sure.

'I believe I love you,' Robert said to me. 'I should be ashamed of myself.'

I wanted to know what it meant – 'love'. I wanted to know how it could be a matter of uncertainty. Surely he loved me or he did not. Either he was speaking the truth or lies. What was more, if he could not help himself, why should he be ashamed?

I asked Robert if 'love' was the same as 'want' or 'need' or 'desire'. He told me that it was the same as all of those, but it was more than all of them as well. When he told me this, I deduced that he did not know its meaning either.

I decided therefore to learn English so well that I would discover the meaning for myself. I told Robert that I wished to 'learn the language of love'. He laughed at this and said I was funny. But I was not joking.

In all my time as a white wife, I learnt more than I would have liked about 'want' and 'need' and 'desire'. But I never learnt the meaning of love to my satisfaction.

English is a language of very many words and I do not think anyone alive knows them all, not even King Edward. I said this once to Robert and he told me that it was because the English imagine themselves scientific and admire precision above almost anything. He said this bitterly, as if he didn't quite believe it himself.

I don't believe it. I believe that the English use their many words not to clarify, but to confuse; to hide meaning in a downpour in which you cannot distinguish one raindrop from *aso amaningi ukungacacisi nje kuphela, kodwa ukudida; ukucashisa incazelo empophomeni lapho ungeke wahlukanisa khona iconsi lemvula elilodwa kwamanye. Empeleni, lapho ngiqhubeka ngifunda isiNgisi, yilapho ngangiqhubeka ngangibona lokhu kudida ngenhloso okwakusenhliziyweni yegrama nasebucikweni bokukhuluma.*

Ngikhumbula isikhulu esixhugayo. Indlela yaso yokukhuluma yayidida kakhulu kangangoba, noma ngangikhuluma isiNgisi kahle kangakanani, kwakuvame ukungithatha isikhathi ukuthola ayekusho. Wathi kimi: 'Tshela abantu bakho ukuthi bakhululekile ukuthi bangabasa umlilo ekhishini eliseningizimu.'

Kungemuva kuphela kokuthi kwase kushaywe abanyama abaningana beshaywa ngonogada lapho ngaqonda khona ukuthi wabe esho okunye; ngokuthi imililo yethu kwakumele ingavunyelwa ekhishini eliseningizimu nokuthi ukukhululeka kwakungahlangene nakho. Ngakhalaza ngokuthi wayengacacile, kodwa naye wabe esengihleka kungathi wayecabanga ukuthi ngiyadlala.

UMnu. John Langalibalele Dube uthi ukufunda isiNgisi ukufunda ukusebenzisa isikhali somuntu omhlophe, kodwa sihlale siyisikhali sakhe. Ukunika isibonelo, uthi useke waba nemihlangano eminingi nabamhlophe abanempumelelo ukuze 'baxoxe ngesimo sobumdabu'. Uthi: 'kungani kumele sixoxe "mayelana" ngesimo sengathi yisakhiwo esimi ngaphandle kwaso? Kungani singakhulumi ngesimo "esikuso" noma "esenzekayo"? Wulimi uqobo oluvumela abamhlophe babalekelane nokukhuluma ngezinkinga baziqonde.' Nomakunjalo, uyakugcizelela ukuthi abesimame bethu kumele balufunde ulimi, ngalokho yiyona ndlela kuphela esingathuthukisa ngayo isikhundla sethu okwesikhashana.

Ngokwami, ngithi angeke. Ngiyamtshela ukuthi sengisifundile isiNgisi, kodwa angeke ngiphinde ngisikhulume ngoba kasingibuyiselanga lutho ngaphandle kwezinkinga. Ngikholelwa wukuthi uma uvela kubantu abangabazingeli, uyokhuluma ulimi oluhlonipha ukuzingela. Uma ningabalimi, ulimi lwenu luyohlonipha ukulima. Uma ningabaqambi bamanga, ngakho-ke, ulimi lwakho luyohlonipha kuphela amanga. Angilangangazeleli ukuqamba amanga kunoma ngubani.

another. In fact, the more English I learnt, the more I came to see this bewildering intention at the heart of grammar and idiom.

I remember the limping officer. His manner of speaking was so confusing that, even when I spoke English quite well, it often took me some time to decipher his meaning. He said to me: 'Tell your people that they are free to light fires at the southern kitchen.'

It was only after several blacks were beaten by the guards that I realized he meant almost the opposite: that our fires were to be restricted to the southern kitchen and freedom had nothing to do with it. I complained that he was not clear, but he, too, laughed at me, as if he thought I was joking.

Mr John Langalibalele Dube says that to learn English is to learn to use the white man's weapon, but it remains *his* weapon. To give an example, he says that he has had many meetings with the progressive whites to 'talk about the native situation'. He says: 'Why must we talk "about" the situation as if it were a building and we were standing outside? Why can't we talk "on" the situation or "in" it? It is the language itself that allows the whites to avoid addressing the problem directly.' Even so, he maintains that our women must learn the language, for that is the only way to improve our position in the short term.

For my part, I say I cannot. I tell him I have already learnt English, but I will no longer speak it because it brought me nothing but problems. I believe that if you are from a hunting people, you will speak a language that honours hunting. If you are farmers, your language will honour farming. If you are liars, therefore, your language will honour only your lies. And I have no desire to lie to anybody.

I learnt English that I might understand Robert and address him as his wife, and that he might understand me as my husband. But I know now that I was never truly Robert's wife (in either tongue) and to speak his language did not make me

Ngafunda isiNgisi esasingangenza ngiqonde u-Robert nokuthi ngikwazi ukukhuluma ngaye njengomkakhe nokuthi naye akwazi ukungiqonda njengomyeni wami. Kodwa, ngiyazi manje ukuthi ngangingakaze ngibe ngumkakhe ngokuseqinisweni (nganoma wuliphi ulimi) nokukhuluma ulimi lwakhe akuzange kwangenza ngaqina, kodwa ngabanteka. IsiNgisi wulimi lwenkohliso, loqhekeko nokubusa. Ngilufisa kabi ulimi lweqiniso, oluhlanganisayo nelokuphenduka! Namanje, ngisabambelele enkolweni ethi, njengoba kudingakala, ngakho ngelinye ilanga liyofika.

stronger, but weaker. English is the language of deceit, division and domination. How I long for a language of honesty, unity and revolution! Still, I hold on to the belief that, as it is required, so it will one day come.

Author's note

I would like to acknowledge several sources that inspired and informed this novel; in particular, *The Magic Spring* by Richard Lewis, my one-time neighbour. It was his passion for English folk music that first sparked my curiosity. I am also, of course, indebted to the work of Rudyard Kipling, William Blake's 'Jerusalem', and J. G. Frazer's extraordinary feat of imagination, *The Golden Bough*.

More specifically, the mumming play in Chapter 21 was recorded by R. J. E. Tiddy and republished as 'Mumming Play from Longborough, Gloucestershire – 1905–1906' on www.folkplay.info. The song cited in Chapter 30 is a corruption of 'I Live Not Where I Love', noted by Cecil J. Sharp from Robert Parish in Exford, Somerset, between 1906 and 1907. A version of Preston Pinner's manifesto, 'Wherefore Cool?' in Chapter 7 first appeared in *Esquire* magazine in November 2005 with the title, 'Cool Is History'. The report quoted by Preston in Chapter 50 was published by the Independent Asylum Commission in March 2008.

This novel would certainly have struggled to surface without key interventions from generous people at important stages. They include Simon Trewin, Juliet Annan, Will Boyd, Derek Safo, Kenny Baraka, Nick Bolton, Charles Beckett, Hazel Marshall, Zack Winfield, Ado Yoshizake and everyone who told me they liked my other books. I am also very thankful to Arts Council England who stepped in when my bank finally lost its sense of humour (along with all the money it never had in the first place).

Finally, I owe particular love and gratitude to the people who support what I do, no matter how daft they secretly think I am: my family, Netsayi Chigwendere, Ilya Colak-Antic, Francesca and Bobby McKenna, Drew Pearce, Sam Bain, Trevor Sather, Elliott Jack and Angela Robertson.